IF

A master sto r of eighteen no ion copies), over scripts, twenty-five major motion pictures and six Broadway plays, ranking him as one of the world's most prolific writers. His first book, *The Naked Face*, was acclaimed by the *New York Times* as 'the best first mystery novel of the year' and subsequently each of his highly popular books have hit No. 1 on the *New York Times* bestseller list. His latest bestseller, *Are You Afraid of the Dark?*, cements Sheldon's reputation as the master of the unexpected.

For more about Sidney Sheldon, visit his website at www.sidneysheldon.com.

For automatic updates on Sidney Sheldon visit HarperCollins.co.uk/sidneysheldon and register for AuthorTracker.

By the same author

The Naked Face
The Other Side of Midnight
A Stranger in the Mirror
Bloodline
Rage of Angels
Master of the Game
If Tomorrow Comes
Windmills of the Gods
The Sands of Time
Memories of Midnight
The Doomsday Conspiracy
The Stars Shine Down
Nothing Lasts Forever
Morning, Noon and Night
The Best Laid Plans
Tell Me Your Dreams
The Sky is Falling
Are You Afraid of the Dark?

SIDNEY SHELDON

If Tomorrow Comes

HarperCollins*Publishers*

This novel is entirely a work of fiction.
The names, characters and incidents portrayed in it are the work of the author's imagination. Any resemblance to actual persons, living or dead, events or localities is entirely coincidental.

HarperCollins*Publishers*
77–85 Fulham Palace Road,
Hammersmith, London W6 8JB

www.harpercollins.co.uk

This paperback edition 2005
1

First published in paperback by Pan 1986

First published in Great Britain by Collins 1985

A catalogue record for this book is available from the British Library

ISBN 978-0-00-783704-5

Typeset in Sabon by Palimpsest Book Production Limited,
Polmont, Stirlingshire

Printed and bound in Great Britain by
Clays Ltd, St Ives plc

ONE

New Orleans
Thursday, 20 February – 11:00 P.M.

She undressed slowly, dreamily, and when she was naked, she selected a bright red negligee to wear so that the blood would not show. Doris Whitney looked around the bedroom for the last time to make certain that the pleasant room, grown dear over the past thirty years, was neat and tidy. She opened the drawer of the bedside table and carefully removed the gun. It was shiny black, and terrifyingly cold. She placed it next to the telephone and dialled her daughter's number in Philadelphia. She listened to the echo of the distant ringing. And then there was a soft 'Hello?'

'Tracy . . . I just felt like hearing the sound of your voice, darling.'

'What a nice surprise, Mother.'

'I hope I didn't wake you up.'

'No. I was reading. Just getting ready to sleep.

Charles and I were going out for dinner, but the weather's too nasty. It's snowing hard here. What's it doing there?'

Dear God, we're talking about the weather, Doris Whitney thought, *when there's so much I want to tell her. And can't.*

'Mother? Are you there?'

Doris Whitney stared out the window. 'It's raining.' And she thought, *How melodramatically appropriate. Like an Alfred Hitchcock movie.*

'What's that noise?' Tracy asked.

Thunder. Too deeply wrapped in her thoughts, Doris had not been aware of it. New Orleans was having a storm. *Continued rain*, the weatherman had said. *Sixty-six degrees in New Orleans. By evening the rain will be turning to thundershowers. Be sure to carry your umbrellas*. She would not need an umbrella.

'That's thunder, Tracy.' She forced a note of cheerfulness into her voice. 'Tell me what's happening in Philadelphia.'

'I feel like a princess in a fairy tale, Mother,' Tracy said. 'I never believed anyone could be so happy. Tomorrow night I'm meeting Charles's parents.' She deepened her voice as though making a pronouncement. 'The Stanhopes, of Chestnut Hill,' she sighed. 'They're an institution. I have butterflies the size of dinosaurs.'

'Don't worry. They'll love you, darling.'

'Charles says it doesn't matter. *He* loves me. And

I adore him. I can't wait for you to meet him. He's fantastic.'

'I'm sure he is.' She would never meet Charles. She would never hold a grandchild in her lap. *No. I must not think about that.* 'Does he know how lucky he is to have you, baby?'

'I keep telling him.' Tracy laughed. 'Enough about me. Tell me what's going on there. How are you feeling?'

You're in perfect health, Doris, were Dr Rush's words. *You'll live to be a hundred.* One of life's little ironies. 'I feel wonderful.' *Talking to you.*

'Got a boyfriend yet?' Tracy teased.

Since Tracy's father had died five years earlier, Doris Whitney had not even considered going out with another man, despite Tracy's encouragement.

'No boyfriends.' She changed the subject. 'How is your job? Still enjoying it?'

'I love it. Charles doesn't mind if I keep working after we're married.'

'That's wonderful, baby. He sounds like a very understanding man.'

'He is. You'll see for yourself.'

There was a loud clap of thunder, like an off-stage cue. It was time. There was nothing more to say except a final farewell. 'Good-bye, my darling.' She kept her voice carefully steady.

'I'll see you at the wedding, Mother. I'll call you as soon as Charles and I set a date.'

'Yes.' There was one final thing to say, after all. 'I love you very, very much, Tracy.' And Doris

Whitney carefully replaced the receiver. She picked up the gun. There was only one way to do it. Quickly. She raised the gun to her temple and squeezed the trigger.

TWO

Philadelphia
Friday, 21 February – 8:00 A.M.

Tracy Whitney stepped out of the lobby of her block of flats into a grey, sleety rain that fell impartially on sleek limousines driven down Market Street by uniformed chauffeurs, and on the abandoned and boarded-up houses huddled together in the slums of North Philadelphia. The rain washed the limousines clean and made sodden messes of the rubbish piled high in front of the neglected row of houses. Tracy Whitney was on her way to work. Her pace was brisk as she walked east on Chestnut Street towards the bank, and it was all she could do to keep from singing aloud. She wore a bright-yellow raincoat, boots, and a yellow rain hat that barely contained a mass of shining chestnut hair. She was in her mid-twenties, with a lively, intelligent face, a full, sensuous mouth, sparkling eyes that could change from a soft moss green to a dark jade in moments, and a trim, athletic figure. Her skin ran the gamut from a translucent white to a deep rose, depending on whether she was angry, tired, or excited. Her mother had once told her, 'Honestly, child, sometimes I don't recognize you. You've got all the colours of the wind in you.'

Now, as Tracy walked down the street, people turned to smile, envying the happiness that shone on her face. She smiled back at them.

It's indecent for anyone to be this happy, Tracy Whitney thought. *I'm marrying the man I love, and I'm going to have his baby. What more could anyone ask?*

As Tracy approached the bank, she glanced at her watch. Eight-twenty. The doors of the Philadelphia Trust and Fidelity Bank would not be open to employees for another ten minutes, but Clarence Desmond, the bank's senior vice-president in charge of the international department, was already turning off the outside alarm and opening the door. Tracy enjoyed watching the morning ritual. She stood in the rain, waiting, as Desmond entered the bank and locked the door behind him.

Banks the world over have arcane safety procedures, and the Philadelphia Trust and Fidelity Bank was no exception. The routine never varied, except for the security signal, which was changed every week. The signal that week was a half-lowered venetian blind, indicating to the employees waiting outside that a search was in progress to make certain that no intruders were concealed on the premises, waiting to hold the employees hostage. Clarence Desmond was checking the lavatories, storeroom, vault and safe-deposit area. Only when he was fully satisfied that he was alone would the venetian blind be raised as a sign that all was well.

The senior bookkeeper was always the first of the employees to be admitted. He would take his place next to the emergency alarm until the other employees were inside, then lock the door behind them.

Promptly at 8:30, Tracy Whitney entered the ornate lobby with her fellow workers, took off her raincoat, hat and boots, and listened with secret amusement to the others complaining about the rainy weather.

'The damned wind carried away my umbrella,' a teller complained. 'I'm soaked.'

'I passed two ducks swimming down Market Street,' the head cashier joked.

'The weatherman says we can expect another week of this. I wish I was in Florida.'

Tracy smiled and went to work. She was in charge of the cable-transfer department. Until recently, the transfer of money from one bank to another and from one country to another had been a slow, laborious process, requiring multiple forms to be filled out and dependent on national and international postal services. With the advent of computers, the situation had changed dramatically, and enormous amounts of money could be transferred instantaneously. It was Tracy's job to extract overnight transfers from the computer and to make computer transfers to other banks. All transactions were in code, changed regularly to prevent unauthorized access. Each day, millions of electronic dollars passed through Tracy's hands. It was fascinating work, the life-blood that fed the arteries of business all over the globe, and until Charles Stanhope III had come into Tracy's life, banking had been the most exciting thing in the world for her. The Philadelphia Trust and Fidelity Bank had a large international division, and at lunch Tracy and her fellow workers would discuss each morning's activities. It was heady conversation.

Deborah, the head bookkeeper, announced, 'We just closed the hundred-million-dollar syndicated loan to Turkey . . .'

Mae Trenton, secretary to the vice-president of the bank, said in a confidential tone, 'At the board meeting this morning they decided to join the new money facility to Peru. The up-front fee is over five million dollars . . .'

Jon Creighton, the bank bigot, added, 'I understand we're going in on the Mexican rescue package for fifty million. Those wetbacks don't deserve a damned cent . . .'

'It's interesting,' Tracy said thoughtfully, 'that the countries that attack America for being too money-oriented are always the first to beg us for loans.'

It was the subject on which she and Charles had had their first argument.

* * *

Tracy had met Charles Stanhope III at a financial symposium where Charles was the guest speaker. He ran the investment house founded by his great-grandfather, and his company did a good deal of business with the bank Tracy worked for. After Charles's lecture, Tracy had gone up to disagree with his analysis of the ability of third-world nations to repay the staggering sums of money they had borrowed from commercial banks worldwide and western governments. Charles at first had been amused, then intrigued by the impassioned arguments of the beautiful young woman before him. Their discussion had continued through dinner at the old Bookbinder's restaurant.

In the beginning, Tracy had not been impressed with Charles Stanhope III, even though she was aware that he was considered Philadelphia's prize catch. Charles was thirty-five and a rich and successful member of one of the oldest families in Philadelphia. Five feet ten inches, with thinning sandy hair, brown eyes, and an earnest, pedantic manner, he was, Tracy thought, one of the boring rich.

As though reading her mind, Charles had leaned across the table and said, 'My father is convinced they gave him the wrong baby at the hospital.'

'What?'

'I'm a throwback. I don't happen to think money is the end-all and be-all of life. But please don't ever tell my father I said so.'

There was such a charming unpretentiousness

about him that Tracy found herself warming to him. *I wonder what it would be like to be married to someone like him – one of the establishment.*

It had taken Tracy's father most of his life to build up a business that the Stanhopes would have sneered at as insignificant. *The Stanhopes and the Whitneys would never mix*, Tracy thought. *Oil and water. And the Stanhopes are the oil. And what am I going on about like an idiot? Talk about ego. A man asks me out to dinner and I'm deciding whether I want to marry him. We'll probably never even see each other again.*

Charles was saying, 'I hope you're free for dinner tomorrow . . . ?'

Philadelphia was a dazzling cornucopia of things to see and do. On Saturday nights Tracy and Charles went to the ballet or watched Riccardo Muti conduct the Philadelphia Orchestra. During the week they explored New Market and the unique collection of shops in Society Hill. They ate cheese steaks at a pavement table at Geno's and dined at the Café Royal, one of the most exclusive restaurants in Philadelphia. They shopped at Head House Square and wandered through the Philadelphia Museum of Art and the Rodin Museum.

Tracy paused in front of the statue of *The Thinker*. She glanced at Charles and grinned. 'It's *you*!'

Charles was not interested in exercise, but Tracy enjoyed it, so on Sunday mornings she jogged along the West River Drive or on the promenade skirting the Schuylkill River. She joined a Saturday afternoon t'ai chi ch'uan class, and after an hour's workout, exhausted but exhilarated, she would meet Charles at his apartment. He was a gourmet cook, and he liked preparing esoteric dishes such as Moroccan *bistilla* and *guo bu li*, the dumplings of northern China, and *tahine de poulet au citron* for Tracy and himself.

Charles was the most punctilious person Tracy had ever known. She had once been fifteen minutes late for a dinner appointment with him, and his displeasure had spoiled the evening for her. After that, she had vowed to be on time for him.

Tracy had had little sexual experience, but it seemed to her that Charles made love the same way he lived his life: meticulously and very properly. Once, Tracy had decided to be daring and unconventional in bed, and had so shocked Charles that she began secretly to wonder if she were some kind of sex maniac.

The pregnancy had been unexpected, and when it happened, Tracy was filled with uncertainty. Charles had not brought up the subject of marriage, and she did not want him to feel he had to marry her because of the baby. She was not certain whether she could go through with an abortion, but the alternative was an equally painful choice. Could she raise a child without the help of its father, and would it be fair to the baby?

She decided to break the news to Charles after

dinner one evening. She had prepared a *cassoulet* for him in her apartment, and in her nervousness she had burned it. As she set the scorched meat and beans in front of him, she forgot her carefully rehearsed speech and wildly blurted out, 'I'm so sorry, Charles. I'm – pregnant.'

There was an unbearably long silence, and as Tracy was about to break it, Charles said, 'We'll get married, of course.'

Tracy was filled with a sense of enormous relief. 'I don't want you to think I – You don't *have* to marry me, you know.'

He raised a hand to stop her. 'I want to marry you, Tracy. You'll make a wonderful wife.' He added, slowly, 'Of course, my mother and father will be a bit surprised.' And he smiled and kissed her.

Tracy quietly asked, 'Why will they be surprised?'

Charles sighed. 'Darling, I'm afraid you don't quite realize what you're letting yourself in for. The Stanhopes always marry – mind you, I'm using quotation marks – "their own kind". Mainline Philadelphia.'

'And they've already selected your wife,' Tracy guessed.

Charles took her in his arms. 'That doesn't matter a damn. It's whom *I've* selected that counts. We'll have dinner with Mother and Father next Friday. It's time you met them.'

At five minutes to 9:00 Tracy became aware of a difference in the noise level in the bank. The employees were beginning to speak a little faster, move a little quicker. The bank doors would open in five minutes and everything had to be in readiness. Through the front window, Tracy could see customers lined up on the pavement outside, waiting in the cold rain.

Tracy watched as the bank guard finished distributing fresh blank deposit and withdrawal slips into the metal trays on the six tables lined up along the centre aisle of the bank. Regular customers were issued deposit slips with a personal magnetized code at the bottom so that each time a deposit was made, the computer automatically credited it to the proper account. But often customers came in without their deposit slips and would fill out blank ones.

The guard glanced up at the clock on the wall, and as the hour hand moved to 9:00, he walked over to the door and ceremoniously unlocked it.

The banking day had begun.

For the next few hours Tracy was too busy at the computer to think about anything else. Every wire transfer had to be double-checked to make sure it had the correct code. When an account was to be debited, she entered the account number, the amount, and the bank to which the money was to be transferred. Each bank had its own code number, the numbers listed in a confidential directory that contained the codes for every major bank in the world.

The morning flew by swiftly. Tracy was planning to use her lunchtime to have her hair done and had made an appointment with Larry Stella Botte. He was expensive, but it would be worth it, for she wanted Charles's parents to see her at her best. *I've got to make them like me. I don't care whom they chose for him*, Tracy thought. *No one can make Charles as happy as I will.*

At 1:00, as Tracy was getting into her raincoat, Clarence Desmond summoned her to his office. Desmond was the image of an important executive. If the bank had used television commercials, he would have been the perfect spokesman. Dressed conservatively, with an air of solid, old-fashioned authority about him, he looked like a person one could trust.

'Sit down, Tracy,' he said. He prided himself on knowing every employee's first name. 'Nasty outside, isn't it?'

'Yes.'

'Ah, well. People still have to do their banking.' Desmond had used up his small talk. He leaned across his desk. 'I understand that you and Charles Stanhope are engaged to be married.'

Tracy was surprised. 'We haven't even announced it yet. How –?'

Desmond smiled. 'Anything the Stanhopes do is news. I'm very happy for you. I assume you'll be returning here to work with us. After the honeymoon, of course. We wouldn't want to lose you. You're one of our most valuable employees.'

'Charles and I talked it over, and we agreed I'd be happier if I worked.'

Desmond smiled, satisfied. Stanhope and Sons was one of the most important investment houses in the financial community, and it would be a nice plum if he could get their exclusive account for his branch. He leaned back in his chair. 'When you return from your honeymoon, Tracy, there's going to be a nice promotion for you, along with a substantial rise.'

'Oh, thank you! That's wonderful.' She knew she had earned it, she felt a thrill of pride. She could hardly wait to tell Charles. It seemed to Tracy that the gods were conspiring to do everything they could to overwhelm her with happiness.

The Charles Stanhope Seniors lived in an impressive old mansion in Rittenhouse Square. It was a city landmark that Tracy had passed often. *And now*, she thought, *it's going to be a part of my life.*

She was nervous. Her beautiful hairdo had succumbed to the dampness of the air. She had changed dresses four times. Should she dress simply? Formally? She had one Yves Saint Laurent she had scrimped to buy at Wanamaker's. *If I wear it, they'll think I'm extravagant. On the other hand, if I dress in one of my sale things from Post Horn, they'll think their son is marrying beneath him. Oh, hell, they're going to think that anyway*, Tracy decided. She finally settled on a simple grey wool skirt and a white silk blouse and fastened around her neck the slender gold chain her mother had sent her for Christmas.

The door to the mansion was opened by a liveried butler. 'Good evening, Miss Whitney.' *The butler knows my name. Is that a good sign? A bad sign?* 'May I take your coat?' She was dripping on their expensive Persian rug.

He led her through a marble hallway that seemed twice as large as the bank. Tracy thought, panicky, *Oh, my God. I'm dressed all wrong! I should have worn the Yves Saint Laurent.* As she turned into the library, she felt a ladder start at the ankle of her pantyhose, and she was face-to-face with Charles's parents.

Charles Stanhope, Sr., was a stern-looking man in his middle sixties. He *looked* a successful man; he was the projection of what his son would be like in thirty years. He had brown eyes, like Charles's, a firm chin, a fringe of white hair, and Tracy loved him instantly. He was the perfect grandfather for their child.

Charles's mother was impressive looking. She was rather short and heavy-set, but despite that, there was a regal air about her. *She looks solid and dependable*, Tracy thought. *She'll make a wonderful grandmother*.

Mrs Stanhope held out her hand. 'My dear, so good of you to join us. We've asked Charles to give us a few minutes alone with you. You don't mind?'

'Of course she doesn't mind,' Charles's father declared. 'Sit down . . . Tracy, isn't it?'

'Yes, sir.'

The two of them seated themselves on a couch facing her. *Why do I feel as though I'm about to undergo an inquisition?* Tracy could hear her mother's voice: *Baby, God will never throw anything at you that you can't handle. Just take it one step at a time.*

Tracy's first step was a weak smile that came out all wrong, because at that instant she could feel the ladder in her hose slither up to her knee. She tried to conceal it with her hands.

'So!' Mr Stanhope's voice was hearty. 'You and Charles want to get married.'

The word *want* disturbed Tracy. Surely Charles had told them they were *going* to be married.

'Yes,' Tracy said.

'You and Charles really haven't known each other long, have you?' Mrs Stanhope asked.

Tracy fought back her resentment. *I was right. It is going to be an inquisition.*

'Long enough to know that we love each other, Mrs Stanhope.'

'*Love?*' Mr Stanhope murmured.

Mrs Stanhope said, 'To be quite blunt, Miss Whitney, Charles's news came as something of a shock to his father and me.' She smiled forbearingly. 'Of course, Charles has told you about Charlotte?' She saw the expression on Tracy's face. 'I see. Well, he and Charlotte grew up together.

They were always very close, and – well, frankly, everyone expected them to announce their engagement this year.'

It was not necessary for her to describe Charlotte. Tracy could have drawn a picture of her. Lived next door. Rich, with the same social background as Charles. All the best schools. Loved horses and won cups.

'Tell us about your family,' Mr Stanhope suggested.

My God, this is a scene from a late-night movie, Tracy thought wildly. *I'm the Rita Hayworth character, meeting Cary Grant's parents for the first time. I need a drink. In the old movies the butler always came to the rescue with a tray of drinks.*

'Where were you born, my dear?' Mrs Stanhope asked.

'In Louisiana. My father was a mechanic.' There had been no need to add that, but Tracy was unable to resist. To hell with them. She was proud of her father.

'A *mechanic*?'

'Yes. He started a small manufacturing plant in New Orleans and built it up into a fairly large company in its field. When father died five years ago, my mother took over the business.'

'What does this – er – company manufacture?'

'Exhaust pipes and other automotive parts.'

Mr and Mrs Stanhope exchanged a look and said in unison, 'I see.'

Their tone made Tracy tense up. *I wonder how long it's going to take me to love them?* she asked herself. She looked into the two unsympathetic faces across from her, and to her horror began babbling inanely. 'You'll really like my mother. She's beautiful, and intelligent, and charming. She's from the South. She's very small, of course, about your height, Mrs Stanhope –' Tracy's words trailed off, weighed down by the oppressive silence. She gave a silly little laugh that died away under Mrs Stanhope's stare.

It was Mr Stanhope who said without expression, 'Charles informs us you're pregnant.'

Oh, how Tracy wished he had not! Their attitude was so nakedly disapproving. It was as though their son had had nothing to do with what had happened. They made her feel it was a stigma. *Now I know what I should have worn*, Tracy thought. *A scarlet letter*.

'I don't understand how in this day and –' Mrs Stanhope began, but she never finished the sentence, because at that moment Charles came into the room. Tracy had never been so glad to see anyone in her entire life.

'Well,' Charles beamed. 'How are you all getting along?'

Tracy rose and hurried into his arms. 'Fine, darling.' She held him close to her, thinking, *Thank goodness Charles isn't like his parents. He could never be like them. They're narrowminded and snobbish and cold.*

There was a discreet cough behind them, and the butler stood there with a tray of drinks. *It's going to be all right*, Tracy told herself. *This movie's going to have a happy ending.*

The dinner was excellent, but Tracy was too nervous to eat. They discussed banking and politics and the distressing state of the world, and it was all very impersonal and polite. No one actually said aloud, 'You trapped our son into marriage.' *In all fairness*, Tracy thought, *they have every right to be concerned about the woman their son marries. One day Charles will own the firm, and it's important that he have the right wife.* And Tracy promised herself, *He will have.*

Charles gently took her hand which had been twisting the napkin under the table and smiled and gave a small wink. Tracy's heart soared.

'Tracy and I prefer a small wedding,' Charles said, 'and afterwards –'

'Nonsense,' Mrs Stanhope interrupted. 'Our family does not have small weddings, Charles. There will be dozens of friends who will want to see you married.' She looked over at Tracy, evaluating her figure. 'Perhaps we should see that the wedding invitations are sent at once.' And as an afterthought, 'That is, if that's acceptable to you?'

'Yes. Yes, of course.' There *was* going to be a wedding. *Why did I even doubt it?*

Mrs Stanhope said, 'Some of the guests will be

coming from abroad. I'll make arrangements for them to stay here at the house.'

Mr Stanhope asked, 'Have you decided where you're going on your honeymoon?'

Charles smiled. 'That's privileged information, Father.' He gave Tracy's hand a squeeze.

'How long a honeymoon are you planning?' Mrs Stanhope enquired.

'About fifty years,' Charles replied. And Tracy adored him for it.

After dinner they moved into the library for brandy, and Tracy looked around at the lovely old oak-panelled room with its shelves of leather-bound volumes, the two Corots, a small Copley, and a Reynolds. It would not have mattered to her if Charles had no money at all, but she admitted to herself that this was going to be a very pleasant way to live.

It was almost midnight when Charles drove her back to her small flat off Fairmount Park.

'I hope the evening wasn't too difficult for you, Tracy. Mother and Father can be a bit stiff sometimes.'

'Oh, no, they were lovely,' Tracy lied.

She was exhausted from the tension of the evening, but when they reached the door of her flat, she asked, 'Are you going to come in, Charles?' She needed to have him hold her in his arms. She wanted him to say, 'I love you, darling. No one in this world will ever keep us apart.'

He said, 'Afraid not tonight. I've got a heavy morning.'

Tracy concealed her disappointment. 'Of course. I understand, darling.'

'I'll talk to you tomorrow.' He gave her a brief kiss, and she watched him disappear down the hallway.

The flat was ablaze and the insistent sound of loud fire bells crashed abruptly through the silence. Tracy jerked upright in her bed, groggy with sleep, sniffing for smoke in the darkened room The ringing continued, and she slowly became aware that it was the telephone. The bedside clock read 2:30 A.M. Her first panicky thought was that something had happened to Charles. She snatched up the phone. 'Hello?'

A distant male voice asked, 'Tracy Whitney?'

She hesitated. If this was an obscene phone call . . . 'Who is this?'

'This is Lieutenant Miller of the New Orleans Police Department. Is this Tracy Whitney?'

'Yes.' Her heart began to pound.

'I'm afraid I have bad news for you.'

Her hand clenched around the phone.

'It's about your mother.'

'Has – has Mother been in some kind of accident?'

'She's dead, Miss Whitney.'

'No!' It was a scream. This *was* an obscene phone call. Some crank trying to frighten her. There was nothing wrong with her mother. Her mother was alive. *I love you very, very much, Tracy.*

'I hate to break it to you this way,' the voice said.

It was real. It was a nightmare, but it was happening. She could not speak. Her mind and her tongue were frozen.

The lieutenant's voice was saying, 'Hello . . . ? Miss Whitney? Hello . . . ?'

'I'll be on the first plane.'

She sat in the tiny kitchen of her flat thinking about her mother. It was impossible that she was dead. She had always been so vibrant, so alive. They had had such a close and loving relationship. From the time Tracy was a small girl, she had been able to go to her mother with her problems, to discuss school and boys and, later, men. When Tracy's father had died, many overtures had been made by people who wanted to buy the business. They had offered Doris Whitney enough money so that she could have lived well for the rest of her life, but she had stubbornly refused to sell. 'Your father built up this business. I can't throw away all his hard work.' And she had kept the business flourishing.

Oh, Mother, Tracy thought. *I love you so much. You'll never meet Charles, and you'll never see your grandchildren*, and she began to weep.

She made a cup of coffee and let it grow cold while she sat in the dark. Tracy wanted desperately to call Charles and tell him what had happened, to have him at her side. She looked at the kitchen clock. It was 3:30 A.M. She did not want to awaken him; she would telephone him from New Orleans. She wondered whether this would affect their wedding plans, and instantly felt guilty at the thought. How could she even think of herself at a time like this? Lieutenant Miller had said, 'When you get here, grab a taxi and come to police headquarters.' *Why police headquarters? Why? What had happened?*

Standing in the crowded New Orleans airport waiting for her suitcase, surrounded by pushing, impatient travellers, Tracy felt suffocated. She tried to move close to the baggage carousel, but no one would let her through. She was becoming increasingly nervous, dreading what she would have to face in a little while. She kept trying to tell herself that it was all some kind of mistake, but the words kept reverberating in her head: *I'm afraid I have bad news for you . . . She's dead, Miss Whitney . . . I hate to break it to you this way . . .*

When Tracy finally retrieved her suitcase, she got into a taxi and repeated the address the lieutenant had given her: 'Seven fifteen South Broad Street, please.'

The driver grinned at her in the rearview mirror. 'Fuzzville, huh?'

No conversation. Not now. Tracy's mind was too filled with turmoil.

The taxi headed east towards the Lake Ponchartrain Causeway. The driver chattered on. 'Come here for the big show, miss?'

She had no idea what he was talking about, but she thought, *No. I came here for death*. She was aware of the drone of the driver's voice, but she did not hear the words. She sat stiffly in her seat, oblivious to the familiar surroundings that sped past. It was only as they approached the French Quarter that Tracy became conscious of the growing noise. It was the sound of a mob gone mad, rioters yelling some ancient berserk litany.

'Far as I can take you,' the driver informed her.

And then Tracy looked up and saw it. It was an incredible sight. There were hundreds of thousands of shouting people, wearing masks, disguised as dragons and giant alligators and pagan gods, filling the streets and pavements ahead with a wild cacophony of sound. It was an insane explosion of bodies and music and floats and dancing.

'Better get out before they turn my cab over,' the driver said. 'Damned Mardi Gras.'

Of course. It was February, the time when the whole city celebrated the beginning of Lent. Tracy got out of the cab and stood at the curb, suitcase in hand, and the next moment she was swept up in the screaming, dancing crowd. It was obscene, a black witches' sabbath, a million Furies celebrating the death of her mother. Tracy's suitcase was torn from her hand and disappeared. She was grabbed by a fat man in a devil's mask and kissed. A deer squeezed her breasts, and a giant panda grabbed her from behind and lifted her up. She struggled free and tried to run, but it was impossible. She was hemmed in, trapped, a part of the singing, dancing celebration. She moved with the chanting mob, tears streaming down her face. There was no escape. When she was finally able to break away and flee to a quiet street, she was near hysteria. She stood still for a long time, leaning against a lamp-post, taking deep breaths, slowly regaining control of herself. She headed for the police station.

Lieutenant Miller was a middle-aged, harassed-looking man with a weather-beaten face, who seemed genuinely uncomfortable in his role. 'Sorry I couldn't meet you at the airport,' he told Tracy, 'but the whole town's gone nuts. We went through your mother's things, and you're the only one we could find to call.'

'Please, Lieutenant, tell me what – what happened to my mother.'

'She committed suicide.'

A cold chill went through her. 'That's – that's impossible! Why would she kill herself? She had everything to live for.' Her voice was ragged.

'She left a note addressed to you.'

The morgue was cold and indifferent and terrifying. Tracy was led down a long white corridor into a large, sterile, empty room, and suddenly she realized that the room was not empty. It was filled with the dead. Her dead.

A white-coated attendant strolled over to a wall,

reached for a handle, and pulled out an oversized drawer. 'Wanna take a look?'

No! I don't want to see the empty, lifeless body lying in that box. She wanted to get out of this place. She wanted to go back a few hours in time when the fire bell was ringing. *Let it be a real fire alarm, not the telephone, not my mother dead.* Tracy moved forward slowly, each step a screaming inside her. Then she was staring down at the lifeless remains of the body that had borne her, nourished her, laughed with her, loved her. She bent over and kissed her mother on the cheek. The cheek was cold and rubbery. 'Oh, Mother,' Tracy whispered. 'Why? Why did you do it?'

'We gotta perform an autopsy,' the attendant was saying. 'It's the state law with suicides.'

The note Doris Whitney left offered no answer.

My darling Tracy,

Please forgive me. I failed, and I couldn't stand being a burden on you. This is the best way. I love you so much.

Mother

The note was as lifeless and devoid of meaning as the body that lay in the drawer.

That afternoon Tracy made the funeral arrangements, then took a taxi to the family home. In the far distance she could hear the roar of the Mardi Gras revellers, like some alien, lurid celebration.

The Whitney residence was a Victorian house located in the Garden District in the residential section known as Uptown. Like most of the homes in New Orleans, it was built of wood and had no basement, for the area was situated below sea level.

Tracy had grown up in that house, and it was filled with warm, comfortable memories. She had not been home in the past year, and as her taxi slowed to a stop in front of the house, she was shocked to see a large sign on the lawn: FOR SALE – NEW ORLEANS REALTY COMPANY. It was impossible. *I'll never sell this old house*, her mother had often told her. *We've all been so happy together here*.

Filled with a strange, unreasoning fire, Tracy moved past a giant magnolia tree towards the front door. She had been given her own key to the house when she was in the seventh grade and had carried it with her since, as a talisman, a reminder of the haven that would always be there waiting for her.

She opened the door and stepped inside. She stood there, stunned. The rooms were completely empty, stripped of furniture. All the beautiful antique pieces were gone. The house was like a barren shell deserted by the people who had once occupied it. Tracy ran from room to room, her disbelief growing. It was as though some sudden disaster had struck. She hurried upstairs and stood in the doorway of the bedroom she had occupied most of her life. It stared back at her, cold and empty. *Oh, God, what could have happened?* Tracy heard the sound of the front doorbell and walked as if in a trance down the stairs to answer it.

Otto Schmidt stood in the doorway. The foreman of the Whitney Automotive Parts Company was an elderly man with a seamed face and a body that was rail-thin, except for a protruding beer belly. A tonsure of straggly grey hair framed his scalp.

'Tracy,' he said in a heavy German accent, 'I just heard the news. I – I can't tell you how sorry I am.'

Tracy clasped his hands. 'Oh, Otto. I'm so glad to see you. Come in.' She led him into the empty living room. 'I'm sorry there's no place to sit down,' she apologized. 'Do you mind sitting on the floor?'

'No, no.'

They sat down across from each other, their eyes dumb with misery. Otto Schmidt had been an employee of the company for as long as Tracy could remember. She knew how much her father had depended on him. When her mother had inherited the business, Schmidt had stayed on to run it for her. 'Otto, I don't understand what's happening. The police say Mother committed suicide, but you know there was no reason for her to kill herself.' A sudden thought stabbed at her. 'She wasn't ill, was she? She didn't have some terrible –'

'No. It wasn't that. Not that.' He looked away, uncomfortable, something unspoken in his words.

Tracy said slowly, 'You know what it was.'

He peered at her through rheumy blue eyes. 'Your mama didn't tell you what's been happening lately. She didn't want to worry you.'

Tracy frowned. 'Worry me about what? Go on . . . *please*.'

His work-worn hands opened and closed. 'Have you heard of a man called Joe Romano?'

'Joe Romano? No. Why?'

Otto Schmidt blinked. 'Six months ago Romano got in touch with your mother and said he wanted to buy the company. She told him she wasn't interested in selling, but he offered her ten times what the company was worth, and she couldn't refuse. She was so excited. She was going to invest all the money in bonds that would bring in an income that both of you could live on comfortably for the rest of your lives. She was going to surprise you. I was so glad for her. I've been ready to retire for the last three years, Tracy, but I couldn't leave Mrs Doris, could I? This Romano –' Otto almost spat out the word. 'This Romano gave her a small down payment. The big money – the balloon payment – was to have come last month.'

Tracy said impatiently, 'Go on, Otto. What happened?'

'When Romano took over, he fired everybody and brought in his own people to run things. Then he began to raid the company. He sold all the assets and ordered a lot of equipment, selling it off but not paying for it. The suppliers weren't worried about the delay in payment because they thought they were still dealing with your mother. When they finally began pressing your mother for their money, she went to Romano and demanded to know what was going on. He told her he had decided not to go ahead with the deal and was returning the company to her. By then, the company was not only worthless but your mother owed half a million dollars she couldn't pay. Tracy, it nearly killed me and the wife to watch how your mother fought to save that company. There was no way. They forced her into bankruptcy. They took everything – the business, this house, even her car.'

'Oh, my God!'

'There's more. The district attorney served your mother notice that he was going to ask for an indictment against her for fraud, that she was facing a prison sentence. That was the day she really died, I think.'

Tracy was seething with a wave of helpless anger. 'But all she had to do was tell them the truth – explain what that man did to her.'

The old foreman shook his head. 'Joe Romano works for a man named Anthony Orsatti. Orsatti runs New Orleans. I found out too late that Romano's done this before with other companies. Even if your mother had taken him to court, it would have been years before it was all untangled, and she didn't have the money to fight him.'

'Why didn't she tell me?' It was a cry of anguish, a cry for her mother's anguish.

'Your mother was a proud woman. And what could you do? There's nothing anyone can do.'

You're wrong, Tracy thought fiercely. 'I want to see Joe Romano. Where can I find him?'

Schmidt said flatly, 'Forget about him. You have no idea how powerful he is.'

'Where does he live, Otto?'

'He has an estate near Jackson Square, but it won't help to go there, Tracy, believe me.'

Tracy did not answer. She was filled with an emotion totally unfamiliar to her: hatred. *Joe Romano is going to pay for killing my mother*, Tracy swore to herself.

THREE

She needed time. Time to think, time to plan her next move. She could not bear to go back to the despoiled house, so she checked into a small hotel on Magazine Street, far from the French Quarter, where the mad parades were still going on. She had no luggage, and the suspicious clerk behind the desk said, 'You'll have to pay in advance. That'll be forty dollars for the night.'

From her room Tracy telephoned Clarence Desmond to tell him she would be unable to come to work for a few days.

He concealed his irritation at being inconvenienced. 'Don't worry about it,' he told Tracy. 'I'll find someone to fill in until you return.' He hoped she would remember to tell Charles Stanhope how understanding he had been.

Tracy's next call was to Charles. 'Charles, darling –'

'Where the devil *are* you, Tracy? Mother has

been trying to reach you all morning. She wanted to have lunch with you today. You two have a lot of arrangements to go over.'

'I'm sorry, darling. I'm in New Orleans.'

'You're *where*? What are you doing in New Orleans?'

'My mother – died.' The word stuck in her throat.

'Oh.' The tone of his voice changed instantly. 'I'm sorry, Tracy. It must have been very sudden. She was quite young, wasn't she?'

She was very young, Tracy thought miserably. Aloud she said, 'Yes. Yes, she was.'

'What happened? Are you all right?'

Somehow Tracy could not bring herself to tell Charles that it was suicide. She wanted desperately to cry out the whole terrible story about what they had done to her mother, but she stopped herself. *It's my problem*, she thought. *I can't throw my burden on Charles*. She said, 'Don't worry. I'm all right, darling.'

'Would you like me to come down there, Tracy?'

'No. Thank you. I can handle it. I'm burying Mama tomorrow. I'll be back in Philadelphia on Monday.'

When she hung up, she lay on the hotel bed, her thoughts unfocused. She counted stained acoustical tiles on the ceiling. One . . . two . . . three . . . Romano . . . four . . . five . . . Joe Romano . . . six . . . seven . . . he was going to pay. She had no plan. She knew only that she was not going to let Joe Romano get away with what he had done, that she would find some way to avenge her mother.

Tracy left her hotel in the late afternoon and walked along Canal Street until she came to a pawn shop. A cadaverous-looking man wearing an old-fashioned green eyeshade sat in a cage behind a counter.

'Help you?'

'I – I want to buy a gun.'

'What kind of gun?'

'You know . . . a . . . revolver.'

'You want a thirty-two, a forty-five, a –'

Tracy had never even held a gun. 'A – a thirty-two will do.'

'I have a nice thirty-two calibre Smith and Wesson here for two hundred and twenty-nine dollars, or a Charter Arms thirty-two for a hundred and fifty-nine . . .'

She had not brought much cash with her. 'Have you got something cheaper?'

He shrugged. '*Cheaper* is a slingshot, lady. Tell you what. I'll let you have the thirty-two for a hundred and fifty, and I'll throw in a box of bullets.'

'All right.' Tracy watched as he moved over to an arsenal on a table behind him and selected a revolver. He brought it to the counter. 'You know how to use it?'

'You – you pull the trigger.'

He grunted. 'Do you want me to show you how to load it?'

She started to say no, that she was not going to

use it, that she just wanted to frighten someone, but she realized how foolish that would sound. 'Yes, please.'

Tracy watched as he inserted the bullets into the chamber. 'Thank you.' She reached in her purse and counted out the money.

'I'll need your name and address for the police records.'

That had not occurred to Tracy. Threatening Joe Romano with a gun was a criminal act. *But he's the criminal, not I.*

The green eyeshade made the man's eyes a pale yellow as he watched her. 'Name?'

'Smith. Joan Smith.'

He made a note on a card. 'Address?'

'Dowman Road. Thirty-twenty Dowman Road.'

Without looking up he said, 'There is no Thirty-twenty Dowman Road. That would be in the middle of the river. We'll make it Fifty-twenty.' He pushed the receipt in front of her.

She signed JOAN SMITH. 'Is that it?'

'That's it.' He carefully pushed the revolver through the cage. Tracy stared at it, then picked it up, put it in her handbag, turned and hurried out of the shop.

'Hey, lady,' he yelled after her. 'Don't forget that gun is loaded!'

Jackson Square is in the heart of the French Quarter, with the beautiful St Louis Cathedral towering over it like a benediction. Lovely old homes and estates in the square are sheltered from the bustling street traffic by tall hedges and graceful magnolia trees. Joe Romano lived in one of those houses.

Tracy waited until dark before she set out. The parades had moved on to Chartres Street, and in the distance Tracy could hear an echo of the pandemonium she had been swept up in earlier.

She stood in the shadows, studying the house, conscious of the heavy weight of the gun in her handbag. The plan she had worked out was simple. She was going to reason with Joe Romano, ask him to clear her mother's name. If he refused, she would threaten him with the gun and force him to write out a confession. She would take it to Lieutenant Miller, and he would arrest Romano, and her mother's name would be protected. She wished desperately that Charles were there with her, but it was best to do it alone. Charles had to be left out of it. She would tell him about it when it was all over and Joe Romano was behind bars, where he belonged. A pedestrian was approaching. Tracy waited until he had walked past and the street was deserted.

She walked up to the house and pressed the doorbell. There was no answer. *He's probably at one of the private krewes balls given during Mardi Gras. But I can wait*, Tracy thought. *I can wait until he gets home*. Suddenly, the porch light snapped on, the front door opened, and a man stood in the doorway. His appearance was a surprise to Tracy. She had visualized a sinister-looking mobster, evil written all over his face. Instead, she found herself facing an attractive, pleasant-looking man who could easily have been mistaken for a university professor. His voice was low and friendly. 'Hello. May I help you?'

'Are you Joseph Romano?' Her voice was shaky.

'Yes. What can I do for you?' He had an easy, engaging manner. *No wonder my mother was taken in by this man*, Tracy thought.

'I – I'd like to talk to you, Mr Romano.'

He studied her figure for a moment. 'Certainly. Please come in.'

Tracy walked into a living room filled with beautiful, burnished antique furniture. Joseph Romano lived well. *On my mother's money*, Tracy thought bitterly.

'I was just about to mix myself a drink. What would you like?'

'Nothing.'

He looked at her curiously. 'What was it you wanted to see me about, Miss –?'

'Tracy Whitney. I'm Doris Whitney's daughter.'

He stared at her blankly for an instant, and then a look of recognition flashed across his face. 'Oh, yes. I heard about your mother. Too bad.'

Too bad! He had caused the death of her mother, and his only comment was: 'Too bad'.

'Mr Romano, the district attorney believes that my mother was guilty of fraud. You know that's not true. I want you to help me clear her name.'

He shrugged. 'I never talk business during Mardi

Gras. It's against my religion.' Romano walked over to the bar and began mixing drinks. 'I think you'll feel better after you've had a drink.'

He was leaving her no choice. Tracy opened her handbag and pulled out the revolver. She pointed it at him. 'I'll tell you what will make me feel better, Mr Romano. Having you confess to exactly what you did to my mother.'

Joseph Romano turned and saw the gun. 'You'd better put that away, Miss Whitney. It could go off.'

'It's *going* to go off if you don't do exactly what I tell you to. You're going to write down how you stripped the company, put it into bankruptcy, and drove my mother to suicide.'

He was watching her carefully now, his dark eyes wary. 'I see. What if I refuse?'

'Then I'm going to kill you.' She could feel the gun shaking in her hand.

'You don't look like a killer, Miss Whitney.' He was moving towards her now, a drink in his hand. His voice was soft and sincere. 'I had nothing to do with your mother's death, and believe me, I –' He threw the drink in her face.

Tracy felt the sharp sting of the alcohol in her eyes, and an instant later the gun was knocked from her hand.

'Your old lady held out on me,' Joe Romano said. 'She didn't tell me she had a horny-looking daughter.'

He was holding her, pinning her arms, and Tracy was blinded and terrified. She tried to move away from him, but he backed her into a wall, pressing against her.

'You have guts, baby. I like that. It turns me on.' His voice was hoarse. Tracy could feel his body hard against hers, and she tried to twist away, but she was helpless in his grip.

'You came here for a little excitement, huh? Well, Joe's going to give it to you.'

She tried to scream, but her voice came out in a gasp. 'Let me go!'

He ripped her blouse away. 'Hey! Look at those tits,' he whispered. He began pinching her nipples. 'Fight me, baby,' he whispered. 'I love it.'

'Let go of me!'

He was squeezing harder, hurting her. She felt herself being forced down to the floor.

'I'll bet you've never been fucked by a real man,' he said. He was astride her now, his body heavy on hers, his hands moving up her thighs. Tracy pushed out blindly, and her fingers touched the gun. She grabbed for it, and there was a sudden, loud explosion.

'Oh, Jesus!' Romano cried. His grip suddenly relaxed. Through a red mist, Tracy watched in horror as he fell off her and slumped to the floor, clutching his side. 'You shot me . . . you bitch. You shot me . . .'

Tracy was transfixed, unable to move. She felt she was going to be sick, and her eyes were blinded by stabbing pain. She pulled herself to her feet, turned, and stumbled to a door at the far end of the room. She pushed it open. It was a bathroom. She staggered over to the sink, filled the basin with cold water, and bathed her eyes until the pain began to subside and her vision cleared. She looked into the cabinet mirror. Her eyes were bloodshot and wild looking. *My God, I've just killed a man.* She ran back into the living room.

Joe Romano lay on the floor, his blood seeping onto the white rug. Tracy stood over him, white-faced. 'I'm sorry,' she said inanely. 'I didn't mean to –'

'Ambulance . . .' His breathing was ragged.

Tracy hurried to the telephone on the desk and dialled the operator. When she tried to speak, her voice was choked. 'Operator, send an ambulance right away. The address is Four-twenty-one Jackson Square. A man has been shot.'

She replaced the receiver and looked down at Joe Romano. *Oh, God*, she prayed, *please don't let him die. You know I didn't mean to kill him.* She knelt beside the body on the floor to see if he was still alive. His eyes were closed, but he was breathing. 'An ambulance is on its way,' Tracy promised.

She fled.

She tried not to run, afraid of attracting attention. She pulled her jacket close around her to conceal her ripped blouse. Four blocks from the house Tracy tried to hail a taxi. Half a dozen sped past her, filled with happy, laughing passengers. In the distance Tracy heard the sound of an approaching siren, and seconds later an ambulance raced past her, headed in the direction of Joe Romano's house. *I've got to get away from here*, Tracy thought. Ahead of her, a taxi pulled to the curb and discharged its passengers. Tracy ran towards it, afraid of losing it. 'Are you free?'

'That depends. Where you goin'?'

'The airport.' She held her breath.

'Get in.'

On the way to the airport, Tracy thought about the ambulance. What if they were too late and Joe Romano was dead? She would be a murderess. She had left the gun back at the house, and her fingerprints were on it. She could tell the police that Romano had tried to rape her and that the gun had gone off accidentally, but they would never believe her. She had purchased the gun that was lying on the floor beside Joe Romano. How much time had passed? Half an hour? An hour? She had to get out of New Orleans as quickly as possible.

'Enjoy the carnival?' the driver asked.

Tracy swallowed. 'I – yes.' She pulled out her hand mirror and did what she could to make herself presentable. She had been stupid to try to make Joe Romano confess. Everything had gone wrong. *How can I tell Charles what happened?* She knew how shocked he would be, but after she explained, he would understand. Charles would know what to do.

When the taxi arrived at New Orleans International Airport, Tracy wondered, *Was it only this morning that I was here? Did all this happen in just one day?* Her mother's suicide . . . the horror of being swept up in the carnival . . . the man snarling, 'You shot me . . . you bitch . . .'

When Tracy walked into the terminal, it seemed to her that everyone was staring at her accusingly. *That's what a guilty conscience does*, she thought. She wished there were some way she could learn about Joe Romano's condition, but she had no idea what hospital he would be taken to or whom she could call. *He's going to be all right. Charles and I will come back for Mother's funeral, and Joe Romano will be fine.* She tried to push from her mind the vision of the man lying on the white rug, his blood staining it red. She had to hurry home to Charles.

Tracy approached the Delta Airlines counter. 'I'd like a one-way ticket on the next flight to Philadelphia, please. Tourist.'

The passenger representative consulted his computer. 'That will be Flight three-o-four. You're in luck. I have one seat left.'

'What time does the plane leave?'

'In twenty minutes. You just have time to board.'

As Tracy reached into her handbag, she sensed rather than saw two uniformed police officers step up on either side of her. One of them said, 'Tracy Whitney?'

Her heart stopped beating for an instant. *It would be stupid to deny my identity.* 'Yes . . .'

'You're under arrest.'

And Tracy felt the cold steel of handcuffs snapped on her wrists.

Everything was happening in slow motion to someone else. Tracy watched herself being led through the airport, manacled to one of the policemen, while passersby turned to stare. She was shoved into the back of a black-and-white squad car with steel mesh separating the front seat from the rear. The police car sped away from the curb with red lights flashing and sirens screaming. She huddled in the back seat, trying to become invisible. She was a murderess. Joseph Romano had died. But it had been an accident. She would explain how it happened. They had to believe her. They *had* to.

The police station Tracy was taken to was in the Algiers district, on the west bank of New Orleans, a grim and foreboding building with a look of hopelessness about it. The booking room was crowded with seedy-looking characters – prostitutes, pimps, muggers and their victims. Tracy was marched to the desk of the sergeant-on-watch.

One of her captors said, 'The Whitney woman, Sarge. We caught her at the airport tryin' to escape.'

'I wasn't –'

'Take the cuffs off.'

The handcuffs were removed. Tracy found her voice. 'It was an accident. I didn't mean to kill him. He tried to rape me and –' She could not control the hysteria in her voice.

The desk sergeant said curtly, 'Are you Tracy Whitney?'

'Yes. I –'

'Lock her up.'

'No! Wait a minute,' she pleaded. 'I have to call someone. I – I'm entitled to make a phone call.'

The desk sergeant grunted, 'You know the routine, huh? How many times you been in the slammer, honey?'

'None. This is –'

'You get one call. Three minutes. What number do you want?'

She was so nervous that she could not remember Charles's telephone number. She could not even recall the area code for Philadelphia. *Was it two-five-one?* No. That was not it. She was trembling.

'Come on. I haven't got all night.'

Two-one-five. That was it! 'Two-one-five-five-five-five-nine-three-zero-one.'

The desk sergeant dialled the number and handed the phone to Tracy. She could hear the phone ringing. And ringing. There was no answer. *Charles had to be home.*

The desk sergeant said, 'Time's up.' He started to take the phone from her.

'Please wait!' she cried. But she suddenly remembered that Charles shut off his phone at night so that he would not be disturbed. She listened to the hollow ringing and realized there was no way she could reach him.

The desk sergeant asked, 'You through?'

Tracy looked up at him and said dully, 'I'm through.'

A policeman in shirt-sleeves took Tracy into a room where she was booked and fingerprinted, then led down a corridor and locked in a holding cell, by herself.

'You'll have a hearing in the morning,' the policeman told her. He walked away, leaving her alone.

None of this is happening, Tracy thought. *This is all a terrible dream. Oh, please, God, don't let any of this be real.*

But the stinking cot in the cell was real, and the seatless toilet in the corner was real, and the bars were real.

The hours of the night dragged by endlessly. *If only I could have reached Charles*. She needed him now more than she had ever needed anyone in her life. *I should have confided in him in the first place. If I had, none of this would have happened.*

At 6:00 A.M. a bored guard brought Tracy a breakfast of tepid coffee and cold oatmeal. She could not touch it. Her stomach was in knots. At 9:00 a matron came for her.

'Time to go, sweetie.' She unlocked the cell door.

'I must make a call,' Tracy said. 'It's very –'

'Later,' the matron told her. 'You don't want to keep the judge waiting. He's a mean son of a bitch.'

She escorted Tracy down a corridor and through a door that led into a courtroom. An elderly judge was seated on the bench. His head and hands kept moving in small, quick jerks. In front of him stood the district attorney, Ed Topper, a slight man in his forties, with crinkly salt-and-pepper hair cut en brosse, and cold, black eyes.

Tracy was led to a seat, and a moment later the bailiff called out, 'People against Tracy Whitney', and Tracy found herself moving towards the bench. The judge was scanning a sheet of paper in front of him, his head bobbing up and down.

Now. Now was Tracy's moment to explain to someone in authority the truth about what had happened. She pressed her hands together to keep them from trembling. 'Your Honour, it wasn't murder. I shot him, but it was an accident. I only meant to frighten him. He tried to rape me and –'

The district attorney interrupted. 'Your Honour, I see no point in wasting the court's time. This woman broke into Mr Romano's home, armed with a thirty-two-calibre revolver, stole a Renoir painting worth half a million dollars, and when Mr Romano caught her in the act, she shot him in cold blood and left him for dead.'

Tracy felt the colour draining from her face. 'What – what are you *talking* about?'

None of this was making any sense.

The district attorney rapped out, 'We have the gun with which she wounded Mr Romano. Her fingerprints are on it.'

Wounded! Then Joseph Romano was alive! She had not killed anyone.

'She escaped with the painting, Your Honour. It's probably in the hands of a fence by now. For that reason, the state is requesting that Tracy Whitney be held for attempted murder and armed robbery and that bail be set at half a million dollars.'

The judge turned to Tracy, who stood there in shock. 'Are you represented by counsel?'

She did not even hear him.

He raised his voice. 'Do you have an attorney?'

Tracy shook her head. 'No. I – what – what this man said isn't true. I never –'

'Do you have money for an attorney?'

There was her employees' fund at the bank. There was Charles. 'I . . . no, Your Honour, but I don't understand –'

'The court will appoint one for you. You are ordered held in jail, in lieu of five hundred thousand dollars bail. Next case.'

'Wait! This is all a mistake! I'm not –'

She had no recollection of being led from the courtroom.

The name of the attorney appointed by the court was Perry Pope. He was in his late thirties, with a craggy, intelligent face and sympathetic blue eyes. Tracy liked him immediately.

He walked into her cell, sat on the cot, and said, 'Well! You've created quite a sensation for a lady who's been in town only twenty-four hours.' He grinned. 'But you're lucky. You're a lousy shot. It's only a flesh wound. Romano's going to live.' He took out a pipe. 'Mind?'

'No.'

He filled his pipe with tobacco, lit it, and studied Tracy. 'You don't *look* like the average desperate criminal, Miss Whitney.'

'I'm not. I *swear* I'm not.'

'Convince me,' he said. 'Tell me what happened. From the beginning. Take your time.'

Tracy told him. Everything. Perry Pope sat quietly listening to her story, not speaking until Tracy had finished. Then he leaned back against the wall of the cell, a grim expression on his face. 'That bastard,' Pope said softly.

'I don't understand what they were talking about.' There was confusion in Tracy's eyes. 'I don't understand anything about a painting.'

'It's really very simple. Joe Romano used you as a patsy, the same way he used your mother. You walked right into a set-up.'

'I still don't understand.'

'Then let me lay it out for you. Romano will put in an insurance claim for half a million dollars for the Renoir he's hidden away somewhere, and he'll collect. The insurance company will be after *you*, not him. When things cool down, he'll sell the painting to a private party and make another half million, thanks to your do-it-yourself approach. Didn't you realise that a confession obtained at the point of a gun is worthless?'

'I – I suppose so. I just thought that if I could

get the truth out of him, someone would start an investigation.'

His pipe had gone out. He relit it. 'How did you enter his house?'

'I rang the front doorbell, and Mr Romano let me in.'

'That's not his story. There's a smashed window at the back of the house, where he says you broke in. He told the police he caught you sneaking out with the Renoir, and when he tried to stop you, you shot him and ran.'

'That's a lie! I –'

'But it's *his* lie, and his house, and your gun. Do you have any idea with whom you're dealing?'

Tracy shook her head mutely.

'Then let me tell you the facts of life, Miss Whitney. This town is sewn up tight by the Orsatti Family. Nothing goes down here without Anthony Orsatti's okay. If you want a permit to put up a building, pave a highway, run girls, numbers, or dope, you see Orsatti. Joe Romano started out as his hit man. Now he's the top man in Orsatti's organisation.' He looked at her in wonder. 'And you walked into Romano's house and pulled a gun on him.'

Tracy sat there, numb and exhausted. Finally she asked, 'Do you believe my story?'

He smiled. 'You're damned right. It's so dumb it has to be true.'

'Can you help me?'

He said slowly, 'I'm going to try. I'd give anything

to put them all behind bars. They own this town and most of the judges in it. If you go to trial, they'll bury you so deep you'll never see daylight again.'

Tracy looked at him, puzzled. '*If* I go to trial?'

Pope stood and paced up and down in the small cell. 'I don't want to put you in front of a jury, because, believe me, it will be *his* jury. There's only one judge Orsatti has never been able to buy. His name is Henry Lawrence. If I can arrange for him to hear this case, I'm pretty sure I can make a deal for you. It's not strictly ethical, but I'm going to speak to him privately. He hates Orsatti and Romano as much as I do. Now all we've got to do is get to Judge Lawrence.'

Perry Pope arranged for Tracy to place a telephone call to Charles. Tracy heard the familiar voice of Charles's secretary. 'Mr Stanhope's office.'

'Harriet. This is Tracy Whitney. Is –?'

'Oh! He's been trying to reach you, Miss Whitney, but we didn't have a telephone number for you. Mrs Stanhope is most anxious to discuss the wedding arrangements with you. If you could call her as soon as possible –'

'Harriet, may I speak to Mr Stanhope, please?'

'I'm sorry, Miss Whitney. He's on his way to Houston for a meeting. If you'll give me your number, I'm sure he'll telephone you as soon as he can.'

'I –' There was no way she could have him telephone her at the jail. Not until she had a chance to explain things to him first.

'I – I'll have to call Mr Stanhope back.' She slowly replaced the receiver.

Tomorrow. Tracy thought wearily. *I'll explain it all to Charles tomorrow.*

That afternoon Tracy was moved to a larger cell. A delicious hot dinner appeared from Galatoire's, and a short time later fresh flowers arrived with a note attached. Tracy opened the envelope and pulled out the card. CHIN UP, WE'RE GOING TO BEAT THE BASTARDS. PERRY POPE.

He came to visit Tracy the following morning. The instant she saw the smile on his face, she knew there was good news.

'We got lucky,' he exclaimed. 'I've just left Judge Lawrence and Topper, the district attorney. Topper screamed like a banshee, but we've got a deal.'

'A deal?'

'I told Judge Lawrence your whole story. He's agreed to accept a guilty plea from you.'

Tracy stared at him in shock. 'A *guilty* plea? But I'm not –'

He raised a hand. 'Hear me out. By pleading guilty, you save the state the expense of a trial. I've persuaded the judge that you didn't steal the painting. He knows Joe Romano, and he believes me.'

'But . . . if I plead guilty,' Tracy asked slowly, 'what will they do to me?'

'Judge Lawrence will sentence you to three months in prison with –'

'Prison!'

'Wait a minute. He'll suspend the sentence, and you can do your probation out of state.'

'But then I'll – I'll have a record.'

Perry Pope sighed. 'If they put you on trial for armed robbery and attempted murder during the commission of a felony, you could be sentenced to ten years.'

Ten years in jail!

Perry Pope was patiently watching her. 'It's your decision,' he said. 'I can only give you my best advice. It's a miracle that I got away with this. They want an answer now. You don't have to take the deal. You can get another lawyer and –'

'No.' She knew that this man was honest. Under the circumstances, considering her insane behaviour, he had done everything possible for her. If only she could talk to Charles. But they needed an answer now. She was probably lucky to get off with a three-month suspended sentence.

'I'll – I'll take the deal,' Tracy said. She had to force the words out.

He nodded. 'Smart girl.'

She was not permitted to make any phone calls before she was returned to the courtroom. Ed Topper stood on one side of her, and Perry Pope on the other. Seated on the bench was a distinguished-looking man in his fifties, with a smooth, unlined face and thick, styled hair.

Judge Henry Lawrence said to Tracy, 'The court has been informed that the defendant wishes to change her plea from not guilty to guilty. Is that correct?'

'Yes, Your Honour.'

'Are all parties in agreement?'

Perry Pope nodded. 'Yes, Your Honour.'

'The state agrees, Your Honour,' the district attorney said.

Judge Lawrence sat there in silence for a long moment. Then he leaned forward and looked into Tracy's eyes. 'One of the reasons this great country of ours is in such pitiful shape is that the streets are crawling with vermin who think they can get away with anything. People who laugh at the law. Some judicial systems in this country coddle criminals. Well, in Louisiana, we don't believe in that. When, during the commission of felony, someone tries to kill in cold blood, we believe that that person should be properly punished.'

Tracy began to feel the first stirrings of panic. She turned to look at Perry Pope. His eyes were fixed on the judge.

'The defendant has admitted that she attempted to murder one of the outstanding citizens of this community – a man noted for his philanthropy and good works. The defendant shot him while in the act of stealing an art object worth half a million dollars.' His voice grew harsher. 'Well, this court is going to see to it that you don't get to enjoy that money – not for the next fifteen years, because for the next fifteen years you're going to be incarcerated in the Southern Louisiana Penitentiary for Women.'

Tracy felt the courtroom begin to spin. Some horrible joke was being played. The judge was an actor typecast for the part, but he was reading the wrong lines. He was not supposed to say any of those things. She turned to explain that to Perry Pope, but his eyes were averted. He was juggling papers in his briefcase, and for the first time, Tracy noticed that his fingernails were bitten to the quick. Judge Lawrence had risen and was gathering up his notes. Tracy stood there, numb, unable to comprehend what was happening to her.

A bailiff stepped to Tracy's side and took her arm. 'Come along,' he said.

'No,' Tracy cried. 'No, please!' She looked up at the judge. 'There's been a terrible mistake, Your Honour. I –'

And as she felt the bailiff's grip tighten on her arm, Tracy realised there had been no mistake. She had been tricked. They were going to destroy her.

Just as they had destroyed her mother.

FOUR

The news of Tracy Whitney's crime and sentencing appeared on the front page of the *New Orleans Courier*, accompanied by a police photograph of her. The major wire services picked up the story and flashed it to correspondent newspapers around the country, and when Tracy was taken from the courtroom to await transport to the state penitentiary, she was confronted by a crew of television reporters. She hid her face in humiliation, but there was no escape from the cameras. Joe Romano was big news, and the attempt on his life by a beautiful female burglar was even bigger news. It seemed to Tracy that she was surrounded by enemies. *Charles will get me out*, she kept repeating to herself. *Oh, please, God, let Charles get me out. I can't have our baby born in prison.*

It was not until the following afternoon that the desk sergeant would permit Tracy to use the telephone. Harriet answered. 'Mr Stanhope's office.'

'Harriet, this is Tracy Whitney. I'd like to speak to Mr Stanhope.'

'Just a moment, Miss Whitney.' She heard the hesitation in the secretary's voice. 'I'll – I'll see if Mr Stanhope is in.'

After a long, harrowing wait, Tracy finally heard Charles's voice. She could have wept with relief. 'Charles –'

'Tracy? Is that you, Tracy?'

'Yes, darling. Oh, Charles, I've been trying to reach –'

'I've been going crazy, Tracy! The newspapers here are full of wild stories about you. I can't believe what they're saying.'

'None of it is true, darling. *None* of it. I –'

'Why didn't you call me?'

'I tried. I couldn't reach you. I –'

'Where are you now?'

'I'm – I'm in jail in New Orleans. Charles, they're going to send me to prison for something I didn't do.' To her horror, she was weeping.

'Hold on. Listen to me. The papers say that you shot a man. That's not true, is it?'

'I did shoot him, but –'

'Then it *is* true.'

'It's not the way it sounds, darling. It's not like that at all. I can explain everything to you. I –'

'Tracy, did you plead guilty to attempted murder and stealing a painting?'

'Yes, Charles, but only because –'

'My God, if you needed money that badly, you

should have discussed it with me . . . And trying to kill someone . . . I can't believe this. Neither can my parents. You're the headline in this morning's Philadelphia *Daily News*. This is the first time a breath of scandal has ever touched the Stanhope family.'

It was the bitter self-control of Charles's voice that made Tracy aware of the depth of his feelings. She had counted on him so desperately, and he was on *their* side. She forced herself not to scream. 'Darling, I need you. Please come down here. You can straighten all this out.'

There was a long silence. 'It doesn't sound like there's much to straighten out. Not if you've confessed to doing all those things. The family can't afford to get mixed up in a thing like this. Surely you can see that. This has been a terrible shock for us. Obviously, I never really knew you.'

Each word was a hammerblow. The world was falling in on her. She felt more alone than she had ever felt in her life. There was no one to turn to now, no one. 'What – what about the baby?'

'You'll have to do whatever you think best with your baby,' Charles said. 'I'm sorry, Tracy.' And the connection was broken.

She stood there holding the dead receiver in her hand.

A prisoner behind her said, 'If you're through with the phone, honey, I'd like to call my lawyer.'

When Tracy was returned to her cell, the matron had instructions for her. 'Be ready to leave in the morning. You'll be picked up at five o'clock.'

She had a visitor. Otto Schmidt seemed to have aged years during the few hours since Tracy had last seen him. He looked ill.

'I just came to tell you how sorry my wife and I are. We know whatever happened wasn't your fault.'

If only Charles had said that!

'The wife and I will be at Mrs Doris's funeral tomorrow.'

'Thank you, Otto.'

They're going to bury both of us tomorrow, Tracy thought miserably.

She spent the night wide awake, lying on her narrow prison bunk, staring at the ceiling. In her mind she replayed the conversation with Charles again and again. He had never even given her a chance to explain.

She had to think of the baby. She had read of women having babies in prison, but the stories had been so remote from her own life that it was as though she were reading about people from another planet. Now it was happening to her. *You'll have to do whatever you think best with your baby*, Charles had said. She wanted to have her baby. *And yet*, she thought, *they won't let me keep it. They'll take it away from me because I'm going to be in prison for the next fifteen years. It's better that it never knows about its mother.*

She wept.

At 5:00 in the morning a male guard, accompanied by a matron, entered Tracy's cell. 'Tracy Whitney?'

'Yes.' She was surprised at how odd her voice sounded.

'By order of the Criminal Court of the State of Louisiana, Orleans Parish, you are forthwith being transferred to the Southern Louisiana Penitentiary for Women. Let's move it, babe.'

She was walked down a long corridor, past cells filled with inmates. There was a series of catcalls.

'Have a good trip, honey . . .'

'You tell me where you got that paintin' hidden, Tracy, baby, and I'll split the money with you . . .'

'If you're headin' for the big house, ask for Ernestine Littlechap. She'll take real good care of you . . .'

Tracy passed the telephone where she had made her call to Charles. *Good-bye, Charles.*

She was outside in a courtyard. A yellow prison bus with barred windows stood there, its engine idling. Half a dozen women already were seated in the bus, watched over by two armed guards. Tracy looked at the faces of her fellow passengers. One was defiant, and another bored; others wore expressions of despair. The lives they had lived were about to come to an end. They were outcasts, headed for cages where they would be locked up like animals. Tracy wondered what crimes they had committed and whether any of them was as innocent as she was, and she wondered what they saw in *her* face.

The ride on the prison bus was interminable, the bus hot and smelly, but Tracy was unaware of it. She had withdrawn into herself, no longer conscious of the other passengers or of the lush green countryside the bus passed through. She was in another time, in another place.

She was a little girl at the shore with her mother and father, and her father was carrying her into the ocean on his shoulders, and when she cried out her father said *Don't be a baby, Tracy*, and he dropped her into the cold water. When the water closed over her head, she panicked and began to choke, and her father lifted her up and did it again, and from that moment on she had been terrified of the water . . .

The college auditorium was filled with students and their parents and relatives. She was class valedictorian. She spoke for fifteen minutes, and her speech was filled with soaring idealism, clever references to the past, and shining dreams for the future. The dean had presented her with a Phi Beta Kappa key. *I want you to keep it*, Tracy told her mother, and the pride on her mother's face was beautiful . . .

I'm going to Philadelphia, Mother. I have a job at a bank there.

Annie Mahler, her best friend, was calling her. *You'll love Philadelphia, Tracy. It's full of all kinds of cultural things. It has beautiful scenery and a shortage of women. I mean, the men here are really hungry! I can get you a job at the bank where I work . . .*

Charles was making love to her. She watched the moving shadows on the ceiling and thought, *How many girls would like to be in my place?* Charles was a prime catch. And she was instantly ashamed of the thought. She loved him. She could feel him inside her, beginning to thrust harder, faster and faster, on the verge of exploding, and he gasped out, *Are you ready?* And she lied and said yes. *Was it wonderful for you? Yes, Charles.* And she thought, *Is that all there is?* and the guilt again . . .

'You! I'm talkin' to you. Are you deaf for Christ's sake? Let's go.'

Tracy looked up and she was in the yellow prison bus. It had stopped in an enclosure surrounded by a gloomy pile of masonry. A series of nine fences topped with barbed wire surrounded the five hundred acres of farm pasture and woodlands that made up the prison grounds of the Southern Louisiana Penitentiary for Women.

'Get out,' the guard said. 'We're here.'

Here was hell.

FIVE

A stocky, stony-faced matron with sable-brown dyed hair was addressing the new arrivals: 'Some of you are gonna be here for a long, long time. There's only one way you're gonna make it, and that's by forgettin' all about the outside world. You can do your time the easy way or the hard way. We have rules here, and you'll follow those rules. We'll tell you when to get up, when to work, when to eat, and when to go to the toilet. You break any of our rules, and you'll wish you was dead. We like to keep things peaceful here, and we know how to handle troublemakers.' Her eyes flicked over to Tracy. 'You'll be taken for your physical examinations now. After that you'll go to the showers and be assigned your cells. In the mornin' you'll receive your work duties. That's all.' She started to turn away.

A pale young girl standing next to Tracy said, 'Excuse me, please, could –'

The matron whirled around, her face filled with

fury. 'Shut your fuckin' mouth. You speak only when you're spoken to, do you understand? That goes for all you assholes.'

The tone, as much as the words, was a shock to Tracy. The matron signalled to two women guards at the back of the room. 'Get these no-good bitches out of here.'

Tracy found herself being herded out of the room with the others, down a long corridor. The prisoners were marched into a large, white-tiled room, where a fat, middle-aged man in a soiled smock stood next to an examination table.

One of the matrons called out, 'Line up', and formed the women into one long line.

The man in the smock said, 'I'm Dr Glasco, ladies. Strip!'

The women turned to look at one another, uncertainly. One of them said, 'How far should we –?'

'Don't you know what the hell *strip* means? Get your clothes off – all of them.'

Slowly, the women began to undress. Some of them were self-conscious, some outraged, some indifferent. On Tracy's left was a woman in her late forties, shivering violently, and on Tracy's right was a pathetically thin girl who looked to be no more than seventeen years old. Her skin was covered with acne.

The doctor gestured to the first woman in line. 'Lie down on the table and put your feet in the stirrups.'

The woman hesitated.

'Come on. You're holding up the line.'

She did as she was told. The doctor inserted a speculum into her vagina. As he probed, he asked, 'Do you have a venereal disease?'

'No.'

'We'll soon find out about that.'

The next woman replaced her on the table. As the doctor started to insert the same speculum into her, Tracy cried out, 'Wait a minute!'

The doctor stopped and looked up in surprise. 'What?'

Everyone was staring at Tracy. She said, 'I . . . you didn't sterilize that instrument.'

Dr Glasco gave Tracy a slow, cold smile. 'Well! We have a gynaecologist in the house. You're worried about germs, are you? Move down to the end of the line.'

'What?'

'Don't you understand English? Move down.'

Tracy, not understanding why, took her place at the end of the line.

'Now, if you don't mind,' the doctor said, 'we'll continue.' He inserted the speculum into the woman on the table, and Tracy suddenly realized why she was the last in line. He was going to examine all of them with the same unsterilized speculum, and she would be the last one on whom he used it. She could feel an anger boiling up inside her. He could have examined them separately, instead of deliberately stripping away their dignity.

And they were letting him get away with it. *If they all protested* – It was her turn.

'On the table, *Ms Doctor*.'

Tracy hesitated, but she had no choice. She climbed up on the table and closed her eyes. She could feel him spread her legs apart, and then the cold speculum was inside her, probing and pushing and hurting. Deliberately hurting. She gritted her teeth.

'You got syphilis or gonorrhoea?' the doctor asked.

'No.' She was not going to tell him about the baby. Not this monster. She would discuss that with the warden.

She felt the speculum being roughly pulled out of her. Dr Glasco was putting on a pair of rubber gloves. 'All right,' he said. 'Line up and bend over. We're going to check your pretty little asses.'

Before she could stop herself, Tracy said, 'Why are you doing this?'

Dr Glasco stared at her. 'I'll tell you why, *Doctor*. Because assholes are great hiding places. I have a whole collection of marijuana and cocaine that I got from ladies like you. Now bend over.' And he went down the line, plunging fingers into anus after anus. Tracy was sickened. She could feel the hot bile rise in her throat and she began to gag.

'You vomit in here, and I'll rub your face in it.' He turned to the guards. 'Get them to the showers. They stink.'

Carrying their clothes, the naked prisoners were

marched down another corridor to a large concrete room with a dozen open shower stalls.

'Lay your clothes in the corner,' a matron ordered. 'And get into the showers. Use the disinfectant soap. Wash every part of your body from head to toe, and shampoo your hair.'

Tracy stepped from the rough cement floor into the shower. The spray of water was cold. She scrubbed herself hard, thinking, *I'll never be clean again. What kind of people are these? How can they treat other human beings in this way? I can't stand fifteen years of this.*

A guard called out to her, 'Hey, you! Time's up. Get out.'

Tracy stepped out of the shower, and another prisoner took her place. Tracy was handed a thin, worn towel and half dried her body.

When the last of the prisoners had showered, they were marched to a large supply room where there were shelves of clothes guarded by a Latino inmate who sized up each prisoner and handed out grey uniforms. Tracy and the others were issued two uniform dresses, two pairs of panties, two brassieres, two pairs of shoes, two nightgowns, a sanitary belt, a hairbrush, and a laundry bag. The matrons stood watching while the prisoners dressed. When they had finished, they were herded to a room where a trusty operated a large portrait camera set on a tripod.

'Stand over there against the wall.'

Tracy moved over to the wall.

'Full face.'

She stared at the camera. Click.

'Turn your head to the right.'

She obeyed. Click.

'Left.' Click. 'Over to the table.'

The table had fingerprint equipment on it. Tracy's fingers were rolled across an inky pad, then pressed onto a white card.

'Left hand. Right hand. Wipe your hands with that rag. You're finished.'

She's right, Tracy thought numbly. *I'm finished. I'm a number. Nameless, faceless.*

A guard pointed to Tracy. 'Whitney? Warden wants to see you. Follow me.'

Tracy's heart suddenly soared. Charles had done something after all! *Of course* he had not abandoned her, any more than she ever could have abandoned him. It was the sudden shock that had made him behave the way he had. He had had time to think it over now and to realize he still loved her. He had talked to the warden and explained the terrible mistake that had been made. She was going to be set free.

She was marched down a different corridor, through two sets of heavily barred doors manned by male and female guards. As Tracy was admitted through the second door, she was almost knocked down by a prisoner. She was a giant, the biggest woman Tracy had ever seen – well over six feet tall, she must have weighed over twenty stone. She had a flat, pockmarked face, with feral yellow eyes.

She grabbed Tracy's arm to steady her and pressed her arm against Tracy's breasts.

'Hey!' the woman said to the guard. 'We got a new fish. How 'bout you put her in with me?' She had a heavy Swedish accent.

'Sorry. She's already been assigned, Bertha.'

The amazon stroked Tracy's face. Tracy jerked away, and the giant woman laughed. 'It's okay, *littbarn*. Big Bertha will see you later. We got plenty of time. You ain't goin' nowhere.'

They reached the warden's office. Tracy was faint with anticipation. Would Charles be there? Or would he have sent his attorney?

The warden's secretary nodded to the guard, 'He's expecting her. Wait here.'

Warden George Brannigan was seated at a scarred desk, studying some papers in front of him. He was in his mid-forties, a thin, careworn-looking man, with a sensitive face and deep-set hazel eyes.

Warden Brannigan had been in charge of the Southern Louisiana Penitentiary for Women for five years. He had arrived with the background of a modern penologist and the zeal of an idealist, determined to make sweeping reforms in the prison. But it had defeated him, as it had defeated others before him.

The prison originally had been built to accommodate two inmates to a cell, and now each cell held as many as four to six prisoners. He knew that the same situation applied everywhere. The country's prisons were all overcrowded and understaffed. Thousands of criminals were penned up day and night with nothing to do but nurse their hatred and plot their vengeance. It was a stupid, brutal system, but it was all there was.

He buzzed his secretary. 'All right. Send her in.'

The guard opened the door to the inner office, and Tracy stepped inside.

Warden Brannigan looked up at the woman standing before him. Dressed in the drab prison uniform, her face bruised with fatigue, Tracy Whitney still looked beautiful. She had a lovely, candid face, and Warden Brannigan wondered how long it would remain that way. He was particularly interested in this prisoner because he had read about her case in the newspapers and had studied her record. She was a first offender, had not killed anyone, and fifteen years was an inordinately harsh sentence. The fact that Joseph Romano was her accuser made her conviction all the more suspect. But the warden was simply the custodian of bodies. He could not buck the system. He *was* the system.

'Please have a seat,' he said.

Tracy was glad to sit down. Her knees were weak. He was going to tell her now about Charles, and how soon she would be released.

'I've been looking over your record,' the warden began.

Charles would have asked him to do that.

'I see you're going to be with us a long time. Your sentence is fifteen years.'

It took a moment for his words to sink in. Something was dreadfully wrong. 'Didn't – didn't you speak to – to Charles?' In her nervousness she was stammering.

He looked at her blankly. 'Charles?'

And she knew. Her stomach turned to water. 'Please,' she said. 'Please listen to me. I'm innocent. I don't belong here.'

How many times had he heard that? A hundred? A thousand? *I'm innocent.*

He said, 'The courts have found you guilty. The best advice I can give you is to try to do easy time. Once you accept the terms of your imprisonment, it will be a lot easier for you. There are no clocks in prison, only calendars.'

I can't be locked up here for fifteen years, Tracy thought in despair. *I want to die. Please, God, let me die. But I can't die, can I? I would be killing my baby. It's your baby, too, Charles. Why aren't you here helping me?* That was the moment she began to hate him.

'If you have any special problems,' Warden Brannigan said, 'I mean, if I can help you in any way, I want you to come and see me.' Even as he spoke, he knew how hollow his words were. She was young and beautiful and fresh. The bull-dykes in the prison would fall on her like animals. There was not even a safe cell to which he could assign her. Nearly every cell was controlled by a stud. Warden Brannigan had heard rumours of rapes in the showers, in the toilets, and in the corridors at night. But they were only rumours, because the victims were always silent afterwards. Or dead.

Warden Brannigan said gently, 'With good behaviour, you might be released in twelve or –'

'No!' It was a cry of black despair, of desperation. Tracy felt the walls of the office closing in on her. She was on her feet, screaming. The guard came hurrying in and grabbed Tracy's arms.

'Easy,' Warden Brannigan commanded him.

He sat there, helpless, and watched as Tracy was led away.

She was taken down a series of corridors past cells filled with inmates of every description. They were black and white and brown and yellow. They stared at Tracy as she passed and called out to her in a dozen accents. Their cries made no sense to Tracy.

'Fish night . . .'

'French mate . . .'

'Fresh mite . . .'

'Flesh meet . . .'

It was not until Tracy reached her cell block that she realized what the women were chanting: 'Fresh meat'.

SIX

There were sixty women in Cell Block C, four to a cell. Faces peered out from behind bars as Tracy was marched down the long, smelly corridor, and the expressions varied from indifference to lust to hatred. She was walking underwater in some strange, unknown land, an alien in a slowly unfolding dream. Her throat was raw from the screaming inside her trapped body. The summons to the warden's office had been her last faint hope. Now there was nothing. Nothing except the mind-numbing prospect of being caged in this purgatory for the next fifteen years.

The matron opened a cell door. 'Inside!'

Tracy blinked and looked around. In the cell were three women, silently watching her.

'Move,' the matron ordered.

Tracy hesitated, then stepped into the cell. She heard the door slam behind her.

She was home.

The cramped cell barely held four bunks, a little

table with a cracked mirror over it, four small lockers, and a seatless toilet in the far corner.

Her cell mates were staring at her. The Puerto Rican woman broke the silence. 'Looks like we got ourselves a new cellie.' Her voice was deep and throaty. She would have been beautiful if it had not been for a livid knife scar that ran from her temple to her throat. She appeared to be no older than fourteen, until you looked into her eyes.

A squat, middle-aged Mexican woman said, '*Que suerte verte!* Nice to see you. What they got you in for, querida?'

Tracy was too paralysed to answer.

The third woman was black. She was almost six feet tall, with narrow, watchful eyes and a cold, hard mask of a face.

Her head was shaved and her skull shone blue-black in the dim light. 'Tha's your bunk over in the corner.'

Tracy walked over to the bunk. The mattress was filthy, stained with the excreta of God only knew how many previous occupants. She could not bring herself to touch it. Involuntarily, she voiced her revulsion. 'I – I can't sleep on this mattress.'

The fat Mexican woman grinned. 'You don't have to, honey. *Hay tiempo*. You can sleep on mine.'

Tracy suddenly became aware of the undercurrents in the cell, and they hit her with a physical force. The three women were watching her, staring, making her feel naked. *Fresh meat*. She was suddenly terrified. *I'm wrong*, Tracy thought. *Oh, please let me be wrong.*

She found her voice. 'Who – who do I see about getting a clean mattress?'

'God,' the black woman grunted. 'But he ain't been around here lately.'

Tracy turned to look at the mattress again. Several large black roaches were crawling across it. *I can't stay in this place*, Tracy thought. *I'll go insane.*

As though reading her mind, the black woman told her, 'You go with the flow, baby.'

Tracy heard the warden's voice. *The best advice I can give you is to try to do easy time . . .*

The black woman continued. 'I'm Ernestine Littlechap.' She nodded towards the woman with the long scar. 'Tha's Lola. She's from Puerto Rico, and fatso here is Paulita, from Mexico. Who are you?'

'I'm – I'm Tracy Whitney.' She had almost said, 'I *was* Tracy Whitney.' She had the nightmarish feeling that her identity was slipping away. A spasm of nausea swept through her, and she gripped the edge of the bunk to steady herself.

'Where you come from, honey?' the fat woman asked.

'I'm sorry, I – I don't feel like talking.' She suddenly felt too weak to stand. She slumped down on the edge of the filthy bunk and wiped the beads of cold perspiration from her face with her skirt. *My baby*, she thought. *I should have told the warden I'm going to have a baby. He'll move me into a clean cell. Perhaps they'll even let me have a cell to myself.*

She heard footsteps coming down the corridor. A matron was walking past the cell. Tracy hurried to the cell door. 'Excuse me,' she said, 'I have to see the warden. I'm –'

'I'll send him right down,' the matron said over her shoulder.

'You don't understand. I'm –'

The matron was gone.

Tracy crammed her knuckles in her mouth to keep from screaming.

'You sick or somethin', honey?' the Puerto Rican asked.

Tracy shook her head, unable to speak. She walked back to the bunk, looked at it a moment, then slowly lay down on it. It was an act of hopelessness, an act of surrender. She closed her eyes.

Her tenth birthday was the most exciting day of her life. *We're going to Antoine's for dinner*, her father announced.

Antoine's! It was a name that conjured up another world, a world of beauty and glamour and wealth. Tracy knew that her father did not have much money: *We'll be able to afford a vacation next year*, was the constant refrain in the house. And now they were going to Antoine's! Tracy's mother dressed her in a new green frock.

Just look at you two, her father boasted. *I'm*

with the two prettiest women in New Orleans. Everyone's going to be jealous of me.

Antoine's was everything Tracy had dreamed it would be, and more. So much more. It was a fairyland, elegant and tastefully decorated, with white napery and gleaming silver-and-gold monogrammed dishes. *It's a palace*, Tracy thought. *I'll bet kings and queens come here.* She was too excited to eat, too busy staring at all the beautifully dressed men and women. *When I'm grown up*, Tracy promised herself, *I'm going to come to Antoine's every night, and I'll bring my mother and father with me.*

You're not eating, Tracy, her mother said.

And to please her, Tracy forced herself to eat a few mouthfuls. There was a cake for her, with ten candles on it, and the waiters sang Happy Birthday and the other guests turned and applauded, and Tracy felt like a princess. Outside she could hear the clang of a street-car bell as it passed.

The clanging of the bell was loud and insistent.

'Suppertime,' Ernestine Littlechap announced.

Tracy opened her eyes. Cell doors were slamming open throughout the cell block. Tracy lay on her bunk, trying desperately to hang on to the past.

'Hey! Chow time,' the young Puerto Rican said.

The thought of food sickened her. 'I'm not hungry.'

Paulita, the fat Mexican woman spoke. '*Es llano.*

It's simple. They don' care if you're hungry or not. Everybody gotta go to mess.'

Inmates were lining up in the corridor outside.

'You better move it, or they'll have your ass,' Ernestine warned.

I can't move, Tracy thought. *I'll stay here.*

Her cell mates left the cell and lined up in a double file. A short, squat matron with peroxided-blonde hair saw Tracy lying on her bunk. 'You!' she said. 'Didn't you hear the bell! Get out here.'

Tracy said, 'I'm not hungry, thank you. I'd like to be excused.'

The matron's eyes widened in disbelief. She stormed inside the cell and strode over to where Tracy lay. 'Who the fuck do you think you are? You waitin' for room service? Get your ass in that line. I could put you on report for this. If it happens again, you go to the bing. Understand?'

She did not understand. She did not understand anything that was happening to her. She dragged herself from the bunk and walked out into the line of women. She was standing next to the black woman. 'Why do I –?'

'Shut up!' Ernestine Littlechap growled out of the corner of her mouth. 'No talkin' in line.'

The women were marched down a narrow, cheerless corridor past two sets of security doors, into an enormous mess hall filled with large wooden tables and chairs. There was a long serving counter with steam tables, where prisoners lined up for their food. The menu of the day consisted of a watery tuna casserole, limp green beans, a pale custard, and a choice of weak coffee or a synthetic fruit drink. Ladles of the unappetizing-looking food were thrown into the tin plates of the prisoners as they moved along the line, and the inmates who were serving behind the counter kept up a steady cry: 'Keep the line moving. Next . . . keep the line moving. Next . . .'

When Tracy was served, she stood there uncertainly, not sure where to go. She looked around for Ernestine Littlechap, but the black woman had disappeared. Tracy walked over to a table where Lola and Paulita, the fat Mexican woman, were seated. There were twenty women at the table, hungrily wolfing down their food. Tracy looked down at what was on her plate, then pushed it away, as the bile rose and welled in her throat.

Paulita reached over and grabbed the plate from Tracy. 'If you ain't gonna eat that, I'll take it.'

Lola said, 'Hey, you gotta eat, or you won't last here.'

I don't want to last, Tracy thought hopelessly. *I want to die. How could these women tolerate living like this? How long had they been here? Months? Years?* She thought of the foetid cell and her verminous mattress, and she wanted to scream. She clenched her jaw shut so that no sound would come out.

The Mexican woman was saying, 'If they catch you not eatin', you go to the bing.' She saw the uncomprehending look on Tracy's face. 'The hole – solitary. You wouldn't like it.' She leaned forward. 'This is your first time in the joint, huh? Well, I'm gonna give you a tip, querida. Ernestine Littlechap runs this place. Be nice to her an' you got it made.'

Thirty minutes from the time the women had entered the room, a loud bell sounded and the women stood up. Paulita snatched a lone green bean from a plate next to her. Tracy joined her in the line, and the women began the march back to their cells. Supper was over. It was four o'clock in the afternoon – five long hours to endure before lights out.

When Tracy returned to the cell, Ernestine Littlechap was already there. Tracy wondered incuriously where she had been at dinnertime. Tracy looked at the toilet in the corner. She desperately needed to use it, but she could not bring herself to do so in front of these women. She would wait until lights went out. She sat down on the edge of her bunk.

Ernestine Littlechap said, 'I understan' you didn't eat none of your supper. Tha's stupid.'

How could she have known that? And why should she care? 'How do I see the warden?'

'You put in a written request. The guards use it for toilet paper. They figure any cunt who wants to see the warden is a troublemaker.' She walked over to Tracy. 'There's lotsa things kin get you in trouble here. What you need is a friend who kin he'p keep you *outta* trouble.' She smiled, showing a gold front tooth. Her voice was soft. 'Someone who knows their way around the zoo.'

Tracy looked up into the black woman's grinning face. It seemed to be floating somewhere near the ceiling.

It was the tallest thing she had ever seen.

That's a giraffe, her father said.

They were at the zoo in Audubon Park. Tracy loved the park. On Sundays they went there to listen to the band concerts, and afterwards her mother and father took her to the aquarium or the zoo. They walked slowly, looking at the animals in their cages.

Don't they hate being locked up, Papa?

Her father laughed. *No, Tracy. They have a wonderful life. They're taken care of and fed, and their enemies can't get at them.*

They looked unhappy to Tracy. She wanted to open their cages and let them out. *I wouldn't ever want to be locked up like that*, Tracy thought.

At 8:45 the warning bells rang throughout the prison. Tracy's cell mates began to undress. Tracy did not move.

Lola said, 'You got fifteen minutes to get ready for bed.'

The women had stripped and put on nightgowns. The peroxided-blonde matron passed the cell. She stopped when she saw Tracy lying on her cot.

'Get undressed,' she ordered. She turned to Ernestine. 'Didn't you tell her?'

'Yeah. We tol' her.'

The matron turned back to Tracy. 'We got a way of takin' care of troublemakers,' she warned. 'You do what you're told here, or I'll bust your ass.' The matron moved down the hall.

Paulita cautioned, 'You better listen to her, baby. Old Iron Pants is one mean bitch.'

Slowly, Tracy rose and began to undress, keeping her back to the others. She took off all her clothes, with the exception of her panties, and slipped the coarse nightgown over her head. She felt the eyes of the other women on her.

'You got a real nice body,' Paulita commented.

'Yeah, real nice,' Lola echoed.

Tracy felt a shiver go through her.

Ernestine moved over to Tracy and looked down at her. 'We're your friends. We gonna take good care of you.' Her voice was hoarse with excitement.

Tracy wildly jerked around. 'Leave me alone! All of you. I'm – I'm not that way.'

The black woman chuckled. 'You'll be any way we want you to be, baby.'

'*Hay tiempo*. There's plenty of time.'

The lights went out.

The dark was Tracy's enemy. She sat on the edge of her bunk, her body tense. She could sense the others waiting to pounce on her. Or was it her imagination? She was so overwrought that everything seemed to be a threat. Had they threatened her? Not really. They were probably just trying to be friendly, and she had read sinister implications into their overtures. She had heard about homosexual activity in prisons, but that had to be the exception rather than the rule. A prison would not permit that sort of behaviour.

Still, there was a nagging doubt. She decided she would stay awake all night. If one of them made a move, she would call for help. It was the responsibility of the guards to see that nothing happened to the inmates. She reassured herself that there was nothing to worry about. She would just have to stay alert.

Tracy sat on the edge of her bunk in the dark, listening to every sound. One by one she heard the three women go to the toilet, use it, and return to their bunks. When Tracy could stand it no longer, she made her way to the toilet. She tried to flush it, but it did not work. The stench was almost unbearable. She hurried back to her cot and sat there. *It will be light soon*, she thought. *In the morning I'll ask to see the warden. I'll tell him about the baby. He'll have me moved to another cell.*

Tracy's body was tense and cramped. She lay back on her bunk and within seconds felt something crawling across her neck. She stifled a scream. *I've got to stand it until morning. Everything will be all right in the morning*, Tracy thought. One minute at a time.

At 3:00 she could no longer keep her eyes open. She slept.

She was awakened by a hand clamped across her mouth and two hands grabbing at her breasts. She tried to sit up and scream, and she felt her nightgown and underpants being ripped away. Hands slid between her thighs, forcing her legs apart. Tracy fought savagely, struggling to rise.

'Take it easy,' a voice in the dark whispered, 'and you won't get hurt.'

Tracy lashed out at the voice with her feet. She connected with solid flesh.

'*Carajo!* Give it to the bitch,' the voice gasped. 'Get her on the floor.'

A hard fist smashed into Tracy's face and another into her stomach. Someone was on top of her, holding her down, smothering her, while obscene hands violated her.

Tracy broke loose for an instant, but one of the women grabbed her and slammed her head against the bars. She felt the blood spurt from her nose. She was thrown to the concrete floor, and her hands and legs were pinned down. Tracy fought like a mad-woman, but she was no match for the three of them. She felt cold hands and hot tongues caressing her body. Her legs were spread apart and a hard, cold object was shoved inside her. She writhed helplessly, desperately trying to call out.

An arm moved across her mouth, and Tracy sank her teeth into it, biting down with all her strength.

There was a muffled cry. 'You cunt!'

Fists pounded her face . . . She sank into the pain, deeper and deeper, until finally she felt nothing.

It was the clanging of the bell that awakened her. She was lying on the cold cement floor of her cell, naked. Her three cell mates were in their bunks.

In the corridor, Iron Pants was calling, 'Rise and shine'. As the matron passed the cell, she saw Tracy lying on the floor in a small pool of blood, her face battered and one eye swollen shut.

'What the hell's goin' on here?' She unlocked the door and stepped inside the cell.

'She musta fell outta her bunk,' Ernestine Littlechap offered.

The matron walked over to Tracy's side and nudged her with her foot. 'You! Get up.'

Tracy heard the voice from a far distance. *Yes*, she thought, *I must get up; I must get out of here*. But she was unable to move. Her body was screaming out with pain.

The matron grabbed Tracy's elbows and pulled her to a sitting position, and Tracy almost fainted from the agony.

'What happened?'

Through one eye Tracy saw the blurred outlines of her cell mates silently waiting for her to answer.

'I – I –' Tracy tried to speak, but no words

would come out. She tried again, and some deep-seated atavistic instinct made her say, 'I fell off my bunk . . .'

The matron snapped, 'I hate smart asses. Let's put you in the bing till you learn some respect.'

It was a form of oblivion, a return to the womb. She was alone in the dark. There was no furniture in the cramped basement cell, only a thin, worn mattress thrown on the cold cement floor. A noisome hole in the floor served as a toilet. Tracy lay there in the blackness, humming folk songs to herself that her father had taught her long ago. She had no idea how close she was to the edge of insanity.

She was not sure where she was, but it did not matter. Only the suffering of her brutalized body mattered. *I must have fallen down and hurt myself, but Mama will take care of it.* She called out in a broken voice, 'Mama . . .', and when there was no answer, she fell asleep again.

She slept for forty-eight hours, and the agony finally receded to pain, and the pain gave way to soreness. Tracy opened her eyes. She was surrounded by nothingness. It was so dark that she could not even make out the outline of the cell. Memories came flooding back. They had carried her to the doctor. She could hear his voice: '. . . a broken rib and a fractured wrist. We'll tape them up . . . The cuts and bruises are bad, but they'll heal. She's lost the baby . . .'

'Oh, my baby,' Tracy whispered. 'They've murdered my baby.'

And she wept. She wept for the loss of her baby. She wept for herself. She wept for the whole sick world.

Tracy lay on the thin mattress in the cold darkness, and she was filled with such an overpowering hatred that it literally shook her body. Her thoughts burned and blazed until her mind was empty of every emotion but one: *vengeance*. It was not a vengeance directed against her three cell mates. They were victims as much as she. No; she was after the men who had done this to her, who had destroyed her life.

Joe Romano: 'Your old lady held out on me. She didn't tell me she had a horny-looking daughter . . .'

Anthony Orsatti: 'Joe Romano works for a man named Anthony Orsatti. Orsatti runs New Orleans . . .'

Perry Pope: 'By pleading guilty, you save the state the expense of a trial . . .'

Judge Henry Lawrence: 'For the next fifteen years you're going to be incarcerated in the Southern Louisiana Penitentiary for Women . . .'

Those were her enemies. And then there was Charles, who had never even listened to her: 'If you needed money that badly, you could have discussed it with me . . . Obviously I never really knew you . . . You'll have to do whatever you think best with your baby . . .'

She was going to make them pay. Every one of them. She had no idea how. But she knew she was going to get revenge. *Tomorrow*, she thought. *If tomorrow comes*.

SEVEN

Time lost all meaning. There was never light in the cell, so there was no difference between night and day, and she had no idea how long she was kept in solitary confinement. From time to time cold meals were shoved through a slot in the bottom of the door. Tracy had no appetite, but she forced herself to eat every morsel. *You gotta eat, or you won't last here*. She understood that now; she knew she would need every bit of her strength for what she planned to do. She was in a situation that anyone else would have considered hopeless: she was locked away for fifteen years, with no money, no friends, no resources of any kind. But there was a wellspring of strength deep within her. *I will survive*, Tracy thought. *I face mine enemies naked, and my courage is my shield*. She would survive as her ancestors had survived. In her was the mixed blood of the English and the Irish and the Scots, and she had inherited the best of their qualities, the intelligence and the courage and the will. *My ancestors survived famine and plagues and floods, and I'm going to survive this.* They were with her now in her stygian cell: the shepherds and trappers, the farmers and shopkeepers, the doctors and teachers. The ghosts of the past, and every one was a part of her. *I won't let you down*, Tracy whispered in the darkness.

She began to plan her escape.

Tracy knew that the first thing she had to do was regain her physical strength. The cell was too cramped for extensive exercise, but it was large enough for t'ai chi ch'uan, the centuries-old martial art that was taught warriors to prepare them for combat. The exercises required little space, and they used every muscle in the body. Tracy stood up and went through the opening moves. Each movement had a name and a significance. She started with the militant Punching the Demons, then into the softer Gathering the Light. The movements were fluid and graceful and done very slowly. Every gesture came from tan tien, the psychic centre, and all the movements were circular. Tracy could hear the voice of her teacher: *Arouse your chi, your vital energy. It starts heavy as a mountain and becomes light as a bird's feather.* Tracy could feel the chi flowing through her fingers, and she concentrated until her whole being was focused on her body moving through the timeless patterns.

Grasp the bird's tail, become the white stork, repulse the monkey, face the tiger, let your hands become clouds and circulate the water of life. Let the white snake creep down and ride the tiger. Shoot the tiger, gather your chi, and go back to tan tien, the centre.

The complete cycle took an hour, and when it was finished Tracy was exhausted. She went through the ritual each morning and afternoon until her body began to respond and grow strong.

When she was not exercising her body, Tracy exercised her mind. She lay in the dark, doing complicated mathematical equations, mentally operating the computer at the bank, reciting poetry, recalling the lines of plays she had been in at college. She was a perfectionist, and when she had got a part in a school play where she had to use different accents, she had studied accents for weeks before the play went on. A talent scout had once approached her to offer her a screen test in Hollywood. 'No, thank you. I don't want the limelight. That's not for me,' Tracy had told him.

Charles's voice: *You're the headline in this morning's* Daily News.

Tracy pushed the memory of Charles away. There were doors in her mind that had to remain closed for now.

She played the teaching game: Name three absolutely impossible things to teach.

To teach an ant the difference between Catholics and Protestants.

To make a bee understand that it is the earth that travels around the sun.

To explain to a cat the difference between communism and democracy.

But she concentrated mostly on how she was going to destroy her enemies, each of them in turn. She remembered a game she had played as a child. By holding up one hand towards the sky, it was possible to blot out the sun. That's what they had done to her. They had raised a hand and blotted out her life.

Tracy had no idea how many prisoners had been broken by their confinement in the bing, nor would it have mattered to her.

On the seventh day, when the cell door opened, Tracy was blinded by the sudden light that flooded the cell. A guard stood outside. 'On your feet. You're going back upstairs.'

He reached down to give Tracy a helping hand, and to his surprise, she rose easily to her feet and walked out of the cell unaided. The other prisoners he had moved from solitary had come out either broken or defiant, but this prisoner was neither. There was an aura of dignity about her, a self-confidence that was alien to this place. Tracy stood in the light, letting her eyes gradually get accustomed to it. *What a great-looking piece of ass*, the guard thought. *Get her cleaned up and you could take her anywhere. I'll bet she'd do anything for a few favours.*

Aloud he said, 'A pretty girl like you shouldn't have to go through this kind of thing. If you and me was friends, I'd see that it didn't happen again.'

Tracy turned to face him, and when he saw the look in her eyes, he hastily decided not to pursue it.

The guard walked Tracy upstairs and turned her over to a matron.

The matron sniffed, 'Jesus, you stink. Go in and take a shower. We'll burn those clothes.'

The cold shower felt wonderful. Tracy shampooed her hair and scrubbed herself from head to foot with the harsh lye soap.

When she had dried herself and put on a change of clothing, the matron was waiting for her. 'Warden wants to see you.'

The last time Tracy had heard those words, she had believed it meant her freedom. Never again would she be that naïve.

Warden Brannigan was standing at the window when Tracy walked into his office. He turned and said, 'Sit down, please.' Tracy took a chair. 'I've been away in Washington at a conference. I just returned this morning and saw a report on what happened. You should not have been put in solitary.'

She sat watching him, her impassive face giving nothing away.

The warden glanced at a paper on his desk. 'According to this report, you were sexually assaulted by your cell mates.'

'No, sir.'

Warden Brannigan nodded understandingly. 'I understand your fear, but I can't allow the inmates to run this prison. I want to punish whoever did this to you, but I'll need your testimony. I'll see that you're protected. Now, I want you to tell me exactly what happened and who was responsible.'

Tracy looked him in the eye. 'I was. I fell off my bunk.'

The warden studied her a long time, and she could see the disappointment cloud his face. 'Are you quite sure?'

'Yes, sir.'

'You won't change your mind?'

'No, sir.'

Warden Brannigan sighed. 'All right. If that's your decision. I'll have you transferred to another cell where –'

'I don't want to be transferred.'

He looked at her in surprise. 'You mean you want to go back to the same cell?'

'Yes, sir.'

He was puzzled. Perhaps he had been wrong about her; maybe she had invited what had happened to her. God only knew what those damned female prisoners were thinking or doing. He wished he could be transferred to some nice, sane men's prison, but his wife and Amy, his small daughter, liked it here. They all lived in a charming cottage, and there were lovely grounds around the prison farm. To them, it was like living in the country, but he had to cope with these crazy women twenty-four hours a day.

He looked at the young woman sitting before him and said awkwardly, 'Very well. Just stay out of trouble in the future.'

'Yes, sir.'

Returning to her cell was the most difficult thing Tracy had ever done. The moment she stepped inside she was assailed by the horror of what had happened there. Her cell mates were away at work. Tracy lay on her bunk, staring at the ceiling, planning. Finally, she reached down to the bottom of her bunk and prised a piece of the metal side loose. She placed it under her mattress. When the 11:00 A.M. lunch bell rang, Tracy was the first to line up in the corridor.

In the mess hall, Paulita and Lola were seated at a table near the entrance. There was no sign of Ernestine Littlechap.

Tracy chose a table filled with strangers, sat down, and finished every bite of the tasteless meal. She spent the afternoon alone in her cell. At 2:45 her three cell mates returned.

Paulita grinned with surprise when she saw Tracy. 'So you came back to us, pretty pussy. You liked what we did to you, huh?'

'Good. We got more for you,' Lola said.

Tracy gave no indication that she heard their taunting. She was concentrating on the black woman. Ernestine Littlechap was the reason Tracy had come back to this cell. Tracy did not trust her. Not for a moment. But she needed her.

I'm gonna give you a tip, querida. Ernestine Littlechap runs this place . . .

That night, when the fifteen-minute warning bell sounded for lights out, Tracy rose from her bunk and began to undress. This time there was no false modesty. She stripped, and the Mexican woman gave a long, low whistle as she looked at Tracy's full, firm breasts and her long, tapering legs and creamy thighs. Lola was breathing hard. Tracy put on a nightgown and lay back on her bunk. The lights went out. The cell was in darkness.

Thirty minutes went by. Tracy lay in the dark listening to the breathing of the others.

Across the cell, Paulita whispered, 'Mama's gonna give you some real lovin' tonight. Take off your nightgown, baby.'

'We're gonna teach you how to eat pussy, and you'll do it till you get it right,' Lola giggled.

Still not a word from the black woman. Tracy felt the rush of wind as Lola and Paulita came at her, but Tracy was ready for them. She lifted the piece of metal she had concealed in her hand and swung with all her might, hitting one of the women in the face. There was a scream of pain, and Tracy kicked out at the other figure and saw her fall to the floor.

'Come near me again and I'll kill you,' Tracy said.

'You bitch!'

Tracy could hear them start for her again, and she raised the piece of metal.

Ernestine's voice came abruptly out of the darkness. 'Tha's enough. Leave her alone.'

'Ernie, I'm bleedin'. I'm gonna fix her –'

'Do what the fuck I tell you.'

There was a long silence. Tracy heard the two women moving back to their bunks, breathing hard. Tracy lay there, tensed, ready for their next move.

Ernestine Littlechap said, 'You got guts, baby.'

Tracy was silent.

'You didn't sing to the warden.' Ernestine laughed softly in the darkness. 'If you had, you'd be dead meat.'

Tracy believed her.

'Why di'n' you let the warden move you to another cell?'

So she even knew about that. 'I wanted to come back here.'

'Yeah? What fo'?' There was a puzzled note in Ernestine Littlechap's voice.

This was the moment Tracy had been waiting for. 'You're going to help me escape.'

EIGHT

A matron came up to Tracy and announced, 'You got a visitor, Whitney.'

Tracy looked at her in surprise. 'A visitor?' Who could it be? And suddenly she knew. *Charles*. He had come after all. But he was too late. He had not been there when she so desperately needed him. *Well, I'll never need him again. Or anyone else.*

Tracy followed the matron down the corridor to the visitors' room.

Tracy stepped inside.

A total stranger was seated at a small wooden table. He was one of the most unattractive men Tracy had ever seen. He was short, with a bloated, androgynous body, a long, pinched-in nose, and a small, bitter mouth. He had a high, bulging forehead and intense brown eyes, magnified by the thick lenses of his glasses.

He did not rise. 'My name is Daniel Cooper. The warden gave me permission to speak to you.'

'About what?' Tracy asked suspiciously.

'I'm an investigator for IIPA – the International Insurance Protection Association. One of our clients insured the Renoir that was stolen from Mr Joseph Romano.'

Tracy drew a deep breath. 'I can't help you. I didn't steal it.' She started for the door.

Cooper's next words stopped her. 'I know that.'

Tracy turned and looked at him, wary, every sense alert.

'No one stole it. You were framed, Miss Whitney.'

Slowly, Tracy sank into a chair.

Daniel Cooper's involvement with the case had begun three weeks earlier when he had been summoned to the office of his superior, J. J. Reynolds, at IIPA headquarters in Manhattan.

'I've got an assignment for you, Dan,' Reynolds said.

Daniel Cooper loathed being called Dan.

'I'll make this brief.' Reynolds intended to make it brief because Cooper made him nervous. In truth, Cooper made everyone in the organization nervous. He was a strange man – *weird*, was how many described him. Daniel Cooper kept entirely to himself. No one knew where he lived, whether he was married or had children. He socialized with no one, and never attended office parties or office meetings. He was a loner, and the only reason Reynolds tolerated him was because the man was a goddamned genius. He was a bulldog, with a computer for a brain. Daniel

Cooper was single-handedly responsible for recovering more stolen merchandise, and exposing more insurance frauds, than all the other investigators put together. Reynolds just wished he knew what the hell Cooper was all about. Merely sitting across from the man with those fanatical brown eyes staring at him made him uneasy. Reynolds said, 'One of our client companies insured a painting for half a million dollars and –'

'The Renoir. New Orleans. Joe Romano. A woman named Tracy Whitney was convicted and sentenced to fifteen years. The painting hasn't been recovered.'

The son of a bitch! Reynolds thought. *If it were anyone else, I'd think he was showing off.* 'That's right,' Reynolds acknowledged grudgingly. 'The Whitney woman has stashed that painting away somewhere, and we want it back. Go to it.'

Cooper turned and left the office without a word. Watching him leave, J. J. Reynolds thought, not for the first time, *Someday I'm going to find out what makes that bastard tick.*

Cooper walked through the office, where fifty employees were working side by side, programming computers, typing reports, answering telephones. It was bedlam.

As Cooper passed a desk, a colleague said, 'I hear you got the Romano assignment. Lucky you. New Orleans is –'

Cooper walked by without replying. Why couldn't they leave him alone? That was all he asked of anybody, but they were always pestering him with their nosey overtures.

It had become a game in the office. They were determined to break through his mysterious reserve and find out who he really was.

'What are you doing for dinner Friday night, Dan . . . ?'

'If you're not married, Sarah and I know a wonderful girl, Dan . . . ?'

Couldn't they see he did not need any of them – didn't *want* any of them?

'Come on, it's only for a drink . . .'

But Daniel Cooper knew what that could lead to. An innocent drink could lead to dinner, and a dinner could start friendships, and friendships could lead to confidences. Too dangerous.

Daniel Cooper lived in mortal terror that one day someone would learn about his past. *Let the dead past bury its dead* was a lie. The dead never stayed buried. Every two or three years one of the scandal sheets would dig up the old scandal, and Daniel Cooper would disappear for several days. Those were the only times he ever got drunk.

Daniel Cooper could have kept a psychiatrist busy full-time had he been able to expose his emotions, but he could never bring himself to speak of the past to anyone. The one piece of physical evidence that he retained from that terrible day long ago was a faded, yellowed newspaper clipping, safely locked away in his room, where no one could ever find it. He looked at it from time to time as a punishment, but every word in the article was emblazoned on his mind.

He showered or bathed at least three times a day, but never felt clean. He firmly believed in hell and hell's fire, and he knew his only salvation on earth was expiation, atonement. He had tried to join the New York police force, but when he had failed the physical because he was four inches too short, he had become a private investigator. He thought of himself as a hunter, tracking down those who broke the law. He was the vengeance of God, the instrument that brought down God's wrath on the heads of wrongdoers. It was the only way he could atone for the past, and prepare himself for eternity.

He wondered if there was time to take a shower before he caught his plane.

Daniel Cooper's first stop was New Orleans. He spent five days in the city, and before he was through, he knew everything he needed to know about Joe Romano, Anthony Orsatti, Perry Pope and Judge Henry Lawrence. Cooper read the transcripts of Tracy Whitney's court hearing and sentencing. He interviewed Lieutenant Miller and learned about the suicide of Tracy Whitney's mother. He talked to Otto Schmidt and found out how Whitney's company had been stripped. During all these meetings, Daniel Cooper made not one note, yet he could have recited every conversation verbatim. He was 99 percent sure that Tracy

Whitney was an innocent victim, but to Daniel Cooper, those were unacceptable odds. He flew to Philadelphia and talked to Clarence Desmond, vice-president of the bank where Tracy Whitney had worked. Charles Stanhope III had refused to meet with him.

Now, as Cooper looked at the woman seated across from him, he was 100 percent convinced that she had had nothing to do with the theft of the painting. He was ready to write his report.

'Romano framed you, Miss Whitney. Sooner or later, he would have put in a claim for the theft of the painting. You just happened to come along at the right moment to make it easy for him.'

Tracy could feel her heartbeat accelerate. This man *knew* she was innocent. He probably had enough evidence against Joe Romano to clear her. He would speak to the warden or the governor, and get her out of this nightmare. She found it suddenly difficult to breathe. 'Then you'll help me?'

Daniel Cooper was puzzled. 'Help you?'

'Yes. Get a pardon or –'

'No.'

The word was like a slap. '*No?* But *why?* If you know I'm innocent –'

How could people be so stupid? 'My assignment is finished.'

When he returned to his hotel room, the first thing Cooper did was to undress and step into the shower. He scrubbed himself from head to foot, letting the steaming-hot spray wash over his body for almost half an hour. When he had dried himself and dressed, he sat down and wrote his report.

TO:
J. J. Reynolds File No. Y-72-830-412

FROM:
Daniel Cooper

SUBJECT: *Deux Femmes dans le Café Rouge*, Renoir – Oil on Canvas

It is my conclusion that Tracy Whitney is in no way involved in the theft of above painting. I believe that Joe Romano took out the insurance policy with the intention of faking a burglary, collecting the insurance, and reselling the painting to a private party, and that by this time the painting is probably out of the country. Since the painting is well known, I would expect it to turn up in Switzerland, which has a good-faith purchase and protection law. If a purchaser says he bought a work of art in good faith, the Swiss government permits him to keep it, even though it is stolen.

Recommendation: Since there is no concrete proof of Romano's guilt, our client will have to pay him off on the policy. Further, it would be useless to look to Tracy Whitney for either the recovery of the painting or damages, since she has neither knowledge of the painting nor any assets that I have been able to uncover. In addition, she will be incarcerated in the Southern Louisiana Penitentiary for Women for the next fifteen years.

Daniel Cooper stopped a moment to think about Tracy Whitney. He supposed other men would consider her beautiful. He wondered, without any real interest, what fifteen years in prison would do to her. It had nothing to do with him.

Daniel Cooper signed the memo and debated whether he had time to take another shower.

NINE

Old Iron Pants had Tracy Whitney assigned to the laundry. Of the thirty-five work assignments available to prisoners, the laundry was the worst. The enormous, hot room was filled with rows of washing machines and ironing boards, and the loads of laundry that poured in were endless. Filling and emptying the washing machines and toting heavy baskets to the ironing section was a mindless, backbreaking job.

Work began at 6:00 A.M., and prisoners were permitted one 10-minute rest period every two hours. By the end of the nine-hour day, most of the women were ready to drop from exhaustion. Tracy went about her work mechanically, speaking to no one, cocooned in her own thoughts.

When Ernestine Littlechap heard about Tracy's assignment, she remarked, 'Old Iron Pants is out for your ass.'

Tracy said, 'She doesn't bother me.'

Ernestine Littlechap was puzzled. This was a

different woman from the terrified young girl who had been brought into prison three weeks earlier. Something had changed her, and Ernestine Littlechap was curious to know what it was.

On Tracy's eighth day working in the laundry, a guard came up to her in the early afternoon. 'I got a transfer here for you. You're assigned to the kitchen.' *The most coveted job in the prison.*

There were two standards of food in the penitentiary: the prisoners ate hash, hot dogs, beans, or inedible casseroles, while the meals for the guards and prison officials were prepared by professional chefs. Their range of meals included steaks, fresh fish, chops, chicken, fresh vegetables and fruits, and tempting desserts. The convicts who worked in the kitchen had access to those meals, and they took full advantage of it.

When Tracy reported to the kitchen, she was somehow not surprised to see Ernestine Littlechap there.

Tracy approached her. 'Thank you.' With difficulty, she forced a friendly note into her voice.

Ernestine grunted and said nothing.

'How did you get me past Old Iron Pants?'

'She ain't with us no mo'.'

'What happened to her?'

'We got a little system. If a guard is hard-ass and starts givin' us too much of a bad time, we get rid of 'em.'

'You mean the warden listens to –'

'Shee-et. What's the warden got to do with it?'

'Then how can you –?'

'It's easy. When the guard you want to get rid of is on duty, hassles begin to happen. Complaints start comin' in. A prisoner reports that Old Iron Pants grabbed her pussy. The next day 'nother prisoner accuses her of brutality. Then someone complains she took somethin' from her cell – say a radio – and sure enough, it turns up in Old Iron Pants's room. Old Iron Pants is gone. The guards don't run this prison, *we* do.'

'What are you in here for?' Tracy asked. She had no interest in the answer. The important thing was to establish a friendly relationship with this woman.

'Through no fault of Ernestine Littlechap, you'd better believe it. I had a whole bunch of girls workin' for me.'

Tracy looked at her. 'You mean as –?' She hesitated.

'Hookers?' She laughed. 'Naw. They worked as maids in big homes. I opened me a employment agency. I had at least twenty girls. Rich folks have a hell of a time findin' maids. I did a lot of fancy advertisin' in the best newspapers, and when they called me I placed my girls with 'em. The girls would size up the houses, and when their employers was at work or outta town, the girls would gather up all the silver and jewellery and furs and whatever other goodies were around and skip.' Ernestine sighed. 'If I told you how much fuckin' tax-free money we was pullin' down, you wouldn't believe me.'

'How did you get caught?'

'It was the fickle finger of fate, honey. One of my maids was servin' a luncheon at the mayor's house, and one of the guests was a old lady the maid had worked for and cleaned out. When the police used hoses on her, my girl began singin', and she sang the whole opera, and here's poor ol Ernestine.'

They were standing at a stove by themselves. 'I can't stay in this place,' Tracy whispered. 'I've got to take care of something on the outside. Will you help me escape? I –'

'Start slicin' up them onions. We're havin' Irish stew tonight.'

And she walked away.

The prison grapevine was incredible. The prisoners knew everything that was going to happen long before it occurred. Inmates known as garbage rats picked up discarded memos, eavesdropped on phone calls, and read the warden's mail, and all information was carefully digested and sent around to the inmates who were important. Ernestine Littlechap was at the head of the list. Tracy was aware of how the guards and prisoners deferred to Ernestine. Since the other inmates had decided that Ernestine had become Tracy's protector, she was left strictly alone. Tracy waited warily for Ernestine to make advances towards her, but the big black kept her distance. *Why?* Tracy wondered.

* * *

Rule number 7 in the official ten-page pamphlet issued to new prisoners read, 'Any form of sex is strictly forbidden. There will be no more than four inmates to a cell. Not more than one prisoner shall be permitted to be on a bunk at one time.'

The reality was so startlingly different that the prisoners referred to the pamphlet as the prison joke book. As the weeks went by, Tracy watched new prisoners – fish – enter the prison every day, and the pattern was always the same. First offenders who were sexually normal never had a chance. They came in timid and frightened, and the bull-dykes were there, waiting. The drama was enacted in planned stages. In a terrifying and hostile world, the bull-dyke was friendly and sympathetic. She would invite her victim to the recreation hall, where they would watch television together, and when the bull-dyke held her hand, the new prisoner would allow it, afraid of offending her only friend. The new prisoner quickly noticed that the other inmates left her alone, and as her dependence on the bull-dyke grew, so did the intimacies, until finally, she was willing to do anything to hold onto her only friend.

Those who refused to give in were raped. Ninety percent of the women who entered the prison were forced into homosexual activity – willingly or unwillingly – within the first thirty days. Tracy was horrified.

'How can the authorities allow it to happen?' she asked Ernestine.

'It's the system,' Ernestine explained, 'and it's the same in every prison, baby. There ain't no way you can separate twelve hundred women from their men and expect them not to fuck somebody. We don't just rape for sex. We rape for power, to show 'em right off who's boss. The new fish who come in here are targets for everybody who wants to gang-fuck 'em. The only protection they got is to become the wife of a bull-dyke. That way, nobody'll mess with 'em.'

Tracy had reason to know she was listening to an expert.

'It ain't only the inmates,' Ernestine went on. 'The guards are just as bad. Some fresh meat comes in and she's on H. She's strung out and needs a fix real bad. She's sweatin' and shakin' herself to pieces. Well, the matron can get heroin for her, but the matron wants a little favour in exchange, see? So the fish goes down on the matron and she gets her fix. The male guards are even worse. They got keys to these cells, and all they have to do is walk in at night and he'p themselves to free pussy. They might get you pregnant, but they can do a lot of favours. You want a candy bar or a visit from your boyfriend, you give the guard a piece of ass. It's called barterin', and it goes on in every prison system in the country.'

'It's horrible!'

'It's survival.' The overhead cell light shone on Ernestine's bald head. 'You know why they don't allow no chewin' gum in this place?'

'No.'

'Because the girls use it to jam up the locks on the doors so they don't close all the way, and at night they slip out and visit one another. We follow the rules we want to follow. The girls who make it out of here may be dumb, but they're *smart* dumb.'

Love affairs within the prison walls flourished, and the protocol between lovers was even more strictly enforced than on the outside. In an unnatural world, the artificial roles of studs and wives were created and played out. The studs assumed a man's role in a world where there were no men. They changed their names. Ernestine was called Ernie; Tessie was Tex; Barbara became Bob; Katherine was Kelly. The stud cut her hair short or shaved her head, and she did no chores. The Mary Femme, the wife, was expected to do the cleaning, mending, and ironing for her stud. Lola and Paulita competed fiercely for Ernestine's attentions, each fighting to outdo the other.

The jealousy was fierce and frequently led to violence, and if the wife was caught looking at another stud or talking to one in the prison yard, tempers would flare. Love letters were constantly flying around the prison, delivered by the garbage rats.

The letters were folded into small triangular shapes, known as kites, so they could easily be hidden in a bra or a shoe. Tracy saw kites being passed among women as they brushed by one another entering the dining hall or on their way to work.

Time after time, Tracy watched inmates fall in love with their guards. It was a love born of despair and helplessness and submissiveness. The prisoners were dependent on the guards for everything: their food, their well-being, and sometimes, their lives. Tracy allowed herself to feel no emotion for anyone.

Sex went on day and night. It ocurred in the shower room, in toilets, in cells, and at night there was oral sex through the bars. The Mary Femmes who belonged to guards were let out of their cells at night to go to the guards' quarters.

After lights out, Tracy would lie in her bunk and put her hands over her ears to shut out the sounds.

One night Ernestine pulled out a box of Rice Krispies from under her bunk and began scattering them in the corridor outside the cell. Tracy could hear inmates from other cells doing the same thing.

'What's going on?' Tracy asked.

Ernestine turned to her and said harshly, 'Non'a your business. Jest stay in your bunk. Jest stay in your fuckin' bunk.'

A few minutes later there was a terrified scream from a nearby cell, where a new prisoner had just arrived. 'Oh, God, no. Don't! Please leave me alone!'

Tracy knew then what was happening, and she was sick inside. The screams went on and on, until they finally diminished into helpless, racking sobs. Tracy squeezed her eyes tightly shut, filled with burning rage. How could women do this to one another? She had thought that prison had hardened her, but when she awoke in the morning, her face was stained with dried tears.

She was determined not to show her feelings to Ernestine. Tracy asked casually, 'What were the Rice Krispies for?'

'That's our early warnin' system. If the guards try sneakin' up on us, we kin hear 'em comin'.'

Tracy soon learned why inmates referred to a term in the penitentiary as 'going to college'. Prison was an educational experience, but what the prisoners learned was unorthodox.

The prison was filled with experts of every conceivable type of crime. They exchanged methods of grifting, shoplifting, and rolling drunks. They brought one another up to date on badger games and exchanged information on snitches and undercover cops.

In the recreation yard one morning, Tracy listened to an older inmate give a seminar on pickpocketing to a fascinated young group.

'The real pros come from Columbia. They got a school in Bogotá, called the school of the ten bells, where you pay twenty-five hundred bucks to learn to be a pickpocket. They hang a dummy from the ceilin', dressed in a suit with ten pockets, filled with money and jewellery.'

'What's the gimmick?'

'The gimmick is that each pocket has a bell on it. You don't graduate till you kin empty every damn pocket without ringin' the bell.'

Lola sighed, 'I used to go with a guy who walked through crowds dressed in an overcoat, with both his hands out in the open, while he picked everybody's pockets like crazy.'

'How the hell could he do that?'

'The right hand was a dummy. He slipped his real hand through a slit in the coat and picked his way through pockets and wallets and purses.'

In the recreation room the education continued.

'I like the locker-key rip-off,' a veteran said. 'You hang around a railway station till you see a little old lady tryin' to lift a suitcase or a big package into one of them lockers. You put it in for her and hand her the key. Only it's the key to an empty locker. When she leaves, you empty her locker and split.'

In the yard another afternoon, two inmates convicted of prostitution and possession of cocaine were talking to a new arrival, a pretty young girl who looked no more than seventeen.

'No wonder you got busted, honey,' one of the older women scolded. 'Before you talk price to a John, you gotta pat him down to make sure he ain't carryin' a gun, and *never* tell him what you're gonna do for him. Make *him* tell you what he wants. Then if he turns out to be a cop, it's entrapment, see?'

The other pro added, 'Yeah. And always look at their hands. If a trick says he's a workin' man, see if his hands are rough. That's the tip-off. A lot of plainsclothes cops wear workin' men's outfits, but when it comes to their hands, they forget, so their hands are smooth.'

Time went neither slowly nor quickly. It was simply time. Tracy thought of St Augustine's aphorism: 'What is time? If no one asks me, I know. But if I have to explain it, I do not know.'

The routine of the prison never varied:

4:40 A.M.	Warning bell
4:45 A.M.	Rise and dress
5:00 A.M.	Breakfast
5:30 A.M.	Return to cell
5:55 A.M.	Warning bell
6:00 A.M.	Work detail lineup
10:00 A.M.	Exercise yard
10:30 A.M.	Lunch
11:00 A.M.	Work detail lineup
3:30 P.M.	Supper
4:00 P.M.	Return to cell
5:00 P.M.	Recreation room
6:00 P.M.	Return to cell
8:45 P.M.	Warning bell
9:00 P.M.	Lights out

The rules were inflexible. All inmates had to go to meals, and no talking was permitted in the lines.

No more than five cosmetic items could be kept in the small cell lockers. Beds had to be made prior to breakfast and kept neat during the day.

The penitentiary had a music all its own: the clanging bells, shuffle of feet on cement, slamming iron doors, day whispers and night screams . . . the hoarse crackle of the guards' walkie-talkies, the clash of trays at mealtime. And always there was the barbed wire and the high walls and the loneliness and isolation and the pervading aura of hate.

Tracy became a model prisoner. Her body responded automatically to the sounds of prison routine: the bat sliding across her cell at count time and sliding back at wake-up time; the bell for reporting to work and the buzzer when work was finished.

Tracy's body was a prisoner in this place, but her mind was free to plan her escape.

Prisoners could make no outside telephone calls, and they were permitted to receive two five-minute calls a month. Tracy received a call from Otto Schmidt.

'I thought you'd want to know,' he said awkwardly. 'It was a real nice funeral. I took care of the bills, Tracy.'

'Thank you, Otto. I – thank you.' There was nothing more for either of them to say.

There were no more phone calls for her.

'Girl, you best forget the outside world,' Ernestine

warned her. 'There ain't nobody out there for you.'

You're wrong, Tracy thought grimly.

Joe Romano
Perry Pope
Judge Henry Lawrence
Anthony Orsatti
Charles Stanhope III

It was in the exercise yard that Tracy encountered Big Bertha again. The yard was a large outdoor rectangle bounded by the high outer prison wall on one side and the inner wall of the prison on the other. The inmates were allowed in the yard for thirty minutes each morning. It was one of the few places where talking was permitted, and clusters of prisoners gathered together exchanging the latest news and gossip before lunch. When Tracy walked into the yard for the first time, she felt a sudden sense of freedom, and she realized it was because she was in the open air. She could see the sun, high above, and cumulus clouds, and somewhere in the distant blue sky she heard the drone of a plane, soaring free.

'You! I been lookin' for you,' a voice said.

Tracy turned to see the huge Swede who had brushed into her on Tracy's first day in prison.

'I hear you got yourself a nigger bull-dyke.'

Tracy started to brush past the woman. Big Bertha grabbed Tracy's arm, with an iron grip. 'Nobody walks away from me,' she breathed. 'Be nice, *littbarn*.' She was backing Tracy towards the wall, pressing her huge body into Tracy's.

'Get away from me.'

'What you need is a real good lickin'. You know what I mean? An' I'm gonna give it to you. You're gonna be all mine, *alskade*.'

A familiar voice behind Tracy rasped, 'Get your fuckin' hands off her, you asshole.'

Ernestine Littlechap stood there, big fists clenched, eyes blazing, the sun reflecting off her shiny shaved skull.

'You ain't man enough for her, Ernie.'

'I'm man enough for *you*,' the black woman exploded. 'You bother her again, and I'll have your ass for breakfast. *Fried*.'

The air was suddenly charged with electricity. The two amazons were eyeing each other with naked hatred. *They're ready to kill each other over me*, Tracy thought. And then she realized it had very little to do with her. She remembered something Ernestine had told her: 'In this place, you have to fight, fuck, or hit the fence. You gotta hold your mud, or you're dead.'

It was Big Bertha who backed down. She gave Ernestine a contemptuous look. 'I ain't in no hurry.' She leered at Tracy. 'You're gonna be here a long time, baby. So am I. I'll be seein' you.'

She turned and walked away.

Ernestine watched her go. 'She's a bad mother. 'Member that nurse in Chicago who killed off all them patients? Stuck 'em full of cyanide and stayed there an' watched 'em die? Well, that angel of mercy is the one who got the hots for you, Whitney.

Sheeet! You need a fuckin' keeper. She ain't gonna let up on you.'

'Will you help me escape?'

A bell rang.

'It's chow time,' Ernestine Littlechap said.

That night, lying in her bunk, Tracy thought about Ernestine.

Even though she had never tried to touch Tracy again, Tracy still did not trust her. She could never forget what Ernestine and her other cell mates had done to her. But she needed the black woman.

Each afternoon after supper, the inmates were allowed to spend one hour in the recreation room, where they could watch television or talk or read the latest magazines and newspapers. Tracy was thumbing through a copy of a magazine when a photograph caught her eye. It was a wedding picture of Charles Stanhope III and his new bride, coming out of a chapel, arm in arm, laughing. It hit Tracy like a blow. Seeing his photograph now, the happy smile on his face, she was filled with a pain that turned to cold fury. She had once planned to share her life with this man, and he had turned his back on her, let them destroy her, let their baby die. But that was another time, another place, another world. *That was fantasy. This is reality.*

Tracy slammed the magazine shut.

On visiting days it was easy to know which inmates had friends or relatives coming to see them. The prisoners would shower and put on fresh clothes and makeup. Ernestine usually returned from the visitors' room smiling and cheerful.

'My Al, he always comes to see me,' she told Tracy. 'He'll be waitin' for me when I get out. You know why? 'Cause I give him what no other woman gives him.'

Tracy could not hide her confusion. 'You mean . . . sexually?'

'You bet your ass. What goes on behind these walls has nothin' to do with the outside. In here, sometimes we need a warm body to hold – somebody to touch us and tell us they love us. We gotta feel there's somebody who gives a damn about us. It don't matter if it ain't real or don't last. It's all we got. But when I get on the outside' – Ernestine broke into a broad grin – 'then I become a fuckin' nymphomaniac, hear?'

There was something that had been puzzling Tracy. She decided to bring it up now. 'Ernie, you keep protecting me. Why?'

Ernestine shrugged. 'Beats the shit out of me.'

'I really want to know.' Tracy chose her words carefully. 'Everyone else who's your – your *friend* belongs to you. They do whatever you tell them to do.'

'If they don't want to walk around with half an ass, yeah.'

'But not me. Why?'

'You complainin'?'

'No. I'm curious.'

Ernestine thought about it for a moment. 'Okay. You got somethin' I want.' She saw the look on Tracy's face. 'No, not that. I get all that I want, baby. You got class. I mean, real, honest-to-God class. Like those cool ladies you see in *Vogue* and *Town and Country*, all dressed up and servin' tea from silver pots. That's where you belong. This ain't your world. I don't know how you got mixed up with all that rat shit on the outside, but my guess is you got suckered by somebody.' She looked at Tracy and said, almost shyly, 'I ain't come across many decent things in my life. You're one of 'em.' She turned away so that her next words were almost inaudible. 'And I'm sorry about your kid. I really am . . .'

That night, after lights out, Tracy whispered in the dark, 'Ernie, I've got to escape. Help me. Please.'

'I'm tryin' to sleep, for Christ's sake! Shut up now, hear?'

Ernestine initiated Tracy into the arcane language of the prison. Groups of women in the yard were talking: 'This bull-dyker dropped the belt on the grey broad, and from then on you had to feed her with a long-handled spoon . . .'

'She was short, but they caught her in a snow-storm, and a stoned cop turned her over to the butcher. That ended her getup. Good-bye, Ruby-do . . .'

To Tracy, it was like listening to a group of Martians. 'What are they talking about?' she asked.

Ernestine roared with laughter. 'Don't you speak no English, girl? When the lesbian "dropped the belt", it meant she switched from bein' the guy to bein' a Mary Femme. She got involved with a "grey broad" – that's a honky, like you. She couldn't be trusted, so that meant you stayed away from her. She was "short", meanin' she was near the end of her prison sentence, but she got caught takin' heroin by a stoned cop – that's someone who lives by the rules and can't be bought – and they sent her to the "butcher", the prison doctor.'

'What's a "Ruby-do" and a "getup"?'

'Ain't you learned nothin'? A "Ruby-do" is a parole. A "getup" is the day of release.'

Tracy knew she would wait for neither.

The explosion between Ernestine Littlechap and Big Bertha happened in the yard the following day. The prisoners were playing a game of softball, supervised by the guards. Big Bertha, at bat with two strikes against her, hit a hard line drive on the third pitch and ran to first base, which Tracy was covering. Big Bertha slammed into Tracy, knocking her down, and then was on top of her. Her hands snaked up between Tracy's legs, and she whispered, 'Nobody says no to me, you cunt. I'm comin' to get you tonight, *littbarn*, and I'm gonna fuck your ass off.'

Tracy fought wildly to get loose. Suddenly she felt Big Bertha being lifted off her. Ernestine had the huge Swede by the neck and was throttling her.

'You goddamn bitch!' Ernestine was screaming. 'I warned you!' She lashed her fingernails across Big Bertha's face, clawing at her eyes.

'I'm blind!' Big Bertha screamed. 'I'm blind!' She grabbed Ernestine's breasts and started pulling them. The two women were punching and clawing at each other as four guards came running up. It took the guards five minutes to pull them apart. Both women were taken to the infirmary. It was late that night when Ernestine was returned to her cell. Lola and Paulita hurried to her bunk to console her.

'Are you all right?' Tracy whispered.

'Damned right,' Ernestine told her. Her voice sounded muffled, and Tracy wondered how badly she had been hurt. 'I made my Ruby-do yesterday. I'm gettin' outta this joint. You got a problem. That mother aint gonna leave you alone now. No way. And when she's finished fuckin' with you, she's gonna kill you.'

They lay there in the silent darkness. Finally, Ernestine spoke again. 'Maybe it's time you and me talked about bustin' you the hell outta here.'

TEN

'You're going to lose your governess tomorrow,' Warden Brannigan announced to his wife.

Sue Ellen Brannigan looked up in surprise. 'Why? Judy's very good with Amy.'

'I know, but her sentence is up. She's being released in the morning.'

They were having breakfast in the comfortable cottage that was one of the perquisites of Warden Brannigan's job. Other benefits included a cook, a maid, a chauffeur, and a governess for their daughter, Amy, who was almost five. All the servants were trusties. When Sue Ellen Brannigan had arrived there five years earlier, she had been nervous about living on the grounds of the penitentiary, and even more apprehensive about having a house full of servants who were all convicted criminals.

'How do you know they won't rob us and cut our throats in the middle of the night?' she had demanded.

'If they do,' Warden Brannigan had promised, 'I'll put them on report.'

He had persuaded his wife, without convincing her, but Sue Ellen's fears had proved groundless. The trusties were anxious to make a good impression and cut their time down as much as possible, so they were very conscientious.

'I was just getting comfortable with the idea of leaving Amy in Judy's care,' Mrs Brannigan complained. She wished Judy well, but she did not want her to leave. Who knew what kind of woman would be Amy's next governess? There were so many horror stories about the terrible things strangers did to children.

'Do you have anyone in particular in mind to replace Judy, George?'

The warden had given it considerable thought. There were a dozen trusties suitable for the job of taking care of their daughter. But he had not been able to get Tracy Whitney out of his mind. There was something about her case that he found deeply disturbing. He had been a professional criminologist for fifteen years, and he prided himself that one of his strengths was his ability to assess prisoners. Some of the convicts in his care were hardened criminals, others were in prison because they had committed crimes of passion or succumbed to a momentary temptation, but it seemed to Warden Brannigan that Tracy Whitney belonged to neither category. He had not been swayed by her protests of innocence, for that was standard operating procedure for all convicts. What bothered him was the people who had conspired to send Tracy Whitney to prison. The warden had been appointed by a New Orleans civil commission headed by the governor of the state, and although he steadfastly refused to become involved in politics, he was aware of all the players. Joe Romano was Mafia, a runner for Anthony Orsatti. Perry Pope, the attorney who had defended Tracy Whitney, was on their payroll, and so was Judge Henry Lawrence. Tracy Whitney's conviction had a decidedly rank odour to it.

Now Warden Brannigan made his decision. He said to his wife, 'Yes. I do have someone in mind.'

There was an alcove in the prison kitchen with a small Formica-topped dining table and four chairs, the only place where it was possible to have a reasonable amount of privacy. Ernestine Littlechap and Tracy were seated there, drinking coffee during their ten-minute break.

'I think it's about time you tol' me what your big hurry is to bust outta here,' Ernestine suggested.

Tracy hesitated. Could she trust Ernestine? She had no choice. 'There – there are some people who did things to my family and me. I've got to get out to pay them back.'

'Yeah? What'd they do?'

Tracy's words came out slowly, each one a drop of pain. 'They killed my mother.'

'Who's *they*?'

'I don't think the names would mean anything to you. Joe Romano, Perry Pope, a judge named Henry Lawrence, Anthony Orsatti –'

Ernestine was staring at her with her mouth open. 'Jesus H. Christ! You puttin' me on, girl?'

Tracy was surprised. 'You've heard of them?'

'*Heard* of 'em! Who hasn't heard of 'em? Nothin' goes down in New Or-fuckin'-leans unless Orsatti or Romano says so. You can't mess with *them*. They'll blow you away like smoke.'

Tracy said tonelessly, 'They've already blown me away.'

Ernestine looked around to make sure they could not be overheard. 'You're either crazy or you're the dumbest broad I've ever met. Talk about the *untouchables*!' She shook her head. 'Forget about 'em. Fast!'

'No. I can't. I have to break out of here. Can it be done?'

Ernestine was silent for a long time. When she finally spoke, she said, 'We'll talk in the yard.'

They were in the yard, off in a corner by themselves.

'There've been twelve bust-outs from this joint,' Ernestine said. 'Two of the prisoners were shot and killed. The other ten were caught and brought back.' Tracy made no comment. 'The tower's manned twenty-four hours by guards with machine guns, and they're mean sons of bitches. If anyone escapes, it costs the guards their jobs, so they'd just as soon kill you as look at you. There's barbed wire all around the prison, and if you get through that and past the machine guns, they got hound dogs that can track a mosquito's fart. There's a National Guard station a few miles away, and when a prisoner escapes from here they send up helicopters with guns and searchlights. Nobody gives a shit if they bring you back dead or alive, girl. They figure dead is better. It discourages anyone else with plans.'

'But people still try,' Tracy said stubbornly.

'The ones who broke out had help from the outside – friends who smuggled in guns and money and clothes. They had getaway cars waitin' for 'em.' She paused for effect. 'And they *still* got caught.'

'They won't catch me,' Tracy swore.

A matron was approaching. She called out to Tracy, 'Warden Brannigan wants you. On the double.'

'We need someone to take care of our young daughter,' Warden Brannigan said. 'It's a voluntary job. You don't have to take it if you don't wish to.'

Someone to take care of our young daughter. Tracy's mind was racing. This might make her escape easier. Working in the warden's house, she could probably learn a great deal more about the prison setup.

'Yes,' Tracy said. 'I'd like to take the job.'

George Brannigan was pleased. He had an odd, unreasonable feeling that he owed this woman something. 'Good. It pays sixty cents an hour. The money will be put in your account at the end of each month.'

Prisoners were not allowed to handle cash, and all monies accumulated were handed over upon the prisoner's release.

I won't be here at the end of the month, Tracy thought, but aloud she said, 'That will be fine.'

'You can start in the morning. The head matron will give you the details.'

'Thank you, Warden.'

He looked at Tracy and was tempted to say something more. He was not quite sure what. Instead, he said, 'That's all.'

When Tracy broke the news to Ernestine, the black woman said thoughtfully, 'That means they gonna make you a trusty. You'll get the run of the prison. That might make bustin' out a little easier.'

'How do I do it?' Tracy asked.

'You got three choices, but they're all risky. The first way is a sneak-out. You use chewin' gum one night to jam the locks on your cell door and the corridor doors. You sneak outside to the yard, throw a blanket over the barbed wire, and you're off and runnin'.'

With dogs and helicopters after her. Tracy could feel the bullets from the guns of the guards tearing into her. She shuddered. 'What are the other ways?'

'The second way's a breakout. That's where you use a gun and take a hostage with you. If they catch you, they'll give you a deuce with a nickel tail.' She saw Tracy's puzzled expression. 'That's another two to five years on your sentence.'

'And the third way?'

'A walkaway. That's for trusties who are out on a work detail. Once you're out in the open, girl, you jest keep movin'.'

Tracy thought about that. Without money and a car and a place to hide out, she would have no chance. 'They'd find out I was gone at the next head count and come looking for me.'

Ernestine sighed. 'There ain't no perfect escape plan, girl. That's why no one's ever made it outta this place.'

I will, Tracy vowed. *I will.*

The morning Tracy was taken to Warden Brannigan's home marked her fifth month as a prisoner. She was nervous about meeting the warden's wife and child, for she wanted this job desperately. It was going to be her key to freedom.

Tracy walked into the large, pleasant kitchen and sat down. She could feel the perspiration bead and roll down from her underarms. A woman clad in a muted rose-coloured housecoat appeared in the doorway.

She said, 'Good morning.'

'Good morning.'

The woman started to sit, changed her mind, and stood. Sue Ellen Brannigan was a pleasant-faced blonde in her middle thirties, with a vague, distracted manner. She was thin and hyper, never quite sure how to treat the convict servants. Should she thank them for doing their jobs, or just give them orders? Should she be friendly, or treat them like prisoners? Sue Ellen still had not got used to the idea of living in the midst of drug addicts and thieves and killers.

'I'm Mrs Brannigan,' she rattled on. 'Amy is almost five years old, and you know how active they are at that age. I'm afraid she has to be watched all the time.' She glanced at Tracy's left hand. There was no wedding ring there, but these days, of course, that meant nothing. *Particularly with the lower classes*, Sue Ellen thought. She paused and asked delicately, 'Do you have children?'

Tracy thought of her unborn baby. 'No.'

'I see.' Sue Ellen was confused by this young woman. She was not at all what she had expected. There was something almost elegant about her. 'I'll bring Amy in.' She hurried out of the room.

Tracy looked around. It was a fairly large cottage, neat and attractively furnished. It seemed to Tracy that it had been years since she had been in anyone's home. That was all part of the other world, the world outside.

Sue Ellen came back into the room holding the hand of a young girl. 'Amy, this is –' Did one call a prisoner by her first or last name? She compromised. 'This is Tracy Whitney.'

'Hi,' Amy said. She had her mother's thinness and deep-set, intelligent hazel eyes. She was not a pretty child, but there was an open friendliness about her that was touching.

I won't let her touch me.

'Are you going to be my new nanny?'

'Well, I'm going to help your mother look after you.'

'Judy went out on parole, did you know that? Are you going out on parole, too?'

No, Tracy thought. She said, 'I'm going to be here for a long while, Amy.'

'That's good,' Sue Ellen said brightly. She coloured in embarrassment and bit her lip. 'I mean –' She whirled around the kitchen and started explaining Tracy's duties to her. 'You'll have your meals with Amy. You can prepare breakfast for her and play with her in the morning. The cook will make lunch here. After lunch, Amy has a nap, and in the afternoon she likes walking around the grounds of the farm. I think it's so good for a child to see growing things, don't you?'

'Yes.'

The farm was on the other side of the main prison, and the twenty acres, planted with vegetables and fruit trees, were tended by trusties. There was a large artificial lake used for irrigation, surrounded by a stone wall that rose above it.

The next five days were almost like a new life for Tracy. Under different circumstances, she would have enjoyed getting away from the bleak prison walls, free to walk around the farm and breathe

the fresh country air, but all she could think about was escaping. When she was not on duty with Amy, she was required to report back to the prison. Each night Tracy was locked in her cell, but in the daytime she had the illusion of freedom. After breakfast in the prison kitchen, she walked over to the warden's cottage and made breakfast for Amy. Tracy had learned a good deal about cooking from Charles, and she was tempted by the varieties of foodstuffs on the warden's shelves, but Amy preferred a simple breakfast of oatmeal or cereal with fruit. Afterwards, Tracy would play games with the little girl or read to her. Without thinking, Tracy began teaching Amy the games her mother had played with her.

Amy loved puppets. Tracy tried to copy Shari Lewis's Lamb Chop for her from one of the warden's old socks, but it turned out looking like a cross between a fox and a duck. 'I think it's beautiful,' Amy said loyally.

Tracy made the puppet speak with different accents: French, Italian, German, and the one Amy adored the most, Paulita's Mexican lilt. Tracy would watch the pleasure on the child's face and think, *I won't become involved. She's just my means of getting out of this place.*

After Amy's afternoon nap, the two of them would take long walks, and Tracy saw to it that they covered areas of the prison grounds she had not seen before. She carefully observed every exit and entrance and how the guard towers were manned and noted when the shifts changed. It became obvious to her that none of the escape plans she had discussed with Ernestine would work.

'Has anyone ever tried to escape by hiding in one of the service trucks that deliver things to the prison? I've seen milk trucks and food –'

'Forget it,' Ernestine said flatly. 'Every vehicle comin' in and goin' out of the gate is searched.'

At breakfast one morning, Amy said, 'I love you, Tracy. Will you be my mother?'

The words sent a pang through Tracy. 'One mother is enough. You don't need two.'

'Yes, I do. My friend Sally Ann's father got married again, and Sally Ann has two mothers.'

'You're not Sally Ann,' Tracy said curtly. 'Finish your breakfast.'

Amy was looking at her with hurt eyes. 'I'm not hungry any more.'

'All right. I'll read to you, then.'

As Tracy started to read, she felt Amy's soft little hand on hers.

'Can I sit on your lap?'

'No.' *Get your affection from your own family*, Tracy thought. *You don't belong to me. Nothing belongs to me.*

The easy days away from the routine of the prison somehow made the nights worse. Tracy loathed returning to her cell, hated being caged in like an animal. She was still unable to get used to the screams that came from nearby cells in the uncaring darkness. She would grit her teeth until her jaws ached. *One night at a time*, she promised herself. *I can stand one night at a time.*

She slept little, for her mind was busy planning. Step one was to escape. Step two was to deal with Joe Romano, Perry Pope, Judge Henry Lawrence, and Anthony Orsatti. Step three was Charles. But that was too painful even to think about yet. *I'll handle that when the time comes*, she told herself.

It was becoming impossible to stay out of the way of Big Bertha. Tracy was sure the huge Swede was having her spied upon. If Tracy went to the recreation room, Big Bertha would show up a few minutes later, and when Tracy went out to the yard, Big Bertha would appear shortly afterwards.

One day Big Bertha walked up to Tracy and said, 'You're looking beautiful today, *littbarn*. I can't wait for us to get together.'

'Stay away from me,' Tracy warned.

The amazon grinned. 'Or what? Your black bitch is gettin' out. I'm arrangin' to have you transferred to my cell.'

Tracy stared at her.

Big Bertha nodded. 'I can do it, honey. Believe it.'

Tracy knew then her time was running out. She had to escape before Ernestine was released.

Amy's favourite walk was through the meadow, rainbowed with colourful wildflowers. The huge artificial lake was nearby, surrounded by a low concrete wall with a long drop to the deep water.

'Let's go swimming,' Amy pleaded. 'Please, let's, Tracy?'

'It's not for swimming,' Tracy said. 'They use the water for irrigation.' The sight of the cold, forbidding-looking lake made her shiver.

Her father was carrying her into the ocean on his shoulders, and when she cried out, her father said, *Don't be a baby, Tracy*, and he dropped her into the cold water, and when the water closed over her head she panicked and began to choke . . .

When the news came, it was a shock, even though Tracy had expected it.

'I'm gettin' outta here a week from Sattiday,' Ernestine said.

The words sent a cold chill through Tracy. She had not told Ernestine about her conversation with Big Bertha. Ernestine would not be here to help her. Big Bertha probably had enough influence to have Tracy transferred to her cell. The only way Tracy could avoid it would be to talk to the warden, and she knew that if she did that, she was as good as dead. Every convict in the prison would turn on her. *You gotta fight, fuck, or hit the fence.* Well, she was going to hit the fence.

She and Ernestine went over the escape possibilities again. None of them was satisfactory.

'You ain't got no car, and you ain't got no one on the outside to he'p you. You're gonna get caught, sure as hell, and then you'll be worse off.

You'd be better doin' cool time and finishin' out your gig.'

But Tracy knew there would be no cool time. Not with Big Bertha after her. The thought of what the giant bull-dyke had in mind for her made her physically ill.

It was Saturday morning, seven days before Ernestine's release. Sue Ellen Brannigan had taken Amy into New Orleans for the weekend, and Tracy was at work in the prison kitchen.

'How's the nursemaid job goin'?' Ernestine asked.

'All right.'

'I seen that little girl. She seems real sweet.'

'She's okay.' Her tone was indifferent.

'I'll sure be glad to get outta here. I'll tell you one thing, I ain't never comin' back to this joint. If there's anythin' Al or me kin do for you on the outside –'

'Coming through,' a male voice called out.

Tracy turned. A laundryman was pushing a huge cart piled to the top with soiled uniforms and linens. Tracy watched, puzzled, as he headed for the exit.

'What I was sayin' was if me and Al can do anythin' for you – you know – send you things or –'

'Ernie, what's a laundry truck doing here? The prison has its own laundry.'

'Oh, that's for the guards,' Ernestine laughed. 'They used to send their uniforms to the prison laundry, but all the buttons managed to get ripped off, sleeves were torn, obscene notes were sewn inside, shirts were shrunk, and the material got mysteriously slashed. Ain't that a fuckin' shame, Miss Scarlett? Now the guards gotta send their stuff to an outside laundry.' Ernestine laughed her Butterfly McQueen imitation.

Tracy was no longer listening. She knew how she was going to escape.

ELEVEN

'George, I don't think we should keep Tracy on.'

Warden Brannigan looked up from his newspaper. 'What's the problem?'

'I'm not sure, exactly. I have the feeling that Tracy doesn't like Amy. Maybe she just doesn't like children.'

'She hasn't been mean to Amy, has she? Hit her, yelled at her?'

'No . . .'

'What, then?'

'Yesterday Amy ran over and put her arms around Tracy, and Tracy pushed her away. It bothered me because Amy's so crazy about her. To tell you the truth, I might be a little jealous. Could that be it?'

Warden Brannigan laughed. 'That could explain a lot, Sue Ellen. I think Tracy Whitney is just right for the job. Now, if she gives you any real problems, let me know, and I'll do something about it.'

'All right, dear.' Sue Ellen was still not satisfied.

She picked up her needlepoint and began stabbing at it. The subject was not closed yet.

'*Why* can't it work?'

'I tol' you, girl. The guards search every truck going through the gate.'

'But a truck carrying a basket of laundry – they're not going to dump out the laundry to check it.'

'They don't have to. The basket is taken to the utility room, where a guard watches it bein' filled.'

Tracy stood there thinking. 'Ernie . . . could someone distract the guard for five minutes?'

'What the hell good would –?' She broke off, a slow grin lighting her face. 'While someone pumps him full of sunshine, you get into the bottom of the hamper and get covered up with laundry!' She nodded. 'You know, I think the damned thing might work.'

'Then you'll help me?'

Ernestine was thoughtful for a moment. Then she said softly, 'Yeah. I'll he'p you. It's my last chance to give Big Bertha a kick in the ass.'

The prison grapevine buzzed with the news of Tracy Whitney's impending escape. A breakout was an event that affected all prisoners. The inmates lived vicariously through each attempt, wishing they had the courage to try it themselves. But there were the guards and the dogs and the helicopters, and, in the end, the bodies of the prisoners who had been brought back.

With Ernestine's help, the escape plan moved ahead swiftly. Ernestine took Tracy's measurements, Lola boosted the material for a dress from the millinery shop, and Paulita had a seamstress in another cell block make it. A pair of prison shoes was stolen from the wardrobe department and dyed to match the dress. A hat, gloves, and handbag appeared, as if by magic.

'Now we gotta get you some ID,' Ernestine informed Tracy. 'You'll need a couple of credit cards and a driver's licence.'

'How can I –?'

Ernestine grinned. 'You just leave it to old Ernie Littlechap.'

The following evening Ernestine handed Tracy three major credit cards in the name of Jane Smith.

'Next, you need a driver's licence.'

Sometime after midnight Tracy heard the door of her cell being opened. Someone had sneaked into the cell. Tracy sat up in her bunk, instantly on guard.

A voice whispered, 'Whitney? Let's go!'

Tracy recognized the voice of Lillian, a trusty. 'What do you want?' Tracy asked.

Ernestine's voice shot out of the darkness. 'What kind of idiot child did your mother raise? Shut up and don't ask questions.'

Lillian said softly, 'We got to do this fast. If we get caught, they'll have my ass. Come on.'

'Where are we going?' Tracy asked, as she followed Lillian down the dark corridor to a stairway. They went up to the landing above and, after making sure there were no guards about, hurried down a hallway until they came to the room where Tracy had been fingerprinted and photographed. Lillian pushed the door open. 'In here,' she whispered.

Tracy followed her into the room. Another inmate was waiting inside.

'Step up against the wall.' She sounded nervous.

Tracy moved against the wall, her stomach in knots.

'Look into the camera. Come on. Try and look relaxed.'

Very funny, Tracy thought. She had never been so nervous in her life. The camera clicked.

'The picture will be delivered in the morning,' the inmate said. 'It's for your driver's licence. Now get out of here – fast.'

Tracy and Lillian retraced their steps. On the way, Lillian said, 'I hear you're changin' cells.'

Tracy froze. 'What?'

'Didn't you know? You're moving in with Big Bertha.'

Ernestine, Lola, and Paulita were waiting up for Tracy when she returned. 'How'd it go?'

'Fine.'

Didn't you know? You're moving in with Big Bertha.

'The dress'll be ready for you Sattiday,' Paulita said.

The day of Ernestine's release. *That's my deadline*, Tracy thought.

Ernestine whispered, 'Everythin' is cool. The laundry pickup Sattiday is two o'clock. You gotta be in the utility room by one-thirty. You don' have to worry about the guard. Lola will keep him busy next door. Paulita will be in the utility room waitin' for you. She'll have your clothes. Your ID will be in your handbag. You'll be drivin' out the prison gates by two-fifteen.'

Tracy found it difficult to breathe. Just talking about the escape made her tremble. *Nobody gives a shit if they bring you back dead or alive . . . They figure dead is better.*

In a few days she would be making her break for freedom. She had no illusions: the odds were against her. They would eventually find her and bring her back. But there was something she had sworn to take care of first.

The prison grapevine knew all about the contest that had been fought between Ernestine Littlechap and Big Bertha over Tracy. Now that the word was out that Tracy was being transferred to Big Bertha's cell, it was no accident that no one had mentioned anything to Big Bertha about Tracy's escape plan: Big Bertha did not like to hear bad news. She was often apt to confuse the news with the bearer and treat that person accordingly. Big Bertha did not learn about Tracy's plan until the morning the escape was to take place, and it was revealed to her by the trusty who had taken Tracy's picture.

Big Bertha took the news in ominous silence. Her body seemed to grow bigger as she listened.

'What time?' was all she asked.

'This afternoon at two o'clock, Bert. They're gonna hide her in the bottom of a laundry hamper in the utility room.'

Big Bertha thought about it for a long time. Then she waddled over to a matron and said, 'I gotta see Warden Brannigan right away.'

Tracy had not slept all night. She was sick with tension. The months she had been in prison seemed like a dozen eternities. Images of the past flashed through her mind as she lay on her bunk, staring into the dark.

I feel like a princess in a fairy tale, Mother. I didn't know anyone could be this happy.

So! You and Charles want to get married.

How long a honeymoon are you planning?

You shot me, you bitch! . . .

Your mother committed suicide . . .

I never really knew you . . .

The wedding picture of Charles smiling at his bride . . .

How many eons ago? How many planets away?

The morning bell clanged through the corridor like a shock wave. Tracy sat up on her bunk, wide awake. Ernestine was watching her. 'How you feelin', girl?'

'Fine,' Tracy lied. Her mouth was dry, and her heart was beating erratically.

'Well, we're both leavin' here today.'

Tracy found it hard to swallow. 'Uh-huh.'

'You sure you kin get away from the warden's house by one-thirty?'

'No problem. Amy always takes a nap after lunch.'

Paulita said, 'You can't be late, or it won't work.'

'I'll be there.'

Ernestine reached under her mattress and took out a roll of bills. 'You're gonna need some walkin' around money. It's only two hundred bucks, but it'll get you on your way.'

'Ernie, I don't know what to –'

'Oh, jest shut up, girl, and take it.'

Tracy forced herself to swallow some breakfast. Her head was pounding, and every muscle in her body ached. *I'll never make it through the day*, she thought. *I've got to make it through the day.*

There was a strained, unnatural silence in the kitchen, and Tracy suddenly realized she was the cause of it. She was the object of knowing looks and nervous whispers. A breakout was about to happen, and she was the heroine of the drama. In a few hours she would be free. Or dead.

She rose from her unfinished breakfast and headed for Warden Brannigan's house. As Tracy waited for a guard to unlock the corridor door, she came face-to-face with Big Bertha. The huge Swede was grinning at her.

She's going to be in for a big surprise, Tracy thought.

She's all mine now, Big Bertha thought.

The morning passed so slowly that Tracy felt she would go out of her mind. The minutes seemed to drag on interminably. She read to Amy and had no idea what she was reading. She was aware of Mrs Brannigan watching from the window.

'Tracy, let's play hide-and-seek.'

Tracy was too nervous to play games, but she dared not do anything to arouse Mrs Brannigan's suspicions. She forced a smile. 'Sure. Why don't you hide first, Amy?'

They were in the front yard of the bungalow. In the far distance Tracy could see the building where the utility room was located. She had to be there at exactly 1:30. She would change into the street clothes that had been made for her, and by 1:45 she would be lying in the bottom of the large clothes hamper, covered over with uniforms and linens. At 2:00 the laundryman would come by for the hamper and wheel it out to his truck. By 2:15 the truck would drive through the gates on its way to the nearby town where the laundry plant was located.

The driver can't see in the back of the truck from the front seat. When the truck gets to town and stops for a red light, just open the door, step out, real cool, and catch a bus to wherever you're goin'.

'Can you see me?' Amy called. She was half-hidden behind the trunk of a magnolia tree. She held her hand over her mouth to stifle a giggle.

I'll miss her, Tracy thought. *When I leave here, the two people I'll miss will be a black, bald-headed bull-dyke and a young girl.* She wondered what Charles Stanhope would have made of that.

'I'm coming to find you,' Tracy said.

Sue Ellen watched the game from inside the house. It seemed to her that Tracy was acting strangely. All morning she had kept looking at her watch, as though expecting someone, and her mind was obviously not on Amy.

I must speak to George about it when he comes home for lunch, Sue Ellen decided. *I'm going to insist that he replace her.*

In the yard, Tracy and Amy played hopscotch for a while, then jacks, and Tracy read to Amy, and finally, blessedly, it was twelve-thirty, time for Amy's lunch. Time for Tracy to make her move. She took Amy into the cottage.

'I'll be leaving now, Mrs Brannigan.'

'What? Oh. Didn't anyone tell you, Tracy? We're having a delegation of VIP visitors today. They'll be having lunch here at the house, so Amy won't be having her nap. You may take her with you.'

Tracy stood there, willing herself not to scream. 'I – I can't do that, Mrs Brannigan.'

Sue Ellen Brannigan stiffened. 'What do you mean you can't do that?'

Tracy saw the anger in her face and thought, *I mustn't upset her. She'll call the warden, and I'll be sent back to my cell.*

Tracy forced a smile. 'I mean . . . Amy hasn't had her lunch. She'll be hungry.'

'I've had the cook prepare a picnic lunch for both of you. You can go for a nice walk in the meadow and have it there. Amy enjoys picnics, don't you darling?'

'I love picnics.' She looked at Tracy pleadingly. 'Can we, Tracy? Can we?'

No! Yes. Careful. It could still work.

Be in the utility room by one-thirty. Don't be late.

Tracy looked at Mrs Brannigan. 'What – what time do you want me to bring Amy back?'

'Oh, about three o'clock. They should be gone by then.'

So would the truck. The world was tumbling in on her. 'I –'

'Are you all right? You look pale.'

That was it. She would say she was ill. Go to the hospital. But then they would want to check her over and keep her there. She would never be able to get out in time. There had to be some other way.

Mrs Brannigan was staring at her.

'I'm fine.'

There's something wrong with her, Sue Ellen

Brannigan decided. *I'm definitely going to have George get someone else.*

Amy's eyes were alight with joy. 'I'll give you the biggest sandwiches, Tracy. We'll have a good time, won't we?'

Tracy had no answer.

The VIP tour was a surprise visit. Governor William Haber himself was escorting the prison reform committee through the penitentiary. It was something that Warden Brannigan had to live with once a year.

'It goes with the territory, George,' the governor had explained. 'Just clean up the place, tell your ladies to smile pretty, and we'll get our budget increased again.'

The word had gone out from the chief guard that morning: 'Get rid of all the drugs, knives, and dildos.'

Governor Haber and his party were due to arrive at 10:00 A.M. They would inspect the interior of the penitentiary first, visit the farm, and then have lunch with the warden at his cottage.

Big Bertha was impatient. When she had put in a request to see the warden, she had been told, 'The warden is very pressed for time this morning. Tomorrow would be easier. He –'

'Fuck tomorrow!' Big Bertha had exploded. 'I want to see him now. It's important.'

There were few inmates in the prison who

could have got away with it, but Big Bertha was one of them. The prison authorities were well aware of her power. They had seen her start riots, and they had seen her stop them. No prison in the world could be run without the cooperation of the inmate leaders, and Big Bertha was a leader.

She had been seated in the warden's outer office for almost an hour, her huge body overflowing the chair she sat in. *She's a disgusting-looking creature*, the warden's secretary thought. *She gives me the creeps.*

'How much longer?' Bertha demanded.

'It shouldn't be too much longer. He has a group of people in with him. The warden's very busy this morning.'

Big Bertha said, 'He's gonna be busier.' She looked at her watch. Twelve-forty-five. *Plenty of time.*

It was a perfect day, cloudless and warm, and the singing breeze carried a tantalizing mixture of scents across the green farmland. Tracy had spread out a tablecloth on a grassy area near the lake, and Amy was happily munching on an egg salad sandwich. Tracy glanced at her watch. It was already 1:00. She could not believe it. The morning had dragged and the afternoon was winging by. She had to think of something quickly, or time was going to steal away her last chance at freedom.

One-ten. In the warden's reception office Warden Brannigan's secretary put down the telephone and said to Big Bertha, 'I'm sorry. The warden says it's impossible for him to see you today. We'll make another appointment for –'

Big Bertha pushed herself to her feet. 'He's *got* to see me! It's –'

'We'll fit you in tomorrow.'

Big Bertha started to say, 'Tomorrow will be too late', but she stopped herself in time. No one but the warden himself must know what she was doing. Snitches suffered fatal accidents. But she had no intention of giving up. There was no way she was going to let Tracy Whitney get away from her. She walked into the prison library and sat down at one of the long tables at the far end of the room. She scribbled a note, and when the matron walked over to an aisle to help an inmate, Big Bertha dropped the note on her desk and left.

When the matron returned, she found the note and opened it. She read it twice:

YOU BETTER CHEK THE LAUNDREY TRUCK TO DAY.

There was no signature. A hoax? The matron had no way of knowing. She picked up the telephone. 'Get me the superintendent of guards . . .'

One-fifteen. 'You're not eating,' Amy said. 'You want some of my sandwich?'

'No! Leave me alone.' She had not meant to speak so harshly.

Amy stopped eating. 'Are you mad at me, Tracy? Please don't be mad at me. I love you so much. I never get mad at you.' Her soft eyes were filled with hurt.

'I'm not angry.' *She was in hell.*

'I'm not hungry if you're not. Let's play ball, Tracy.' And Amy pulled her rubber ball out of her pocket.

One-sixteen. She should have been on her way. It would take her at least fifteen minutes to get to the utility room. She could just make it if she hurried. But she could not leave Amy alone. Tracy looked around, and in the far distance she saw a group of trusties picking crops. Instantly, Tracy knew what she was going to do.

'Don't you want to play ball, Tracy?'

Tracy rose to her feet. 'Yes. Let's play a new game. Let's see who can throw the ball the farthest. I'll throw the ball, and then it will be your turn.' Tracy picked up the hard rubber ball and threw it as far as she could in the direction of the workers.

'Oh, that's good,' Amy said admiringly. 'That's real far.'

'I'll go get the ball,' Tracy said. 'You wait here.'

And she was running, running for her life, her feet flying across the fields. It was 1:18. If she was late, they would wait for her. *Or would they?* She ran faster. Behind her, she heard Amy calling, but she paid no attention. The farm workers were moving in the other direction now. Tracy yelled at them, and they stopped. She was breathless when she reached them.

'Anythin' wrong?' one of them asked.

'No, n-nothing.' She was panting, fighting for breath. 'The little girl back there. One of you look after her. I have something important to do. I –'

She heard her name called from a distance and turned. Amy was standing on top of the concrete wall surrounding the lake. She waved. 'Look at me, Tracy.'

'No! Get down!' Tracy screamed.

And as Tracy watched in horror, Amy lost her balance and plunged into the lake.

'Oh, dear God!' The blood drained from Tracy's face. She had a choice to make, but there was no choice. *I can't help her. Not now. Someone will save her. I have to save myself. I've got to get out of this place or I'll die*. It was 1:20.

Tracy turned and began running as fast as she had ever run in her life. The others were calling after her, but she did not hear them. She flew through the air, unaware that her shoes had fallen off, not caring that the sharp ground was cutting into her feet. Her heart was pounding, and her lungs were bursting, and she pushed herself to run faster, faster. She reached the wall around the lake and vaulted on top of it. Far below, she could see Amy in the deep, terrifying water, struggling to stay afloat. Without a second's hesitation, Tracy jumped in after her. And as she hit the water, Tracy thought, *Oh, my God! I can't swim . . .*

BOOK TWO

TWELVE

New Orleans
Friday, 25 August – 10:00 A.M.

Lester Torrance, a cashier at the First Merchants Bank of New Orleans, prided himself on two things: his sexual prowess with the ladies and his ability to size up his customers. Lester was in his late forties, a lanky, sallow-faced man with a Tom Selleck moustache and long sideburns. He had been passed over for promotion twice, and in retaliation, Lester used the bank as a personal dating service. He could spot hookers a mile away, and he enjoyed trying to persuade them to give him their favours for nothing. Lonely widows were an especially easy prey. They came in all shapes, ages and states of desperation, and sooner or later they would appear in front of Lester's cage. If they were temporarily overdrawn, Lester would lend a sympathetic ear and delay bouncing their cheques. In return, perhaps they could have a quiet little dinner together? Many of his female customers sought his help and confided delicious secrets to him: they needed a loan without their husbands' knowledge . . . They wanted to keep confidential certain cheques they had written . . . They were contemplating a divorce, and could Lester help them close out their joint account right away? . . . Lester was only too eager to please. And to be pleased.

On this particular Friday morning, Lester knew he had hit the jackpot. He saw the woman the moment she walked in the door of the bank. She was an absolute stunner. She had sleek black hair falling to her shoulders, and she wore a tight skirt and sweater that outlined a figure a Las Vegas chorine would have envied.

There were four other cashiers in the bank, and the young woman's eyes went from one cage to the other, as though seeking help. When she glanced at Lester, he nodded eagerly and gave her an encouraging smile. She walked over to his cage, just as Lester had known she would.

'Good *morning*,' Lester said warmly. 'What may I do for you?' He could see her nipples pushing against her cashmere sweater, and he thought, *Baby, what I'd like to do for you!*

'I'm afraid I have a problem,' the woman said softly. She had the most delightful southern accent Lester had ever heard.

'That's what I'm here for,' he said heartily, 'to solve problems.'

'Oh, I do hope so. I'm afraid I've done somethin' just terrible.'

Lester gave her his best paternal, you-can-lean-on-me smile. 'I can't believe a lovely lady like you could do anything terrible.'

'Oh, but I *have*.' Her soft brown eyes were wide with panic. 'I'm Joseph Romano's secretary, and he told me to order new blank cheques for his current account a week ago, and I simply forgot all about it, and now we've just about run out, and when he finds out, I don't know what he'll do to me.' It came out in a soft, velvety rush.

Lester was only too familiar with the name of Joseph Romano. He was a prized customer of the bank's, even though he kept relatively small amounts in his account. Everyone knew that his real money was laundered elsewhere.

He sure has great taste in secretaries, Lester thought. He smiled again. 'Well, now, that's not too serious, Mrs –?'

'Miss. Hartford. Lureen Hartford.'

Miss. This was his lucky day. Lester sensed that this was going to work out splendidly. 'I'll just order those new cheques for you right now. You should have them in two or three weeks and –'

She gave a little moan, a sound that seemed to Lester to hold infinite promise. 'Oh, that's too late, and Mr Romano's already so upset with me. I just can't seem to keep my mind on my work, you know?' She leaned forward so that her breasts were touching the front of the cage. She said breathlessly,

'If you could just rush those cheques out, I'd be happy to pay extra.'

Lester said ruefully, 'Gee, I'm sorry, Lureen, it would be impossible to –' He saw that she was near to tears.

'To tell you the truth, this might cost me my job. Please . . . I'll do *anything*.'

The words fell like music on Lester's ears.

'I'll tell you what I'll do,' Lester declared. 'I'll phone in a special rush on them, and you'll have them Monday. How's that?'

'Oh, you're just *wonderful*!' Her voice was filled with gratitude.

'I'll send them to the office and –'

'It would be better if I picked them up myself. I don't want Mr Romano to know how stupid I was.'

Lester smiled indulgently. 'Not stupid, Lureen. We all get a little forgetful sometimes.'

She said softly, 'I'll never forget *you*. See you Monday.'

'I'll be here.' It would take a broken back to keep him home.

She gave him a dazzling smile and walked slowly out of the bank, and her walk was a sight to behold. Lester was grinning as he went over to a file cabinet, got the number of Joseph Romano's account, and phoned in a rush order for the new cheques.

The hotel in Carmen Street was indistinguishable from a hundred other hotels in New Orleans, which was why Tracy had chosen it. She had been in the small, cheaply furnished room for a week. Compared to her cell, it was a palace.

When Tracy returned from her encounter with Lester, she took off the black wig, ran her fingers through her own luxuriant hair, removed the soft contact lenses, and creamed off her dark makeup. She sat down on the single straight chair in the room and breathed deeply. It was going well. It had been easy to learn where Joe Romano kept his bank account. Tracy had looked up the cancelled cheque from her mother's estate, issued by Romano. 'Joe Romano? You can't touch him,' Ernestine had said.

Ernestine was wrong and Joe Romano was just the first. The others would follow. Every one of them.

She closed her eyes and relived the miracle that had brought her there . . .

She felt the cold, dark waters closing over her head. She was drowning, and she was filled with terror. She dived down, and her hands found the child and grabbed her and pulled her to the surface. Amy struggled in blind panic to break free, dragging them both under again, her arms and legs flailing wildly. Tracy's lungs were bursting. She fought her way out of the watery grave, hanging on to the little girl in a death grip, and she felt her strength ebbing. *We're not going to make it*, she thought. *We're dying*. Voices were calling out, and she felt Amy's body torn from her arms and she screamed, 'Oh, God, no!'

Strong hands were around Tracy's waist and a voice said, 'Everything's fine now. Take it easy. It's over.'

Tracy looked around frantically for Amy and saw that she was safe in a man's arms. Moments later they were both hauled up from the deep, cruel water . . .

The incident would have been worth no more than a paragraph on the inside page of the morning newspapers, except for the fact that a prisoner who could not swim had risked her life to save the child of the warden. Overnight the newspapers and television commentators turned Tracy into a heroine. Governor Haber himself visited the prison hospital with Warden Brannigan to see Tracy.

'That was a very brave thing you did,' the warden said. 'Mrs Brannigan and I want you to know how grateful we are.' His voice was choked with emotion.

Tracy was still weak and shaken from her experience. 'How is Amy?'

'She's going to be fine.'

Tracy closed her eyes. *I couldn't have borne it if anything had happened to her*, she thought. She remembered her coldness, when all the child had wanted was love, and Tracy felt bitterly ashamed. The incident had cost her her chance to escape, but she knew that if she had to do it over again, she would do the same thing.

There was a brief inquiry into the accident.

'It was my fault,' Amy told her father. 'We were playing ball, and Tracy ran after the ball and told me to wait, but I climbed up on the wall so I could see her better and I fell in the water. But Tracy saved me, Daddy.'

They kept Tracy in the hospital that night for observation, and the next morning she was taken to Warden Brannigan's office. The media was waiting for her. They knew a human-interest story when they saw one, and stringers from UPI and the Associated Press were present; the local television station had sent a news team.

That evening the report of Tracy's heroism unfolded, and the account of the rescue went on national television and began to snowball. *Time*, *Newsweek*, *People*, and hundreds of newspapers all over the country carried the story. As the press coverage continued, letters and telegrams poured into the penitentiary, demanding that Tracy Whitney be pardoned.

Governor Haber discussed it with Warden Brannigan.

'Tracy Whitney is in here for some serious crimes,' Warden Brannigan observed.

The governor was thoughtful. 'But she has no previous record, right, George?'

'That's right, sir.'

'I don't mind telling you, I'm getting a hell of a lot of pressure to do something about her.'

'So am I, Governor.'

'Of course, we can't let the public tell us how to run our prisons, can we?'

'Certainly not.'

'On the other hand,' the governor said judiciously, 'the Whitney girl has certainly demonstrated a remarkable amount of courage. She's become quite a heroine.'

'No question about it,' Warden Brannigan agreed.

The governor paused to light a cigar. 'What's your opinion, George?'

George Brannigan chose his words carefully. 'You're aware, of course, Governor, that I have a very personal interest in this. It was my child she saved. But, putting that aside, I don't think Tracy Whitney is the criminal type, and I can't believe she would be a danger to society if she were out in the world. My strong recommendation is that you give her a pardon.'

The governor, who was about to announce his candidacy for a new term, recognized a good idea when he heard it. 'Let's play this close to the chest for a bit.' In politics, timing was everything.

After discussing it with her husband, Sue Ellen said to Tracy, 'Warden Brannigan and I would like it very much if you moved into the cottage. We have a spare bedroom in the back. You could take care of Amy full-time.'

'Thank you,' Tracy said gratefully. 'I would like that.'

It worked out perfectly. Not only did Tracy not have to spend each night locked away in a cell, but her relationship with Amy changed completely. Amy adored Tracy, and Tracy responded. She enjoyed being with this bright, loving little girl. They played their old games and watched Disney films on television and read together. It was almost like being part of a family.

But whenever Tracy had an errand that took her into the cell blocks, she invariably ran into Big Bertha.

'You're a lucky bitch,' Big Bertha growled. 'But you'll be back here with the common folks one day soon. I'm workin' on it, *littbarn*.'

Three weeks after Amy's rescue Tracy and Amy were playing tag in the yard when Sue Ellen Brannigan hurried out of the house. She stood there a moment watching them. 'Tracy, the warden just telephoned. He would like to see you in his office right away.'

Tracy was filled with a sudden fear. *Did it mean that she was going to be transferred back to the prison?* Had Big Bertha used her influence to arrange it? Or had Mrs Brannigan decided that Amy and Tracy were getting too close?

'Yes, Mrs Brannigan.'

The warden was standing in the doorway of his office when Tracy was escorted in. 'You'd better sit down,' he said.

Tracy tried to read the answer to her fate from the tone of his voice.

'I have some news for you.' He paused, filled with some emotion that Tracy did not understand.

'I have just received an order from the governor of Louisiana,' Warden Brannigan went on, 'giving you a full pardon, effective immediately.'

Dear God, did he say what I think he said? She was afraid to speak.

'I want you to know,' the warden continued, 'that this is not being done because it was my child you saved. You acted instinctively in the way any decent citizen would have acted. By no stretch of the imagination could I ever believe that you would be a threat to society.' He smiled and added, 'Amy is going to miss you. So are we.'

Tracy had no words. If the warden only knew the truth: that if the accident had not happened, the warden's men would have been out hunting her as a fugitive.

'You'll be released the day after tomorrow.'

Her 'getup'. And still Tracy could not absorb it. 'I – I don't know what to say.'

'You don't have to say anything. Everyone here is very proud of you. Mrs Brannigan and I expect you to do great things on the outside.'

So it was true: she was free. Tracy felt so weak that she had to steady herself against the arm of the chair. When she finally spoke, her voice was firm. 'There's a lot I want to do, Warden Brannigan.'

On Tracy's last night in prison an inmate from Tracy's old cell block walked up to her. 'So you're getting out.'

'That's right.'

The woman, Betty Franciscus, was in her early forties, still attractive, with an air of pride about her.

'If you need any help on the outside, there's a man you should see in New York. His name is Conrad Morgan.' She slipped Tracy a piece of paper. 'He's into criminal reform. He likes to give a hand to people who've been in prison.'

'Thank you, but I don't think I'll need –'

'You never know. Keep his address.'

Two hours later, Tracy was walking through the penitentiary gates, moving past the television cameras. She would not speak to the reporters, but when Amy broke away from her mother and threw herself into Tracy's arms, the cameras whirred. That was the picture that came out over the evening news.

Freedom to Tracy was no longer simply an abstract word. It was something tangible, physical, a condition to be enjoyed and savoured. Freedom meant breathing fresh air, privacy, not standing in lines for meals, not listening for bells. It meant hot baths and good-smelling soaps, soft lingerie, pretty dresses and high-heeled shoes. It meant having a name instead of a number. Freedom meant escape from Big Bertha and fear of gang rapes and the deadly monotony of prison routine.

Tracy's newfound freedom took getting used to. Walking along a street, she was careful not to jostle anyone. In the penitentiary bumping into another prisoner could be the spark that set off a conflagration. It was the absence of constant menace that Tracy found most difficult to adjust to. No one was threatening her.

She was free to carry out her plans.

In Philadelphia, Charles Stanhope III saw Tracy on television, leaving the prison. *She's still beautiful*, he thought. Watching her, it seemed impossible that she had committed any of the crimes for which she had been convicted. He looked at his exemplary wife, placidly seated across the room, knitting. *I wonder if I made a mistake.*

Daniel Cooper watched Tracy on the television news in his apartment in New York. He was totally indifferent to the fact that she had been released from prison. He clicked off the television set and returned to the file he was working on.

When Joe Romano saw the television news, he laughed aloud. The Whitney girl was a lucky bitch. *I'll bet prison was good for her. She must be really horny by now. Maybe one day we'll meet again.*

Romano was pleased with himself. He had already passed the Renoir to a fence, and it had been purchased by a private collector in Zurich. Five hundred grand from the insurance company, and another two hundred thousand from the fence. Naturally, Romano had split the money with Anthony Orsatti. Romano was very meticulous in his dealings with him, for he had seen examples of what happened to people who were *not* correct in their transactions with Orsatti.

At noon on Monday Tracy, in her Lureen Hartford persona, returned to the First Merchants Bank of New Orleans. At that hour it was crowded with customers. There were several people in front of Lester Torrance's window. Tracy joined the line, and when Lester saw her, he beamed and nodded. She was even more goddamned beautiful than he had remembered.

When Tracy finally reached his window, Lester crowed, 'Well, it wasn't easy, but I did it for you, Lureen.'

A warm, appreciative smile lit Lureen's face. 'You're just too wonderful.'

'Yes, sir, got 'em right here.' Lester opened a drawer, found the box of cheques he had carefully put away, and handed it to her. 'There you are. Four hundred blank cheques. Will that be enough?'

'Oh, more than enough, unless Mr Romano goes on a cheque-writing spree.' She looked into Lester's eyes and sighed, 'You saved my life.'

Lester felt a pleasurable stirring in his groin. 'I believe people have to be nice to people, don't you, Lureen?'

'You're so right, Lester.'

'You know, you should open your account here. I'd take real good care of you. *Real* good.'

'I just know you would,' Tracy said softly.

'Why don't you and me talk about it over a nice quiet dinner somewhere?'

'I'd surely love that.'

'Where can I call you, Lureen?'

'Oh, I'll call *you*, Lester.' She moved away.

'Wait a min –' The next customer stepped up and handed the frustrated Lester a sackful of coins.

In the centre of the bank were four tables that held containers of blank deposit and withdrawal slips, and the tables were crowded with people busily filling out forms. Tracy moved away from Lester's view. As a customer made room at a table, Tracy took her place. The box that Lester had given her contained eight packets of blank cheques. But it was not the cheques Tracy was interested in: it was the deposit slips at the back of the packets.

She carefully separated the deposit slips from the cheques and, in fewer than three minutes, she was holding eighty deposit slips in her hand. Making sure she was unobserved, Tracy put twenty slips in the metal container.

She moved on to the next table, where she placed twenty more deposit slips. Within a few minutes, all of them had been left on the various tables. The deposit slips were blank, but each one contained a magnetized code at the bottom, which the computer used to credit the various accounts. No matter who deposited money, because of the magnetic code, the computer would automatically credit Joe Romano's account with each deposit. From her experience working in a bank, Tracy knew that within two days all the magnetized deposit slips would be used up and that it would take at least five days before the mix-up was noticed. That would give her more than enough time for what she planned to do.

On the way back to her hotel, Tracy threw the blank cheques into a rubbish bin. Mr Joe Romano would not be needing them.

Tracy's next stop was at the New Orleans Holiday Travel Agency. The young woman behind the desk asked, 'May I help you?'

'I'm Joseph Romano's secretary. Mr Romano would like to make a reservation for Rio de Janeiro. He wants to leave this Friday.'

'Will that be one ticket?'

'Yes. First class. An aisle seat. Smoking, please.'

'Round trip?'

'One way.'

The travel agent turned to her desk computer. In a few seconds, she said, 'We're all set. One first-class seat on Pan American's Flight seven twenty-eight, leaving at six-thirty P.M. on Friday, with a short stopover in Miami.'

'He'll be very pleased,' Tracy assured the woman.

'That will be nineteen hundred and twenty-nine dollars. Will that be cash or charge?'

'Mr Romano always pays cash. COD. Could you have the ticket delivered to his office on Thursday, please?'

‘We could have it delivered tomorrow, if you like.’

‘No. Mr Romano won’t be there tomorrow. Would you make it Thursday at eleven A.M.?’

‘Yes. That will be fine. And the address?’

‘Mr Joseph Romano, Two-seventeen Poydras Street, Suite four-zero-eight.’

The woman made a note of it. ‘Very well. I’ll see that it’s delivered Thursday morning.’

‘Eleven sharp,’ Tracy said. ‘Thank you.’

Half a block down the street was Acme Luggage Store. Tracy studied the display in the window before she walked inside.

A clerk approached her. ‘Good morning. And what can I do for you this morning?’

‘I want to buy some luggage for my husband.’

‘You’ve come to the right place. We’re having a sale. We have some nice, inexpensive –’

‘No,’ Tracy said. ‘Nothing inexpensive.’

She stepped over to a display of Vuitton suitcases stacked against a wall. ‘That’s more what I’m looking for. We’re going away on a trip.’

‘Well, I’m sure he’ll be pleased with one of these. We have three different sizes. Which one would –?’

‘I’ll take one of each.’

‘Oh. Fine. Will that be charge or cash?’

‘COD. The name is Joseph Romano. Could you have them delivered to my husband’s office on Thursday morning?’

‘Why, certainly, Mrs Romano.’

‘At eleven o’clock?’

'I'll see to it personally.'

As an afterthought, Tracy added, 'Oh . . . would you put his initials on them – in gold? That's J. R.'

'Of course. It will be a pleasure, Mrs Romano.'

Tracy smiled and gave him the office address.

At a nearby Western Union office, Tracy sent a paid cable to the Rio Othon Place on Copacabana Beach in Rio de Janeiro. It read: REQUEST YOUR BEST SUITE COMMENCING THIS FRIDAY FOR TWO MONTHS. PLEASE CONFIRM BY COLLECT CABLE. JOSEPH ROMANO, 217 POYDRAS STREET, SUITE 408, NEW ORLEANS, LOUISIANA, USA.

Three days later Tracy telephoned the bank and asked to speak to Lester Torrance. When she heard his voice, she said softly, 'You probably don't remember me, Lester, but this is Lureen Hartford, Mr Romano's secretary, and –'

Not remember her! His voice was eager. 'Of *course* I remember you, Lureen. I –'

'You do? Why, I'm flattered. You must meet so many people.'

'Not like you,' Lester assured her. 'You haven't forgotten about our dinner date, have you?'

'You don't know how much I'm lookin' forward to it. Would next Tuesday suit you, Lester?'

'Great!'

'Then it's a date. Oh. I'm such an idiot! You got me so excited talkin' to you I almost forgot why I called. Mr Romano asked me to check on his bank balance. Would you give me that figure?'

'You bet. No trouble at all.'

Ordinarily, Lester Torrance would have asked for a birth date or some form of identification from the caller, but in this case it was certainly not necessary. No, sir. 'Hang on, Lureen,' he said.

He walked over to the file, pulled out Joseph Romano's sheet, and studied it in surprise. There had been an extraordinary number of deposits made to Romano's acount in the past several days. Romano had never kept so much money in his account before. Lester Torrance wondered what was going on. Some big deal, obviously. When he had dinner with Lureen Hartford, he intended to pump her. A little inside information never hurt. He returned to the phone.

'Your boss has been keeping us busy,' he told Tracy. 'He has just over three hundred thousand dollars in his current account.'

'Oh, good. That's the figure I have.'

'Would he like us to transfer it to an investment account? It's not drawing any interest sitting here, and I could –'

'No. He wants it right where it is,' Tracy assured him.

'Okay.'

'Thank you so much, Lester. You're a darlin'.'

'Wait a minute! Should I call you at the office about the arrangements for Tuesday?'

'I'll call you, honey,' Tracy told him.

And the connection was broken.

* * *

The modern high-rise office building owned by Anthony Orsatti stood on Poydras Street between the riverfront and the gigantic Louisiana Superdrome, and the offices of the Pacific Import-Export Company occupied the entire fourth floor of the building. At one end of the suite were Orsatti's offices, and at the other end, Joe Romano's rooms. The space in between was occupied by four young receptionists who were available evenings to entertain Anthony Orsatti's friends and business acquaintances. In front of Orsatti's suite sat two very large men whose lives were devoted to guarding their boss. They also served as chauffeurs, masseurs and errand boys for the capo.

On this Thursday morning Orsatti was in his office checking out the previous day's receipts from running numbers, book-making, prostitution, and a dozen other lucrative activities that the Pacific Import-Export Company controlled.

Anthony Orsatti was in his late sixties. He was a strangely built man with a large, heavy torso and short, bony legs that seemed to have been designed for a smaller man. Standing up he looked like a seated frog. He had a face criss-crossed with an erratic web of scars that could have been woven by a drunken spider, an oversized mouth and black, bulbous eyes. He had been totally bald from the age of fifteen after an attack of alopecia, and had worn a black wig ever since. It fitted him badly, but in all the years no one had dared mention it to his face. Orsatti's cold eyes were gambler's eyes, giving away nothing, and his face, except when he was with his five daughters, whom he adored, was expressionless. The only clue to Orsatti's emotions was his voice. He had a hoarse, raspy voice, the result of a wire having been tightened around his throat on his twenty-first birthday, when he had been left for dead. The two men who had made that mistake had turned up in the morgue the following week. When Orsatti got really upset, his voice lowered to a strangled whisper that could barely be heard.

Anthony Orsatti was a king who ran his fiefdom with bribes, guns and blackmail. He ruled New Orleans, and it paid him obeisance in the form of untold riches. The capos of the other Families across the country respected him and constantly sought his advice.

At the moment, Anthony Orsatti was in a benevolent mood. He had had breakfast with his mistress, whom he kept in an block of flats he owned in Lake Vista. He visited her three times a week, and this morning's visit had been particularly satisfactory. She did things to him in bed that other women never dreamed of, and Orsatti sincerely believed it was because she loved him so much. His organization was running smoothly. There were no problems, because Anthony Orsatti knew how to solve difficulties before they became problems. He had once explained his philosophy to Joe Romano: 'Never let a little problem become a big problem, Joe, or it grows like a fuckin' snowball. You got a precinct captain who thinks he oughta get a bigger cut – you *melt* him, see? No more snowball. You get some hot-shot from Chicago who asks permission to open up his own little operation here in New Orleans? You know that pretty soon that "little" operation is gonna turn into a *big* operation and start cuttin' into your profits. So you say yes, and then when he gets here, you *melt* the son of a bitch. No more snowball. Get the picture?'

Joe Romano got the picture.

Anthony Orsatti loved Romano. He was like a son to him. Orsatti had picked him up when Romano was a punk kid rolling drunks in alleys. He himself had trained Romano, and now the kid could tap-dance his way around with the best of them. He was fast, he was smart and he was honest. In ten years Romano had risen to the rank of Anthony Orsatti's chief lieutenant. He supervised all the Family's operations and reported only to Orsatti.

Lucy, Orsatti's private secretary, knocked and came into the office. She was twenty-four years old, a college graduate, with a face and figure that had won several local beauty contests. Orsatti enjoyed having beautiful young women around him.

He looked at the clock on his desk. It was

10:45. He had told Lucy he did not want any interruptions before noon. He scowled at her. 'What?'

'I'm sorry to bother you, Mr Orsatti. There's a Miss Gigi Dupres on the phone. She sounds hysterical, but she won't tell me what she wants. She insists on speaking with you personally. I thought it might be important.'

Orsatti sat there, running the name through the computer in his brain. *Gigi Dupres?* One of the broads he had up in his suite his last time in Vegas? *Gigi Dupres?* Not that he could remember, and he prided himself on a mind that forgot nothing. Out of curiosity, Orsatti picked up the phone and waved a dismissal at Lucy.

'Yeah? Who's this?'

'Is thees Mr Anthony Orsatti?' She had a French accent.

'So?'

'Oh, thank God I got hold of you, Meester Orsatti!'

Lucy was right. The dame was hysterical. Anthony Orsatti was not interested. He started to hang up, when her voice went on.

'You must stop him, please!'

'Lady, I don't know who you're talkin' about, and I'm busy –'

'My Joe. Joe Romano. He promised to take me with him, *comprenez vous?*'

'Hey, you got a beef with Joe, take it up with him. I ain't his nursemaid.'

'He lie to me! I just found out he is leave for Brazil without me. Half of that three hundred thousand dollars is mine.'

Anthony Orsatti suddenly found he was interested, after all. 'What three hundred thousand you talkin' about?'

'The money Joe is hiding in his current account. The money – how you say? – *skimmed.*'

Anthony Orsatti was *very* interested.

'Please tell Joe he must take me to Brazil with him. Please! Weel you do thees?'

'Yeah,' Anthony Orsatti promised. 'I'll take care of it.'

Joe Romano's office was modern, all white and chrome, done by one of New Orleans's most fashionable decorators. The only touches of colour were the three expensive French Impressionist paintings on the walls. Romano prided himself on his good taste. He had fought his way up from the slums of New Orleans, and on the way he had educated himself. He had an eye for paintings and an ear for music. When he dined out, he had long, knowledgeable discussions with the sommelier about wines. Yes, Joe Romano had every reason to be proud. While his contemporaries had survived by using their fists, he had succeeded by using his brains. If it was true that Anthony Orsatti owned New Orleans, it was also true that it was Joe Romano who ran it for him.

His secretary walked into his office. 'Mr Romano,

there's a messenger here with an airplane ticket for Rio de Janeiro. Shall I write out a cheque? It's COD.'

'*Rio de Janeiro?*' Romano shook his head. 'Tell him there's some mistake.'

The uniformed messenger was in the doorway. 'I was told to deliver this to Joseph Romano at this address.'

'Well, you were told wrong. What is this, some kind of a new airline promotion gimmick?'

'No, sir. I –'

'Let me see that.' Romano took the ticket from the messenger's hand and looked at it. 'Friday. Why would I be going to Rio on Friday?'

'That's a good question,' Anthony Orsatti said. He was standing behind the messenger. 'Why would you, Joe?'

'It's some kind of dumb mistake, Tony.' Romano handed the ticket back to the messenger. 'Take this back where it came from and –'

'Not so fast.' Anthony Orsatti took the ticket and examined it. 'It says here one first-class ticket, aisle seat, smoking, to Rio de Janeiro for Friday. One way.'

Joe Romano laughed. 'Someone made a mistake.' He turned to his secretary. 'Madge, call the travel agency and tell them they goofed. Some poor slob is going to be missing his plane ticket.'

Joleen, the assistant secretary, walked in. 'Excuse me, Mr Romano. The luggage has arrived. Do you want me to sign for it?'

Joe Romano stared at her. 'What luggage? I didn't order any luggage.'

'Have them bring it in,' Anthony Orsatti commanded.

'Jesus!' Joe Romano said. 'Has everyone gone nuts?'

A messenger walked in carrying three Vuitton suitcases.

'What's all this? I never ordered those.'

The messenger checked his delivery slip. 'It says Mr Joseph Romano, Two-seventeen Poydras Street, Suite four-zero-eight?'

Joe Romano was losing his temper. 'I don't care what the fuck it says. I didn't order them. Now get them out of here.'

Orsatti was examining the luggage. 'They have your initials on them, Joe.'

'What? Oh. Wait a minute! It's probably some kind of present.'

'Is it your birthday?'

'No. But you know how broads are, Tony. They're always givin' you gifts.'

'Have you got somethin' going in Brazil?' Anthony Orsatti enquired.

'*Brazil?*' Joe Romano laughed. 'This must be someone's idea of a joke, Tony.'

Orsatti smiled gently, then turned to the secretaries and the two messengers. 'Out.'

When the door was closed behind them, Anthony Orsatti spoke. 'How much money you got in your bank account, Joe?'

Joe Romano looked at him, puzzled. 'I don't know. Fifteen hundred, I guess, maybe a couple of grand. Why?'

'Just for fun, why don't you call your bank and check it out?'

'What for? I –'

'Check it out, Joe.'

'Sure. If it'll make you happy.' He buzzed his secretary. 'Get me the head bookkeeper over at First Merchants.'

A minute later she was on the line.

'Hello, honey. Joseph Romano. Would you give me the current balance in my current account? My birth date is October fourteenth.'

Anthony Orsatti picked up the extension phone. A few moments later the bookkeeper was back on the line.

'Sorry to keep you waiting, Mr Romano. As of this morning, your current account balance is three hundred and ten thousand, nine hundred and five dollars and thirty-two cents.'

Romano could feel the blood draining from his face. 'It's *what*?'

'Three hundred and ten thousand, nine hundred and five –'

'You stupid bitch!' he yelled. 'I don't have that kind of money in my account. You made a mistake. Let me talk to the –'

He felt the telephone being taken out of his hand, as Anthony Orsatti replaced the receiver. 'Where'd that money come from, Joe?'

Joe Romano's face was pale. 'I swear to God, Tony, I don't know anything about that money.'

'No?'

'Hey, you've got to believe me! You know what's happening? Someone is setting me up.'

'It must be someone who likes you a lot. He gave you a going-away present of three hundred and ten thousand dollars.' Orsatti sat down heavily on the Scalamander silk-covered armchair and looked at Joe Romano for a long moment, then spoke very quietly. 'Everything was all set, huh? A one-way ticket to Rio, new luggage . . . Like you was planning a whole new life.'

'No!' There was panic in Joe Romano's voice. 'Jesus, you know me better than that, Tony. I've always been on the level with you. You're like a father to me.'

He was sweating now. There was a knock at the door, and Madge poked her head in. She held an envelope.

'I'm sorry to interrupt, Mr Romano. There's a cable for you, but you have to sign for it yourself.'

With the instincts of a trapped animal, Joe Romano said, 'Not now. I'm busy.'

'I'll take it,' Anthony Orsatti said, and he was out of the chair before the woman could close the door. He took his time reading the cable, then he focused his eyes on Joe Romano.

In a voice so low that Romano could barely hear him, Anthony Orsatti said, 'I'll read it out to you, Joe. "Pleased to confirm your reservation for our Princess Suite for two months this Friday, first September." It's signed, "S. Montalband, manager, Rio Othon Palace, Copacabana Beach, Rio de Janeiro." It's your reservation, Joe. You won't be needin' it, will you?'

THIRTEEN

Andre Gillian was in the kitchen making preparations for *spaghetti alla carbonara*, a large Italian salad, and a pear torte when he heard a loud, ominous popping sound, and a moment later the comfortable hum of the central air conditioner trailed off into silence.

Andre stamped his foot and said, '*Merde!* Not the night of the *game*.'

He hurried to the utility cupboard where the breaker box was located and flicked the electrical switches, one by one. Nothing happened.

Oh, Mr Pope was going to be furious. Simply *furious*! Andre knew how much his employer looked forward to his weekly Friday-night poker game. It was a tradition that had been going on for years, and it was always with the same elite group of players. Without air-conditioning, the house would be unbearable. *Simply unbearable!* New Orleans in September was only for the uncivilized. Even after the sun went down, there was no relief from the heat and humidity.

Andre returned to the kitchen and consulted the kitchen clock. Four o'clock. The guests would be arriving at 8:00. Andre thought about telephoning Mr Pope and telling him the problem, but then he remembered that the lawyer had said he was going to be tied up in court all day. *The dear man was so busy. He needed his relaxation. And now this!*

Andre took a small black telephone book from a kitchen drawer, looked up a number and dialled.

After three rings, a metallic voice intoned, 'You have reached the Eskimo Air-Conditioning Service. Our technicians are not available at this time. If you will leave your name and number and a brief message, we will get back to you as soon as possible. Please wait for the beep.'

Foutre! Only in America were you forced to hold a conversation with a machine.

A shrill, annoying beep sounded in Andre's ear. He spoke into the mouthpiece: 'This is the residence of Monsieur Perry Pope, Forty-two Charles Street. Our air-conditioning has ceased to function. You must send someone here as quickly as possible. *Vite!*'

He slammed down the receiver. *Of course no one was available. Air-conditioning was probably going off all over this dreadful city. It was impossible for air conditioners to cope with the damnable heat and humidity. Well, someone had better come soon*. Mr Pope had a temper. A nasty temper.

In the three years Andre Gillian had worked as a cook for the attorney, he had learned how influential his employer was. *It was amazing. All that brilliance in one so young*. Perry Pope knew simply everybody. When he snapped his fingers, people jumped.

It seemed to Andre Gillian that the house was already feeling warmer. *Ça va chier dur. If something is not done quickly, the shit's going to hit the fan.*

As Andre went back to cutting paper-thin slices of salami and provolone cheese for the salad, he could not shake the terrible feeling that the evening was fated to be a disaster.

When the doorbell rang thirty minutes later, Andre's clothes were soaked with perspiration, and the kitchen was like an oven. Gillian hurried to open the back door.

Two workmen in overalls stood in the doorway, carrying tool-boxes. One of them was a tall black man. His companion was white, several inches shorter, with a sleepy, bored look on his face. In the rear driveway stood their service truck.

'Gotta problem with your air-conditioning?' the black man asked.

'*Oui!* Thank heaven you're here. You've just got to get it working right away. There'll be guests arriving soon.'

The black man walked over to the oven, sniffed the baking torte and said, 'Smells good.'

'Please!' Gillian urged. '*Do* something!'

'Let's take a look in the furnace room,' the short man said. 'Where is it?'

'This way.'

Andre hurried them down a corridor to a utility room, where the air-conditioning unit stood.

'This is a good unit, Ralph,' the black man said to his companion.

'Yeah, Al. They don't make 'em like this any more.'

'Then for heaven's sake why isn't it *working*?' Gillian demanded.

They both turned to stare at him.

'We just got here,' Ralph said reprovingly. He knelt down and opened a small door at the bottom of the unit, took out a flashlight, got down on his stomach and peered inside. After a moment, he rose to his feet. 'The problem's not here.'

'Where is it, then?' Andre asked.

'Must be a short in one of the outlets. Probably shorted out the whole system. How many air-conditioning vents do you have?'

'Each room has one. Let's see. That must be at least nine.'

'That's probably the problem. Transduction overload. Let's go take a look.'

The three of them trooped back down the hall. As they passed the living room, Al said, 'This is sure a beautiful place Mr Pope has got here.'

The living room was exquisitely furnished, filled with signed antiques worth a fortune. The floors were covered with muted-coloured Persian rugs. To the left of the living room was a large, formal dining room, and to the right a den, with a large, green baize-covered gaming table in the centre. In one corner of the room was a round table, already set up for supper. The two servicemen walked into the den, and Al shone his flashlight into the air-conditioning vent high on the wall.

'Hmm,' he muttered. He looked up at the ceiling over the card table. 'What's above this room?'

'The attic.'

'Let's take a look.'

The workmen followed Andre up to the attic, a long, low-ceilinged room, dusty and spattered with cobwebs.

Al walked over to an electrical box set in the wall. He inspected the tangle of wires. 'Ha!'

'Did you find something?' Andre asked anxiously.

'Condenser problem. It's the humidity. We musta had a hundred calls this week. It's shorted out. We'll have to replace the condenser.'

'Oh, my God! Will it take long?'

'Naw. We got a new condenser out in the truck.'

'Please hurry,' Andre begged them. 'Mr Pope is going to be home soon.'

'You leave everything to us,' Al said.

Back in the kitchen, Andre confided, 'I must finish preparing my salad dressing. Can you find your way back up to the attic?'

Al raised a hand. 'No sweat, pal. You just go on about your business, and we'll go on about ours.'

'Oh, thank you. *Thank* you.'

Andre watched the men go out to the truck and return with two large canvas bags. 'If you need anything,' he told them, 'just call me.'

'You betcha!'

The workmen went up the stairs, and Andre returned to his kitchen.

When Ralph and Al reached the attic, they opened their canvas bags and removed a small folding camp chair, a drill with a steel bit, a tray of sandwiches, two cans of beer, a pair of 12 by 40 Zeiss binoculars for viewing distant objects in a dim light, and two live hamsters that had been injected with three quarters of a milligramme of acetyl promazine.

The two men went to work.

'Ol Ernestine is gonna be proud of me,' Al chortled as they started.

In the beginning, Al had stubbornly resisted the idea.

'You must be outta your mind, woman. I ain't gonna fuck around with no Perry Pope. That dude'll come down on my ass so hard I'll never see daylight again.'

'You don't gotta worry about him. He won't never be botherin' *no one* again.'

They were naked on the water bed in Ernestine's apartment.

'What you gettin' out of this deal, anyway, honey?' Al demanded.

'He's a prick.'

'Hey baby, the world's full of pricks, but you don't spend your life goin' round cuttin' off their balls.'

'All right. I'm doin' it for a friend.'

'Tracy?'

'That's right.'

Al liked Tracy. They had all had dinner together the day she got out of prison.

'She's a classy dame,' Al admitted. 'But why we stickin' our necks out for her?'

'Because if we don't he'p her, she's gonna have to settle for someone who ain't half as good as you, and if she gets caught, they'll cart her ass right back to the joint.'

Al sat up in bed and looked at Ernestine curiously. 'Does it mean that much to you, baby?'

'Yeah, hon.'

She would never be able to make him understand it, but the truth was simply that Ernestine could not stand the thought of Tracy back in prison at the mercy of Big Bertha. It was not only Tracy whom Ernestine was concerned about: it was herself. She had made herself Tracy's protector, and if Big Bertha got her hands on her, it would be a defeat to Ernestine.

So all she said now was, 'Yeah. It means a lot to me, honey. You gonna do it?'

'I damn sure can't do it alone,' Al grumbled.

And Ernestine knew she had won. She started nibbling her way down his long, lean body. And she murmured, 'Wasn't ol Ralph due to be released a few days ago . . . ?'

It was 6:30 before the two men returned to Andre's kitchen, grimy with sweat and dust.

'Is it fixed?' Andre asked anxiously.

'It was a real bitch,' Al informed him. 'You see, what you got here is a condenser with an AC/DC cutoff that –'

'Never mind that,' Andre interrupted impatiently. 'Did you *fix* it?'

'Yeah. It's all set. In five minutes we'll have it goin' again as good as new.'

'*Formidable!* If you'll just leave your bill on the kitchen table –'

Ralph shook his head. 'Don't worry about it. The company'll bill you.'

'Bless you both. *Au 'voir*.'

Andre watched the two men leave by the back door, carrying their canvas bags. Out of his sight, they walked around to the yard and opened the casing that housed the outside condenser of the air-conditioning unit. Ralph held the flashlight while Al reconnected the wires he had loosened a couple of hours earlier. The air-conditioning unit immediately sprang into life.

Al copied down the telephone number on the service tag attached to the condenser. When he telephoned the number a short time later and reached the recorded voice of the Eskimo Air-Conditioning Company, Al said, 'This is Perry Pope's residence at Forty-two Charles Street. Our air-conditioning is workin' fine now. Don't bother to send anyone. Have a nice day.'

The weekly Friday-night poker game at Perry Pope's house was an event to which all the players looked forward. It was always the same carefully selected group: Anthony Orsatti, Joe Romano, Judge Henry Lawrence, an alderman, a state senator, and of course their host. The stakes were high, the food was great, and the company was raw power.

Perry Pope was in his bedroom changing into white silk slacks and matching sports shirt. He hummed happily, thinking of the evening ahead. He had been on a winning streak lately. *In fact, my whole life is just one big winning streak*, he thought.

If anyone needed a legal favour in New Orleans, Perry Pope was the attorney to see. His power came from his connections with the Orsatti Family. He was known as The Arranger, and could fix anything from a traffic ticket to a drug-dealing charge to a murder rap. Life was good.

When Anthony Orsatti arrived, he brought a guest with him. 'Joe Romano won't be playin' any more,' Orsatti announced. 'You all know Inspector Newhouse.'

The men shook hands all round.

'Drinks are on the sideboard, gentlemen,' Perry Pope said. 'We'll have supper later. Why don't we start a little action going?'

The men took their accustomed chairs around the green felt table in the den. Orsatti pointed to Joe Romano's vacant chair and said to Inspector Newhouse, 'That'll be your seat from now on, Mel.'

While one of the men opened fresh packs of cards, Pope began distributing poker chips. He explained to Inspector Newhouse, 'The black chips are five dollars, red chips ten dollars, blue chips fifty dollars, white chips a hundred. Each man starts out buying five hundred dollars' worth of chips. We play table stakes, three raises, dealer's choice.'

'Sounds good to me,' the inspector said.

Anthony Orsatti was in a bad mood. 'Come on. Let's get started.' His voice was a strangled whisper. Not a good sign.

Perry Pope would have given a great deal to learn what had happened to Joe Romano, but the lawyer knew better than to bring up the subject. Orsatti would discuss it with him when he was ready.

Orsatti's thoughts were black: *I been like a father to Joe Romano. I trusted him, made him my chief lieutenant. And the son of a bitch stabbed me in the back. If that dizzy French dame hadn't telephoned, he might have got away with it, too. Well, he won't ever get away with nothin' again. Not where he is. If he's so clever, let him fuck around with the fish down there.*

'Tony, are you in or out?'

Anthony Orsatti turned his attention back to the game. Huge sums of money had been won and lost at this table. It always upset Anthony Orsatti to lose, and it had nothing to do with money. He could not bear to be on the losing end of anything. He thought of himself as a natural-born winner. Only winners rose to his position in life. For the last six weeks, Perry Pope had been on some kind of crazy winning streak, and tonight Anthony Orsatti was determined to break it.

Since they played dealer's choice, each dealer chose the game in which he felt the strongest. Hands were dealt for five-card stud, seven-card stud, low ball, draw poker – but tonight, no matter which game was chosen, Anthony Orsatti kept finding himself on the losing end. He began to increase his bets, playing recklessly, trying to recoup his losses. By midnight when they stopped to have the meal Andre had prepared, Orsatti was out $50,000, with Perry Pope the big winner.

The food was delicious. Usually Orsatti enjoyed the free midnight snack, but this evening he was impatient to get back to the table.

'You're not eating, Tony,' Perry Pope said.

'I'm not hungry.' Orsatti reached for the silver coffee urn at his side, poured coffee into a Victoria-patterned Herend-china cup, and sat down at the poker table. He watched the others eat and wished they would hurry. He was impatient to win his money back. As he started to stir his coffee, a small particle fell into his cup. Distastefully, Orsatti removed the particle with a spoon and examined it. It appeared to be a piece of plaster. He looked up at the ceiling, and something hit him on the forehead. He suddenly became aware of a scurrying noise overhead.

'What the hell's goin' on upstairs?' Anthony Orsatti asked.

Perry Pope was in the middle of telling an anecdote to Inspector Newhouse. 'I'm sorry, what did you say, Tony?'

The scurrying noise was more noticeable now. Bits of plaster began to trickle onto the green felt.

'It sounds to me like you have mice,' the senator said.

'Not in *this* house.' Perry Pope was indignant.

'Well, you sure as hell got somethin',' Orsatti growled.

A larger piece of plaster fell on the green felt table.

'I'll have Andre take care of it,' Pope said. 'If we're finished eating, why don't we get back to the game?'

Anthony Orsatti was staring up at a small hole in the ceiling directly above his head. 'Hold it. Let's go take a look up there.'

'What for, Tony? Andre can –'

Orsatti had already risen and started for the stairway. The others looked at one another, then hurried after him.

'A squirrel probably got into the attic,' Perry Pope guessed. 'This time of year they're all over the place. Probably hiding his nuts for the winter.' He laughed at his little joke.

When they reached the door to the attic, Orsatti pushed it open, and Perry Pope turned on the light. They caught a glimpse of two white hamsters frantically racing around the room.

'Jesus!' Perry Pope said. 'I've got rats!'

Anthony Orsatti was not listening. He was staring at the room. In the middle of the attic was a camp chair with a packet of sandwiches on top of it and two open cans of beer. On the floor next to the chair was a pair of binoculars.

Orsatti walked over to them, picked up the objects one by one, and examined them. Then he got down on his knees on the dusty floor and moved the tiny wooden cylinder that concealed a peephole that had been drilled into the ceiling. Orsatti put his eye to the peephole. Directly beneath him the card table was clearly visible.

Perry Pope was standing in the middle of the attic, dumb-founded. 'Who the hell put all this junk up here? I'm going to raise hell with Andre about this.'

Orsatti rose slowly to his feet and brushed the dust from his trousers.

Perry Pope glanced down at the floor. 'Look!' he exclaimed. 'They left a goddamned hole in the ceiling. Workmen today aren't worth a shit.'

He crouched down and took a look through the hole, and his face suddenly lost its colour. He stood up and looked around wildly, to find all the men staring at him.

'Hey!' Perry Pope said. 'You don't think I –?

Come on, fellas, this is *me*. I don't know anything about this. I wouldn't cheat you. My God, we're *friends*!' His hand flew to his mouth, and he began biting furiously at his cuticles.

Orsatti patted him on the arm. 'Don't worry about it.' His voice was almost inaudible.

Perry Pope kept gnawing desperately at the raw flesh of his right thumb.

FOURTEEN

'That's two down, Tracy,' Ernestine Littlechap chortled. 'The word on the street is that your lawyer friend Perry Pope ain't practisin' law no more. He had a real bad accident.'

They were having *café au lait* and *beignets* at a small pavement café off Royal Street.

Ernestine gave a high giggle. 'You got a brain, girl. You wouldn't like to go into business with me, would you?'

'Thanks, Ernestine. I have other plans.'

Ernestine asked eagerly, 'Who's next?'

'Lawrence. Judge Henry Lawrence.'

Henry Lawrence had begun his career as a small-town lawyer in Leesville, Louisiana. He had very little aptitude for the law, but he had two very important attributes: he was impressive looking, and he was morally flexible. His philosophy was that the law was a frail rod, meant to be bent to suit the needs of his clients. With that in mind, it was not surprising that shortly after he moved to New Orleans, Henry Lawrence's law practice began to flourish with a special group of clients. He went from handling misdemeanours and traffic accidents to handling felonies and capital crimes, and by the time he reached the big leagues, he was an expert at suborning juries, discrediting witnesses, and bribing anyone who could help his case. In short, he was Anthony Orsatti's kind of man, and it was inevitable that the paths of the two should cross. It was a marriage made in Mafia heaven. Lawrence became the mouthpiece for the Orsatti Family, and when the timing was right, Orsatti had him elevated to a judgeship.

'I don't know how you kin nail the judge,' Ernestine said. 'He's rich an' powerful an' untouchable.'

'He's rich and powerful,' Tracy corrected her, 'but he's not untouchable.'

Tracy had worked out her plan, but when she telephoned Judge Lawrence's chambers, she knew, immediately, that she would have to change it.

'I'd like to speak to Judge Lawrence, please.'

A secretary said, 'I'm sorry, Judge Lawrence is not in.'

'When do you expect him?' Tracy asked.

'I really couldn't say.'

'It's very important. Will he be in tomorrow morning?'

'No. Judge Lawrence is out of town.'

'Oh. Perhaps I can reach him somewhere?'

'I'm afraid that would be impossible. His Honour is out of the country.'

Tracy carefully kept the disappointment from her voice. 'I see. May I ask where?'

'His Honour is in Europe, attending an international judiciary symposium.'

'What a shame,' Tracy said.

'Who's calling, please?'

Tracy's mind was racing. 'This is Elizabeth Rowane Dastin, chairwoman of the southern division of the American Trial Lawyers' Association. We're having our annual awards dinner in New Orleans on the twentieth of this month, and we've chosen Judge Henry Lawrence to be our man of the year.'

'That's lovely,' the judge's secretary said, 'but I'm afraid His Honour won't be back by then.'

'What a pity. We were all so looking forward to hearing one of his famous speeches. Judge Lawrence was the unanimous choice of our selection committee.'

'He'll be disappointed to miss it.'

'Yes. I'm sure you know what a great honour this is. Some of our country's most prominent judges have been chosen in the past. Wait a minute! I have an idea. Do you suppose the judge might tape a brief acceptance speech for us – a few words of thanks, perhaps?'

'Well, I – I really can't say. He has a very busy schedule –'

'There'll be a great deal of national television and newspaper coverage.'

There was a silence. Judge Lawrence's secretary knew how much His Honour enjoyed media coverage. In fact, as far as she could see, the tour he was presently on seemed to be mainly for that purpose.

She said, 'Perhaps he might find time to record a few words for you. I could ask him.'

'Oh, that would be wonderful,' Tracy enthused. 'It would really make the whole evening.'

'Would you like His Honour to address his remarks towards anything specific?'

'Oh, definitely. We'd like him to talk about –' She hesitated. 'I'm afraid it's a bit complicated. It would be better if I could explain to him directly.'

There was a momentary silence. The secretary faced a dilemma. She had orders not to reveal her boss's itinerary. On the other hand, it would be just like him to blame her if he missed receiving an award as important as this.

She said, 'I'm really not supposed to give out any information, but I'm sure he would want me to make an exception for something as prestigious as this. You can reach him in Moscow, at the Rossia Hotel. He'll be there for the next five days, and after that –'

'Wonderful. I'll get in touch with him right away. Thank you so much.'

'Thank *you*, Miss Dastin.'

The cables were addressed to Judge Henry Lawrence, Rossia Hotel, Moscow. The first cable read:

NEXT JUDICIARY COUNCIL MEETING CAN NOW BE ARRANGED. CONFIRM CONVENIENT DATE AS SPACE MUST BE REQUESTED.
BORIS

The second cable, which arrived the next day, read:

ADVISE PROBLEM TRAVEL PLANS. YOUR SISTER'S PLANE ARRIVED LATE BUT LANDED SAFELY. LOST PASSPORT AND MONEY. SHE WILL BE PLACED IN FIRST-CLASS SWISS HOTEL. WILL SETTLE ACCOUNT LATER.
BORIS

The last cable read:

YOUR SISTER WILL TRY AMERICAN EMBASSY TO OBTAIN TEMPORARY PASSPORT. NO INFORMATION AVAILABLE YET ON NEW VISA. SWISS MAKE RUSSIANS SEEM SAINTS. WILL SHIP SISTER TO YOU SOONEST.
BORIS

The NKVD sat back and waited to see if there were any further cables. When no more were forthcoming, they arrested Judge Lawrence.

The interrogation lasted for ten days and nights.

'To whom did you send the information?'

'*What* information? I don't know what you're talking about.'

'We're talking about plans. Who gave you the plans?'

'What plans?'

'The plans for the Soviet atomic submarine.'

'You must be crazy. What do I know about Soviet submarines?'

'That's what we intend to find out. Who were your secret meetings with?'

'*What* secret meetings? I have no secrets.'

'Good. Then you can tell us who Boris is.'

'Boris, who?'

'The man who deposited money in your Swiss account.'

'*What* Swiss account?'

They were furious. 'You're a stubborn fool,' they told him. 'We're going to make an example of you and all the other American spies trying to undermine our great motherland.'

By the time the American ambassador was permitted to visit him, Judge Henry Lawrence had lost fifteen pounds. He could not remember the last time his captors had allowed him to sleep, and he was a trembling wreck of a man.

'Why are they doing this to me?' the judge croaked. 'I'm an American citizen. I'm a judge. For God's sake, get me out of here!'

'I'm doing everything I can,' the ambassador assured him. He was shocked by Lawrence's appearance. The ambassador had greeted Judge Lawrence and the other members of the Judiciary Committee when they had arrived two weeks earlier. The man the ambassador met then bore no resemblance to the cringing, terrified creature who grovelled before him now.

What the hell are the Russians up to this time? the ambassador wondered. *The judge is no more a spy than I am.* Then he thought wryly, *I suppose I could have chosen a better example.*

The ambassador demanded to see the president of the Politburo, and when the request was refused, he settled for one of the ministers.

'I must make a formal protest,' the ambassador angrily declared. 'Your country's behaviour in the treatment of Judge Henry Lawrence is inexcusable. To call a man of his stature a spy is ridiculous.'

'If you're quite finished,' the minister said coldly, 'you will please take a look at these.'

He handed copies of the cables to the ambassador.

The ambassador read them and looked up, bewildered. 'What's wrong with them? They're perfectly innocent.'

'Really? Perhaps you had better read them again. Decoded.' He handed the ambassador another copy of the cables. Every fourth word had been underlined.

NEXT JUDICIARY COUNCIL MEETING CAN NOW BE ARRANGED. CONFIRM CONVENIENT DATE AS SPACE MUST BE REQUESTED.
BORIS

ADVISE PROBLEM TRAVEL PLANS. YOUR SISTER'S PLANE ARRIVED LATE BUT LANDED SAFELY. LOST PASSPORT AND MONEY. SHE WILL BE PLACED IN FIRST-CLASS SWISS HOTEL. WILL SETTLE ACCOUNT LATER.

BORIS

YOUR SISTER WILL TRY AMERICAN EMBASSY TO OBTAIN TEMPORARY PASSPORT. NO INFORMATION AVAILABLE YET ON NEW VISA. SWISS MAKE RUSSIANS SEEM SAINTS. WILL SHIP SISTER TO YOU SOONEST.

BORIS

I'll be a son of a bitch, the ambassador thought.

The press and public were barred from the trial. The prisoner remained stubborn to the last, continuing to deny he was in the Soviet Union on a spying mission. The prosecution promised him leniency if he would divulge who his bosses were, and Judge Lawrence would have given his soul to have been able to do so, but alas, he could not.

The day after the trial there was a brief mention in *Pravda* that the notorious American spy Judge Henry Lawrence had been convicted of espionage and sentenced to Siberia for fourteen years of hard labour.

The American intelligence community was

baffled by the Lawrence case. Rumours buzzed among the CIA, the FBI, the Secret Service and the Treasury Department.

'He's not one of ours,' the CIA said. 'He probably belongs to Treasury.'

The Treasury Department disclaimed any knowledge of the case. 'No, sir. Lawrence isn't our baby. Probably the fucking FBI butting into our territory again.'

'Never heard of him,' the FBI said. 'He was probably run by State, or the Defence Intelligence Agency.'

The Defence Intelligence Agency, as much in the dark as the others, cannily said, 'No comment.'

Each agency was sure that Judge Henry Lawrence had been sent abroad by one of the others.

'Well, you've got to admire his guts,' the head of the CIA said. 'He's tough. He hasn't confessed and he hasn't named names. To tell you the truth, I wish we had a lot more like him.'

Things were not going well for Anthony Orsatti, and the capo was unable to figure out why. For the first time in his life, his luck was going bad. It had started with Joe Romano's defection, then Perry Pope, and now the judge was gone, mixed up in some crazy spy deal. They had all been an intrinsic part of Orsatti's machine – people he had relied on.

Joe Romano had been the linchpin in the Family organization, and Orsatti had not found anyone to take his place. The business was being run sloppily, and complaints were coming in from people who had never dared complain before. The word was out that Tony Orsatti was getting old, that he couldn't keep his men in line, that his organization was coming apart.

The final straw was a telephone call from New Jersey.

'We hear you're in a little trouble back there. Tony. We'd like to help you out.'

'I ain't in no trouble,' Orsatti bristled. 'Sure, I've had a couple of problems lately, but they're all straightened out.'

'That's not what we hear, Tony. The word's out that your town's goin' a little wild; there's no one controlling it.'

'*I'm* controlling it.'

'Maybe it's too much for you. Could be you're working too hard. Maybe you need a little rest.'

'This is *my* town. No one's takin' it away from me.'

'Hey, Tony, who said anything about taking it away from you? We just want to help. The Families back east got together and decided to send a few of our people down there to give you a little hand. There's nothing wrong with that between old friends, is there?'

Anthony Orsatti felt a deep chill go through him. There was only one thing wrong with it: the little hand was going to become a big hand, and it was going to snowball.

* * *

Ernestine had prepared shrimp gumbo for dinner, and it was simmering on the stove while she and Tracy waited for Al to arrive. The September heat wave had burned itself deeply into everyone's nerves, and when Al finally walked into the small flat, Ernestine screamed, 'Where the hell you been? The fuckin' dinner's burnin', and so am I.'

But Al's spirits were too euphoric to be affected. 'I been busy diggin' the scam, woman. An' wait'll you hear what I got.' He turned to Tracy. 'The mob's puttin' the arm on Tony Orsatti. The Family from New Jersey's comin' in to take over.' His face split into a broad grin. 'You *got* the son of a bitch!' He looked into Tracy's eyes, and his smile died. 'Ain't you happy, Tracy?'

What a strange word, Tracy thought. *Happy*. She had forgotten what it meant. She wondered whether she would ever be happy again, whether she would ever feel any normal emotions again. For so long now, her every waking thought had been to avenge what had been done to her mother and herself. And now that it was almost finished, there was only an emptiness inside her.

The following morning Tracy stopped at a florist. 'I want some flowers delivered to Anthony Orsatti. A funeral wreath of white carnations on a stand, with a wide ribbon. I want the ribbon to read: "REST IN PEACE".' She wrote out a card. It said, FROM DORIS WHITNEY'S DAUGHTER.

BOOK THREE

FIFTEEN

Philadelphia
Tuesday, 7 October – 4:00 P.M.

It was time to deal with Charles Stanhope III. The others had been strangers. Charles had been her lover, the father of her unborn child, and he had turned his back on both of them.

Ernestine and Al had been at the New Orleans Airport to see Tracy off.

'I'm gonna miss you,' Ernestine had said. 'You sure set this town on its ass. They oughta run you for people's mayor.'

'Whatcha gonna do in Philly?' Al had asked.

She had told them half the truth. 'Go back to my old job at the bank.'

Ernestine and Al had exchanged a glance. 'They – er – know you're comin'?'

'No. But the vice-president likes me. There won't

be a problem. Good computer operators are hard to find.'

'Well, good luck. Keep in touch, ya hear? And stay out of trouble, girl.'

Thirty minutes later Tracy had been in the air, bound for Philadelphia.

She checked into the Hilton Hotel and steamed out her one good dress over the hot tub. At 11:00 the following morning she walked into the bank and approached Clarence Desmond's secretary.

'Hello, Mae.'

The girl stared at Tracy as though she were seeing a ghost. 'Tracy!' She did not know where to look. 'I – how are you?'

'Fine. Is Mr Desmond in?'

'I – I don't know. Let me see. Excuse me.' She rose from her chair, flustered, and hurried into the vice-president's office.

She came out a few moments later. 'You may go in.' She edged away as Tracy walked towards the door.

What's the matter with her? Tracy wondered.

Clarence Desmond was standing next to his desk.

'Hello, Mr Desmond. Well, I've come back,' Tracy said brightly.

'What for?' His tone was unfriendly. Definitely unfriendly.

It caught Tracy by surprise. She pressed on. 'Well, you said I was the best computer operator you had ever seen, and I thought –'

'You thought I'd give you back your old job?'

'Well, yes, sir. I haven't forgotten any of my skills. I can still –'

'Miss Whitney.' It was no longer Tracy. 'I'm sorry, but what you're asking is quite out of the question. I'm sure you can understand that our customers would not wish to deal with someone who served time in the penitentiary for armed robbery and attempted murder. That would hardly fit in with our high ethical image. I think it unlikely that given your background, *any* bank would hire you. I would suggest that you try to find employment more suitable to your circumstances. I hope you understand there is nothing personal in this.'

Tracy listened to his words, first with shock and then with growing anger. He made her sound like an outcast, a leper. *We wouldn't want to lose you. You're one of our most valuable employees.*

'Was there anything else, Miss Whitney?' It was a dismissal.

There were a hundred things Tracy wanted to say, but she knew they would do no good. 'No. I think you've said it all.' Tracy turned and walked out the office door, her face burning. All the bank employees seemed to be staring at her. Mae had spread the word: the convict had come back. Tracy moved towards the exit, head held high, dying inside. *I can't let them do this to me. My pride is all I have left, and no one is going to take that away from me.*

* * *

Tracy stayed in her room all day, miserable. How could she have been naïve enough to believe that they would welcome her back with open arms? She was notorious now. 'You're the headline in the Philadelphia *Daily News.*' *Well, to hell with Philadelphia*, Tracy thought. She had some unfinished business there, but when that was done, she would leave. She would go to New York, where she would be anonymous. The decision made her feel better.

That evening, Tracy treated herself to dinner at the Café Royal. After the sordid meeting with Clarence Desmond that morning, she needed the reassuring atmosphere of soft lights, elegant surroundings, and soothing music. She ordered a vodka martini, and as the waiter brought it to her table, Tracy glanced up, and her heart suddenly skipped a beat. Seated in a booth across the room were Charles and his wife. They had not yet seen her. Tracy's first impulse was to get up and leave. She was not ready to face Charles, not until she had a chance to put her plan into action.

'Would you like to order now?' the head waiter was asking.

'I'll – I'll wait, thank you.' She had to decide whether she was going to stay.

She looked over at Charles again, and an astonishing phenomenon occurred: it was as though she were looking at a stranger. She was seeing a sallow, drawn-looking, middle-aged, balding man, with stooped shoulders and an air of ineffable boredom on his face. It was impossible to believe that she had once thought she loved this man, that she had slept with him, planned to spend the rest of her life with him. Tracy glanced at his wife. She wore the same bored expression as Charles. They gave the impression of two people trapped together for eternity, frozen in time. They simply sat there, speaking not one word to each other. Tracy could visualize the endless, tedious years ahead of the two of them. No love. No joy. *That is Charles's punishment*, Tracy thought, and she felt a sudden surge of release, a freedom from the deep, dark, emotional chains that had bound her.

Tracy signalled to the head waiter and said, 'I'm ready to order now.'

It was over. The past was finally buried.

It was not until Tracy returned to her hotel room that evening that she remembered she was owed money from the bank's employees' fund. She sat down and calculated the amount. It came to $1,375.65.

She composed a letter to Clarence Desmond, and two days later she received a reply from Mae.

> Dear Miss Whitney:
> In response to your request, Mr Desmond has asked me to inform you that because of the morals policy in the employees' financial plan, your share has reverted to the general fund.

He wants to assure you that he bears no personal ill will towards you.

Sincerely,

Mae Trenton

Secretary to the Senior Vice-president

Tracy could not believe it. They were stealing her money, and doing it under the pretext of protecting the morals of the bank! She was outraged. *I'm not going to let them cheat me*, she vowed. *No one is ever going to cheat me again.*

Tracy stood outside the familiar entrance to the Philadelphia Trust and Fidelity Bank. She wore a long black wig and heavy, dark makeup, with a raw red scar on her chin. If anything went wrong, it would be the scar they remembered. Despite her disguise, Tracy felt naked, for she had worked in this bank for five years, and it was staffed with people who knew her well. She would have to be very careful not to give herself away.

She removed a bottle cap from her handbag, placed it in her shoe, and limped into the bank. The bank was crowded with customers, for Tracy had carefully chosen a time when the bank would be doing peak business. She limped over to one of the customer-service desks, and the man seated behind it finished a phone call and said, 'Yes?'

It was Jon Creighton, the bank bigot. He hated Jews, blacks, and Puerto Ricans, but not necessarily in that order. He had been an irritant to

Tracy during the years she had worked there. Now there was no sign of recognition on his face.

'*Buenas dias, señor*. I would like to open a current account, *ahora*,' Tracy said. Her accent was Mexican, the accent she had heard for all those months from her cell mate Paulita.

There was a look of disdain on Creighton's face. 'Name?'

'Rita Gonzales.'

'And how much would you like to put in your account?'

'Ten dollars.'

His voice was a sneer. 'Will that be by cheque or cash?'

'Cash, I theenk.'

She carefully took a crumpled, half-torn ten-dollar bill from her purse and handed it to him. He shoved a white form towards her.

'Fill this out –'

Tracy had no intention of putting anything in her hand-writing. She frowned. 'I'm sorry, señor. I hurt *mi mano* – my hand – in an accident. Would you min' writin' it for me, *si se puede*?'

Creighton snorted. *These illiterate wetbacks!* 'Rita Gonzales, you said?'

'*Sí.*'

'Your address?'

She gave him the address and telephone number of her hotel.

'Your mother's maiden name?'

'Gonzales. My mother, she married her uncle.'

'And your date of birth?'

'December twentieth, 1958.'

'Place of birth?'

'Ciudad de Mexico.'

'Mexico City. Sign here.'

'I will have to use my left hand,' Tracy said. She picked up a pen and clumsily scrawled out an illegible signature. Jon Creighton wrote out a deposit slip.

'I'll give you a temporary chequebook. Your printed cheques will be mailed to you in three or four weeks.'

'Bueno. Muchas gracias, señor.'

'Yeah.'

He watched her walk out of the bank. *Fuckin' spic.*

There are numerous illegal ways to gain entry to a computer, and Tracy was an expert. She had helped set up the security system at the Philadelphia Trust and Fidelity Bank, and now she was about to circumvent it.

Her first step was to find a computer shop, where she could use a terminal to tap into the bank's computer. The shop, some distance from the bank, was almost empty.

An eager salesman approached Tracy. 'May I help you, miss?'

'*Eso si que no, señor*. I am just looking.'

His eye was caught by a teenager playing a computer game. 'Excuse me.' He hurried away.

Tracy turned to the desk-model computer in front of her, which was connected to a telephone. Getting into the system would be easy, but without the proper access code, she was stymied, and the access code was changed daily. Tracy had been at the meeting when the original authorization code had been decided on.

'We must keep changing it,' Clarence Desmond had said, 'so no one can break in; yet we want to keep it simple enough for people who are authorized to use it.'

The code they had finally settled on used the four seasons of the year and the current day's date.

Tracy turned on the terminal and tapped out the code for the Philadelphia Trust and Fidelity Bank. She heard a high-pitched whine and placed the telephone receiver into the terminal modem. A sign flashed on the small screen: YOUR AUTHORIZATION CODE, PLEASE?

Today was the tenth.

AUTUMN 10, Tracy tapped out.

THAT IS AN IMPROPER AUTHORIZATION CODE. The computer screen went blank.

Had they changed the code? Out of the corner of her eye, Tracy saw the salesman coming towards her again. She moved over to another computer, gave it a casual glance, and ambled along the aisle. The salesman checked his stride. *A looker*, he decided. He hurried forward to greet a prosperous-looking couple coming in the door. Tracy returned to the desk-model computer.

She tried to put herself into Clarence Desmond's mind. He was a creature of habit, and Tracy was sure he would not have varied the code too much. He had probably kept the original concept of the seasons and the numbers, but how had he changed them? It would have been too complicated to reverse all the numbers, so he had probably shifted the seasons around.

Tracy tried again.

YOUR AUTHORIZATION CODE, PLEASE?

WINTER 10.

THAT IS AN IMPROPER AUTHORIZATION CODE.

The blank screen again.

It's not going to work, Tracy thought despairingly. *I'll give it one more try.*

YOUR AUTHORIZATION CODE, PLEASE?

SPRING 10.

The screen went blank for a moment, and then the message appeared: PLEASE PROCEED.

So he *had* switched the seasons. She quickly typed out: DOMESTIC MONEY TRANSACTION.

Instantly, the bank menu, the category of available transactions, flashed onto the screen:

DO YOU WISH TO

A DEPOSIT MONEY

B TRANSFER MONEY

C WITHDRAW MONEY FROM SAVINGS ACCOUNT

D INTERBRANCH TRANSFER

E WITHDRAW MONEY FROM CURRENT ACCOUNT

PLEASE ENTER YOUR CHOICE

Tracy chose B. The screen went blank and a new menu appeared.

AMOUNT OF TRANSFER?

WHERE TO?

WHERE FROM?

She typed in: FROM GENERAL RESERVE FUND TO RITA GONZALES. When she came to the amount, she hesitated for an instant. *Tempting*, Tracy thought. Since she had access, there was no limit to the amount the now subservient computer would give her. She could have taken millions. But she was no thief. All she wanted was what was rightfully owed her.

She typed in $1,375.65, and added Rita Gonzales's account number.

The screen flashed: TRANSACTION COMPLETED. DO YOU WISH OTHER TRANSACTIONS?

NO.

SESSION COMPLETED. THANK YOU.

The money would automatically be transferred by CHIPS, the Clearing House Interbank Payment System that kept track of the $220 billion shifted from bank to bank every day.

The store clerk was approaching Tracy again, frowning. Tracy hurriedly pressed a key, and the screen went blank.

'Are you interested in purchasing this machine, miss?'

'No, *gracias*,' Tracy apologized. 'I don' understan' these computers.'

She telephoned the bank from a corner drug store and asked to speak to the head cashier.

'*Hola*. Thees is Rita Gonzales. I would like to have my current account transferred to the main branch of the First Hanover Bank of New York City, *por favor*.'

'Your account number, Miss Gonzales?'

Tracy gave it to her.

An hour later Tracy had checked out of the Hilton and was on her way to New York City.

When the first Hanover Bank of New York opened at 10:00 the following morning, Rita Gonzales was there to withdraw all the money from her account.

'How much ees in it?' she asked.

The cashier checked. 'Thirteen hundred and eighty-five dollars and sixty-five cents.'

'*Sí*, that ees correct.'

'Would you like a certified cheque for that, Miss Gonzales?'

'No, *gracias*,' Tracy said. 'I don' trust banks. I weel take the cash.'

Tracy had received the standard two hundred dollars from the state prison upon her release, plus the small amount of money she had earned taking care of Amy, but even with her money from the bank fund, she had no financial security. It was imperative she get a job as quickly as possible.

She checked into an inexpensive hotel on Lexington Avenue and began sending out applications to New York banks, applying for a job as a computer expert. But Tracy found that the computer had suddenly become her enemy. Her life was no longer private. The computer banks held her life's story, and readily told it to everyone who pressed the right buttons. The moment Tracy's criminal record was revealed, her application was automatically rejected.

I think it unlikely that given your background, any bank would hire you. Clarence Desmond had been right.

Tracy sent in more job applications to insurance companies and dozens of other computer-oriented businesses. The replies were always the same: *negative.*

Very well, Tracy thought, *I can always do something else.* She bought a copy of *The New York Times* and began searching the situations vacant ads.

There was a position listed as secretary in an export firm.

The moment Tracy walked in the door, the personnel manager said, 'Hey, I seen you on television. You saved a kid in prison, didn't you?'

Tracy turned and fled.

The following day she was hired as a saleswoman in the children's department at Saks Fifth Avenue. The salary was a great deal less than she had been used to, but at least it was enough to support herself.

On her second day, an hysterical customer recognized her and informed the floor manager that she refused to be waited on by a murderess who had drowned a small child. Tracy was given no chance to explain. She was discharged immediately.

It seemed to Tracy that the men upon whom she had exacted vengeance had had the last word after all. They had turned her into a public criminal, an outcast. The unfairness of what was happening to her was corrosive. She had no idea how she was going to live, and for the first time she began to have a feeling of desperation. That night she looked through her purse to see how much money remained, and tucked away in a corner of her wallet she came across a slip of paper that Betty Franciscus had given her in prison. CONRAD MORGAN, JEWELLER, 640 FIFTH AVENUE, NEW YORK CITY. *He's into criminal reform. He likes to give a hand to people who've been in prison.*

Conrad Morgan et Cie Jewellers was an elegant establishment, with a liveried doorman on the outside and an armed guard on the inside. The shop itself was tastefully understated, but the jewels were exquisite and expensive.

Tracy told the receptionist, 'I'd like to see Mr Conrad Morgan, please.'

'Do you have an appointment?'

'No. A – a mutual friend suggested that I see him.'

'Your name?'

'Tracy Whitney.'

'Just a moment, please.'

The receptionist picked up a telephone and murmured something into it that Tracy could not hear.

She replaced the receiver. 'Mr Morgan is occupied just now. He wonders if you could come back at six o'clock.'

'Yes, thank you,' Tracy said.

She walked out of the shop and stood on the pavement, uncertainly. Coming to New York had been a mistake. There was probably nothing Conrad could do for her. And why should he? She was a complete stranger to him. *He'll give me a lecture and a handout. Well, I don't need either. Not from him or anyone else. I'm a survivor. Somehow I'm going to make it. To hell with Conrad Morgan. I won't go back to see him.*

Tracy wandered the streets aimlessly, passing the glittering salons of Fifth Avenue, the guarded apartment buildings on Park Avenue, the bustling shops on Lexington and Third. She walked the streets of New York mindlessly, seeing nothing, filled with a bitter frustration.

At 6:00 she found herself back on Fifth Avenue, in front of Conrad Morgan et Cie Jewellers. The doorman was gone, and the door was locked. Tracy pounded on the door in a gesture of defiance and then turned away, but to her surprise, the door suddenly opened.

An avuncular-looking man stood there looking at her. He was bald, with ragged tufts of grey hair above his ears, and he had a jolly, rubicund face and twinkling blue eyes. He looked like a cheery little gnome. 'You must be Miss Whitney?'

'Yes . . .'

'I'm Conrad Morgan. Please, do come in, won't you?'

Tracy entered the deserted shop.

'I've been waiting for you,' Conrad Morgan said. 'Let's go into my office where we can talk.'

He led her through the shop to a closed door, which he unlocked with a key. His office was elegantly furnished, and it looked more like a flat than a place of business, with no desk, just couches, chairs, and tables artfully placed. The walls were covered with old masters.

'Would you care for a drink?' Conrad Morgan offered. 'Whisky, cognac, or perhaps sherry?'

'No, nothing, thank you.'

Tracy was suddenly nervous. She had dismissed the idea that this man would do anything to help her, yet at the same time she found herself desperately hoping that he could.

'Betty Franciscus suggested that I look you up, Mr Morgan. She said you – you helped people who have been in . . . trouble.' She could not bring herself to say *prison*.

Conrad Morgan clasped his hands together, and Tracy noticed how beautifully manicured they were.

'Poor Betty. Such a lovely lady. She was unlucky, you know.'

'Unlucky?'

'Yes. She got caught.'

'I – I don't understand.'

'It's really quite simple, Miss Whitney. Betty used to work for me. She was well protected. Then the poor dear fell in love with a chauffeur from New Orleans and went off on her own. And, well . . . they caught her.'

Tracy was confused. 'She worked for you here as a saleslady?'

Conrad Morgan sat back and laughed until his eyes filled with tears. 'No, my dear,' he said, wiping the tears away. 'Obviously, Betty didn't explain everything to you.' He leaned back in his chair and steepled his fingers. 'I have a very profitable little sideline, Miss Whitney, and I take great pleasure in sharing those profits with my colleagues. I have been most successful employing people like yourself – if you'll forgive me – who have served time in prison.'

Tracy studied his face, more puzzled than ever.

'I'm in a unique position, you see. I have an extremely wealthy clientele. My clients become my friends. They confide in me.' He tapped his fingers together delicately. 'I know when my customers take trips. Very few people travel with jewellery in these parlous times, so their jewels are locked away at home. I recommend to them the security measures they should take to protect them. I know exactly what jewels they own because they purchased them from me. They –'

Tracy found herself on her feet. 'Thank you for your time, Mr Morgan.'

'Surely you're not leaving already?'

'If you're saying what I think you're saying –'

'Yes. Indeed, I am.'

She could feel her cheeks burning. 'I'm not a criminal. I came here looking for a job.'

'And I'm offering you one, my dear. It will take an hour or two of your time, and I can promise you twenty-five thousand dollars.' He smiled impishly. 'Tax free, of course.'

Tracy was fighting hard to control her anger. 'I'm not interested. Would you let me out, please?'

'Certainly, if that is your wish.' He rose to his feet and showed her to the door. 'You must understand, Miss Whitney, that if there were the slightest danger of anyone's being caught, I would not be involved in this. I have my reputation to protect.'

'I promise you I won't say anything about it,' Tracy said coldly.

He grinned. 'There's really nothing you could say, my dear, is there? I mean, who would believe you? *I* am Conrad Morgan.'

As they reached the front entrance of the store, Morgan said, 'You will let me know if you change your mind, won't you? The best time to telephone me is after six o'clock in the evening. I'll wait for your call.'

'Don't,' Tracy said curtly, and she walked out into the approaching night. When she reached her room, she was still trembling.

She sent the hotel's one bellboy out for a sandwich and coffee. She did not feel like facing anyone. The meeting with Conrad Morgan had made her feel unclean. He had lumped her with all the sad, confused and beaten criminals she had been surrounded by at the Southern Louisiana Penitentiary for Women. She was not one of them. She was Tracy Whitney, a computer expert, a decent, law-abiding citizen.

Whom no one would hire.

Tracy lay awake all night thinking about her future. She had no job, and very little money left. She made two resolutions: in the morning she would move to a cheaper place and she would find a job. Any kind of job.

The cheaper place turned out to be a dreary fourth-floor walk-up, one-room flat on the Lower East Side. From her room, through the paper-thin walls, Tracy could hear her neighbours screaming at one another in foreign languages. The windows and doors of the small shops that lined the streets were heavily barred, and Tracy could understand why. The neighbourhood seemed to be populated by drunks, prostitutes and bag ladies.

On her way to the market to shop, Tracy was accosted three times – twice by men and once by a woman.

I can stand it. I won't be here long, Tracy assured herself.

She went to a small employment agency a short distance from her flat. It was run by a Mrs Murphy, a matronly looking, heavy-set lady. She put down Tracy's résumé and studied her quizzically. 'I don't know what you need me for. There must be a dozen companies that'd give their eyeteeth to get someone like you.'

Tracy took a deep breath. 'I have a problem,' she said. She explained as Mrs Murphy sat listening quietly, and when Tracy was finished, Mrs Murphy said flatly, 'You can forget about looking for a computer job.'

'But you said –'

'Companies are jumpy these days about computer crimes. They're not gonna hire anybody with a record.'

'But I *need* a job. I –'

'There are other kinds of jobs. Have you thought about working as a saleslady?'

Tracy remembered her experience at the department store. She could not bear to go through that again. 'Is there anything else?'

The woman hesitated. Tracy Whitney was obviously overqualified for the job Mrs Murphy had in mind. 'Look,' she said. 'I know this isn't up your alley, but there's a waitress job open at Jackson Hole. It's a hamburger place on the Upper East Side.'

'A waitress job?'

'Yeah. If you take it, I won't charge you any commission. I just happened to hear about it.'

Tracy sat there, debating. She had waited on tables in college. Then it had been fun. Now it was a question of surviving.

'I'll try it,' she said.

* * *

Jackson Hole was bedlam, packed with noisy impatient customers, and harassed, irritable fry cooks. The food was good and the prices reasonable, and the place was always jammed. The waitresses worked at a frantic pace with no time to relax, and by the end of the first day Tracy was exhausted. But she was earning money.

At noon on the second day, as Tracy was serving a table filled with salesmen, one of the men ran his hand up her skirt, and Tracy dropped a bowl of chili on his head. That was the end of the job.

She returned to Mrs Murphy and reported what had happened.

'I may have some good news,' Mrs Murphy said. 'The Wellington Arms needs an assistant housekeeper. I'm going to send you over there.'

The Wellington Arms was a small, elegant hotel on Park Avenue that catered to the rich and famous. Tracy was interviewed by the housekeeper and hired. The work was not difficult, the staff was pleasant, and the hours reasonable.

A week after she started, Tracy was summoned to the housekeeper's office. The assistant manager was also there.

'Did you check Suite eight-twenty-seven today?' the housekeeper asked Tracy. The suite was occupied by Jennifer Marlowe, a Hollywood actress. Part of Tracy's job was to inspect each suite and see that the maids had done their work properly.

'Why, yes,' she said.

'What time?'

'At two o'clock. Is something wrong?'

The assistant manager spoke up. 'At three o'clock Miss Marlowe returned and discovered that a valuable diamond ring was missing.'

Tracy could feel her body grow tense.

'Did you go into the bedroom, Tracy?'

'Yes. I checked every room.'

'When you were in the bedroom, did you see any jewellery lying around?'

'Why . . . no. I don't think so.'

The assistant manager pounced on it. 'You don't *think* so? You're not *sure*?'

'I wasn't looking for jewellery,' Tracy said. 'I was checking the beds and towels.'

'Miss Marlowe insists that her ring was on the dressing table when she left the suite.'

'I don't know anything about it.'

'No one else has access to that room. The maids have been with us for many years.'

'I didn't take it.'

The assistant manager sighed. 'We're going to have to call in the police to investigate.'

'It *had* to be someone else,' Tracy cried. 'Or perhaps Miss Marlowe misplaced it.'

'With your record –' the assistant manager said.

And there it was, out in the open. *With your record . . .*

'I'll have to ask you to please wait in the security office until the police get here.'

Tracy felt her face flush. 'Yes, sir.'

She was accompanied to the office by one of

the security guards, and she felt as though she were back in prison again. She had read of convicts being hounded because they had prison records, but it had never occurred to her that this kind of thing could happen to her. They had stuck a label on her, and they expected her to live up to it. *Or down to it*, Tracy thought bitterly.

Thirty minutes later the assistant manager walked into the office, smiling. 'Well!' he said. 'Miss Marlowe found her ring. She had misplaced it, after all. It was just a little mistake.'

'Wonderful,' Tracy said.

She walked out of the office and headed for Conrad Morgan et Cie Jewellers.

'It's ridiculously simple,' Conrad Morgan was saying. 'A client of mine, Lois Bellamy, has gone to Europe. Her house is in Sea Cliff on Long Island. On weekends the servants are off, so there's no one there. A private patrol makes a check every four hours. You can be in and out of the house in a few minutes.'

They were seated in Conrad Morgan's office.

'I know the alarm system, and I have the combination to the safe. All you have to do, my dear, is walk in, pick up the jewels, and walk out again. You bring the jewels to me, I take them out of their settings, recut the larger ones, and sell them again.'

'If it's so simple, why don't you do it yourself?' Tracy asked bluntly.

His blue eyes twinkled. 'Because I'm going to be out of town on business. Whenever one of these little "incidents" occurs, I'm always out of town on business.'

'I see.'

'If you have any scruples about the robbery hurting Mrs Bellamy, you needn't have. She's really quite a horrible woman, who has houses all over the world filled with expensive goodies. Besides, she's insured for twice the amount the jewels are worth. Naturally, I did all the appraisals.'

Tracy sat there looking at Conrad Morgan, thinking, *I must be crazy. I'm sitting here calmly discussing a jewel robbery with this man.*

'I don't want to go back to prison, Mr Morgan.'

'There's no danger of that. Not one of my people has ever been caught. Not while they were working for me. Well . . . what do you say?'

That was obvious. She was going to say no. The whole idea was insane.

'You said twenty-five thousand dollars?'

'Cash on delivery.'

It was a fortune, enough to take care of her until she could figure out what to do with her life. She thought of the dreary little room she lived in, of the screaming tenants, and the customer yelling, 'I don't want a murderess waiting on me', and the assistant manager saying, 'We're going to have to call in the police to investigate.'

But Tracy still could not bring herself to say yes.

'I would suggest this Saturday night,' Conrad

Morgan said. 'The staff leaves at noon on Saturdays. I'll arrange a driver's licence and a credit card for you in a false name. You'll rent a car here in Manhattan and drive out to Long Island, arriving at eleven o'clock. You'll pick up the jewellery, drive back to New York, and return the car . . . You do drive, don't you?'

'Yes.'

'Excellent. There's a train leaving for St Louis at seven-forty-five A.M. I'll reserve a compartment for you. I'll meet you at the station in St Louis, you'll turn over the jewels, and I'll give you your twenty-five thousand.'

He made it all sound so simple.

This was the moment to say no, to get up and walk out. *Walk out to where?*

'I'll need a blonde wig,' Tracy said slowly.

When Tracy had left, Conrad Morgan sat in the dark in his office, thinking about her. A beautiful woman. Very beautiful indeed. It was a shame. Perhaps he should have warned her that he was not really that familiar with that particular burglar-alarm system.

SIXTEEN

With the thousand dollars that Conrad Morgan advanced her, Tracy purchased two wigs – one blonde and one black, with a multitude of tiny braids. She bought a dark-blue pants suit, black overalls, and an imitation Gucci valise from a street vendor on Lexington Avenue. So far everything was going smoothly. As Morgan had promised, Tracy received an envelope containing a driver's licence in the name of Ellen Branch, a diagram of the security system in the Bellamy house, the combination to the bedroom safe, and an Amtrak ticket to St Louis, in a private compartment. Tracy packed her few belongings and left. *I'll never live in a place like this again*, Tracy promised herself. She rented a car and headed for Long Island. She was on her way to commit a burglary.

What she was doing had the unreality of a dream, and she was terrified. What if she were caught? Was the risk worth what she was about to do?

It's ridiculously simple, Conrad Morgan had said.

He wouldn't be involved in anything like this if he weren't sure about it. He has his reputation to protect. I have a reputation, too, Tracy thought bitterly, *and it's all bad. Any time a piece of jewellery is missing, I'll be guilty until proven innocent.*

Tracy knew what she was doing: she was trying to work herself up into a rage, trying to psych herself up to commit a crime. It did not work. By the time she reached Sea Cliff, she was a nervous wreck. Twice, she almost ran the car off the road. *Maybe the police will pick me up for reckless driving*, she thought hopefully, *and I can tell Mr Morgan that things went wrong.*

But there was not a police car in sight. *Sure*, Tracy thought in disgust. *They're never around when you need them.*

She headed towards Long Island Sound, following Conrad Morgan's directions. *The house is right on the water. It's called the Embers. It's an old Victorian mansion.* You can't miss it.

Please let me miss it, Tracy prayed.

But there it was, looming up out of the dark like some ogre's castle in a nightmare. It looked deserted. *How dare the servants take the weekend off*, Tracy thought indignantly. *They should all be discharged.*

She drove the car behind a stand of giant willow trees, where it was hidden from view, and turned off the engine, listening to the nocturnal sounds of insects. Nothing else disturbed the silence. The house was off the main road, and there was no traffic at that time of night.

The property is screened by trees, my dear, and the nearest neighbour is acres away, so you don't have to be concerned about being seen. The security patrol makes its check at ten P.M. *and again at two* A.M. *You'll be long gone by the two* A.M. *check.*

Tracy looked at her watch. It was 11:00. The first patrol had gone. She had three hours before the patrol was due to arrive for its second check. Or three seconds to turn the car around and head back to New York and forget about this insanity. But head back to *what*? The images flashed unbidden into her mind. The assistant manager at Saks: 'I'm terribly sorry, Miss Whitney, but our customers must be humoured . . .'

'You can forget about running a computer. They're not going to hire anybody with a record . . .'

'Twenty-five thousand tax-free dollars for an hour or two. If you have scruples, she's really a horrible woman.'

What am I doing? Tracy thought. *I'm not a burglar. Not a real one. I'm a dumb amateur who's about to have a nervous breakdown.*

If I had half a brain, I'd get away from here while there's still time. Before the SWAT team catches me and there's a shoot-out and they carry my riddled body to the morgue. I can see the headline: DANGEROUS CRIMINAL KILLED DURING BUNGLED BURGLARY ATTEMPT.

Who would be there to cry at her funeral? Ernestine and Amy. Tracy looked at her watch. 'Oh, my God.' She had been sitting there, daydreaming, for twenty minutes. *If I'm going to do it, I'd better move.*

She could not move. She was frozen with fear. *I can't sit here forever*, she told herself. *Why don't I just go take a look at the house? A quick look.*

Tracy took a deep breath and got out of the car. She was wearing black overalls; her knees were shaking. She approached the house slowly, and she could see that it was completely dark.

Be sure to wear gloves.

Tracy reached in her pocket and took out a pair of gloves, and put them on. *Oh, God, I'm doing it*, she thought. *I'm really going ahead with it.* Her heart was pounding so loudly she could no longer hear any other sounds.

The alarm is to the left of the front door. There are five buttons. The red light will be on, which means the alarm is activated. The code to turn it off is three-two-four-one-one. When the red light goes off, you'll know the alarm is deactivated. Here's the key to the front door. When you enter, be sure to close the door after you. Use this flashlight. Don't turn on any of the lights in the house in case someone happens to drive past. The master bedroom is upstairs, to your left, overlooking the bay. You'll find the safe behind a portrait of Lois Bellamy. It's a very simple safe. All you have to do is follow this combination.

Tracy stood stock-still, trembling, ready to flee at the slightest sound. Silence. Slowly, she reached out and pressed the sequence of alarm buttons, praying that it would not work. The red light went out. The next step would commit her. She remembered that airplane pilots had a phrase for it: the point of no return.

Tracy put the key in the lock, and the door swung open. She waited a full minute before she stepped inside. Every nerve in her body throbbed to a savage beat as she stood in the hallway, listening, afraid to move. The house was filled with a deserted silence. She took out a flashlight, turned it on, and saw the staircase. She moved forward and started up. All she wanted to do now was get it over with as quickly as possible and run.

The upstairs hallway looked eerie in the glow of her flash-light, and the wavering beam made the walls seem to pulse back and forth. Tracy peered into each room she passed. They were all empty.

The master bedroom was at the end of the hallway, looking out over the bay, just as Morgan had described it. The bedroom was beautiful, done in dusky pink, with a canopied bed and a commode decorated with pink roses. There were two love seats, a fireplace, and a table in front of it for dining. *I almost lived in a house like this with Charles and our baby*, Tracy thought.

She walked over to the picture window and looked out at the distant boats anchored in the bay. *Tell me, God, what made you decide that Lois*

Bellamy should live in this beautiful house and that I should be here robbing it? Come on, girl, she told herself, don't get philosophical. This is a one-time thing. It will be over in a few minutes, but not if you stand here doing nothing.

She turned from the window and walked over to the portrait Morgan had described. Lois Bellamy had a hard, arrogant look. *It's true. She does look like a horrible woman.* The painting swung outward, away from the wall, and behind it was a small safe. Tracy had memorized the combination. *Three turns to the right, stop at forty-two. Two turns to the left, stop at ten. One turn to the right, stop at thirty.* Her hands were trembling so much that she had to start again twice. She heard a click. The door was open.

The safe was filled with thick envelopes and papers, but Tracy ignored them. At the back, resting on a small shelf, was a chamois jewellery bag. Tracy reached for it and lifted it from the shelf. At that instant the burglar alarm went off, and it was the loudest sound Tracy had ever heard. It seemed to reverberate from every corner of the house, screaming out its warning. She stood there, paralysed, in shock.

What had gone wrong? Had Conrad Morgan not known about the alarm inside the safe that was activated when the jewels were removed?

She had to get out quickly. She scooped the chamois bag into her pocket and started running towards the stairs. And then, over the sound of the alarm, she heard another sound, the sound of an approaching siren. Tracy stood at the top of the staircase, terrified, her heart racing, her mouth dry. She hurried to a window, raised the curtain and peered out. A black-and-white patrol car was pulling up in front of the house. As Tracy watched, a uniformed policeman ran towards the back of the house, while a second one moved towards the front door. There was no escape. The alarm bells were still clanging, and suddenly they sounded like the terrible bells in the corridors of the Southern Louisiana Penitentiary for Women.

No! thought Tracy. *I won't let them send me back there.*

The front doorbell shrilled.

Lieutenant Melvin Durkin had been on the Sea Cliff police force for ten years. Sea Cliff was a quiet town, and the main activity of the police was handling vandalism, a few car thefts, and occasional Saturday-night drunken brawls. The setting-off of the Bellamy alarm was in a different category. It was the type of criminal activity for which Lieutenant Durkin had joined the force. He knew Lois Bellamy and was aware of what a valuable collection of paintings and jewellery she owned. With her away, he had made it a point to check the house from time to time, for it was a tempting target for a cat burglar. *And now*, Lieutenant Durkin thought, *it looks like I've caught one*. He had been only a short distance away when the radio call had come in from the security company. *This is going to look good on my record. Damned good.*

Lieutenant Durkin pressed the front doorbell again. He wanted to be able to state in his report that he had rung it three times before making a forcible entry. His partner was covering the back, so there was no chance of the burglar's escaping. He would probably try to conceal himself on the premises, but he was in for a surprise. No one could hide from Melvin Durkin.

As the lieutenant reached for the bell for the third time, the front door suddenly opened. The policeman stood there staring. In the doorway was a woman dressed in a filmy nightgown that left little to the imagination. Her face was covered with a mudpack, and her hair was tucked into a curler cap.

She demanded, 'What on earth is going on?'

Lieutenant Durkin swallowed. 'I . . . who are you?'

'I'm Ellen Branch. I'm a houseguest of Lois Bellamy's. She's away in Europe.'

'I know that.' The lieutenant was confused. 'She didn't tell us she was having a houseguest.'

The woman in the doorway nodded knowingly. 'Isn't that just like Lois? Excuse me, I can't stand that noise.'

As Lieutenant Durkin watched, Lois Bellamy's houseguest reached over to the alarm buttons, pressed a sequence of numbers, and the sound stopped.

'That's better,' she sighed. 'I can't tell you how glad I am to see you.' She laughed shakily. 'I was just getting ready for bed when the alarm went off. I was sure there were burglars in the house and I'm all alone here. The servants left at noon.'

'Do you mind if we look around?'

'Please, I insist!'

It took the lieutenant and his partner only a few minutes to make sure there was no one lurking on the premises.

'All clear,' Lieutenant Durkin said. 'False alarm. Something must have set it off. Can't always depend on these electronic things. I'd call the security company and have them check out the system.'

'I most certainly will.'

'Well, guess we'd better be running along,' the lieutenant said.

'Thank you so much for coming by. I feel safer now.'

She sure has a great body, Lieutenant Durkin thought. He wondered what she looked like under that mudpack and without the curler cap. 'Will you be staying here long, Miss Branch?'

'Another week or two, until Lois returns.'

'If there's anything I can do for you, just let me know.'

'Thank you, I will.'

Tracy watched as the police car drove away into the night. She felt faint with relief. When the car was out of sight, she hurried upstairs, washed off the mudpack she had found in the bathroom, stripped off Lois Bellamy's curler cap and nightgown, changed into her own black overalls, and left by the front door, carefully resetting the alarm.

It was not until Tracy was halfway back to Manhattan that the audacity of what she had done struck her. She giggled, and the giggle turned into a shaking, uncontrollable laughter, until she finally had to pull the car off onto the side of the road. She laughed until the tears streamed down her face. It was the first time she had laughed in a year. It felt wonderful.

SEVENTEEN

It was not until the Amtrak train pulled out of Pennsylvania Station that Tracy began to relax. At every second she had expected a heavy hand to grip her shoulder, a voice to say, 'You're under arrest.'

She had carefully watched the other passengers as they boarded the train, and there was nothing alarming about them. Still, Tracy's shoulders were knots of tension. She kept assuring herself that it was unlikely anyone would have discovered the burglary this soon, and even if they had, there was nothing to connect her with it. Conrad Morgan would be waiting in St Louis with $25,000. Twenty-five thousand dollars to do with as she pleased! She would have had to work at the bank for a year to earn that much money. *I'll travel to Europe*, Tracy thought, *Paris*. No. Not Paris. *Charles and I were going to honeymoon there. I'll go to London. There, I won't be a jail-bird*. In a curious way, the experience she had just gone through had made Tracy feel like a different person. It was as though she had been reborn.

She locked the door to the compartment and took out the chamois bag and opened it. A cascade of glittering colours spilled into her hands. There were three large diamond rings, an emerald pin, a sapphire bracelet, three pairs of earrings, and two necklaces, one of rubies, one of pearls.

There must be more than a million dollars' worth of jewellery here, Tracy marvelled. As the train rolled through the countryside, she leaned back in her seat and replayed the evening in her mind. Renting the car . . . the drive to Sea Cliff . . . the stillness of the night . . . turning off the alarm and entering the house . . . opening the safe . . . the shock of the alarm going off, and the police appearing. It had never occurred to them that the woman in the nightgown with a mudpack on her face and a curler cap on her head was the burglar they were looking for.

Now, seated in her compartment on the train to St Louis, Tracy allowed herself a smile of satisfaction. She had enjoyed outwitting the police. There was something wonderfully exhilarating about being on the edge of danger. She felt daring and clever and invincible. She felt absolutely great.

There was a knock at the door of her compartment. Tracy hastily put the jewels back into the chamois bag and placed the bag in her suitcase. She took out her train ticket and unlocked the compartment door for the conductor.

Two men in grey suits stood in the corridor. One appeared to be in his early thirties, the other one about ten years older. The younger man was attractive, with the build of an athlete. He had a strong chin, a small, neat moustache, and wore horn-rimmed glasses behind which were intelligent blue eyes. The older man had a thick head of black hair and was heavy-set. His eyes were a cold brown.

'Can I help you?' Tracy asked.

'Yes, ma'am,' the older man replied. He pulled out a wallet and held up an identification card:

FEDERAL BUREAU OF INVESTIGATION
UNITED STATES DEPARTMENT OF JUSTICE

'I'm Special Agent Dennis Trevor. This is Special Agent Thomas Bowers.'

Tracy's mouth was suddenly dry. She forced a smile. 'I – I'm afraid I don't understand. Is something wrong?'

'I'm afraid there is, ma'am,' the younger agent said. He had a soft, southern accent. 'A few minutes ago this train crossed into New Jersey. Transporting stolen merchandise across a state line is a federal offence.'

Tracy felt suddenly faint. A red film appeared in front of her eyes, blurring everything.

The older man, Dennis Trevor, was saying, 'Would

you open your luggage, please?' It was not a question but an order.

Her only hope was to try to bluff it out. 'Of course I won't! How dare you come barging into my compartment like this!' Her voice was filled with indignation. 'Is that all you have to do – go around bothering innocent citizens? I'm going to call the conductor.'

'We've already spoken to the conductor,' Trevor said.

Her bluff was not working. 'Do – do you have a search warrant?'

The younger man said gently, 'We don't need a search warrant, Miss Whitney. We're apprehending you during the commission of a crime.' They even knew her name. She was trapped. There was no way out. *None.*

Trevor was at her suitcase, opening it. It was useless to try to stop him. Tracy watched as he reached inside and pulled out the chamois bag. He opened it, looked at his partner, and nodded. Tracy sank down onto the seat, suddenly too weak to stand.

Trevor took a list from his pocket, checked the contents of the bag against the list, and put the bag in his pocket. 'It's all here, Tom.'

'How – how did you find out?' Tracy asked miserably.

'We're not permitted to give out any information,' Trevor replied. 'You're under arrest. You have the right to remain silent, and to have an attorney present before you say anything. Anything you say now may be used as evidence against you. Do you understand?'

Her answer was a whispered, 'Yes.'

Tom Bowers said, 'I'm sorry about this. I mean, I know about your background, and I'm really sorry.'

'For Christ's sake,' the older man said, 'this isn't a social visit.'

'I know, but still –'

The older man held out a pair of handcuffs to Tracy. 'Hold out your wrists, please.'

Tracy felt her heart twisting in agony. She remembered the airport in New Orleans when they had handcuffed her, the staring faces. 'Please! Do you – do you have to do that?'

'Yes, ma'am.'

The younger man said, 'Can I talk to you alone for a minute, Dennis?'

Dennis Trevor shrugged. 'Okay.'

The two men stepped outside into the corridor. Tracy sat there, dazed, filled with despair. She could hear snatches of their conversation.

'For God's sake, Dennis, it isn't necessary to put cuffs on her. She's not going to run away . . .'

'When are you going to stop being such a boy scout? When you've been with the Bureau as long as I have . . .'

'Come on. Give her a break. She's embarrassed enough, and . . .'

'That's nothing to what she's going to . . .'

She could not hear the rest of the conversation. She did not want to hear the rest of the conversation.

In a moment they returned to the compartment. The older man seemed angry. 'All right,' he said. 'We're not cuffing you. We're taking you off at the next station. We're going to radio ahead for a Bureau car. You're not to leave this compartment. Is that clear?'

Tracy nodded, too miserable to speak.

The younger man, Tom Bowers, gave her a sympathetic shrug, as though to say, 'I wish there was something more I could do.'

There was nothing anyone could do. Not now. It was too late. She had been caught red-handed. Somehow the police had traced her and informed the FBI.

The agents were outside in the corridor talking to the conductor. Bowers pointed to Tracy and said something she could not hear. The conductor nodded. Bowers closed the door of the compartment, and to Tracy, it was like a cell door slamming.

The countryside sped by, flashing vignettes briefly framed by the window, but Tracy was unaware of the scenery. She sat there, paralysed by fear. There was a roaring in her ears that had nothing to do with the sounds of the train. She would get no second chance. She was a convicted felon. They would give her the maximum sentence, and this time there would be no warden's daughter to rescue, there would be nothing but the deadly, endless years of prison facing her. And the Big Berthas. *How had they caught her?* The only person who knew about the robbery was Conrad Morgan, and he could have no possible reason to turn her and the jewellery over to the FBI. Possibly some clerk in his shop had learned of the plan and tipped off the police. But how it happened made no difference. She had been caught. At the next stop she would be on her way to prison again. There would be a preliminary hearing and then the trial, and then . . .

Tracy squeezed her eyes tightly shut, refusing to think about it any further. She felt hot tears brush her cheeks.

The train began to lose speed. Tracy started to hyperventilate. She could not get enough air. The two FBI agents would be coming for her at any moment. A station came into view, and a few seconds later the train jerked to a stop. It was time to go. Tracy closed her suitcase, put on her coat, and sat down. She stared at the closed compartment door, waiting for it to open. Minutes went by. The two men did not appear. What could they be doing? She recalled their words, 'We're taking you off at the next station. We're going to radio ahead for a Bureau car. You're not to leave this compartment.'

She heard the conductor call, 'All aboard . . .'

Tracy started to panic. Perhaps they had meant

they would wait for her on the platform. *That must be it*. If she stayed on the train, they would accuse her of trying to run away from them, and it would make things even worse. Tracy grabbed her suitcase, opened the compartment door, and hurried out into the corridor.

The conductor was approaching. 'Are you getting off here, miss?' he asked. 'You'd better hurry. Let me help you. A woman in your condition shouldn't be lifting things.'

She stared. 'In my condition?'

'You don't have to be embarrassed. Your brothers told me you're pregnant and to sort of keep an eye on you.'

'My brothers –?'

'Nice chaps. They seemed really concerned about you.'

The world was spinning around. Everything was topsy-turvy.

The conductor carried the suitcase to the end of the carriage and helped Tracy down the steps. The train began to move.

'Do you know where my brothers went?' Tracy called.

'No, ma'am. They jumped into a taxi when the train stopped.'

With a million dollars' worth of stolen jewellery.

Tracy headed for the airport. It was the only place she could think of. If the men had taken a taxi, it meant they did not have their own transportation, and they would surely want to get out of town as fast as possible. She sat back in the cab, filled with rage at what they had done to her and with shame at how easily they had conned her. Oh, they were good, both of them. Really good. They had been so convincing. She blushed to think how she had fallen for the ancient good cop-bad cop routine.

For God's sake, Dennis, it isn't necessary to put cuffs on her. She's not going to run away . . .

When are you going to stop being such a boy scout? When you've been with the Bureau as long as I have . . .

The Bureau? They were probably both fugitives from the law. Well, she was going to get those jewels back. She had gone through too much to be outwitted by two con artists. She *had* to get to the airport in time.

She leaned forward in her seat and said to the driver, 'Could you go faster, please.'

They were standing in the boarding line at the departure gate, and she did not recognize them immediately. The younger man, who had called himself Thomas Bowers, no longer wore glasses, his eyes had changed from blue to grey, and his moustache was gone. The other man, Dennis Trevor, who had had thick black hair, was now totally bald. But still, there was no mistaking them. They had not had time to change their clothes. They were almost at the boarding gate when Tracy reached them.

'You forgot something,' Tracy said.

They turned to look at her, startled. The younger man frowned. 'What are you doing here? A car from the Bureau was supposed to have been at the station to pick you up.' His southern accent was gone.

'Then why don't we go back and find it?' Tracy suggested.

'Can't. We're on another case,' Trevor explained. 'We have to catch this plane.'

'Give me back the jewellery, first,' Tracy demanded.

'I'm afraid we can't do that,' Thomas Bowers told her. 'It's evidence. We'll send you a receipt for it.'

'No. I don't want a receipt. I want the jewellery.'

'Sorry,' said Trevor. 'We can't let it out of our possession.'

They had reached the gate. Trevor handed his boarding pass to the attendant. Tracy looked around, desperate, and saw an airport policeman standing nearby. She called out, '*Officer! Officer!*'

The two men looked at each other, startled.

'What the hell do you think you're doing?' Trevor hissed. 'Do you want to get us all arrested?'

The policeman was moving towards them. 'Yes, miss? Any problem?'

'Oh, no problem,' Tracy said gaily. 'These two wonderful gentlemen found some valuable jewellery I lost, and they're returning it to me. I was afraid I was going to have to go to the FBI about it.'

The two men exchanged a frantic look.

'They suggested that perhaps you wouldn't mind escorting me to a taxi.'

'Certainly. Be happy to.'

Tracy turned towards the men. 'It's safe to give the jewels to me now. This nice officer will take care of me.'

'No, really,' Tom Bowers objected. 'It would be much better if we –'

'Oh, no, I insist,' Tracy urged. 'I know how important it is for you to catch your plane.'

The two men looked at the policeman, and then at each other, helpless. There was nothing they could do. Reluctantly, Tom Bowers pulled out the chamois bag from his pocket.

'That's it!' Tracy said. She took the bag from his hand, opened it, and looked inside. 'Thank goodness. It's all here.'

Tom Bowers made one last-ditch try. 'Why don't we keep it safe for you until –'

'That won't be necessary,' Tracy said cheerfully. She opened her handbag, put the jewellery inside, and took out two $5.00 bills. She handed one to each of the men. 'Here's a little token of my appreciation for what you've done.'

The other passengers had all departed through the gate. The airline attendant said, 'That was the last call. You'll have to board now, gentlemen.'

'Thank you again,' Tracy beamed as she walked away with the policeman at her side. 'It's so rare to find an honest person these days.'

EIGHTEEN

Thomas Bowers – née Jeff Stevens – sat at the plane window looking out as the aircraft took off. He raised his handkerchief to his eyes, and his shoulders heaved up and down.

Dennis Taylor – a.k.a. Brandon Higgins – seated next to him, looked at him in surprise. 'Hey,' he said, 'it's only money. It's nothing to cry about.'

Jeff Stevens turned to him with tears streaming down his face, and Higgins, to his astonishment, saw that Jeff was convulsed with laughter.

'What the hell's the matter with you?' Higgins demanded. 'It's nothing to *laugh* about, either.'

To Jeff, it was. The manner in which Tracy Whitney had outwitted them at the airport was the most ingenious con he had ever witnessed. A scam on top of a scam. Conrad Morgan had told them the woman was an amateur. *My God*, Jeff thought, *what would she be like if she were a professional?* Tracy Whitney was without doubt the most beautiful woman Jeff Stevens had ever seen. And clever.

Jeff prided himself on being the best confidence artist in the business, and she had outsmarted him. *Uncle Willie would have loved her*, Jeff thought.

It was Uncle Willie who had educated Jeff. Jeff's mother was the trusting heiress to a farm-equipment fortune, married to an improvident schemer filled with get-rich-quick projects that never quite worked out. Jeff's father was a charmer, darkly handsome and persuasively glib, and in the first five years of marriage he had managed to run through his wife's inheritance. Jeff's earliest memories were of his mother and father quarrelling about money and his father's extramarital affairs. It was a bitter marriage, and the young boy had resolved, *I'm never going to get married. Never.*

His father's brother, Uncle Willie, owned a small travelling carnival, and whenever he was near Marion, Ohio, where the Stevenses lived, he came to visit them. He was the most cheerful man Jeff had ever known, filled with optimism and promises of a rosy tomorrow. He always managed to bring the boy exciting gifts, and he taught Jeff wonderful magic tricks. Uncle Willie had started out as a magician at a carnival and had taken it over when it went broke.

When Jeff was fourteen, his mother died in an car accident. Two months later Jeff's father married a nineteen-year-old cocktail waitress. 'It isn't natural for a man to live by himself,' his father had explained. But the boy was filled with a deep resentment, feeling betrayed by his father's callousness.

Jeff's father had been hired as a siding salesman and was on the road three days a week. One night when Jeff was alone in the house with his stepmother, he was awakened by the sound of his bedroom door opening. Moments later he felt a soft, naked body next to his. Jeff sat up in alarm.

'Hold me, Jeffie,' his stepmother whispered. 'I'm afraid of thunder.'

'It – it isn't thundering,' Jeff stammered.

'But it *could* be. The paper said rain.' She pressed her body close to his. 'Make love to me, baby.'

The boy was in a panic. 'Sure. Can we do it in Dad's bed?'

'Okay.' She laughed. 'Kinky, huh?'

'I'll be right there,' Jeff promised.

She slid out of bed and went into the other bedroom. Jeff had never dressed faster in his life. He went out the window and headed for Cimarron, Kansas, where Uncle Willie's carnival was playing. He never looked back.

When Uncle Willie asked Jeff why he had run away from home all he would say was, 'I don't get along with my stepmother.'

Uncle Willie telephoned Jeff's father, and after a long conversation, it was decided that the boy should remain with the carnival. 'He'll get a better education here than any school could ever give him,' Uncle Willie promised.

* * *

The carnival was a world unto itself. 'We don't run a Sunday school show,' Uncle Willie explained to Jeff. 'We're flimflam artists. But remember, sonny, you can't con people unless they're greedy to begin with. W. C. Fields had it right. You can't cheat an honest man.'

The carnies became Jeff's friends. There were the 'front-end' men, who had the concessions, and the 'back-end' people, who ran shows like the fat woman and the tattooed lady, and the flatstore operators, who operated the games. The carnival had its share of nubile girls, and they were attracted to the young boy. Jeff had inherited his mother's sensitivity and his father's dark, good looks, and the ladies fought over who was going to relieve Jeff of his virginity. His first sexual experience was with a pretty contortionist, and for years she was the high-water mark that other women had to live up to.

Uncle Willie arranged for Jeff to work at various jobs around the carnival.

'Someday all this will be yours,' Uncle Willie told the boy, 'and the only way you're gonna hang on to it is to know more about it than anybody else does.'

Jeff started out with the six-cat 'hanky-pank', a scam where customers paid to throw balls to try to knock six cats made out of canvas with a wood-base bottom into a net. The operator running the joint would demonstrate how easy it was to knock them over, but when the customer tried it, a 'gunner' hiding in the back of the canvas lifted a rod to keep the wooden base on the cats steady. Not even Sandy Koufax could have downed the cats.

'Hey, you hit it too low,' the operator would say. 'All you have to do is hit it nice and easy.'

Nice and easy was the password, and the moment the operator said it, the hidden gunner would drop the rod, and the operator would knock the cat off the board. He would then say, 'See what I mean?' and that was the gunner's signal to put up the rod again. There was always another rube who wanted to show off his pitching arm to his giggling girl friend.

Jeff worked the 'count stores', where clothespins were arranged in a line. The customer would pay to throw rubber rings over the clothespins, which were numbered, and if the total added up to twenty-nine, he would win an expensive toy. What the sucker did not know was that the clothespins had different numbers at both ends, so that the man running the count store could conceal the number that would add up to twenty-nine and make sure the mark never won.

One day Uncle Willie said to Jeff, 'You're doin' real good, kid, and I'm proud of you. You're ready to move up to the skillo.'

The skillo operators were the *crème de la crème*, and all the other carnies looked up to them. They made more money than anyone else in the carnival, stayed at the best hotels, and drove flashy cars. The skillo game consisted of a flat wheel with an arrow balanced very carefully on glass with a thin piece of paper in the centre. Each section was numbered, and when the customer spun the wheel and it stopped on a number, that number would be blocked off. The customer would pay again for another spin of the wheel, and another space would be blocked off. The skillo operator explained that when all the spaces were blocked off, the customer would win a large sum of money. As the customer got closer to filling in all the spaces, the skillo operator would encourage him to increase his bets. The operator would look around nervously and whisper, 'I don't own this game, but I'd like to win. If you do, maybe you'll give me a small piece.'

The operator would slip the customer five or ten dollars and say, 'Bet this for me, will you? You can't lose now.' And the mark would feel as though he had a confederate. Jeff became an expert at milking the customers. As the open spaces on the board became smaller and the odds of winning grew greater, the excitement would intensify.

'You can't miss now!' Jeff would exclaim, and the player would eagerly put up more money. Finally, when there was only one tiny space left to fill, the excitement would peak. The mark would put up all the money he had, and often hurry home to get more. The customer never won, however, because the operator or his shill would give the table an imperceptible nudge, and the arrow would invariably land at the wrong place.

Jeff quickly learned all the carnie terms: The 'gaff' was a term for fixing the games so that the marks could not win. The men who stood in front of a sideshow making their spiel were called 'barkers' by outsiders, but the carnie people called them 'talkers'. The talker got 10 percent of the take for building the tip – the 'tip' being a crowd. 'Slum' was the prize given away. The 'postman' was a cop who had to be paid off.

Jeff became an expert at the 'blow-off'. When customers paid to see a sideshow exhibition, Jeff would make his spiel: 'Ladies and gentlemen: everything that's pictured, painted and advertised outside, you will see within the walls of this tent for the price of your general admission. *However*, immediately after the young lady in the electric chair gets finished being tortured, her poor body racked by fifty thousand watts of electricity, we have an extra added attraction that has absolutely nothing to do with the show and is not advertised outside. Behind this enclosure you are going to see something so truly remarkable, so chilling and hair-raising, that we dare not portray it outside, because it might come under the eyes of innocent children or susceptible women.'

And after the suckers had paid an extra dollar Jeff would usher them inside to see a girl with no middle, or a two-headed baby, and of course it was all done with mirrors.

One of the most profitable carnival games was the 'mouse running'. A live mouse was put in the centre of a table and a bowl was placed over it. The rim of the table had ten holes around its perimeter into any one of which the mouse could run when the bowl was lifted. Each patron bet on a numbered hole. Whoever selected the hole into which the mouse would run won the prize.

'How do you gaff a thing like that?' Jeff asked Uncle Willie. 'Do you use trained mice?'

Uncle Willie roared with laughter. 'Who the hell's got time to train mice? No, no. It's simple. The operator sees which number no one has bet on, and he puts a little vinegar on his finger and touches the edge of the hole he wants the mouse to run into. The mouse will head for that hole every time.'

Karen, an attractive belly dancer, introduced Jeff to the 'key' game.

'When you've made your spiel on Saturday night,' Karen told him, 'call some of the men customers aside, one at a time, and sell them a key to my trailer.'

The keys cost five dollars. By midnight, a dozen or more men would find themselves milling around outside her trailer. Karen, by that time, was at a hotel in town, spending the night with Jeff. When the marks came back to the carnival the following morning to get their revenge, the show was long gone.

During the next four years Jeff learned a great deal about human nature. He found out how easy it was to arouse greed, and how gullible people could be. They believed incredible tales because their greed made them *want* to believe. At eighteen, Jeff was strikingly handsome. Even the most casual woman observer would instantly note and approve his grey, well-spaced eyes, tall build, and curly dark hair. Men enjoyed his wit and air of easy good humour. Even children, as if speaking to some answering child in him, gave him their confidence immediately. Customers flirted outrageously with Jeff, but Uncle Willie cautioned, 'Stay away from the townies, my boy. Their fathers are always the sheriff.'

It was the knife thrower's wife who caused Jeff to leave the carnival. The show had just arrived at Milledgeville, Georgia, and the tents were being set up. A new act had signed on, a Sicilian knife thrower called the Great Zorbini and his attractive blonde wife. While the Great Zorbini was at the carnival setting up his equipment, his wife invited Jeff to their hotel room in town.

'Zorbini will be busy all day,' she told Jeff. 'Let's have some fun.'

It sounded good.

'Give me an hour and then come up to the room,' she said.

'Why wait an hour?' Jeff asked.

She smiled and said, 'It will take me that long to get everything ready.'

Jeff waited, his curiosity increasing, and when he finally arrived at the hotel room, she greeted him at the door, half naked. He reached for her, but she took his hand and said, 'Come in here.'

He walked into the bathroom and stared in disbelief. She had filled the bath with six flavours of Jell-O, mixed with warm water.

'What's that?' Jeff asked.

'It's dessert. Get undressed baby.'

Jeff undressed.

'Now, into the bath.'

He stepped into the bath and sat down, and it was the wildest sensation he had ever experienced. The soft, slippery Jell-O seemed to fill every crevice of his body, massaging him all over. The blonde joined him in the bath.

'Now,' she said, 'lunch.'

She started down his chest towards his groin, licking the Jell-O as she went. 'Mmmm, you taste delicious. I like the strawberry best . . .'

Between her rapidly flicking tongue and the friction of the warm, viscous Jell-O, it was an erotic experience beyond description. In the middle of it, the bathroom door flew open and the Great Zorbini strode in. The Sicilian took one look at his wife and the startled Jeff, and howled, '*Tu sei una puttana! Vi ammazzo tutti e due! Dove sono i miei coltelli?*'

Jeff did not recognize any of the words, but the tone was familiar. As the Great Zorbini raced out of the room to get his knives, Jeff leaped out of the bath, his body looking like a rainbow with the multicoloured Jell-O clinging to it, and grabbed his clothes. He jumped out of the window, naked, and began running down the alley. He heard a shout behind him and felt a knife sing past his head. Zing! Another, and then he was out of range. He dressed in a culvert, pulling his shirt and pants over the sticky Jell-O, and squished his way to the depot, where he caught the first bus out of town.

Six months later, he was in Vietnam.

Every soldier fights a different war, and Jeff came out of his Vietnam experience with a deep contempt for bureaucracy and a lasting resentment of authority. He spent two years in a war that could never be won, and he was appalled by the waste of money and matériel and lives, and sickened by the treachery and deceit of the generals and politicians who performed their verbal sleight of hand. *We've been suckered into a war that nobody wants*, Jeff thought. *It's a con game. The biggest con game in the world.*

A week before Jeff's discharge, he received the news of Uncle Willie's death. The carnival had folded. The past was finished. It was time for him to enjoy the future.

The years that followed were filled with a series of adventures. To Jeff, the whole world was a carnival, and the people in it were his marks. He devised his own con games. He placed ads in newspapers offering a colour picture of the President for a dollar. When he received a dollar, he sent his victim a postage stamp with a picture of the President on it.

He put announcements in magazines warning

the public that there were only sixty days left to send in five dollars, that after that it would be too late. The ad did not specify what the five dollars would buy, but the money poured in.

For three months Jeff worked in a boiler room, selling phony oil stocks over the telephone.

He loved boats, and when a friend offered him a job working on a sailing schooner bound for Tahiti, Jeff signed on as a seaman.

The ship was a beauty, a 165-foot white schooner, glistening in the sun, all sails drawing well. It had teak decking, long, gleaming Oregon fir for the hull, with a main salon that sat twelve and a galley forward, with electric ovens. The crew's quarters were in the forepeak. In addition to the captain, the steward, and a cook, there were five deckhands. Jeff's job consisted of helping hoist the sails, polishing the brass port-holes, and climbing up the ratlines to the lower spreader to mast the sails. The schooner was carrying a party of eight.

'The owner is named Hollander,' Jeff's friend informed him.

Hollander turned out to be Louise Hollander, a twenty-five-year-old, golden-haired beauty, whose father owned half of Central America. The other passengers were her friends, whom Jeff's buddies sneeringly referred to as the 'jest set'.

The first day out Jeff was working in the hot sun, polishing the brass on deck. Louise Hollander stopped beside him.

'You're new on board.'

He looked up. 'Yes.'

'Do you have a name?'

'Jeff Stevens.'

'That's a nice name.' He made no comment. 'Do you know who I am?'

'No.'

'I'm Louise Hollander. I own this boat.'

'I see. I'm working for you.'

She gave him a slow smile. 'That's right.'

'Then if you want to get your money's worth, you'd better let me get on with my work.' Jeff moved on to the next stanchion.

In their quarters at night, the crew members disparaged the passengers and made jokes about them. But Jeff admitted to himself that he was envious of them – their backgrounds, their educations, and their easy manners. They had come from monied families and had attended the best schools. *His* school had been Uncle Willie and the carnival.

One of the carnies had been a professor of archaeology until he was thrown out of college for stealing and selling valuable relics. He and Jeff had had long talks, and the professor had imbued Jeff with an enthusiasm for archaeology. 'You can read the whole future of mankind in the past,' the professor would say. 'Think of it, son. Thousands of years ago there were people just like you and me dreaming dreams, spinning tales, living out their lives, giving birth to our ancestors.' His eyes had taken on a faraway look. 'Carthage – that's where

I'd like to go on a dig. Long before Christ was born, it was a great city, the Paris of ancient Africa. The people had their games, and baths, and chariot racing. The Circus Maximus was as large as five football fields.' He had noted the interest in the boy's eyes. 'Do you know how Cato the Elder used to end his speeches in the Roman Senate? He'd say, "*Delenda est cartaga*"; "Carthage must be destroyed". His wish finally came true. The Romans reduced the place to rubble and came back twenty-five years later to build a great city on its ashes. I wish I could take you there on a dig one day, my boy.'

A year later the professor had died of alcoholism, but Jeff had promised himself that one day he would go on a dig. Carthage, first, for the professor.

On the last night before the schooner was to dock in Tahiti, Jeff was summoned to Louise Hollander's stateroom. She was wearing a sheer silk robe.

'You wanted to see me, ma'am?'

'Are you a homosexual, Jeff?'

'I don't believe it's any of your business, Miss Hollander, but the answer is no. What I am is choosy.'

Louise Hollander's mouth tightened. 'What kind of women do you like? Whores, I suppose.'

'Sometimes,' Jeff said agreeably. 'Was there anything else Miss Hollander?'

'Yes. I'm giving a dinner party tomorrow night. Would you like to come?'

Jeff looked at the woman for a long moment before he answered. 'Why not?'

And that was the way it began.

Louise Hollander had had two husbands before she was twenty-one, and her lawyer had just made a settlement with her third husband when she met Jeff. The second night they were moored at the harbour in Papeete, and as the passengers and crew were going ashore, Jeff received another summons to Louise Hollander's quarters. When Jeff arrived, she was dressed in a colourful silk pareu slit all the way up to the thigh.

'I'm trying to get this off,' she said. 'I'm having a problem with the zipper.'

Jeff walked over and examined the costume. 'It doesn't have a zipper.'

She turned to face him, and smiled. 'I know. That's my problem.'

They made love on the deck, where the soft tropical air caressed their bodies like a blessing. Afterwards, they lay on their sides, facing each other. Jeff propped himself up on an elbow and looked down at Louise. 'Your daddy's not the sheriff, is he?' Jeff asked.

She sat up in surprise. 'What?'

'You're the first townie I ever made love to. Uncle Willie used to warn me that their daddies always turned out to be the sheriff.'

They were together every night after that. At first Louise's friends were amused. *He's another one of Louise's playthings*, they thought. But when she informed them that she intended to marry Jeff, they were frantic.

'For Christ's sake, Louise, he's a *nothing*. He worked in a carnival. My God, you might as well be marrying a stable hand. He's handsome – granted. And he has a fab bod. But outside of sex, you have absolutely nothing in common, darling.'

'Louise, Jeff's for breakfast, not *dinner*.'

'You have a social position to uphold.'

'Frankly, angel, he just won't fit in, will he?'

But nothing her friends said could dissuade Louise. Jeff was the most fascinating man she had ever met. She had found that men who were outstandingly handsome were either monumentally stupid or unbearably dull. Jeff was intelligent and amusing, and the combination was irresistible.

When Louise mentioned the subject of marriage to Jeff, he was as surprised as her friends had been.

'Why marriage? You've already got my body. I can't give you anything you don't have.'

'It's very simple, Jeff. I love you. I want to share the rest of my life with you.'

Marriage had been an alien idea, and suddenly it no longer was. Beneath Louise Hollander's worldly, sophisticated veneer, there was a vulnerable, lost little girl. *She needs me*, Jeff thought. The idea of a stable homelife and children was suddenly immensely appealing. It seemed to him that ever since he could remember, he had been running. It was time to stop.

They were married in the town hall in Tahiti three days later.

When they returned to New York, Jeff was summoned to the office of Scott Fogarty, Louise Hollander's attorney, a small, frigid man, tight-lipped and probably, Jeff thought, tight-assed.

'I have a paper here for you to sign,' the attorney announced.

'What kind of paper?'

'It's a release. It simply states that in the event of the dissolution of your marriage to Louise Hollander –'

'Louise Stevens.'

'– Louise Stevens, that you will not participate financially in any of her –'

Jeff felt the muscles of his jaw tightening. 'Where do I sign?'

'Don't you want me to finish reading?'

'No. I don't think you get the point. I didn't marry her for her fucking money.'

'Really, Mr Stevens! I just –'

'Do you want me to sign it or don't you?'

The lawyer placed the paper in front of Jeff. He scrawled his signature and stormed out of the office. Louise's limousine and driver were waiting for him downstairs. As Jeff climbed in, he had to laugh to himself. *What the hell am I so pissed off about? I've been a con artist all my life, and when*

I go straight for the first time and someone thinks I'm out to take them, I behave like a fucking Sunday school teacher.

Louise took Jeff to the best tailor in Manhattan. 'You'll look fantastic in a dinner jacket,' she coaxed. And he did. Before the second month of the marriage, five of Louise's best friends had tried to seduce the attractive newcomer in their circle, but Jeff ignored them. He was determined to make this marriage work.

Budge Hollander, Louise's brother, put Jeff up for membership in the exclusive New York Pilgrim Club, and Jeff was accepted. Budge was a beefy, middle-aged man who had obtained his sobriquet playing right tackle on the Harvard football team, where he got the reputation of being a player his opponents could not budge. He owned a shipping line, a banana plantation, cattle ranches, a meat-packing company, and more corporations than Jeff could count. Budge Hollander was not subtle in concealing his contempt for Jeff Stevens.

'You're really out of our class, aren't you, old boy? But as long as you amuse Louise in bed, that will do nicely. I'm fond of my sister.'

It took every ounce of willpower for Jeff to control himself. *I'm not married to this prick. I'm married to Louise.*

The other members of the Pilgrim Club were equally obnoxious. They found Jeff terribly amusing.

All of them dined at the club every noontime, and pleaded for Jeff to tell them stories about his 'carnie days', as they liked to call them. Perversely, Jeff made the stories more and more outrageous.

Jeff and Louise lived in a twenty-room townhouse filled with servants, on the East Side of Manhattan. Louise had estates in Long Island and the Bahamas, a villa in Sardinia, and a large apartment on Avenue Foch in Paris. Aside from the yacht, Louise owned a Maserati, a Rolls Corniche, a Lamborghini and a Daimler.

It's fantastic, Jeff thought.

It's great, Jeff thought.

It's boring, Jeff thought. *And degrading*.

One morning he got up from his eighteenth-century four-poster bed, put on a Sulka robe, and went looking for Louise. He found her in the breakfast room.

'I've got to get a job,' he told her.

'For heaven's sake, darling, why? We don't need the money.'

'It has nothing to do with money. You can't expect me to sit around on my hands and be spoon-fed. I have to work.'

Louise gave it a moment's thought. 'All right, angel. I'll speak to Budge. He owns a stockbrokerage firm. Would you like to be a stockbroker, darling?'

'I just want to get off my ass,' Jeff muttered.

* * *

He went to work for Budge. He had never had a job with regular hours before. *I'm going to love it*, Jeff thought.

He hated it. He stayed with it because he wanted to bring home a salary cheque to his wife.

'When are you and I going to have a baby?' he asked Louise, after a lazy Sunday brunch.

'Soon, darling. I'm trying.'

'Come to bed. Let's try again.'

Jeff was seated at the luncheon table reserved for his brother-in-law and half a dozen other captains of industry at the Pilgrim Club.

Budge announced, 'We just issued our annual report for the meat-packing company, fellas. Our profits are up forty percent.'

'Why shouldn't they be?' one of the men at the table laughed. 'You've got the fucking inspectors bribed.' He turned to the others at the table. 'Old clever Budge, here, buys inferior meat and has it stamped prime and sells it for a bloody fortune.'

Jeff was shocked. 'People *eat* meat, for Christ's sake. They feed it to their children. He's kidding, isn't he, Budge?'

Budge grinned and whooped, 'Look who's being moral!'

Over the next three months Jeff became very well acquainted with his table companions. Ed Zeller had paid a million in bribes in order to build a factory in Libya. Mike Quincy, the head of a conglomerate, was a raider who bought companies and illegally tipped off his friends when to buy and sell the stock. Alan Thompson, the richest man at the table, boasted of his company's policy. 'Before they changed the damn law, we used to fire the old grey hairs one year before their pensions were due. Saved a fortune.'

All the men cheated on taxes, had insurance scams, falsified expense accounts, and put their current mistresses on their payroll as secretaries or assistants.

Christ, Jeff thought. *They're just dressed-up carnies. They all run flat stores.*

The wives were no better. They grabbed everything they could get their greedy hands on and cheated on their husbands. *They're playing the key game*, Jeff marvelled.

When he tried to tell Louise how he felt, she laughed. 'Don't be naïve, Jeff. You're enjoying your life, aren't you?'

The truth was that he was not. He had married Louise because he believed she needed him. He felt that children would change everything.

'Let's have one of each. It's time. We've been married a year now.'

'Angel, be patient. I've been to the doctor, and he told me I'm fine. Maybe you should have a checkup and see if *you're* all right.'

Jeff went.

'You should have no trouble producing healthy children,' the doctor assured him.

And still nothing happened.

On Black Monday Jeff's world fell apart. It started in the morning when he went into Louise's medicine chest for an aspirin. He found a shelf full of birth control pills. One of the cases was almost empty. Lying innocently next to it was a vial of white powder and a small golden spoon. And that was only the start of the day.

At noon, Jeff was seated in a deep armchair in the Pilgrim Club, waiting for Budge to appear, when he heard two men behind him talking.

'She swears that her Italian singer's cock is over ten inches long.'

There was a snicker. 'Well, Louise always liked them big.'

They're talking about another Louise, Jeff told himself.

'That's probably why she married that carnival person in the first place. But she does tell the most amusing stories about him. You won't believe what he did the other day . . .'

Jeff rose and blindly made his way out of the club.

He was filled with a rage such as he had never known. He wanted to kill. He wanted to kill the unknown Italian. He wanted to kill Louise. How many other men had she been sleeping with during the past year? They had been laughing at him all this time. Budge and Ed Zeller and Mike Quincy and Alan Thompson and their wives had been having an enormous joke at his expense. And Louise, the woman he had wanted to protect. Jeff's immediate reaction was to pack up and leave. But that was not good enough. He had no intention of letting the bastards have the last laugh.

That afternoon when Jeff arrived home, Louise was not there. 'Madame went out this morning,' Pickens, the butler, said. 'I believe she had several appointments.'

I'll bet she did, Jeff thought. *She's out fucking that ten-inch-cock Italian. Jesus Christ!*

By the time Louise arrived home, Jeff had himself under tight control. 'Did you have a nice day?' Jeff asked.

'Oh, the usual boring things, darling. A beauty appointment, shopping . . . How was your day, angel?'

'It was interesting,' Jeff said truthfully. 'I learned a lot.'

'Budge tells me you're doing beautifully.'

'I am,' Jeff assured her. 'And very soon I'm going to be doing even better.'

Louise stroked his hand. 'My bright husband. Why don't we go to bed early?'

'Not tonight,' Jeff said. 'I have a headache.'

He spent the next week making his plans.

He began at lunch at the club. 'Do any of you know anything about computer frauds?' Jeff asked.

'Why?' Ed Zeller wanted to know. 'You planning to commit one?'

There was a sputter of laughter.

'No, I'm serious,' Jeff insisted. 'It's a big problem. People are tapping into computers and ripping off banks and insurance companies and other businesses for billions of dollars. It gets worse all the time.'

'Sounds right up your alley,' Budge murmured.

'Someone I met has come up with a computer he says can't be tampered with.'

'And you want to have him knocked off,' Mike Quincy kidded.

'As a matter of fact, I'm interested in raising money to back him. I just wondered if any of you might know something about computers.'

'No,' Budge grinned, 'but we know everything about backing inventors, don't we fellas?'

There was a burst of laughter.

Two days later at the club, Jeff passed by the usual table and explained to Budge, 'I'm sorry I won't be able to join you fellows today. I'm having a guest for lunch.'

When Jeff moved to another table, Alan Thompson grinned, 'He's probably having lunch with the bearded lady from the circus.'

A stooped, grey-haired man entered the dining room and was ushered to Jeff's table.

'Jesus!' Mike Quincy said. 'Isn't that Professor Ackerman?'

'Who's Professor Ackerman?'

'Don't you ever read anything but financial reports, Budge? Vernon Ackerman was on the cover of *Time* last month. He's chairman of the President's National Scientific Board. He's the most brilliant scientist in our country.'

'What the hell is he doing with my dear brother-in-law?'

Jeff and the professor were engrossed in a deep conversation all during lunch, and Budge and his friends grew more and more curious. When the professor left, Budge motioned Jeff over to his table.

'Hey, Jeff. Who was that?'

Jeff looked guilty. 'Oh . . . you mean Vernon?'

'Yeah. What were you two talking about?'

'We . . . ah . . .' The others could almost watch Jeff's thought processes as he tried to dodge the question. 'I . . . ah . . . might write a book about him. He's a very interesting character.'

'I didn't know you were a writer.'

'Well, I guess we all have to start sometime.'

Three days later Jeff had another luncheon guest. This time it was Budge who recognized him. 'Hey! That's Seymour Jarrett, chairman of the board of Jarrett International Computer. What the hell would he be doing with Jeff?'

Again, Jeff and his guest held a long, animated conversation. When the luncheon was over, Budge sought Jeff out.

'Jeffrey, boy, what's with you and Seymour Jarrett?'

'Nothing,' Jeff said quickly. 'Just having a chat.' He started to walk away. Budge stopped him.

'Not so fast, old buddy. Seymour Jarrett is a very busy fellow. He doesn't sit around having long chats about nothing.'

Jeff said earnestly, 'All right. The truth is, Budge, that Seymour collects stamps, and I told him about a stamp I might be able to acquire for him.'

The truth, my ass, Budge thought.

The following week, Jeff lunched at the Club with Charles Bartlett, the president of Bartlett & Bartlett, one of the largest private capital venture groups in the world. Budge, Ed Zeller, Alan Thompson, and Mike Quincy watched in fascination as the two men talked, their heads close together.

'Your brother-in-law is sure in high-flying company lately,' Zeller commented. 'What kind of deal has he got cooking, Budge?'

Budge said testily, 'I don't know, but I'm sure in hell going to find out. If Jarrett and Bartlett are interested, there must be a pot of money involved.'

They watched as Bartlett rose, enthusiastically pumped Jeff's hand, and left. As Jeff passed their table, Budge caught his arm. 'Sit down, Jeff. We want to have a little talk with you.'

'I should get back to the office,' Jeff protested. 'I –'

'You work for *me*, remember? Sit down.' Jeff sat. 'Who were you having lunch with?'

Jeff hesitated. 'No one special. An old friend.'

'Charlie Bartlett's an old friend?'

'Kind of.'

'What were you and your old friend Charlie discussing, Jeff?'

'Uh . . . cars, mostly. Old Charlie likes antique cars, and I heard about this '37 Packard, four-door convertible –'

'Cut the horseshit!' Budge snapped. 'You're not collecting stamps or selling cars, or writing any fucking book. What are you really up to?'

'Nothing. I –'

'You're raising money for something, aren't you, Jeff?' Ed Zeller asked.

'No!' But he said it a shade too quickly.

Budge put a beefy arm around Jeff. 'Hey, buddy, this is your brother-in-law. We're family, remember?' He gave Jeff a bear hug. 'It's something about that tamperproof computer you mentioned last week, right?'

They could see by Jeff's face that they had trapped him.

'Well, yes.'

It was like pulling teeth to get anything out of the son of a bitch. 'Why didn't you tell us Professor Ackerman was involved?'

'I didn't think you'd be interested.'

'You were wrong. When you need capital, you go to your friends.'

'The professor and I don't need capital,' Jeff said. 'Jarrett and Bartlett –'

'Jarrett and Bartlett are fuckin' sharks! They'll eat you alive,' Alan Thompson exclaimed.

Ed Zeller picked it up. 'Jeff, when you deal with friends, you don't get hurt.'

'Everything is already arranged,' Jeff told them. 'Charlie Bartlett –'

'Have you signed anything yet?'

'No, but I gave my word –'

'Then *nothing*'s arranged. Hell, Jeff boy, in business people change their minds every hour.'

'I shouldn't even be discussing this with you,' Jeff protested. 'Professor Ackerman's name can't be mentioned. He's under contract to a government agency.'

'We know that,' Thompson said soothingly. 'Does the professor think this thing will work?'

'Oh, he *knows* it works.'

'If it's good enough for Ackerman, it's good enough for us, right fellows?'

There was a chorus of assent.

'Hey, I'm not a scientist,' Jeff said. 'I can't guarantee anything. For all I know, this thing may have no value at all.'

'Sure. We understand. But say it *does* have a value, Jeff. How big could this thing be?'

'Budge, the market for this is worldwide. I couldn't even begin to put a value on it. Everybody will be able to use it.'

'How much initial financing are you looking for?'

'Two million dollars, but all we need is two hundred and fifty thousand dollars down. Bartlett promised –'

'Forget Bartlett. That's chicken feed, old buddy. We'll put that up ourselves. Keep it in the family. Right, fellas?'

'Right!'

Budge looked up and snapped his fingers, and a waiter came hurrying over to the table. 'Dominick, bring Mr Stevens some paper and a pen.'

It was produced almost instantly.

'We can wrap up this little deal right here,' Budge said to Jeff. 'You just make out this paper, giving us the rights, and we'll sign it, and in the morning you'll have a certified cheque for two hundred and fifty thousand dollars. How does that suit you?'

Jeff was biting his lower lip. 'Budge, I promised Mr Barlett –'

'Fuck Barlett,' Budge snarled. 'Are you married to his sister or mine? Now *write*.'

'We don't have a patent on this, and –'

'*Write*, goddamn it!' Budge shoved the pen in Jeff's hand.

Reluctantly, Jeff began to write. 'This will transfer all my rights, title and interest to a mathematical computer called SUCABA, to the buyers, Donald "Budge" Hollander, Ed Zeller, Alan Thompson and Mike Quincy, for the consideration of two million dollars, with a payment of two hundred and fifty thousand dollars on signing. SUCABA has been extensively tested, is inexpensive, trouble-free, and uses less power than any computer currently on the market. SUCABA will require no maintenance or parts for a minimum period of ten years.' They were all looking over Jeff's shoulder as he wrote.

'Jesus!' Ed Zeller said. 'Ten years! There's not a computer on the market that can claim that!'

Jeff continued. 'The buyers understand that neither Professor Vernon Ackerman nor I holds a patent on SUCABA –'

'We'll take care of all that,' Alan Thompson interrupted impatiently. 'I've got one hell of a patent attorney.'

Jeff kept writing. 'I have explained to the buyers that SUCABA may have no value of any kind, and that neither Professor Vernon Ackerman nor I makes any representations or warranties about SUCABA except as written above.' He signed it and held up the paper. 'Is that satisfactory?'

'You sure about the ten years?' Budge asked.

'Guaranteed. I'll just make a copy of this,' Jeff said. They watched as he carefully made a copy of what he had written.

Budge snatched the papers out of Jeff's hand and signed them. Zeller, Quincy and Thompson followed suit.

Budge was beaming. 'A copy for us and a copy for you. Old Seymour Jarrett and Charlie Bartlett are sure going to have egg on their faces, huh, boys? I can't wait until they hear that they got screwed out of this deal.'

The following morning Budge handed Jeff a certified cheque for $250,000.

'Where's the computer?' Budge asked.

'I arranged for it to be delivered here at the club at noon. I thought it only fitting that we should all be together when you receive it.'

Budge clapped him on the shoulder. 'You know, Jeff, you're a smart fellow. See you at lunch.'

At the stroke of noon a messenger carrying a box appeared in the dining room of the Pilgrim Club and was ushered to Budge's table, where he was seated with Zeller, Thompson, and Quincy.

'Here it is!' Budge exclaimed. 'Jesus! The damned thing's even portable.'

'Should we wait for Jeff?' Thompson asked.

'Fuck him. This belongs to us now.' Budge ripped the paper away from the box. Inside was a nest of straw. Carefully, almost reverently, he lifted out the object that lay in the nest. The men sat there, staring at it. It was a square frame about a foot in diameter, holding a series of wires across which were strung rows of beads. There was a long silence.

'What is it?' Quincy finally asked.

Alan Thompson said, 'It's an abacus. One of those things Orientals use to count –' The expression on his face changed. 'Jesus! SUCABA is *abacus* spelled backwards!' He turned to Budge. 'Is this some kind of joke?'

Zeller was sputtering. 'Low power, trouble-free, uses less power than any computer currently on the market . . . Stop the goddamned cheque!'

There was a concerted rush to the telephone.

'Your certified cheque?' the head bookkeeper said. 'There's nothing to worry about. Mr Stevens cashed it this morning.'

Pickens, the butler, was very sorry, indeed, but Mr Stevens had packed and left. 'He mentioned something about an extended journey.'

That afternoon, a frantic Budge finally managed to reach Professor Vernon Ackerman.

'Of course. Jeff Stevens. A charming man. Your brother-in-law, you say?'

'Professor, what were you and Jeff discussing?'

'I suppose it's no secret. Jeff is eager to write a book about me. He has convinced me that the world wants to know the human being behind the scientist . . .'

Seymour Jarrett was reticent. 'Why do you want to know what Mr Stevens and I discussed? Are you a rival stamp collector?'

'No, I –'

'Well, it won't do you any good to snoop around. There's only one stamp like it in existence, and Mr Stevens has agreed to sell it to me when he acquires it.'

And he slammed down the receiver.

Budge knew what Charlie Bartlett was going to say before the words were out. 'Jeff Stevens? Oh, yes.

I collect antique cars. Jeff knows where this '37 Packard four-door convertible in mint condition –'

This time it was Budge who hung up.

'Don't worry,' Budge told his partners. 'We'll get our money back and put the son of a bitch away for the rest of his life. There are laws against fraud.'

The group's next stop was at the office of Scott Fogarty.

'He took us for two hundred and fifty thousand dollars,' Budge told the attorney. 'I want him put behind bars for the rest of his life. Get a warrant out for –'

'Do you have the contract with you, Budge?'

'It's right here.' He handed Fogarty the paper Jeff had written out.

The lawyer scanned it quickly, then read it again, slowly. 'Did he forge your names to this paper?'

'Why, no,' Mike Quincy said. 'We signed it.'

'Did you read it first?'

Ed Zeller angrily said, 'Of course we read it. Do you think we're stupid?'

'I'll let you be the judge of that, gentlemen. You signed a contract stating that you were informed that what you were purchasing with a down payment of two hundred and fifty thousand dollars was an object that had not been patented and could be completely worthless. In the legal parlance of an old professor of mine, "You've been royally fucked."'

* * *

Jeff had obtained the divorce in Reno. It was while he was establishing residence there that he had run into Conrad Morgan. Morgan had once worked for Uncle Willie. 'How would you like to do me a small favour, Jeff?' Conrad Morgan had asked. 'There's a young lady travelling on a train from New York to St Louis with some jewellery . . .'

Jeff looked out of the plane window and thought about Tracy. There was a smile on his face.

When Tracy returned to New York, her first stop was at Conrad Morgan et Cie Jewellers. Conrad Morgan ushered Tracy into his office and closed the door. He rubbed his hands together and said, 'I was getting very worried, my dear. I waited for you in St Louis and –'

'You weren't in St Louis.'

'What? What do you mean?' His blue eyes seemed to twinkle.

'I mean, you didn't go to St Louis. You never intended to meet me.'

'But of course I did! You have the jewels and I –'

'You sent two men to take them away from me.'

There was a puzzled expression on Morgan's face. 'I don't understand.'

'At first I thought there might be a leak in your organization, but there wasn't, was there? It was you. You told me that you personally arranged for my train ticket, so you were the only one who knew the number of my compartment. I used a different name and a disguise, but your men knew exactly where to find me.'

There was a look of surprise on his cherubic face. 'Are you trying to tell me that some men robbed you of the jewels?'

Tracy smiled. 'I'm trying to tell you that they *didn't*.'

This time the surprise on Morgan's face was genuine. '*You* have the jewels?'

'Yes. Your friends were in such a big hurry to catch a plane that they left them behind.'

Morgan studied Tracy a moment. 'Excuse me.'

He went through a private door, and Tracy sat down on the couch, perfectly relaxed.

Conrad Morgan was gone for almost fifteen minutes, and when he returned, there was a look of dismay on his face. 'I'm afraid a mistake has been made. A *big* mistake. You're a very clever young lady, Miss Whitney. You've earned your twenty-five thousand dollars.' He smiled admiringly. 'Give me the jewels and –'

'Fifty thousand.'

'I beg your pardon?'

'I had to steal them twice. That's fifty thousand dollars, Mr Morgan.'

'No,' he said flatly. His eyes had lost their twinkle. 'I'm afraid I can't give you that much for them.'

Tracy rose. 'That's perfectly all right. I'll try to find someone in Las Vegas who thinks they're worth that.' She moved towards the door.

'Fifty thousand dollars?' Conrad Morgan asked.

Tracy nodded.

'Where are the jewels?'

'In a locker at Penn Station. As soon as you give me the money – in cash – and put me in a taxi, I'll hand you the key.'

Conrad Morgan gave a sigh of defeat. 'You've got a deal.'

'Thank you,' Tracy said cheerfully. 'It's been a pleasure doing business with you.'

NINETEEN

Daniel Cooper was already aware of what the meeting in J. J. Reynolds's office that morning was about, for all the company's investigators had been sent a memo the day before regarding the Lois Bellamy burglary that had taken place a week earlier. Daniel Cooper loathed conferences. He was too impatient to sit around listening to stupid chatter.

He arrived in J. J. Reynolds's office forty-five minutes late, while Reynolds was in the middle of a speech.

'Nice of you to drop by,' J. J. Reynolds said sarcastically. There was no response. *It's a waste of time*, Reynolds decided. Cooper did not understand sarcasm – or anything else, as far as Reynolds was concerned. Except how to catch criminals. There, he had to admit, the man was a goddamned genius.

Seated in the office were three of the agency's top investigators: David Swift, Robert Schiffer, and Jerry Davis.

'You've all read the report on the Bellamy burglary,' Reynolds said, 'but something new has been added. It turns out that Lois Bellamy is a cousin of the police commissioner. He's raising holy hell.'

'What are the police doing?' Davis asked.

'Hiding from the press. Can't blame them. The investigating officers acted like the Keystone Kops. They actually *talked* to the burglar they caught in the house and let her get away.'

'Then they should have a good description of her,' Swift suggested.

'They have a good description of her nightgown,' Reynolds retorted witheringly. 'They were so goddamned impressed with her figure that their brains melted. They don't even know the colour of her hair. She wore some kind of curler cap, and her face was covered with a mudpack. Their description is of a woman somewhere in her middle twenties, with a fantastic ass and tits. There's not one single clue. We have no information to go on. Nothing.'

Daniel Cooper spoke for the first time. 'Yes, we have.'

They all turned to look at him, with varying degrees of dislike.

'What are you talking about?' Reynolds asked.

'I know who she is.'

When Cooper had read the memo the morning before, he had decided to take a look at the Bellamy house, as a logical first step. To Daniel Cooper, logic was the orderliness of God's mind, the basic solution to every problem, and to apply logic, one always started at the beginning. Cooper drove out to the Bellamy estate in Long Island, took one look at it, and, without getting out of his car, turned around and drove back to Manhattan. He had learned all he needed to know. The house was isolated, and there was no public transportation nearby, which meant that the burglar could have reached the house only by car.

He was explaining his reasoning to the men assembled in Reynolds's office. 'Since she probably would have been reluctant to use her own car, which could have been traced, the vehicle either had to be stolen or rented. I decided to try the rental agencies first. I assumed that she would have rented the car in Manhattan, where it would be easier for her to cover her trail.'

Jerry Davis was not impressed. 'You've got to be kidding, Cooper. There must be thousands of cars a day rented in Manhattan.'

Cooper ignored the interruption. 'All car-rental operations are computerized. Relatively few cars are rented by women. I checked them all out. The lady in question went to Budget Rent a Car at Pier Sixty-one on West twenty-third Street, rented a Chevy Caprice at eight P.M. the night of the burglary, and returned it to the office at two A.M.'

'How do you know it was the getaway car?' Reynolds asked sceptically.

Cooper was getting bored with the stupid

questions. 'I checked the elapsed mileage. It's thirty-two miles to the Lois Bellamy estate and another thirty-two miles back. That checks exactly with the odometer on the Caprice. The car was rented in the name of Ellen Branch.'

'A phony,' David Swift surmised.

'Right. Her real name is Tracy Whitney.'

They were all staring at him. 'How the hell do you know that?' Schiffer demanded.

'She gave a false name and address, but she had to sign a rental agreement. I took the original down to One Police Plaza and had them run it through for fingerprints. They matched the prints of Tracy Whitney. She served time at the Southern Louisiana Penitentiary for Women. If you remember, I talked to her about a year ago about a stolen Renoir.'

'I remember,' Reynolds nodded. 'You said then that she was innocent.'

'She was – then. She's not innocent any more. She pulled the Bellamy job.'

The little bastard had done it again! And he had made it seem so simple. Reynolds tried not to sound grudging. 'That's – that's fine work, Cooper. Really fine work. Let's nail her. We'll have the police pick her up and –'

'On what charge?' Cooper asked mildly. 'Renting a car? The police can't identify her, and there's not a shred of evidence against her.'

'What are we supposed to do?' Schiffer asked. 'Let her walk away scot-free?'

'This time, yes,' Cooper said. 'But I know who

she is now. She'll try something again. And when she does, I'll catch her.'

The meeting was finally over. Cooper desperately wanted a shower. He took out a little black book and wrote in it very carefully: TRACY WHITNEY.

TWENTY

It's time to begin my new life, Tracy decided. *But what kind of life? I've gone from an innocent, naïve victim to a . . . what? A thief – that's what.* She thought of Joe Romano and Anthony Orsatti and Perry Pope and Judge Lawrence. *No. An avenger. That's what I've become. And an adventuress, perhaps.* She had outwitted the police, two professional con artists, and a double-crossing jeweller. She thought of Ernestine and Amy and felt a pang. On an impulse, Tracy went to F.A.O. Schwarz and bought a puppet theatre, complete with half a dozen characters, and had it mailed to Amy. The card read: SOME NEW FRIENDS FOR YOU. MISS YOU. LOVE TRACY.

Next she visited a furrier on Madison Avenue and bought a blue fox boa for Ernestine and mailed it with a money order for two hundred dollars. The card simply read: THANKS, ERNIE. TRACY.

All my debts are paid now, Tracy thought. It

was a good feeling. She was free to go anywhere she liked, do anything she pleased.

She celebrated her independence by checking into a Tower Suite in The Helmsley Palace Hotel. From her forty-seventh-floor living room, she could look down at St Patrick's Cathedral and see the George Washington Bridge in the distance. Only a few miles in another direction was the dreary place she had recently lived in. *Never again*, Tracy swore.

She opened the bottle of champagne that the management had sent up and sat sipping it, watching the sun set over the skyscrapers of Manhattan. By the time the moon had risen, Tracy had made up her mind. She was going to London. She was ready for all the wonderful things life had to offer. *I've paid my dues*, Tracy thought. *I deserve some happiness.*

She lay in bed and turned on the late television news. Two men were being interviewed. Boris Melnikov was a short, stocky Russian, dressed in an ill-fitting brown suit, and Pietr Negulesco was his opposite, tall and thin and elegant-looking. Tracy wondered what the two men could possibly have in common.

'Where is the chess match going to be held?' the news anchorman asked.

'At Sochi, on the beautiful Black Sea,' Melnikov replied.

'You are both international grand masters, and this one has created quite a stir, gentlemen. In your previous matches you have taken the title from each other, and your last one was a draw. Mr Negulesco, Mr Melnikov currently holds the title. Do you think you will be able to take it away from him again?'

'Absolutely,' the Romanian replied.

'He has no chance,' the Russian retorted.

Tracy knew nothing about chess, but there was an arrogance about both men that she found distasteful. She pressed the remote-control button that turned off the television set and went to sleep.

Early the following morning Tracy stopped at a travel agency and reserved a suite on the Signal Deck of the *Queen Elizabeth II*. She was as excited as a child about her first trip abroad, and spent the next three days buying clothes and luggage.

On the morning of the sailing Tracy hired a limousine to drive her to the pier. When she arrived at Pier 90, Berth 3, at West Fifty-fifth and Twelfth Avenue, where the *QE II* was docked, it was crowded with photographers and television reporters, and for a moment, Tracy was panic-stricken. Then she realized they were interviewing the two men posturing at the foot of the gangplank – Melnikov and Negulesco, the international grand masters. Tracy brushed past them, showed her passport to a ship's officer at the gangplank, and walked up onto the ship. On deck, a steward looked at Tracy's ticket and directed her to her stateroom. It was a lovely suite, with a private terrace. It had been ridiculously expensive, but Tracy decided it was going to be worth it.

She unpacked and then wandered along the corridor. In almost every cabin there were farewell parties going on, with laughter and champagne and conversation. She felt a sudden ache of loneliness. There was no one to see her off, no one for her to care about, no one who cared about her. *That's not true*, Tracy told herself. *Big Bertha wants me*. And she laughed aloud.

She made her way up to the Boat Deck and had no idea of the admiring glances of the men and the envious stares of the women cast her way.

Tracy heard the sound of a deep-throated boat whistle and calls of 'All ashore who's going ashore', and she was filled with a sudden excitement. She was sailing into a completely unknown future. She felt the huge ship shudder as the tugs started to pull it out of the harbour, and she stood among the passengers on the Boat Deck, watching the Statue of Liberty slide out of sight, and then she went exploring.

The *QE II* was a city, more than nine hundred feet long and thirteen storeys high. It had four restaurants, six bars, two ballrooms, two nightclubs, and a 'Golden Door Spa at Sea'. There were scores of shops, four swimming pools, a gymnasium, a golf driving range, a jogging track. *I may never want to leave the ship*, Tracy marvelled.

She had reserved a table upstairs in the Princess Grill, which was smaller and more elegant than the main dining room. She barely had been seated when a familiar voice said, 'Well, hello there!'

She looked up, and there stood Tom Bowers, the bogus FBI man. *Oh, no. I don't deserve this*, Tracy thought.

'What a pleasant surprise. Do you mind if I join you?'

'Very much.'

He slid into the chair across from her and gave her an engaging smile. 'We might as well be friends. After all, we're both here for the same reason, aren't we?'

Tracy had no idea what he was talking about. 'Look, Mr Bowers –'

'Stevens,' he said easily. 'Jeff Stevens.'

'Whatever.' Tracy started to rise.

'Wait. I'd like to explain about the last time we met.'

'There's nothing to explain,' Tracy assured him. 'An idiot child could have figured it out – and did.'

'I owed Conrad Morgan a favour.' He grinned ruefully. 'I'm afraid he wasn't too happy with me.'

There was that same easy, boyish charm that had completely taken her in before. *For God's sake, Dennis, it isn't necessary to put cuffs on her. She's not going to run away . . .*

She said hostilely, 'I'm not too happy with you, either. What are you doing aboard this ship? Shouldn't you be on a riverboat?'

He laughed. 'With Maximilian Pierpont on board, this *is* a riverboat.'

'Who?'

He looked at her in surprise. 'Come on. You mean you really don't know?'

'Know what?'

'Max Pierpont is one of the richest men in the world. His hobby is forcing competitive companies out of business. He loves slow horses and fast women, and he owns a lot of both. He's the last of the big-time spenders.'

'And you intend to relieve him of some of his excess wealth.'

'Quite a lot of it, as a matter of fact.' He was eyeing her speculatively. 'Do you know what you and I should do?'

'I certainly do, Mr Stevens. We should say goodbye.'

And he sat there watching as Tracy got up and walked out of the dining room.

She had dinner in her cabin. As she ate, she wondered what ill fate had placed Jeff Stevens in her path again. She wanted to forget the fear she had felt on that train when she thought she was under arrest. *Well, I'm not going to let him spoil this trip. I'll simply ignore him.*

After dinner Tracy went up on deck. It was a fantastic night, with a magic canopy of stars sprayed against a velvet sky. She was standing at the rail in the moonlight, watching the soft phosphorescence of the waves and listening to the sounds of the night wind, when he moved up beside her.

'You have no idea how beautiful you look

standing there. Do you believe in shipboard romances?'

'Definitely. What I don't believe in is *you*.' She started to walk away.

'Wait. I have some news for you. I just found out that Max Pierpont isn't on board, after all. He cancelled at the last minute.'

'Oh, what a shame. You wasted your fare.'

'Not necessarily.' He eyed her speculatively. 'How would you like to pick up a small fortune on this voyage?'

The man is unbelievable. 'Unless you have a submarine or a helicopter in your pocket, I don't think you'll get away with robbing anyone on this ship.'

'Who said anything about robbing anyone? Have you ever heard of Boris Melnikov or Pietr Negulesco?'

'What if I have?'

'Melnikov and Negulesco are on their way to Russia for a championship match. If I can arrange for you to play the two of them,' Jeff said earnestly, 'we can win a lot of money. It's a perfect setup.'

Tracy was looking at him incredulously. 'If you can arrange for *me* to play the two of them? *That's* your perfect setup?'

'Uh-huh. How do you like it?'

'I love it. There's just one tiny hitch.'

'What's that?'

'I don't play chess.'

He smiled benignly. 'No problem. I'll teach you.'

'You're insane,' Tracy said. 'If you want some

advice, you'll find yourself a good psychiatrist. Good night.'

The following morning Tracy literally bumped into Boris Melnikov. He was jogging on the Boat Deck, and as Tracy rounded a corner, he ran into her, knocking her off her feet.

'Watch where you're going,' he growled. And he kept running.

Tracy sat on the deck, looking after him. 'Of all the rude –!' She stood up and brushed herself off.

A steward approached. 'Are you hurt, miss? I saw him –'

'No, I'm fine, thank you.'

Nobody was going to spoil this trip.

When Tracy returned to her cabin, there were six messages to call Mr Jeff Stevens. She ignored them. In the afternoon she swam and read and had a massage, and by the time she went into the bar that evening to have a cocktail before dinner, she was feeling wonderful. Her euphoria was short-lived. Pietr Negulesco, the Romanian, was seated at the bar. When he saw Tracy, he stood up and said, 'May I buy you a drink, beautiful lady?'

Tracy hesitated, then smiled. 'Why, yes, thank you.'

'What would you like?'

'A vodka and tonic, please.'

Negulesco gave the order to the barman and turned back to Tracy. 'I'm Pietr Negulesco.'

'I know.'

'Of course. Everyone knows me. I am the greatest chess player in the world. In my country, I am a national hero.' He leaned close to Tracy, put a hand on her knee, and said, 'I am also a great fuck.'

Tracy thought she had misunderstood him. 'What?'

'I am a great fuck.'

Her first reaction was to throw her drink in his face, but she controlled herself. She had a better idea. 'Excuse me,' she said, 'I have to meet a friend.'

She went to look for Jeff Stevens. She found him in the Princess Grill, but as Tracy started towards his table, she saw that he was dining with a lovely looking blonde with a spectacular figure, dressed in an evening gown that looked as if it had been painted on. *I should have known better*, Tracy thought. She turned and headed down the corridor. A moment later Jeff was at her side.

'Tracy . . . did you want to see me?'

'I don't want to take you away from your . . . dinner.'

'She's dessert,' Jeff said lightly. 'What can I do for you?'

'Were you serious about Melnikov and Negulesco?'

'Absolutely. Why?'

'I think they both need a lesson in manners.'

'So do I. And we'll make money while we teach them.'

'Good. What's your plan?'

'You're going to beat them at chess.'

'I'm serious.'

'So am I.'

'I told you, I don't play chess. I don't know a pawn from a king. I –'

'Don't worry,' Jeff promised her. 'A couple of lessons from me, and you'll slaughter them both.'

'*Both?*'

'Oh, didn't I tell you? You're going to play them simultaneously.'

Jeff was seated next to Boris Melnikov in the Double Down Piano Bar.

'The woman is a fantastic chess player,' Jeff confided to Melnikov. 'She's travelling incognito.'

The Russian grunted. 'Women know nothing about chess. They cannot think.'

'This one does. She says she could beat you easily.'

Boris Melnikov laughed aloud. '*Nobody* beats me – easily or not.'

'She's willing to bet you ten thousand dollars that she can play you and Pietr Negulesco at the same time and get a draw with at least one of you.'

Boris Melnikov choked on his drink. '*What!* That's – that's ridiculous! Play *two* of us at the same time? This – this female *amateur*?'

'That's right. For ten thousand dollars each.'

'I should do it just to teach the stupid idiot a lesson.'

'If you win, the money will be deposited in any country you choose.'

A covetous expression flitted across the Russian's face. 'I've never even heard of this person. And to play the *two* of us! My God, she must be insane.'

'She has the twenty thousand dollars in cash.'

'What nationality is she?'

'American.'

'Ah, that explains it. All rich Americans are crazy, especially their women.'

Jeff started to rise. 'Well, I guess she'll just have to play Pietr Negulesco alone.'

'*Negulesco* is going to play her?'

'Yes, didn't I tell you? She wanted to play the two of you, but if you're afraid . . .'

'*Afraid!* Boris Melnikov *afraid*?' His voice was a roar. 'I will *destroy* her. When is this ridiculous match to take place?'

'She thought perhaps Friday night. The last night out.'

Boris Melnikov was thinking hard. 'The best two out of three?'

'No. Only one game.'

'For ten thousand dollars?'

'That is correct.'

The Russian sighed. 'I do not have that much cash with me.'

'No problem,' Jeff assured him. 'All Miss Whitney really wants is the glory of playing the great Boris Melnikov. If you lose, you give her a personally autographed picture. If you win, you get ten thousand dollars.'

'Who holds the stakes?' There was a sharp note of suspicion in his voice.

'The ship's purser.'

'Very well,' Melnikov decided. 'Friday night. We will start at ten o'clock, promptly.'

'She'll be so pleased,' Jeff assured him.

The following morning Jeff was talking to Pietr Negulesco in the gymnasium, where the two men were working out.

'She's an American?' Pietr Negulesco said. 'I should have known. All Americans are cuckoo.'

'She's a great chess player.'

Pietr Negulesco made a gesture of contempt. 'Great is not good enough. *Best* is what counts. And I am the best.'

'That's why she's so eager to play against you. If you lose, you give her an autographed picture. If you win, you get ten thousand dollars in cash . . .'

'Negulesco does not play amateurs.'

'. . . deposited in any country you like.'

'Out of the question.'

'Well, then, I guess she'll have to play only Boris Melnikov.'

'*What?* Are you saying Melnikov has agreed to play against this woman?'

'Of course. But she was hoping to play you both at once.'

'I've never heard of anything so – so –' Negulesco sputtered, at a loss for words. 'The arrogance! Who is she that she thinks she can defeat the two top chess masters in the world? She must have escaped from some lunatic asylum.'

'She's a little erratic,' Jeff confessed, 'but her money is good. All cash.'

'You said ten thousand dollars for defeating her?'

'That's right.'

'And Boris Melnikov gets the same amount?'

'*If* he defeats her.'

Pietr Negulesco grinned. 'Oh, he will defeat her. And so will I.'

'Just between us, I wouldn't be a bit surprised.'

'Who will hold the stakes?'

'The ship's purser.'

Why should Melnikov be the only one to take money from this woman? thought Pietr Negulesco.

'My friend, you have a deal. Where and when?'

'Friday night. Ten o'clock. The Queen's Room.'

Pietr Negulesco smiled wolfishly. 'I will be there.'

'You mean they *agreed*?' Tracy cried.

'That's right.'

'I'm going to be sick.'

'I'll get you a cold towel.'

Jeff hurried into the bathroom of Tracy's suite, ran cold water on a towel, and brought it back to her. She was lying on the chaise longue. He placed the towel on her forehead. 'How does that feel?'

'Terrible. I think I have a migraine.'

'Have you ever had a migraine before?'

'No.'

'Then you don't have one now. Listen to me, Tracy, it's perfectly natural to be nervous before something like this.'

She leapt up and flung down the towel. 'Something like *this*? There's never *been* anything like this! I'm playing two international master chess players with *one* chess lesson from you and –'

'Two,' Jeff corrected her. 'You have a natural talent for chess.'

'My God, why did I ever let you talk me into this?'

'Because we're going to make a lot of money.'

'I don't want to make a lot of money,' Tracy wailed. 'I want this boat to sink. Why couldn't this be the *Titanic*?'

'Now, just stay calm,' Jeff said soothingly. 'It's going to be –'

'It's going to be a *disaster*! Everyone on this ship is going to be watching.'

'That's exactly the point, isn't it?' Jeff beamed.

Jeff had made all the arrangements with the ship's purser. He had given the purser the stakes to hold – $20,000 in traveller's cheques – and asked him to set up two chess tables for Friday evening. The word spread rapidly throughout the ship, and passengers kept approaching Jeff to ask if the matches were actually going to take place.

'Absolutely,' Jeff assured all who enquired. 'It's incredible. Poor Miss Whitney believes she can win. In fact, she's betting on it.'

'I wonder,' a passenger asked, 'if I might place a small bet?'

'Certainly. As much money as you like. Miss Whitney is asking only ten-to-one odds.'

A million-to-one odds would have made more sense. From the moment the first bet was accepted, the floodgates opened. It seemed that everyone on board, including the engine-room crew and the ship's officers, wanted to place bets on the game. The amounts varied from five dollars to five thousand dollars and every single bet was on the Russian and the Romanian.

The suspicious purser reported to the captain. 'I've never seen anything like it, sir. It's a stampede. Nearly all the passengers have placed wagers. I must be holding two hundred thousand dollars in bets.'

The captain studied him thoughtfully. 'You say Miss Whitney is going to play Melnikov and Negulesco at the same time?'

'Yes, Captain.'

'Have you verified that the two men are really Pietr Negulesco and Boris Melnikov?'

'Oh, yes, of course, sir.'

'There's no chance they would deliberately throw the chess game, is there?'

'Not with *their* egos. I think they'd rather die first. And if they lost to this woman, that's probably exactly what would happen to them when they got home.'

The captain ran his fingers through his hair, a

puzzled frown on his face. 'Do you know anything about Miss Whitney or this Mr Stevens?'

'Not a thing, sir. As far as I can determine, they're travelling separately.'

The captain made his decision. 'It smells like some kind of con game, and ordinarily I would put a stop to it. However, I happen to be a bit of an expert myself, and if there was one thing I'd stake my life on, it's the fact that there is *no* way to cheat at chess. Let the match go on.' He walked over to his desk and withdrew a black leather wallet. 'Put down fifty pounds for me. On the masters.'

By 9:00 Friday evening the Queen's Room was packed with passengers from first class, those who had sneaked in from second and third class, and the ship's officers and members of the crew who were off duty. At Jeff Stevens's request, two rooms had been set up for the tournament. One table was in the centre of the Queen's Room, and the other table was in the adjoining salon. Curtains had been drawn to separate the two rooms.

'So that the players aren't distracted by each other,' Jeff explained. 'And we would like the spectators to remain in whichever room they choose.'

Velvet ropes had been placed around the tables to keep the crowds back. The spectators were about to witness something they were sure they would never see again. They knew nothing about the beautiful young American woman, except that it would be impossible for her – or anyone else –

to play the great Negulesco and Melnikov simultaneously and obtain a draw with either of them.

Jeff introduced Tracy to the two grand masters shortly before the game was to begin. Tracy looked like a Grecian painting in a muted green chiffon Galanos gown which left one shoulder bare. Her eyes seemed tremendous in her pale face.

Pietr Negulesco looked her over carefully. 'Have you won all the national tournaments you have played in?' he asked.

'Yes,' Tracy replied truthfully.

He shrugged. 'I have never heard of you.'

Boris Melnikov was equally rude. 'You Americans do not know what to do with your money,' he said. 'I wish to thank you in advance. My winnings will make my family very happy.'

Tracy's eyes were green jade. 'You haven't won, yet, Mr Melnikov.'

Melnikov's laugh boomed out through the room. 'My dear lady, I don't know who you are, but I know who *I* am. I am the great Boris Melnikov.'

It was 10:00. Jeff looked around and saw that both salons had filled up with spectators. 'It's time for the match to start.'

Tracy sat down across the table from Melnikov and wondered for the hundredth time how she had got herself into this.

'There's nothing to it,' Jeff had assured her. 'Trust me.'

And like a fool she had trusted him. *I must have been out of my mind*, Tracy thought. She was playing the two greatest chess players in the world, and she knew nothing about the game, except what Jeff had spent four hours teaching her.

The big moment had arrived. Tracy felt her legs trembling. Melnikov turned to the expectant crowd and grinned. He made a hissing noise at a steward. 'Bring me a brandy. Napoleon.'

'In order to be fair to everyone,' Jeff said to Melnikov, 'I suggest you play the white so that you go first, and in the game with Mr Negulesco, Miss Whitney will play the white and she will go first.'

Both grand masters agreed.

While the audience stood hushed, Boris Melnikov reached across the board and played the queen's gambit decline opening, moving his queen's pawn two squares. *I'm not simply going to beat this woman. I'm going to crush her.*

He glanced up at Tracy. She studied the board, nodded, and stood up, without moving a piece. A steward cleared the way through the crowd as Tracy walked into the second salon, where Pietr Negulesco was seated at a table waiting for her. There were at least a hundred people crowding the room as Tracy took her seat opposite Negulesco.

'Ah, my little pigeon. Have you defeated Boris yet?' Pietr Negulesco laughed uproariously at his joke.

'I'm working on it, Mr Negulesco,' Tracy said quietly.

She reached forward and moved her white queen's pawn two squares. Negulesco looked up at her and grinned. He had arranged for a massage in one hour, but he planned to finish this game before then. He reached down and moved his black queen's pawn two squares. Tracy studied the board a moment, then rose. The steward escorted her back to Boris Melnikov.

Tracy sat down at the table and moved her black queen's pawn two squares. In the background she saw Jeff's almost imperceptible nod of approval.

Without hesitation, Boris Melnikov moved his white queen's bishop pawn two squares.

Two minutes later, at Negulesco's table, Tracy moved her white queen's bishop two squares.

Negulesco played his king's pawn square.

Tracy rose and returned to the room where Boris Melnikov was waiting. Tracy played her king's pawn square.

So! She is not a complete amateur, Melnikov thought in surprise. *Let us see what she does with this*. He played his queen's knight to queen's bishop 3.

Tracy watched his move, nodded, and returned to Negulesco, where she copied Melnikov's move.

Negulesco moved the queen's bishop pawn two squares, and Tracy went back to Melnikov and repeated Negulesco's move.

With growing astonishment, the two grand masters realized they were up against a brilliant opponent. No matter how clever their moves, this amateur managed to counteract them.

Because they were separated, Boris Melnikov and

Pietr Negulesco had no idea that, in effect, they were playing against each other. Every move that Melnikov made with Tracy, Tracy repeated with Negulesco. And when Negulesco countered with a move, Tracy used that move against Melnikov.

By the time the grand masters entered the middle game, they were no longer smug. They were fighting for their reputations. They paced the floor while they contemplated moves and puffed furiously on cigarettes. Tracy appeared to be the only calm one.

In the beginning, in order to end the game quickly, Melnikov had tried a knight's sacrifice to allow his white bishop to put pressure on the black king's side. Tracy had carried the move to Negulesco. Negulesco had examined the move carefully, then refuted the sacrifice by covering his exposed side, and when Negulesco had sacked a bishop to advance a rook to white's seventh rank, Melnikov had refuted it before the black rook could damage his own structure.

There was no stopping Tracy. The game had been going on for four hours, and not one person in either audience had stirred.

Every grand master carries in his head hundreds of games played by other grand masters. It was as this particular match was going into the end game that both Melnikov and Negulesco recognized the hallmark of the other.

The bitch, Melnikov thought. *She has studied with Negulesco. He has tutored her.*

And Negulesco thought, *She is Melnikov's protégée. The bastard has taught her his game.*

The harder they fought Tracy, the more they came to realize there was simply no way they could beat her. The match was appearing drawish.

In the sixth hour of play, at 4:00 A.M., when the players had reached the end game, the pieces on each board had been reduced to three pawns, one rook and a king. There was no way for either side to win. Melnikov studied the board for a long time, then took a deep, choked breath and said, 'I offer a draw.'

Over the hubbub, Tracy said, 'I accept.'

The crowd went wild.

Tracy rose and made her way through the crowd into the next room. As she started to take her seat, Negulesco, in a strangled voice said, 'I offer a draw.'

And the uproar from the other room was repeated. The crowd could not believe what it had just witnessed. A woman had come out of nowhere to simultaneously stalemate the two greatest chess masters in the world.

Jeff appeared at Tracy's side. 'Come on,' he grinned. 'We both need a drink.'

When they left, Boris Melnikov and Pietr Negulesco were still slumped in their chairs, mindlessly staring at their boards.

Tracy and Jeff sat at a table for two in the Upper Deck bar.

'You were beautiful,' Jeff laughed. 'Did you

notice the look on Melnikov's face? I thought he was going to have a heart attack.'

'I thought *I* was going to have a heart attack,' Tracy said. 'How much did we win?'

'About two hundred thousand dollars. We'll collect it from the purser in the morning when we dock at Southampton. I'll meet you for breakfast in the dining room.'

'Fine.'

'I think I'll turn in now. Let me walk you to your stateroom.'

'I'm not ready to go to bed yet, Jeff. I'm too excited. You go ahead.'

'You were a champion,' Jeff told her. He leaned over and kissed her lightly on the cheek. 'Good night, Tracy.'

'Good night, Jeff.'

She watched him leave. Go to sleep? Impossible! It had been one of the most fantastic nights of her life. The Russian and the Romanian had been so sure of themselves, so arrogant. Jeff had said, 'Trust me', and she had. She had no illusions about what he was. He was a con artist. He was bright and amusing and clever, easy to be with. But of course she could never be seriously interested in him.

Jeff was on the way to his stateroom when he encountered one of the ship's officers.

'Good show, Mr Stevens. The word about the match has already gone out over the wireless. I imagine the press will be meeting you both at

Southampton. Are you Miss Whitney's manager?'

'No, we're just shipboard acquaintances,' Jeff said easily, but his mind was racing. If he and Tracy were linked together, it would look like a setup. There could even be an investigation. He decided to collect the money before any suspicions were aroused.

Jeff wrote a note to Tracy. HAVE PICKED UP MONEY AND WILL MEET YOU FOR A CELEBRATION BREAKFAST AT THE SAVOY HOTEL. YOU WERE MAGNIFICENT. JEFF. He sealed it in an envelope and handed it to a steward. 'Please see that Miss Whitney gets this first thing in the morning.'

'Yes, sir.'

Jeff headed for the purser's office.

'Sorry to bother you,' Jeff apologized, 'but we'll be docking in a few hours, and I know how busy you're going to be, so I wondered whether you'd mind paying me off now?'

'No trouble at all,' the purser smiled. 'Your young lady is really wizard, isn't she?'

'She certainly is.'

'If you don't mind my asking, Mr Stevens, where in the world did she learn to play chess like that?'

Jeff leaned close and confided, 'I heard she studied with Bobby Fischer.'

The purser took two large manila envelopes out of the safe. 'This is a lot of cash to carry around. Would you like me to give you a cheque for this amount?'

'No, don't bother. The cash will be fine,' Jeff assured him. 'I wonder if you could do me a favour? The mail boat comes out to meet the ship before it docks, doesn't it?'

'Yes, sir. We're expecting it at six A.M.'

'I'd appreciate it if you could arrange for me to leave on the mail boat. My mother is seriously ill, and I'd like to get to her before it's' – his voice dropped – 'before it's too late.'

'Oh, I'm dreadfully sorry, Mr Stevens. Of course I can handle that for you. I'll make the arrangements with customs.'

At 6:15 A.M. Jeff Stevens, with the two envelopes carefully stashed away in his suitcase, climbed down the ship's ladder into the mail boat. He turned to take one last look at the outline of the huge ship towering above him. The passengers on the liner were sound asleep. Jeff would be on the dock long before the *QE II* landed. 'It was a beautiful voyage,' Jeff said to one of the crewmen on the mail boat.

'Yes, it was, wasn't it?' a voice agreed.

Jeff turned around. Tracy was seated on a coil of rope, her hair blowing softly around her face.

'Tracy! What are you doing here?'

'What do you think I'm doing?'

He saw the expression on her face. 'Wait a minute! You didn't think I was going to run out on you?'

'Why would I think that?' Her tone was bitter.

'Tracy, I left a note for you. I was going to meet you at the Savoy and –'

'Of course you were,' she said cuttingly. 'You never give up, do you?'

He looked at her, and there was nothing more for him to say.

In Tracy's suite at the Savoy, she watched carefully as Jeff counted out the money. 'Your share comes to one hundred and one thousand dollars.'

'Thank you.' Her tone was icy.

Jeff said, 'You know, you're wrong about me, Tracy. I wish you'd give me a chance to explain. Will you have dinner with me tonight?'

She hesitated, then added. 'All right.'

'Good. I'll pick you up at eight o'clock.'

When Jeff Stevens arrived at the hotel that evening and asked for Tracy, the room clerk said, 'I'm sorry, sir. Miss Whitney checked out early this afternoon. She left no forwarding address.'

TWENTY-ONE

It was the handwritten invitation, Tracy decided later, that changed her life.

After collecting her share of the money from Jeff Stevens, Tracy checked out of the Savoy and moved into 47 Park Street, a quiet, semi-residential hotel with large, pleasant rooms and superb service.

On her second day in London the invitation was delivered to her suite by the hall porter. It was written in a fine, copperplate handwriting: 'A mutual friend has suggested that it might be advantageous for us to become acquainted. Won't you join me for tea at the Ritz this afternoon at 4:00? If you will forgive the cliché, I will be wearing a red carnation.' It was signed 'Gunther Hartog'.

Tracy had never heard of him. Her first inclination was to ignore the note, but her curiosity got the better of her, and at 4:15 she was at the entrance of the elegant dining hall of the Ritz Hotel. She noticed him immediately. He was in his sixties, Tracy guessed, an interesting-looking man with a lean, intellectual face. His skin was smooth and clear, almost translucent. He was dressed in an expensively tailored grey suit and wore a red carnation in his lapel.

As Tracy walked towards his table, he rose and bowed slightly. 'Thank you for accepting my invitation.'

He seated her with an old-fashioned gallantry that Tracy found attractive. He seemed to belong to another world. Tracy could not imagine what on earth he wanted with her.

'I came because I was curious,' Tracy confessed, 'but are you sure you haven't confused me with some other Tracy Whitney?'

Gunther Hartog smiled. 'From what I have heard, there is only one Tracy Whitney.'

'What exactly have you heard?'

'Shall we discuss that over tea?'

Tea consisted of finger sandwiches, filled with chopped egg, salmon, cucumber, watercress and chicken. There were hot scones with clotted cream and jam, and freshly made pastries, accompanied by Twinings tea. As they ate, they talked.

'Your note mentioned a mutual friend,' Tracy began.

'Conrad Morgan. I do business with him from time to time.'

I did business with him once, Tracy thought grimly. *And he tried to cheat me.*

'He's a great admirer of yours,' Gunther Hartog was saying.

Tracy looked at her host more closely. He had the bearing of an aristocrat and the look of wealth. *What does he want with me?* Tracy wondered again. She decided to let him pursue the subject, but there was no further mention of Conrad Morgan or of what possible mutual benefit there could be between Gunther Hartog and Tracy Whitney.

Tracy found the meeting enjoyable and intriguing. Gunther told her about his background. 'I was born in Munich. My father was a banker. He was wealthy, and I'm afraid I grew up rather spoiled, surrounded by beautiful paintings and antiques. My mother was Jewish, and when Hitler came to power, my father refused to desert my mother, and so he was stripped of everything. They were both killed in the bombings. Friends smuggled me out of Germany to Switzerland, and when the war was over, I decided not to return to Germany. I moved to London and opened a small antique shop on Mount Street. I hope that you will visit it one day.'

That's what this is all about, Tracy thought in surprise. *He wants to sell me something.*

As it turned out, she was wrong.

As Gunther Hartog was paying the bill, he said, casually, 'I have a little country house in Hampshire. I'm having a few friends down for the weekend, and I'd be delighted if you would join us.'

Tracy hesitated. The man was a complete

stranger, and she still had no idea what he wanted from her. She decided she had nothing to lose.

The weekend turned out to be fascinating. Gunther Hartog's 'little country house' was a beautiful seventeenth-century manor home on a thirty-acre estate. Gunther was a widower, and except for his servants, he lived alone. He took Tracy on a tour of the grounds. There was a barn stabling half a dozen horses, and a yard where he raised chickens and pigs.

'That's so we'll never go hungry,' he said gravely. 'Now, let me show you my real hobby.'

He led Tracy to a cote full of pigeons. 'These are homing pigeons.' Gunther's voice was filled with pride. 'Look at these little beauties. See that slate-grey one over there? That's Margo.' He picked her up and held her. 'You really are a dreadful girl, do you know that? She bullies the others, but she's the brightest.' He gently smoothed the feathers over the small head and carefully set her down.

The colours of the birds were spectacular. There was a variety of blue-black, blue-grey with checked patterns, and silver.

'But no white ones,' Tracy noticed.

'Homing pigeons are never white,' Gunther explained, 'because white feathers come off too easily, and when pigeons are homing, they fly at an average of forty miles an hour.'

Tracy watched Gunther as he fed the birds a special racing feed with added vitamins.

'They are an amazing species,' Gunther said. 'Do you know they can find their way home from over five hundred miles away?'

'That's fascinating.'

The guests were equally fascinating. There was a cabinet minister, with his wife; an earl; a general and his girlfriend; and the Maharani of Morvi, a very attractive, friendly young woman. 'Please call me V. J.,' she said, in an almost unaccented voice. She wore a deep-red sari shot with golden threads, and the most beautiful jewels Tracy had ever seen.

'I keep most of my jewellery in a vault,' V. J. explained. 'There are so many robberies these days.'

On Sunday afternoon, shortly before Tracy was to return to London, Gunther invited her into his study. They sat across from each other over a tea tray. As Tracy poured the tea into the wafer-thin Belleek cups, she said, 'I don't know why you invited me here, Gunther, but whatever the reason, I've had a wonderful time.'

'I'm pleased, Tracy.' Then, after a moment, he continued. 'I've been observing you.'

'I see.'

'Do you have any plans for the future?'

She hesitated. 'No. I haven't decided what I'm going to do yet.'

'I think we could work well together.'

'You mean in your antique shop?'

He laughed. 'No, my dear. It would be a shame

to waste your talents. You see, I know about your escapade with Conrad Morgan. You handled it brilliantly.'

'Gunther . . . all that's behind me.'

'But what's ahead of you? You said you have no plans. You must think about your future. Whatever money you have is surely going to run out one day. I'm suggesting a partnership. I travel in very affluent, international circles. I attend charity balls and hunting parties and yachting parties. I know the comings and goings of the rich.'

'I don't see what that has to do with me –'

'I can introduce you into that golden circle. And I do mean golden, Tracy. I can supply you with information about fabulous jewels and paintings, and how you can safely acquire them. I can dispose of them privately. You would be balancing the ledgers of people who have become wealthy at the expense of others. Everything would be divided evenly between us. What do you say?'

'I say no.'

He studied her thoughtfully. 'I see. You will call me if you change your mind?'

'I won't change my mind, Gunther.'

Late that afternoon Tracy returned to London.

Tracy adored London. She dined at Le Gavroche and Bill Bentley's and Coin du Feu, and went to Drones after the theatre, for real American hamburgers and hot chili. She went to the National Theatre and the Royal Opera House and attended auctions at Christie's and Sotheby's. She shopped at Harrods, and Fortnum and Mason's, and browsed for books at Hatchards and Foyles, and W. H. Smith. She hired a car and driver and spent a memorable weekend at the Chewton Glen Hotel in Hampshire, on the fringe of the New Forest, where the setting was spectacular and the service impeccable.

But all these things were expensive. *Whatever money you have is sure to run out some day.* Gunther Hartog was right. Her money was not going to last forever, and Tracy realized she would have to make plans for the future.

She was invited back for more weekends at Gunther's country home, and she thoroughly enjoyed each visit and delighted in Gunther's company.

One Sunday evening at dinner a member of Parliament turned to Tracy and said, 'I've never met a real Texan, Miss Whitney. What are they like?'

Tracy went into a wicked imitation of a noveau riche Texas dowager and had the company roaring with laughter.

Later, when Tracy and Gunther were alone, he asked, 'How would you like to make a small fortune doing that imitation?'

'I'm not an actress, Gunther.'

'You underestimate yourself. There's a jewellery firm in London – Parker and Parker – that takes a delight in – as you Americans would say – ripping off their customers. You've given me an idea how to make them pay for their dishonesty.' He told Tracy his idea.

'No,' Tracy said. But the more she thought about it, the more intrigued she was. She remembered the excitement of outwitting the police in Long Island, and Boris Melnikov and Pietr Negulesco, and Jeff Stevens. It had been a thrill that was indescribable. Still, that was part of the past.

'No, Gunther,' she said again. But this time there was less certainty in her voice.

London was unseasonably warm for October, and Englishmen and tourists alike took advantage of the bright sunshine. The noon traffic was heavy with hold-ups at Trafalgar Square, Charing Cross, and Piccadilly Circus. A white Daimler turned off Oxford Street to New Bond Street and threaded its way through the traffic, passing Roland Cartier, Geigers, and the Royal Bank of Scotland. A few doors further on, it coasted to a stop in front of a jewellery shop. A discreet, polished sign at the side of the door read: PARKER & PARKER. A liveried chauffeur stepped out of the limousine and hurried around to open the rear door for his passenger. A young woman with blonde Sassooned hair, wearing far too much makeup and a tight-fitting Italian knit dress under a sable coat, totally inappropriate for the weather, jumped out of the car.

'Which way's the joint, junior?' she asked. Her voice was loud, with a grating Texas accent.

The chauffeur indicated the entrance. 'There, madame.'

'Okay, honey. Stick around. This ain't gonna take long.'

'I may have to circle the block, madame. I won't be permitted to park here.'

She clapped him on the back and said, 'You do what you gotta do, sport.'

Sport! The chauffeur winced. It was his punishment for being reduced to chauffeuring rental cars. He disliked all Americans, particularly Texans. They were savages; but savages with money. He would have been astonished to learn that his passenger had never even seen the Lone Star State.

Tracy checked her reflection in the display window, smiled broadly, and strutted towards the door, which was opened by a uniformed attendant.

'Good afternoon, madame.'

'Afternoon, sport. You sell anythin' besides costume jewellery in this joint?' She chuckled at her joke.

The doorman blanched. Tracy swept into the shop, trailing an overpowering scent of Chloé behind her.

Arthur Chilton, a salesman in a morning coat, moved towards her. 'May I help you, madame?'

'Maybe, maybe not. Old P. J. told me to buy myself a little birthday present, so here I am. Whatcha got?'

'Is there something in particular Madame is interested in?'

'Hey, pardner, you English fellows are fast workers, ain'cha?' She laughed raucously and clapped him on the shoulder. He forced himself to remain impassive. 'Mebbe somethin' in emeralds. Old P. J. loves to buy me emeralds.'

'If you'll step this way, please . . .'

Chilton led her to a vitrine where several trays of emeralds were displayed.

The bleached blonde gave them one disdainful glance. 'These're the babies. Where are the mamas and papas?'

Chilton said stiffly, 'These range in price up to thirty thousand dollars.'

'Hell, I tip my hairdresser that.' The woman guffawed. 'Old P. J. would be insulted if I came back with one of them little pebbles.'

Chilton visualized old P. J. Fat and paunchy and as loud and obnoxious as this woman. They deserved each other. *Why did money always flow to the undeserving?* he wondered.

'What price range was Madame interested in?'

'Why don't we start with somethin' around a hundred G's.'

He looked blank. 'A hundred *G*'s?'

'Hell, I thought you people was supposed to speak the king's English. A hundred grand. A hundred thou.'

He swallowed. 'Oh. In that case, perhaps it would be better if you spoke with our managing director.'

The managing director, Gregory Halston,

insisted on personally handling all large sales, and since the employees of Parker & Parker received no commission, it made no difference to them. With a customer as distasteful as this one, Chilton was relieved to let Halston deal with her. Chilton pressed a button under the counter, and a moment later a pale, reedy-looking man bustled out of a back room. He took a look at the outrageously dressed blonde and prayed that none of his regular customers appeared until the woman had departed.

Chilton said, 'Mr Halston, this is Mrs . . . er . . . ?' He turned to the woman.

'Benecke, honey. Mary Lou Benecke. Old P. J. Benecke's wife. Betcha you all have heard of P. J. Benecke.'

'Of course.' Gregory Halston gave her a smile that barely touched his lips.

'Mrs Benecke is interested in purchasing an emerald, Mr Halston.'

Gregory Halston indicated the trays of emeralds. 'We have some fine emeralds here that –'

'She wanted something for approximately a hundred thousand dollars.'

This time the smile that lit Gregory Halston's face was genuine. What a nice way to start the day.

'You see, it's my birthday, and old P. J. wants me to buy myself somethin' pretty.'

'Indeed,' Halston said. 'Would you follow me, please?'

'You little rascal, what you got in mind?' The blonde giggled.

Halston and Chilton exchanged a pained look. *Bloody Americans!*

Halston led the woman to a locked door and opened it with a key. They entered a small, brightly lit room, and Halston carefully locked the door behind them.

'This is where we keep our merchandise for our valued customers,' he said.

In the centre of the room was a showcase filled with a stunning array of diamonds, rubies and emeralds, flashing their bright colours.

'Well, this is more like it. Old P. J.'d go crazy in here.'

'Does Madame see something she likes?'

'Well, let's jest see what we got here.' She walked over to the jewellery case containing emeralds. 'Let me look at that there bunch.'

Halston extracted another small key from his pocket, unlocked the case, lifted out a tray of emeralds, and placed it on top of the table. There were ten emeralds in the velvet case. Halston watched as the woman picked up the largest of them, an exquisite pin in a platinum setting.

'As old P. J. would say, "This here one's got my name writ on it."'

'Madame has excellent taste. This is a ten-carat grass-green Colombian. It's flawless and –'

'Emeralds ain't never flawless.'

Halston was taken aback for an instant. 'Madame

is correct, of course. What I meant was –' For the first time he noticed that the woman's eyes were as green as the stone she twisted in her hands, turning it around, studying its facets.

'We have a wider selection if –'

'No sweat, sweetie. I'll take this here one.'

The sale had taken fewer than three minutes.

'Splendid,' Halston said. Then he added delicately, 'In dollars it comes to one hundred thousand. How will Madame be paying?'

'Don't you worry, Ralston, old sport, I have a dollar account at a bank here in London. I'll write out a little ol personal cheque. Then P. J. can jest pay me back.'

'Excellent. I'll have the stone cleaned for you and delivered to your hotel.'

The stone did not need cleaning, but Halston had no intention of letting it out of his possession until her cheque had cleared, for too many jewellers he knew had been bilked by clever swindlers. Halston prided himself on the fact that he had never been cheated out of one pound.

'Where shall I have the emerald delivered?'

'We got ourselves the Oliver Messel Suite at the Dorch.'

Halston made a note. 'The Dorchester.'

'I call it the Oliver *Messy* Suite,' she laughed. 'Lots of people don't like the hotel any more because it's full of A-rabs, but old P. J. does a lot of business with them. "Oil is its own country", he always says. P. J. Benecke's one smart fella.'

'I'm sure he is,' Halston replied dutifully.

He watched as she tore out a cheque and began writing. He noted that it was a Barclays Bank cheque. Good. He had a friend there who would verify the Beneckes' account.

He picked up the cheque. 'I'll have the emerald delivered to you personally tomorrow morning.'

'Old P. J.'s gonna love it,' she beamed.

'I am sure he will,' Halston said politely.

He walked her to the front door.

'Ralston –'

He almost corrected her, then decided against it. Why bother? He was never going to lay eyes on her again, thank God! 'Yes, madame?'

'You gotta come up and have tea with us some afternoon. You'll love old P. J.'

'I am sure I would. Unfortunately, I work afternoons.'

'Too bad.'

He watched as his customer walked out to the kerb. A white Daimler slithered up, and a chauffeur got out and opened the door for her. The blonde turned to give Halston the thumbs-up sign as she drove off.

When Halston returned to his office, he immediately picked up the telephone and called his friend at Barclays. 'Peter, dear, I have a cheque here for a hundred thousand dollars drawn on the account of a Mrs Mary Lou Benecke. Is it good?'

'Hold on, old boy.'

Halston waited. He hoped the cheque was good,

for business had been slow lately. The miserable Parker brothers, who owned the store, were constantly complaining, as though it were he who was responsible for the recession. Of course, profits were not down as much as they *could* have been, for Parker & Parker had a department that specialized in cleaning jewellery, and at frequent intervals the jewellery that was returned to the customer was inferior to the original that had been brought in. Complaints had been lodged, but nothing had ever been proven.

Peter was back on the line. 'No problem, Gregory. There's more than enough money in the account to cover the cheque.'

Halston felt a little frisson of relief. 'Thank you, Peter.'

'Not at all.'

'Lunch next week – on me.'

The cheque cleared the following morning, and the Colombian emerald was delivered by bonded messenger to Mrs P. J. Benecke at the Dorchester Hotel.

That afternoon, shortly before closing time, Gregory Halston's secretary said, 'A Mrs Benecke is here to see you, Mr Halston.'

His heart sank. She had come to return the pin, and he could hardly refuse to take it back. *Damn all women, all Americans, and all Texans!* Halston put on a smile and went out to greet her.

'Good afternoon, Mrs Benecke. I assume your husband didn't like the pin.'

'You assume wrong, buster. Old P. J. was just plain crazy about it.'

Halston's heart began to sing. 'He was?'

'In fact, he liked it so much he wants me to get another one so we can have 'em made into a pair of earrings. Let me have a twin to the one I got.'

A small frown appeared on Gregory Halston's face. 'I'm afraid we might have a little problem there, Mrs Benecke.'

'What kinda problem, honey?'

'Yours is a unique stone. There's not another one like it. Now, I have a lovely set in a different style I could –'

'I don't want a different style. I want one jest like the one I bought.'

'To be perfectly candid, Mrs Benecke, there aren't very many ten-carat Colombian flawless' – he saw her look – '*nearly* flawless stones available.'

'Come on, sport. There's gotta be one somewhere.'

'In all honesty, I've seen very few stones of that quality, and to try to duplicate it exactly in shape and colour would be almost impossible.'

'We got a sayin' in Texas that the impossible jest takes a little longer. Saturday's my birthday. P. J. wants me to have those earrings, and what P. J. wants, P. J. gets.'

'I don't think I can –'

'How much did I pay for that pin – a hundred grand? I know old P. J. will go up to two hundred or three hundred thousand for another one.'

Gregory Halston was thinking fast. There *had* to be a duplicate of that stone somewhere, and if P. J. Benecke was willing to pay an extra $200,000 for it, that would mean a tidy profit. *In fact*, Halston thought, *I can work it out so that it means a tidy profit for me*.

Aloud he said, 'I'll enquire around, Mrs Benecke. I'm sure that no other jeweller in London has the identical emerald, but there are always estates coming up for auction. I'll do some advertising and see what results I get.'

'You got till the end of the week,' the blonde told him. 'And jest between you and me and the lamp-post, old P. J. will probably be willin' to go up to three hundred and fifty thousand for it.'

And Mrs Benecke was gone, her sable coat billowing out behind her.

Gregory Halston sat in his office in a daydream. Fate had placed in his hands a man who was so besotted with his blonde tart that he was willing to pay $350,000 for a $100,000 emerald. That was a net profit of $250,000. Gregory Halston saw no need to burden the Parker brothers with the details of the transaction. It would be a simple matter to record the sale of the second emerald at $100,000 and pocket the rest. The extra $250,000 would set him up for life.

All he had to do now was to find a twin to the emerald he had sold to Mrs P. J. Benecke.

It turned out to be even more difficult than

Halston had anticipated. None of the jewellers he telephoned had anything in stock that resembled what he required. He placed advertisements in the London *Times* and the *Financial Times*, and he called Christie's and Sotheby's, and a dozen estate agents. In the next few days Halston was inundated with a flood of inferior emeralds, good emeralds, and a few first-quality emeralds, but none of them came close to what he was looking for.

On Wednesday Mrs Benecke telephoned. 'Old P. J.'s gettin' mighty restless,' she warned. 'Did you find it yet?'

'Not yet, Mrs Benecke,' Halston assured her, 'but don't worry, we will.'

On Friday she telephoned again. 'Tomorrow's my birthday,' she reminded Halston.

'I know, Mrs Benecke. If I only had a few more days, I know I could –'

'Well, never mind sport. If you don't have that emerald by tomorrow mornin', I'll return the one I bought from you. Old P. J. – bless his heart – says he's gonna buy me a big ol country estate instead. Ever hear of a place called Sussex?'

Halston broke out in perspiration, 'Mrs Benecke,' he moaned earnestly, 'you would *hate* living in Sussex. You would loathe living in a country house. Most of them are in deplorable condition. They have no central heating and –'

'Between you and I,' she interrupted, 'I'd rather have them earrings. Old P. J. even mentioned somethin' about bein' willin' to pay four hundred thousand dollars for a twin to that stone. You got no idea how stubborn old P. J. can be.'

Four hundred thousand! Halston could feel the money slipping between his fingers. 'Believe me, I'm doing everything I can,' he pleaded. 'I need a little more time.'

'It ain't up to me, honey,' she said. 'It's up to P. J.'

And the line went dead.

Halston sat there cursing fate. Where could he find an identical ten-carat emerald? He was so busy with his bitter thoughts that he did not hear his intercom until the third buzz. He pushed down the button and snapped, 'What is it?'

'There's a Contessa Marissa on the telephone, Mr Halston. She's calling about our advertisement for the emerald.'

Another one! He had had at least ten calls that morning, every one of them a waste of time. He picked up the telephone and said ungraciously, 'Yes?'

A soft female voice with an Italian accent said, '*Buon giorno, signore*. I have read you are interested possibly in buying an emerald, *sì*?'

'If it's my qualifications, yes.' He could not keep the impatience out of his voice.

'I have an emerald that has been in my family for many years. It is a *peccato* – a pity – but I am in a situation now where I am forced to sell it.'

He had heard *that* story before. *I must try*

Christie's again, Halston thought. *Or Sotheby's. Maybe something came in at the last minute, or –*

'*Signore?* You are looking for a ten-carat emerald, *sì*?'

'Yes.'

'I have a ten-carat verde – green – Colombian.'

When Halston started to speak, he found that his voice was choked. 'Would – would you say that again, please?'

'*Sì*. I have a ten-carat grass-green Colombian. Would you be interested in that?'

'I might be,' he said carefully. 'I wonder if you could drop by and let me have a look at it.'

'No, *scusi*, I am afraid I am very busy right now. We are preparing a party at the embassy for my husband. Perhaps next week I could –'

No! Next week would be too late. 'May I come to see you?' He tried to keep the eagerness out of his voice. 'I could come up now.'

'*Ma, no. Sono occupata stamani.* I was planning to go shopping –'

'Where are you staying, Contessa?'

'At the Savoy.'

'I can be there in fifteen minutes. *Ten*.' His voice was feverish.

'*Molto bene*. And your name is –'

'Halston. Gregory Halston.'

'Suite *ventisei* – twenty-six.'

The taxi ride was interminable. Halston transported himself from the heights to the depths of hell, and back again. If the emerald was indeed similar to the other one, he would be wealthy beyond his wildest dreams. *Four hundred thousand dollars, he'll pay.* A $300,000 profit. He would buy a place on the Riviera. Perhaps get a cruiser. With a villa and his own boat, he would be able to attract as many handsome young men as he liked . . .

Gregory Halston was an atheist, but as he walked down the corridor of the Savoy Hotel to Suite 26, he found himself praying, *Let the stone be similar enough to satisfy old P. J. Benecke.*

He stood in front of the door of the contessa's room taking slow, deep breaths, fighting to get control of himself. He knocked on the door, and there was no answer.

Oh, my God, Halston thought. *She's gone; she didn't wait for me. She went out shopping and –*

The door opened, and Halston found himself facing an elegant-looking lady in her fifties, with dark eyes, a lined face, and black hair laced with grey.

When she spoke, her voice was soft, with the familiar melodic Italian accent. '*Sì?*'

'I'm G-Gregory Halston. You t-telephoned me.' In his nervousness he was stuttering.

'Ah, *sì*. I am the Contessa Marissa. Come in, *signore, per favore*.'

'Thank you.'

He entered the suite, pressing his knees together to keep them from trembling. He almost blurted out, 'Where's the emerald?' But he knew he must control himself. He must not seem too eager. If the stone was satisfactory, he would have the advantage of bargaining. After all, he was the expert. She was an amateur.

'Please to sit yourself,' the contessa said.

He took a chair.

'*Scusi. Non parlo molto bene inglese.* I speak poor English.'

'No, no. It's charming, charming.'

'*Grazie.* Would you take perhaps coffee? Tea?'

'No, thank you, Contessa.'

He could feel his stomach quivering. Was it too soon to bring up the subject of the emerald? He could not wait another second. 'The emerald –'

She said, 'Ah, *sì*. The emerald was given to me by my grandmother. I wish to pass it on to my daughter when she is twenty-five, but my husband is going into a new business in Milano, and I –'

Halston's mind was elsewhere. He was not interested in the boring life story of the stranger sitting across from him. He was burning to see the emerald. The suspense was more than he could bear.

'*Credo che sia importante* to help my husband get started in his business.' She smiled ruefully. 'Perhaps I am making a mistake –'

'No, no,' Halston said hastily. 'Not at all, Contessa. It's a wife's duty to stand by her husband. Where is the emerald now?'

'I have it here,' the contessa said.

She reached into her pocket, pulled out a jewel wrapped in a tissue, and held it out to Halston. He stared at it, and his spirits soared. He was looking at the most exquisite ten-carat grass-green Colombian emerald he had ever seen. It was so close in appearance, size, and colour to the one he had sold Mrs Benecke that the difference was almost impossible to detect. *It is not exactly the same*, Halston told himself, *but only an expert would be able to tell the difference*. His hands began to tremble. He forced himself to appear calm.

He turned the stone over, letting the light catch the beautiful facets, and said casually, 'It's a rather nice little stone.'

'*Splendente, sì*. I have loved it very much all these years. I will hate to part with it.'

'You're doing the right thing,' Halston assured her. 'Once your husband's business is successful, you will be able to buy as many of these as you wish.'

'That is exactly what I feel. You are *molto simpatico*.'

'I'm doing a little favour for a friend, Contessa. We have much better stones than this in our shop, but my friend wants one to match an emerald that his wife bought. I imagine he would be willing to pay as much as sixty thousand dollars for this stone.'

The contessa sighed. 'My grandmother would haunt me from her grave if I sold it for sixty thousand dollars.'

Halston pursed his lips. He could afford to go higher. He smiled. 'I'll tell you what . . . I think I might persuade my friend to go as high as one hundred thousand. That's a great deal of money, but he's anxious to have the stone.'

'That sounds fair,' the contessa said.

Gregory Halston's heart swelled within his breast. '*Bene!* I brought my chequebook with me, so I'll just write out a cheque –'

'*Ma, no* . . . I am afraid it will not solve my problem.' The contessa's face was sad.

Halston stared at her. 'Your problem?'

'*Sì*. As I explain, my husband is going into his new business, and he needs three hundred and fifty thousand dollars. I have a hundred thousand of my money to give him, but I need two hundred and fifty thousand more. I was hope to get it for this emerald.'

He shook his head. 'My dear Contessa, no emerald in the world is worth that kind of money. Believe me, one hundred thousand dollars is more than a fair offer.'

'I am sure it is so, Mr Halston,' the contessa told him, 'but it will not help my husband, will it?' She rose to her feet. 'I will save this to give to our daughter.' She held out a slim, delicate hand. '*Grazie, signore*. Thank you for coming.'

Halston stood there in panic. 'Wait a minute,' he said. His greed was duelling with his common sense, but he knew he must not lose the emerald now. 'Please sit down, Contessa. I'm sure we can come to some equitable arrangement. If I can persuade my client to pay a hundred and fifty thousand –?'

'Two hundred and fifty thousand dollars.'

'Let's say, two hundred thousand?'

'Two hundred and fifty thousand dollars.'

There was no budging her. Halston made his decision. A $150,000 profit was better than nothing. It would mean a smaller villa and a boat, but it was still a fortune. It would serve the Parker brothers right for the shabby way they treated him. He would wait a day or two and then give them his notice. By next week he would be on the Côte d'Azur.

'You have a deal,' he said.

'Meraviglioso! Sono contenta!'

You should be contented, you bitch, Halston thought. But he had nothing to complain about. He was set for life. He took one last look at the emerald and slipped it into his pocket. 'I'll give you a cheque written on the shop's account.'

'Bene, signore.'

Halston wrote out the cheque and handed it to her. He would have Mrs P. J. Benecke make out her $400,000 cheque to cash. Peter would cash the cheque for him, and he would exchange the contessa's cheque for the Parker brothers' cheque and pocket the difference. He would arrange it with Peter so that the $250,000 cheque would not appear on the Parker brothers' monthly statement. One hundred and fifty thousand dollars.

He could already feel the warm French sun on his face.

The taxi ride back to the shop seemed to take only seconds. Halston visualized Mrs Benecke's happiness when he broke the good news to her. He had not only found the jewel she wanted, he had spared her from the excruciating experience of living in a draughty, rundown country house.

When Halston floated into the shop, Chilton said, 'Sir, a customer here is interested in –'

Halston cheerfully waved him aside. 'Later.'

He had no time for customers. Not now, not ever again. From now on people would wait on *him*. He would shop at Hermes and Gucci and Lanvin.

Halston fluttered into his office, closed the door, set the emerald on the desk in front of him, and dialled a number.

An operator's voice said, 'Dorchester Hotel.'

'The Oliver Messel Suite, please.'

'To whom did you wish to speak?'

'Mrs P. J. Benecke.'

'One moment, please.'

Halston whistled softly while he waited.

The operator came back on the line. 'I'm sorry, Mrs Benecke has checked out.'

'Then ring whatever suite she's moved to.'

'Mrs Benecke has checked out of the hotel.'

'That's impossible. She –'

'I'll connect you with reception.'

A male voice said, 'Reception. May I help you?'

'Yes. What suite is Mrs P. J. Benecke in?'

'Mrs Benecke checked out of the hotel this morning.'

There had to be an explanation. Some unexpected emergency.

'May I have her forwarding address, please. This is –'

'I'm sorry. She didn't leave one.'

'*Of course* she left one.'

'I checked Mrs Benecke out myself. She left no forwarding address.'

It was a jab to the pit of his stomach. Halston slowly replaced the receiver and sat there, bewildered. He *had* to find a way to get in touch with her, to let her know that he had finally located the emerald. In the meantime, he had to get back the $250,000 cheque from the Contessa Marissa.

He hurriedly dialled the Savoy Hotel. 'Suite twenty-six.'

'Whom are you calling, please?'

'The Contessa Marissa.'

'One moment, please.'

But even before the operator came back on the line, some terrible premonition told Gregory Halston the disastrous news he was about to hear.

'I'm sorry. The Contessa Marissa has checked out.'

He hung up. His fingers were trembling so hard that he was barely able to dial the number of the bank. 'Give me the head bookkeeper . . . quickly! I wish to stop payment on a cheque.'

But, of course, he was too late. He had sold an emerald for $100,000 and had bought back the same emerald for $250,000. Gregory Halston sat there slumped in his chair, wondering how he was going to explain it to the Parker brothers.

TWENTY-TWO

It was the beginning of a new life for Tracy. She purchased a beautiful old Georgian house at 45 Eaton Square that was bright and cheerful and perfect for entertaining. It had a Queen Anne – British slang for a front garden – and a Mary Anne – a back garden – and in season the flowers were magnificent. Gunther helped Tracy furnish the house, and before the two of them were finished, it was one of the showplaces of London.

Gunther introduced Tracy as a wealthy young widow whose husband had made his fortune in the import-export business. She was an instant success; beautiful, intelligent and charming, she was soon inundated with invitations.

At intervals, Tracy made short trips to France and Switzerland and Belgium and Italy, and each time she and Gunther Hartog profited.

Under Gunther's tutelage, Tracy studied the *Almanach de Gotha* and *Debrett's Peerage and Baronetage*, the authoritative books listing detailed information on all the royalty and titles in Europe. Tracy became a chameleon, an expert in make-up and disguises and accents. She acquired half a dozen passports. In various countries, she was a British duchess, a French airline stewardess, and a South American heiress. In a year she had accumulated more money than she would ever need. She set up a fund from which she made large, anonymous contributions to organizations that helped former women prisoners, and she arranged for a generous pension to be sent to Otto Schmidt every month. She no longer entertained the thought of quitting. She loved the challenge of outwitting clever, successful people. The thrill of each daring escapade acted like a drug, and Tracy found that she constantly needed new and bigger challenges. There was one credo she lived by: she was careful never to hurt the innocent. The people who jumped at her swindles were greedy or immoral, or both. *No one will ever commit suicide because of what I've done to them*, Tracy promised herself.

The newspapers began to carry stories of the daring escapades that were occurring all over Europe, and because Tracy used different disguises, the police were convinced that a rash of ingenious swindles and burglaries was being carried out by a gang of women. Interpol began to take an interest.

At the Manhattan headquarters of the International Insurance Protection Association, J. J. Reynolds sent for Daniel Cooper.

'We have a problem,' Reynolds said. 'A large number of our European clients are being hit – apparently by a gang of women. Everybody's screaming bloody murder. They want the gang caught. Interpol has agreed to cooperate with us. It's your assignment, Dan. You leave for Paris in the morning.'

Tracy was having dinner with Gunther at Scott's on Mount Street.

'Have you ever heard of Maximilian Pierpont, Tracy?'

The name sounded familiar. Where had she heard it before? She remembered. Jeff Stevens, on board the *QE II*, had said, 'We're here for the same reason. Maximilian Pierpont.'

'Very rich, isn't he?'

'And quite ruthless. He specializes in buying up companies and stripping them.'

When Joe Romano took over the business, he fired everybody and brought in his own people to run things. Then he began to raid the company . . . They took everything – the business, this house, your mother's car . . .

Gunther was looking at her oddly. 'Tracy, are you all right?'

'Yes. I'm fine.' *Sometimes life can be unfair*, she thought, *and it's up to us to even things out*. 'Tell me more about Maximilian Pierpont.'

'His third wife just divorced him, and he's alone now. I think it might be profitable if you made the gentleman's acquaintance. He's booked on the *Orient Express* Friday, from London to Istanbul.'

Tracy smiled. 'I've never been on the *Orient Express*. I think I'd enjoy it.'

Gunther smiled back. 'Good. Maximilian Pierpont has the only important Fabergé egg collection outside of the Hermitage Museum in Leningrad. It's conservatively estimated to be worth twenty million dollars.'

'If I managed to get some of the eggs for you,' Tracy asked, curious, 'what would you do with them, Gunther? Wouldn't they be too well known to sell?'

'Private collectors, dear Tracy. You bring the little eggs to me, and I will find a nest for them.'

'I'll see what I can do.'

'Maximilian Pierpont is not an easy man to approach. However, there are two other pigeons also booked on the *Orient Express* Friday, bound for the film festival in Venice. I think they're ripe for plucking. Have you heard of Silvana Luadi?'

'The Italian movie star? Of course.'

'She's married to Alberto Fornati, who produces those terrible epic films. Fornati is infamous for hiring actors and directors for very little cash, promising them big percentages of the profits, and keeping all the profits for himself. He manages to make enough to buy his wife very expensive jewels. The more unfaithful he is to her, the more jewellery he gives her. By this time Silvana should be able to open her own jewellery shop. I'm sure you'll find all of them interesting company.'

'I'm looking forward to it,' Tracy said.

The *Venice Simplon Orient Express* departs from Victoria Station in London every Friday morning at 11:44, travelling from London to Istanbul, with intermediate stops in Boulogne, Paris, Lausanne, Milan and Venice. Thirty minutes before departure a portable check-in counter is set up at the entrance to the boarding platform in the terminal, and two burly uniformed men roll a red rug up to the counter, elbowing aside eagerly waiting passengers.

The new owners of the *Orient Express* had attempted to recreate the golden age of rail travel as it existed in the late nineteenth century, and the rebuilt train was a duplicate of the original, with a British Pullman car, wagon-lit restaurants, a bar-salon car, and sleeping cars.

An attendant in a 1920's marine-blue uniform with gold braid carried Tracy's two suitcases and her vanity case to her cabin, which was disappointingly small. There was a single seat, upholstered with a flower-patterned mohair. The rug, as well as the ladder that was used to reach the top berth, was covered in the same green plush. It was like being in a chocolate box.

Tracy read the card accompanying a small bottle of champagne in a silver bucket: OLIVER AUBERT, TRAIN MANAGER.

I'll save it until I have something to celebrate, Tracy decided. *Maximilian Pierpont*. Jeff Stevens had failed. It would be a wonderful feeling to top Mr Stevens. Tracy smiled at the thought.

She unpacked in the cramped space and hung up the clothes she would be needing. She preferred travelling on a Pan American jet rather than a train, but this journey promised to be an exciting one.

Exactly on schedule, the *Orient Express* began to move out of the station. Tracy sat back in her seat and watched the southern suburbs of London roll by.

At 1:15 that afternoon the train arrived at the port of Folkestone, where the passengers transferred to the Sealink ferry, which would take them across the channel to Boulogne, where they would board another *Orient Express* heading south.

Tracy approached one of the attendants. 'I understand Maximilian Pierpont is travelling with us. Could you point him out to me?'

The attendant shook his head. 'I wish I could, ma'am. He booked his cabin and paid for it, but he never showed up. Very unpredictable gentleman, so I'm told.'

That left Silvana Luadi and her husband, the producer of forgettable epics.

In Boulogne, the passengers were escorted onto the continental *Oriental Express*. Unfortunately, Tracy's cabin on the second train was identical to the one she had left, and the rough railway track made the journey even more uncomfortable. She remained in her cabin all day making her plans, and at 8:00 in the evening she began to dress.

The dress code of the *Orient Express* recommended evening clothes, and Tracy chose a stunning dove-grey chiffon gown with grey hose and grey satin shoes. Her only jewellery was a single strand of matched pearls. She checked herself in the mirror before she left her quarters, staring at her reflection for a long time. Her green eyes had a look of innocence, and her face looked guileless and vulnerable. *The mirror is lying*, Tracy thought. *I'm not that woman any more. I'm living a masquerade. But an exciting one.*

As Tracy left her cabin, her handbag slipped out of her hand, and as she knelt down to retrieve it, she quickly examined the outside locks on the door. There were two of them: a Yale lock and a Universal lock. *No problem*. Tracy rose and moved on towards the dining cars.

There were three dining cars aboard the train. The seats were plush-covered, the walls were veneered, and the soft lights came from brass sconces topped with Lalique shades. Tracy entered the first dining room and noted several empty tables. The maître d' greeted her. 'A table for one, mademoiselle?'

Tracy looked around the room. 'I'm joining some friends, thank you.'

She continued on to the next dining car. This one was more crowded, but there were still several unoccupied tables.

'Good evening,' the maître d' said. 'Are you dining alone?'

'No, I'm meeting someone. Thank you.'

She moved on to the third dining car. There, every table was occupied.

The maître d' stopped her at the door. 'I'm afraid there will be a wait for a table, madame. There are available tables in the other dining cars, however.'

Tracy looked around the room, and at a table in the far corner she saw what she was looking for. 'That's all right,' Tracy said. 'I see friends.'

She moved past the maître d' and walked over to the corner table. 'Excuse me,' she said apologetically. 'All the tables seem to be occupied. Would you mind if I joined you?'

The man quickly rose to his feet, took a good look at Tracy, and exclaimed, '*Prego! Con piacere!* I am Alberto Fornati and this is my wife, Silvana Luadi.'

'Tracy Whitney.' She was using her own passport.

'Ah! *È Americana!* I speak the excellent English.'

Alberto Fornati was short, bald and fat. Why Silvana Luadi had ever married him had been the most lively topic in Rome for the twelve years they had been together. Silvana Luadi was a classic beauty, with a sensational figure and a compelling, natural talent. She had won an Oscar and a Silver Palm award and was always in great demand. Tracy recognized that she was dressed in a

Valentino evening gown that sold for five thousand dollars, and the jewellery she wore must have been worth close to a million. Tracy remembered Gunther Hartog's words: *The more unfaithful he is to her, the more jewellery he gives her. By this time Silvana should be able to open her own jewellery shop.*

'This is your first time on the *Orient Express*, signorina?' Fornati opened the conversation, after Tracy was seated.

'Yes, it is.'

'Ah, it is a very romantic train, filled with legend.' His eyes were moist. 'There are many *interessante* tales about it. For instance, Sir Basil Zaharoff, the arms tycoon, used to ride the old *Orient Express* – always in the seventh compartment. One night he hears a scream and a pounding on his door. A *bellissima* young Spanish duchess throws herself upon him.' Fornati paused to butter a roll and take a bite. 'Her husband was trying to murder her. The parents had arranged the marriage, and the poor girl now realized her husband was insane. Zaharoff restrained the husband and calmed the hysterical young woman and thus began a romance that lasted forty years.'

'How exciting,' Tracy said. Her eyes were wide with interest.

'*Si*. Every year after that they meet on the *Orient Express*, he in compartment number seven, she in number eight. When her husband died, the lady and Zaharoff were married, and as a token of his love, he bought her the casino at Monte Carlo as a wedding gift.'

'What a beautiful story, Mr Fornati.'

Silvana Luadi sat in stony silence.

'*Mangia*,' Fornati urged Tracy. 'Eat.'

The menu consisted of six courses, and Tracy noted that Alberto Fornati ate each one and finished what his wife left on her plate. In between bites he kept up a constant chatter.

'You are an actress, perhaps?' he asked Tracy.

She laughed. 'Oh no. I'm just a tourist.'

He beamed at her. '*Bellissima*. You are beautiful enough to be an actress.'

'She said she is not an actress,' Silvana said sharply.

Alberto Fornati ignored her. 'I produce motion pictures,' he told Tracy. 'You have heard of them, of course: *Wild Savages*, *The Titans versus Superwoman* . . .'

'I don't see many movies,' Tracy apologized. She felt his fat leg press against hers under the table.

'Perhaps I can arrange to show you some of mine.'

Silvana turned white with anger.

'Do you ever get to Rome, my dear?' His leg was moving up and down against Tracy's.

'As a matter of fact, I'm planning to go to Rome after Venice.'

'Splendid! *Benissimo!* We will all get together for dinner. Won't we, *cara?*' He gave a quick glance towards Silvana before he continued. 'We have a lovely villa off the Appian Way. Ten acres of –'

His hand made a sweeping gesture and knocked a bowl of gravy into his wife's lap. Tracy could not be sure whether it was deliberate or not.

Silvana Luadi rose to her feet and looked at the spreading stain on her dress. '*Sei un mascalzone!*' she screamed. '*Tieni le tue puttane lontano da me.*'

She stormed out of the dining car, every eye following her.

'What a shame,' Tracy murmured. 'It's such a beautiful dress.' She could have slapped the man for degrading his wife. *She deserves every carat of jewellery she has*, Tracy thought, *and more*.

He sighed. 'Fornati will buy her another one. Pay no attention to her manners. She is very jealous of Fornati.'

'I'm sure she has good reason to be.' Tracy covered her irony with a small smile.

He peered. 'It is true. Women find Fornati very attractive.'

It was all Tracy could do to keep from bursting out laughing at the pompous little man. 'I can understand that.'

He reached across the table and took her hand. 'Fornati likes you,' he said. 'Fornati likes you very much. What do you do for a living?'

'I'm a legal secretary. I saved up all my money for this trip. I hope to get an interesting position in Europe.'

His bulging eyes roved over her body. 'You will have no problem, Fornati promises you. He is very nice to people who are very nice to him.'

'How wonderful of you,' Tracy said shyly.

He lowered his voice. 'Perhaps we could discuss this later this evening in your cabin?'

'That might be embarrassing.'

'*Perché?* Why?'

'You're so famous. Everyone on the train probably knows who you are.'

'Naturally.'

'If they see you come to my cabin – well, you know, some people might misunderstand. Of course, if your cabin is near mine . . . What number are you in?'

'*E settanta* – seventy.' He looked at her hopefully.

Tracy sighed. 'I'm in another car. Why don't we meet in Venice?'

He beamed. '*Bene!* My wife, she stays in her room most of the time. She cannot stand the sun on her face. Have you ever been to Venezia?'

'No.'

'Ah. You and I shall go to Torcello, a beautiful little island with a wonderful restaurant, the Locanda Cipriani. It is also a small hotel.' His eyes gleamed. '*Molto privato*.'

Tracy gave him a slow, understanding smile. 'It sounds exciting.' She lowered her eyes, too overcome to say more.

Fornati leaned forward, squeezed her hand, and whispered wetly, 'You do not know what excitement is yet, *cara*.'

Half an hour later Tracy was back in her cabin.

* * *

The *Orient Express* sped through the lonely night, past Paris and Dijon and Vallarbe, while the passengers slept. They had turned in their passports the evening before, and the border formalities would be handled by the conductors.

At 3:30 in the morning Tracy quietly left her compartment. The timing was critical. The train would cross the Swiss border and reach Lausanne at 5:21 A.M. and was due to arrive in Milan, Italy, at 9:15 A.M.

Clad in pyjamas and robe, and carrying a sponge bag, Tracy moved down the corridor, every sense alert, the familiar excitement making her pulse leap. There were no toilets in the cabins of the train, but there were some located at the end of each carriage. If Tracy was questioned, she was prepared to say that she was looking for the ladies' room, but she encountered no one. The conductors and porters were taking advantage of the early-morning hours to catch up on their sleep.

Tracy reached Cabin E 70 without incident. She quietly tried the doorknob. The door was locked. Tracy opened the sponge bag and took out a metallic object and a small bottle with a syringe, and went to work.

Ten minutes later she was back in her cabin, and thirty minutes after that she was asleep, with the trace of a smile on her freshly scrubbed face.

At 7:00 A.M., two hours before the *Orient Express* was due to arrive in Milan, a series of piercing screams rang out. They came from Cabin E 70, and they awakened the entire carriage. Passengers poked their heads out of their cabins to see what was happening. A conductor came hurrying along the carriage and entered E 70.

Silvana Luadi was in hysterics. '*Aiuto! Help!*' she screamed. 'All my jewellery is gone! This miserable train is full of *ladri* – thieves!'

'Please calm down, madame,' the conductor begged. 'The other –'

'*Calm down!*' Her voice went up an octave. 'How dare you tell me to calm down, *stupido maiale!* Someone has stolen more than a million dollars' worth of my jewels!'

'How could this have happened?' Alberto Fornati demanded. 'The door was locked – and Fornati is a light sleeper. If anyone had entered, I would have awakened instantly.'

The conductor sighed. He knew only too well how it had happened, because it had happened before. During the night someone had crept down the corridor and sprayed a syringe full of ether through the keyhole. The locks would have been child's play for someone who knew what he was doing. The thief would have closed the door behind him, looted the room, and, having taken what he wanted, quietly crept back to his compartment while his victims were still unconscious. But there was one thing about this burglary that was different from the others. In the past the thefts had not been discovered until *after* the train had reached its destination, so the thieves had had a chance to escape. This was a different situation. No one had disembarked since the robbery, which meant that the jewellery still had to be on board.

'Don't worry,' the conductor promised the Fornatis. 'You'll get your jewels back. The thief is still on this train.'

He hurried forward to telephone the police in Milan.

When the *Orient Express* pulled into the Milan terminal, twenty uniformed policemen and plain-clothes detectives lined the station platform, with orders not to let any passengers or baggage off the train.

Luigi Ricci, the inspector in charge, was taken directly to the Fornati compartment.

If anything, Silvana Luadi's hysteria had increased. 'Every bit of jewellery I owned was in that jewel case,' she screamed. 'And none of it was insured!'

The inspector examined the empty jewel case. 'You are sure you put your jewels in there last night, signora?'

'*Of course* I am sure. I put them there every night.' Her luminous eyes, which had thrilled millions of adoring fans, pooled over with large tears, and Inspector Ricci was ready to slay dragons for her.

He walked over to the compartment door, bent down, and sniffed the keyhole. He could detect the lingering odour of ether. There had been a robbery, and he intended to catch the unfeeling bandit.

Inspector Ricci straightened up and said, 'Do not worry, signora. There is no way the jewels can be removed from this train. We will catch the thief, and your gems will be returned to you.'

Inspector Ricci had every reason to be confident. The trap was tightly sealed, and there was no possibility for the culprit to get away.

One by one, the detectives escorted the passengers to a station waiting room that had been roped off, and they were expertly body searched. The passengers, many of them people of prominence, were outraged by this indignity.

'I'm sorry,' Inspector Ricci explained to each of them, 'but a million-dollar theft is a very serious business.'

As each passenger was led from the train, detectives turned their cabins upside down. Every inch of space was examined. This was a splendid opportunity for Inspector Ricci, and he intended to make the most of it. When he recovered the stolen jewels, it would mean a promotion and a rise. His imagination became inflamed. Silvana Luadi would be so grateful to him that she would probably invite him to . . . He gave orders with renewed vigour.

There was a knock at Tracy's cabin door and a detective entered. 'Excuse me, signorina. There has been a robbery. It is necessary to search all passengers. If you will come with me, please . . .'

'A robbery?' Her voice was shocked. 'On this train?'

'I fear so, signorina.'

When Tracy stepped out of her compartment, two detectives moved in, opened her suitcases, and began carefully sifting through the contents.

At the end of four hours the search had turned up several packets of marijuana, five ounces of cocaine, a knife, and an illegal gun. There was no sign of the missing jewellery.

Inspector Ricci could not believe it. 'Have you searched the entire train?' he demanded of his lieutenant.

'Inspector, we have searched every inch. We have examined the engine, the dining rooms, the bar, the toilets, the compartments. We have searched the passengers and crew and examined every piece of luggage. I can swear to you that the jewellery is not on board this train. Perhaps the lady imagined the theft.'

But Inspector Ricci knew better. He had spoken to the waiters, and they had confirmed that Silvana Luadi had indeed worn a dazzling display of jewellery at dinner the evening before.

A representative of the *Orient Express* had flown to Milan. 'You cannot detain this train any longer,' he insisted. 'We are already far behind schedule.'

Inspector Ricci was defeated. He had no excuse for holding the train any further. There was nothing more he could do. The only explanation he could think of was that somehow, during the night, the thief had tossed the jewels off the train to a waiting confederate. But could it have happened that way?

The timing would have been impossible. The thief could not have known in advance when the corridor would be clear, when a conductor or passenger might be prowling about, what time the train would be at some deserted assignation point. This was a mystery beyond the inspector's power to solve.

'Let the train go on,' he ordered.

He stood watching helplessly as the *Orient Express* slowly pulled out of the station. With it went his promotion, his rise, and a blissful orgy with Silvana Luadi.

The sole topic of conversation in the breakfast car was the robbery.

'It's the most exciting thing that's happened to me in years,' confessed a prim teacher at a girls' school. She fingered a small gold necklace with a tiny diamond chip. 'I'm lucky they didn't take this.'

'Very,' Tracy gravely agreed.

When Alberto Fornati walked into the dining car, he caught sight of Tracy and hurried over to her. 'You know what happened, of course. But did you know it was Fornati's wife who was robbed?'

'No!'

'Yes! My life was in great danger. A gang of thieves crept into my cabin and chloroformed me. Fornati could have been murdered in his sleep.'

'How terrible.'

'*È una bella fregatura!* Now I shall have to replace all of Silvana's jewellery. It's going to cost me a fortune.'

'The police didn't find the jewels?'

'No, but Fornati knows how the thieves got rid of them.'

'Really! How?'

He looked around and lowered his voice. 'An accomplice was waiting at one of the stations we passed during the night. The *ladri* threw the jewels out of the train, and – *ecco* – it was done.'

Tracy said admiringly, 'How clever of you to figure that out.'

'*Sì*.' He raised his brows meaningfully. 'You will not forget our little tryst in Venezia?'

'How could I?' Tracy smiled.

He squeezed her arm hard. 'Fornati is looking forward to it. Now I must go console Silvana. She is hysterical.'

When the *Orient Express* arrived at the Santa Lucia station in Venice, Tracy was among the first passengers to disembark. She had her luggage taken directly to the airport and was on the next plane to London with Silvana Luadi's jewellery.

Gunther Hartog was going to be pleased.

TWENTY-THREE

The seven-storey headquarters building of Interpol, the International Criminal Police Organization, is at 26 Rue Armengaud, in the hills of St Cloud, about six miles west of Paris, discreetly hidden behind a high green fence and white stone walls. The gate at the street entrance is locked twenty-four hours a day, and visitors are admitted only after being scrutinized through a closed-circuit television system. Inside the building, at the head of the stairs at each floor, are white iron gates which are locked at night, and every floor is equipped with a separate alarm system and closed-circuit television.

The extraordinary security is mandatory, for within this building are kept the world's most elaborate dossiers with files on two and a half million criminals. Interpol is a clearinghouse of information for 126 police forces in 78 countries, and coordinates the worldwide activities of police forces in dealing with swindlers, counterfeiters, narcotics smugglers, robbers, and murderers. It disseminates up-to-the-second information by an updated bulletin called a *circulation*; by radio, phototelegraphy, and early-bird satellite. The Paris headquarters is manned by former detectives from the Sûreté Nationale or the Paris Préfecture.

On an early May morning a conference was under way in the office of Inspector Andre Trignant, in charge of Interpol headquarters. The office was comfortable and simply furnished, and the view was breathtaking. In the far distance to the east, the Eiffel Tower loomed, and in another direction the white dome of the Sacré Coeur in Montmartre was clearly visible. The inspector was in his mid-forties, an attractive, authoritative figure, with an intelligent face, dark hair, and shrewd brown eyes behind black horn-rimmed glasses. Seated in the office with him were detectives from England, Belgium, France and Italy.

'Gentlemen,' Inspector Trignant said, 'I have received urgent requests from each of your countries for information about the rash of crimes that has recently sprung up all over Europe. Half a dozen countries have been hit by an epidemic of ingenious swindles and burglaries, in which there are several similarities. The victims are of unsavoury reputation, there is never violence involved, and the perpetrator is always a female. We have reached the conclusion that we are facing an international gang of women. We have identi-kit pictures based on the descriptions by victims and random witnesses.

As you will see, none of the women in the pictures is alike. Some are blonde, some brunette. They have variously been reported as being English, French, Spanish, Italian, American – or Texan.'

Inspector Trignant pressed a switch, and a series of pictures began to appear on the wall screen. 'Here you see an identi-kit sketch of a brunette with short hair.' He pressed the button again. 'Here is a young blonde with a shag cut . . . Here is another blonde with a perm . . . a brunette with a pageboy . . . Here is an older woman with a French twist . . . a young woman with blonde streaks . . . an older woman with a *coup sauvage*.' He turned off the projector. 'We have no idea who the gang's leader is or where their headquarters is located. They never leave any clues behind, and they vanish like smoke rings. Sooner or later we will catch one of them, and when we do, we shall get them all. In the meantime, gentlemen, until one of you can furnish us with some specific information, I am afraid we are at a dead end . . .'

When Daniel Cooper's plane landed in Paris, he was met at Charles de Gaulle Airport by one of Inspector Trignant's assistants, and driven to the Prince de Galles, next door to its more illustrious sister hotel, the George V.

'It is arranged for you to meet Inspector Trignant tomorrow,' his escort told Cooper. 'I will pick you up at eight-fifteen.'

* * *

Daniel Cooper had not been looking forward to the trip to Europe. He intended to finish his assignment as quickly as possible and return home. He knew about the fleshpots of Paris, and he had no intention of becoming involved.

He checked into his room and went directly into the bathroom. To his surprise, the bath was satisfactory. In fact, he admitted to himself, it was much larger than the one at home. He ran the bath water and went into the bedroom to unpack. Near the bottom of his suitcase was the small locked box, safe between his extra suit and his underwear. He picked up the box and held it in his hands, staring at it, and it seemed to pulse with a life of its own. He carried it into the bathroom and placed it on the sink. With the tiny key dangling from his key ring, he unlocked the box and opened it, and the words screamed up at him from the yellowed newspaper clipping.

BOY TESTIFIES IN MURDER TRIAL

> Twelve-year-old Daniel Cooper today testified in the trial of Fred Zimmer, accused of the rape-murder of the young boy's mother. According to his testimony, the boy returned home from school and saw Zimmer, a next-door neighbour, leaving the Cooper home with blood on his hands and face. When the boy entered his home, he discovered the body of his mother in the bath. She had been savagely

stabbed to death. Zimmer confessed to being Mrs Cooper's lover, but denied that he had killed her.

The young boy has been placed in the care of an aunt.

Daniel Cooper's trembling hands dropped the clipping back into the box and locked it. He looked around wildly. The walls and ceiling of the hotel bathroom were spattered with blood. He saw his mother's naked body floating in the red water. He felt a wave of vertigo and clutched the sink. The screams inside him became guttural moans, and he frantically tore off his clothes and sank down into the blood-warm bath.

'I must inform you, Mr Cooper,' Inspector Trignant said, 'that your position here is most unusual. You are not a member of any police force, and your presence here is unofficial. However, we have been requested by the police departments of several European countries to extend our cooperation.'

Daniel Cooper said nothing.

'As I understand it, you are an investigator for the International Protective Association, a consortium of insurance companies.'

'Some of our European clients have had heavy losses lately. I was told there are no clues.'

Inspector Trignant sighed. 'I'm afraid that is the case. We know we are dealing with a gang of very clever women, but beyond that –'

'No information from informers?'

'No. Nothing.'

'Doesn't that strike you as odd?'

'What do you mean, monsieur?'

It seemed so obvious to Cooper that he did not bother to keep the impatience out of his voice. 'When a gang is involved, there's always someone who talks too much, drinks too much, spends too much. It's impossible for a large group of people to keep a secret. Would you mind giving me your files on this gang?'

The inspector started to refuse. He thought Daniel Cooper was one of the most physically unattractive men he had ever met. And certainly the most arrogant. He was going to be a *chierie*, 'a pain in the ass'; but the inspector had been asked to cooperate fully.

Reluctantly, he said, 'I will have copies made for you.' He spoke into an intercom and gave the order. To make conversation, Inspector Trignant said, 'An interesting report just crossed my desk. Some valuable jewels were stolen aboard the *Orient Express* while it –'

'I read about it. The thief made a fool of the Italian police.'

'No one has been able to figure out how the robbery was accomplished.'

'It's obvious,' Daniel Cooper said rudely. 'A matter of simple logic.'

Inspector Trignant looked over his glasses in surprise. *Mon Dieu, he has the manners of a pig.* He continued, coolly, 'In this case, logic does not help. Every inch of that train was examined, and the employees, passengers, and all the luggage searched.'

'No,' Daniel Cooper contradicted.

This man is crazy, Inspector Trignant decided. 'No – *what*?'

'They didn't search all the luggage.'

'And I tell you they did,' Inspector Trignant insisted. 'I have seen the police report.'

'The woman from whom the jewels were stolen – Silvana Luadi?'

'Yes?'

'She had placed her jewels in an overnight case from which they were taken?'

'That is correct.'

'Did the police search Miss Luadi's luggage?'

'Only her overnight case. She was the victim. Why should they search her luggage?'

'Because that's logically the only place the thief could have hidden the jewels – in the bottom of one of her other suitcases. He probably had a duplicate case, and when all the luggage was piled on the platform at the Venice station, all he had to do was exchange suitcases and disappear.' Daniel Cooper rose. 'If those reports are ready, I'll be running along.'

Thirty minutes later, Inspector Trignant was speaking to Alberto Fornati in Venice.

'Monsieur,' the inspector said, 'I was calling to enquire whether there happened to be any problem with your wife's luggage when you arrived in Venice.'

'*Sì, sì,*' Fornati complained. 'The idiot porter got her suitcases mixed up with someone else's. When my wife opened her bag at the hotel, it contained nothing but a lot of old magazines. I reported it to the office of the *Orient Express*. Have they located my wife's suitcase?' he asked hopefully.

'No, monsieur,' the inspector said. And he added silently to himself, *Nor would I expect it, if I were you*.

When he completed the telephone call, he sat back in his chair thinking, *This Daniel Cooper is très formidable*. Very formidable, indeed.

TWENTY-FOUR

Tracy's house in Eaton Square was a haven. It was in one of the most beautiful areas in London, with the old Georgian houses facing tree-filled private parks. Nannies in stiffly starched uniforms wheeled their small charges in status-named prams along the gravelled paths, and children played their games. *I miss Amy*, Tracy thought.

Tracy walked along the storied old streets and shopped at the greengrocers and the chemist on Elizabeth Street; she marvelled at the variety of brilliantly coloured flowers sold outside the little shops.

Gunther Hartog saw to it that Tracy contributed to the right charities and met the right people. She dated wealthy dukes and impoverished earls and had numerous proposals of marriage. She was young and beautiful and rich, and she seemed so vulnerable.

'Everyone thinks you're a perfect target,' Gunther laughed. 'You've really done splendidly for yourself, Tracy. You're set now. You have everything you'll ever need.'

It was true. She had money in safe-deposit boxes all over Europe, the house in London, and a chalet in St Moritz. Everything she would ever need. Except for someone to share it with. Tracy thought of the life she had almost had, with a husband and a baby. Would that ever be possible for her again? She could never reveal to any man who she really was, nor could she live a lie by concealing her past. She had played so many parts, she was no longer sure who she really was, but she did know that she could never return to the life she had once had. *It's all right*, Tracy thought defiantly. *A lot of people are lonely. Gunther is right. I have everything.*

She was giving a cocktail party the following evening, the first since her return from Venice.

'I'm looking forward to it,' Gunther told her. 'Your parties are the hottest ticket in London.'

Tracy said fondly, 'Look who my sponsor is.'

'Who's going to be there?'

'Everybody,' Tracy told him.

Everybody turned out to be one more guest than Tracy had anticipated. She had invited the Baroness Howarth, an attractive young heiress, and when Tracy saw the baroness arrive, she walked over to greet her. The greeting died on Tracy's lips. With the baroness was Jeff Stevens.

'Tracy, darling, I don't believe you know Mr Stevens. Jeff, this is Mrs Tracy Whitney, your hostess.'

Tracy said stiffly, 'How do you do, Mr Stevens?'

Jeff took Tracy's hand, holding it a fraction longer than necessary. 'Mrs Tracy Whitney?' he said. 'Of course! I was a friend of your husband's. We were together in India.'

'Isn't that exciting!' Baroness Howarth exclaimed.

'Strange, he never mentioned you,' Tracy said coolly.

'Didn't he, really? I'm surprised. Interesting old fella. Pity he had to go the way he did.'

'Oh, what happened?' Baroness Howarth asked.

Tracy glared at Jeff. 'It was nothing, really.'

'*Nothing!*' Jeff said reproachfully. 'If I remember correctly, he was hanged in India.'

'Pakistan,' Tracy said tightly. 'And I believe I *do* remember my husband mentioning you. How is your wife?'

Baroness Howarth looked at Jeff. 'You never mentioned that you were married, Jeff.'

'Cecily and I are divorced.'

Tracy smiled sweetly. 'I meant Rose.'

'Oh, *that* wife.'

Baroness Howarth was astonished. 'You've been married twice?'

'Once,' he said easily. 'Rose and I got an annulment. We were very young.' He started to move away.

Tracy asked, 'But weren't there twins?'

Baroness Howarth exclaimed, 'Twins?'

'They live with their mother,' Jeff told her. He looked at Tracy. 'I can't tell you how pleasant it's been talking to you, Mrs Whitney, but we mustn't monopolize you.' And he took the baroness's hand and walked away.

The following morning Tracy ran into Jeff in an elevator at Harrods. The store was crowded with shoppers. Tracy got off at the second floor. As she left the elevator, she turned to Jeff and said in a loud, clear voice, 'By the way, how did you ever come out on that morals charge?' The door closed, and Jeff was trapped in an elevator filled with indignant strangers.

Tracy lay in bed that night thinking of Jeff, and she had to laugh. He really was a charmer. A scoundrel, but an engaging one. She wondered what his relationship with Baroness Howarth was: she knew very well what his relationship with Baroness Howarth was. *Jeff and I are two of a kind*, Tracy thought. Neither of them would ever settle down. The life they led was too exciting and stimulating and rewarding.

She turned her thoughts towards her next job. It was going to take place in the South of France, and it would be a challenge. Gunther had told her that the police were looking for a gang. She fell asleep with a smile on her lips.

In his hotel room in Paris, Daniel Cooper was reading the reports Inspector Trignant had given him. It was 4:00 A.M., and Cooper had been poring over the papers for hours, analysing the imaginative mix of robberies and swindles. Some of the scams Cooper was familiar with, but others were new to him. As Inspector Trignant had mentioned, all the victims had unsavoury reputations. *This gang apparently thinks they're Robin Hoods*, Cooper reflected.

He had nearly finished. There were only three reports left. The one on top was headed BRUSSELS. Cooper opened the cover and glanced at the report. Two million dollars' worth of jewellery had been stolen from the wall safe of a Mr Van Ruysen, a Belgian stock-broker, who had been involved in some questionable financial dealings.

The owners were away on vacation, and the house was empty, and – Cooper caught something on the page that made his heart quicken. He went back to the first sentence and began rereading the report, focusing on every word. This one varied from the others in one significant respect: the burglar had set off an alarm, and when the police arrived, they were greeted at the door by a woman wearing a filmy négligée. Her hair was tucked into a curler cap, and her face was thickly covered with cold cream. She claimed to be a houseguest of the Van Ruysens'. The police accepted her story, and by the time they were able to check it out with the absent owners, the woman and the jewellery had vanished.

Cooper laid down the report. Logic, logic.

Inspector Trignant was losing his patience. 'You're wrong. I tell you it is impossible for one woman to be responsible for all these crimes.'

'There's a way to check it out,' Daniel Cooper said.

'How?'

'I'd like to see a computer run on the dates and locations of the last few burglaries and swindles that fit into this category.'

'That's simple enough, but –'

'Next, I would like to get an immigration report on every female American tourist who was in those same cities at the times the crimes were committed. It's possible that she uses false passports some of the time, but the probabilities are that she also uses her real identity.'

Inspector Trignant was thoughtful. 'I see your line of reasoning, monsieur.' He studied the little man before him and found himself half hoping that Cooper was mistaken. He was much too sure of himself. 'Very well. I will set the wheels in motion.'

The first burglary in the series had been committed in Stockholm. The report from Interpol Sektionen Rikspolis Styrelsen, the Interpol branch in Sweden, listed the American tourists in Stockholm that week, and the names of the women were fed into a computer. The next city checked was Milan. When the names of American women tourists in Milan at the time of the burglary was cross-checked with the names of women who had been in Stockholm during that burglary, there were fifty-five names on the list. That list was checked against the names of female Americans who had been in Ireland during a swindle, and the list was reduced to fifteen. Inspector Trignant handed the printout to Daniel Cooper.

'I'll start checking these names against the Berlin swindle,' Inspector Trignant said, 'and –'

Daniel Cooper looked up. 'Don't bother.'

The name at the top of the list was *Tracy Whitney*.

With something concrete finally to go on, Interpol went into action. Red *circulations*, which meant top priority, were sent to each member nation, advising them to be on the lookout for Tracy Whitney.

'We're also Teletyping green notices,' Inspector Trignant told Cooper.

'Green notices?'

'We use a colour-code system. A red *circulation* is top priority, blue is an enquiry for information about a suspect, a green notice puts police departments on warning that an individual is under suspicion and should be watched, black is an enquiry into unidentified bodies. X-D signals that a message is very urgent, while D is urgent. No matter what country Miss Whitney goes to, from the moment she checks through customs, she will be under observation.'

The following day Telephoto pictures of Tracy Whitney from the Southern Louisiana Penitentiary for Women were in the hands of Interpol.

Daniel Cooper put in a call to J. J. Reynolds's home. The phone rang a dozen times before it was answered.

'Hello . . .'

'I need some information.'

'Is that you, Cooper? For Christ's sake, it's four o'clock in the morning here. I was sound –'

'I want you to send me everything you can find on Tracy Whitney. Press clippings, videotapes – everything.'

'What's happening over –?'

Cooper had hung up.

One day I'll kill the son of a bitch, Reynolds swore.

Before, Daniel Cooper had been only casually interested in Tracy Whitney. Now she was his assignment. He taped her photographs on the walls of his small Paris hotel room and read all the newspaper accounts about her. He rented a video cassette player and ran and reran the television news shots of Tracy after her sentencing, and after her release from prison. Cooper sat in his darkened room hour after hour, looking at the film, and the first glimmering of suspicion became a certainty. 'You're the gang of women, Miss Whitney,' Daniel Cooper said aloud. Then he flicked the rewind button of the cassette player once more.

TWENTY-FIVE

Every year, on the first Saturday in June, the Count de Matigny sponsored a charity ball for the benefit of the Children's Hospital in Paris. Tickets for the white-tie affair were a thousand dollars apiece, and society's élite flew in from all over the world to attend.

The Château de Matigny, at Cap d'Antibes, was one of the showplaces of France. The carefully manicured grounds were superb, and the château itself dated back to the fifteenth century. On the evening of the fête, the grand ballroom and the petit ballroom were filled with beautifully dressed guests and smartly liveried servants offering endless glasses of champagne. Huge buffet tables were set up, displaying an astonishing array of hors d'oeuvres on Georgian silver platters.

Tracy, looking ravishing in a white lace gown, her hair dressed high and held in place by a diamond tiara, was dancing with her host, Count de Matigny, a widower in his late sixties, small and trim, with pale, delicate features. *The benefit ball the count gives each year for the Children's Hospital is a racket*, Gunther Hartog had told Tracy. *Ten percent of the money goes to the children – ninety percent goes into his pocket.*

'You are a superb dancer, Duchess,' the count said.

Tracy smiled. 'That's because of my partner.'

'How is it that you and I have not met before?'

'I've been living in South America,' Tracy explained. 'In the jungles, I'm afraid.'

'Why on earth!'

'My husband owns a few mines in Brazil.'

'Ah. And is your husband here this evening?'

'No. Unfortunately, he had to stay in Brazil and take care of business.'

'Unlucky for him. Lucky for me.' His arm tightened around her waist. 'I look forward to our becoming very good friends.'

'And I, too,' Tracy murmured.

Over the count's shoulder Tracy suddenly caught sight of Jeff Stevens, looking suntanned and ridiculously fit. He was dancing with a beautiful, willowy brunette in crimson taffeta, who was clinging to him possessively. Jeff saw Tracy at the same moment and smiled.

The bastard has every reason to smile, Tracy thought grimly. During the previous two weeks Tracy had meticulously planned two burglaries. She had broken into the first house and opened the safe, only to find it empty. Jeff Stevens had been there first. On the second occasion Tracy was moving through the grounds towards the targeted house when she heard the sudden acceleration of a car and caught a glimpse of Jeff as he sped away. He had beaten her to it again. He was infuriating. *Now he's here at the house I'm planning to burgle next*, Tracy thought.

Jeff and his partner danced nearer. Jeff smiled and said, 'Good evening, Count.'

The Count de Matigny smiled. 'Ah, Jeffrey. Good evening. I'm so pleased that you could come.'

'I wouldn't have missed it.' Jeff indicated the voluptuous-looking woman in his arms. 'This is Miss Wallace. The Count de Matigny.'

'*Enchanté!*' The count indicated Tracy. 'Duchess, may I present Miss Wallace and Mr Jeffrey Stevens? The Duchess de Larosa.'

Jeff's eyebrows raised questioningly. 'Sorry. I didn't hear the name.'

'De Larosa,' Tracy said evenly.

'De Larosa . . . De Larosa.' Jeff was studying Tracy. 'That name seems so familiar. Of *course*! I know your husband. Is the dear fellow here with you?'

'He's in Brazil.' Tracy found that she was gritting her teeth.

Jeff smiled. 'Ah, too bad. We used to go hunting together. Before he had his accident, of course.'

'Accident?' the count asked.

'Yes.' Jeff's tone was rueful. 'His gun went off and shot him in a very sensitive area. It was one of those stupid things.' He turned to Tracy. 'Is there any hope that he'll be normal again?'

Tracy said tonelessly. 'I'm sure that one day he'll be as normal as you are, Mr Stevens.'

'Oh, good. You will give him my best regards when you talk to him, won't you, Duchess?'

The music stopped. The Count de Matigny apologized to Tracy. 'If you'll excuse me, my dear, I have a few hostly duties to attend to.' He squeezed her hand. 'Don't forget you're seated at my table.'

As the count moved away, Jeff said to his companion, 'Angel, you put some aspirin in your bag, didn't you? Could you get one for me? I'm afraid I'm getting a terrible headache.'

'Oh, my poor darling.' There was an adoring look in her eyes. 'I'll be right back, sweetheart.'

Tracy watched her slink across the floor. 'Aren't you afraid she'll give you diabetes?'

'She is sweet, isn't she? And how have you been lately, Duchess?'

Tracy smiled for the benefit of those around them. 'That's really none of your concern, is it?'

'Ah, but it is. In fact, I'm concerned enough to give you some friendly advice. Don't try to rob this château.'

'Why? Are you planning to do it first?'

Jeff took Tracy's arm and walked her over to a deserted spot near the piano, where a dark-eyed young man was soulfully massacring American show tunes.

Only Tracy could hear Jeff's voice over the

music. 'As a matter of fact, I *was* planning a little something, but it's too dangerous.'

'Really?' Tracy was beginning to enjoy the conversation.

It was a relief to be herself, to stop playacting. *The Greeks had the right word for it*, Tracy thought. *Hypocrite* was from the Greek word for 'actor'.

'Listen to me, Tracy.' Jeff's tone was serious. 'Don't try this. First of all, you'd never get through the grounds alive. A killer guard dog is let loose at night.'

Suddenly, Tracy was listening intently. Jeff *was* planning to rob the place.

'Every window and door is wired. The alarms connect directly to the police station. Even if you did manage to get inside the house, the whole place is crisscrossed with invisible infra-red beams.'

'I know all that.' Tracy was a little smug.

'Then you must also know that the beam doesn't sound the alarm when you step into it. It sounds the alarm when you step *out* of it. It senses the heat change. There's no way you can get through it without setting it off.'

She had not known that. *How had Jeff learned it?*

'Why are you telling me all this?'

He smiled, and she thought he had never looked more attractive. 'I really don't want you to get caught, Duchess. I like having you around. You know, Tracy, you and I could become very good friends.'

'You're wrong,' Tracy assured him. She saw Jeff's date hurrying towards them. 'Here comes Ms Diabetes. Enjoy yourself.'

As Tracy walked away, she heard Jeff's date say, 'I brought you some champagne to wash it down with, poor baby.'

The dinner was sumptuous. Each course was accompanied by the appropriate wine, impeccably served by white-gloved footmen. The first course was a native asparagus with a white truffle sauce, followed by a consommé with delicate morels. After that came a saddle of lamb with an assortment of fresh vegetables from the count's gardens. A crisp endive salad was next. For dessert there were individually moulded ice-cream servings and a silver epergne, piled high with petits fours. Coffee and brandy came last. Cigars were offered to the men, and the women were given Joy perfume in a Baccarat crystal *flacon*.

After dinner, the Count de Matigny turned to Tracy. 'You mentioned that you were interested in seeing some of my paintings. Would you like to take a look now?'

'I'd love to,' Tracy assured him.

The picture gallery was a private museum filled with Italian masters, French Impressionists, and Picassos. The long hall was ablaze with the bewitching colours and forms painted by immortals. There were Monets and Renoirs, Canalettos and Guardis and Tintorettos. There was an exquisite Tiepolo and a Guercino and a Titian, and there was almost a full wall of Cezannes. There was no calculating the value of the collection.

Tracy stared at the paintings a long time, savouring their beauty. 'I hope these are well guarded.'

The count smiled. 'On three occasions thieves have tried to get at my treasures. One was killed by my dog, the second was maimed, and the third is serving a life term in prison. The château is an invulnerable fortress, Duchess.'

'I'm so relieved to hear that, Count.'

There was a bright flash of light outside. 'The fireworks display is beginning,' the count said. 'I think you'll be amused.' He took Tracy's soft hand in his papery, dry one and led her out of the picture gallery. 'I'm leaving for Deauville in the morning, where I have a villa on the sea. I've invited a few friends down next weekend. You might enjoy it.'

'I'm sure I would,' Tracy said regretfully, 'but I'm afraid my husband is getting restless. He insists that I return.'

The fireworks display lasted for almost an hour, and Tracy took advantage of the distraction to reconnoitre the house. What Jeff had said was true: the odds against a successful burglary were formidable, but for that very reason Tracy found the challenge irresistible. She knew that upstairs in the count's bedroom were $2 million in jewels, and half a dozen masterpieces, including a Leonardo.

The château is a treasure house, Gunther Hartog

had told her, *and it's guarded like one. Don't make a move unless you have a foolproof plan.*

Well, I've worked out a plan, Tracy thought. *Whether it's foolproof or not, I'll know tomorrow.*

The following night was chilly and cloudy, and the high walls around the château appeared grim and forbidding as Tracy stood in the shadows, wearing black overalls, rubber-soled shoes, and supple black kid gloves, carrying a shoulder bag. For an unguarded moment Tracy's mind embraced the memory of the walls of the penitentiary, and she gave an involuntary shiver.

She had driven the rented van alongside the stone wall at the back of the estate. From the other side of the wall came a low, fierce growl that developed into a frenzied barking, as the dog leapt into the air, trying to attack. Tracy visualized the Doberman's powerful, heavy body and deadly teeth.

She called out softly to someone in the van, 'Now.'

A slight, middle-aged man, also dressed in black, with a rucksack on his back, came out of the van holding onto a female Doberman. The dog was in season, and the tone of barking from the other side of the stone wall suddenly changed to an excited whine.

Tracy helped lift the bitch to the top of the van, which was almost the exact height of the wall.

'One, two, three,' she whispered.

And the two of them tossed the bitch over the

wall into the grounds of the estate. There were two sharp barks, followed by a series of snuffling noises, then the sound of the dogs running. After that all was quiet.

Tracy turned to her confederate. 'Let's go.'

The man, Jean Louis, nodded. She had found him in Antibes. He was a thief who had spent most of his life in prison. Jean Louis was not bright, but he was a genius with locks and alarms, perfect for this job.

Tracy stepped from the roof of the van onto the top of the wall. She unrolled a scaling ladder and hooked it to the edge of the wall. They both moved down it onto the grass below. The estate appeared vastly different from the way it had looked the evening before, when it was brightly lit and crowded with laughing guests. Now, everything was dark and bleak.

Jean Louis trailed behind Tracy, keeping a fearful watch for the Dobermans.

The château was covered with centuries-old ivy clinging to the wall up to the rooftop. Tracy had casually tested the ivy the evening before. Now, as she put her weight on a vine, it held. She began to climb, scanning the grounds below. There was no sign of the dogs. *I hope they stay busy for a long time*, she prayed.

When Tracy reached the roof, she signalled to Jean Louis and waited until he climbed up beside her. From the pinpoint light Tracy switched on, they saw a glass skylight, securely locked from below. As Tracy watched, Jean Louis reached into the rucksack on his back and pulled out a small glass cutter. It took him less than a minute to remove the glass.

Tracy glanced down and saw that their way was blocked by a spiderweb of alarm wires. 'Can you handle that, Jean?' she whispered.

'*Je peux faire ça*. No problem.' He reached into his pack and pulled out a foot-long wire with an alligator clamp on each end. Moving slowly, he traced the beginning of the alarm wire, stripped it, and connected the alligator clamp to the end of the alarm. He pulled out a pair of pliers and carefully cut the wire. Tracy tensed herself, waiting for the sound of the alarm, but all was quiet. Jean Louis looked up and grinned. '*Voilà. Fini*.'

Wrong, Tracy thought. *This is just the beginning*.

They used a second scaling ladder to climb down through the skylight. So far so good. They had made it safely into the attic. But when Tracy thought of what lay ahead, her heart began to pound.

She pulled out two pairs of red-lens goggles and handed one of them to Jean Louis. 'Put these on.'

She had figured out a way to distract the Doberman, but the infra-red ray alarms had proved to be a more difficult problem to solve. Jeff had been correct: the house was criss-crossed with invisible beams. Tracy took several long, deep breaths. *Centre your energy, your chi. Relax*. She forced her mind into a crystal clarity: *When a person moves into a beam, the sensor detects the difference in temperature and the alarm is set off. It has been devised to go off before the burglar opens the safe, leaving him no time to do anything before the police arrive.*

And there, Tracy had decided, was the weakness in the system. She had needed to devise a way to keep the alarm silent until *after* the safe was opened. At 6:30 in the morning she had found the solution. The burglary was possible, and Tracy had felt that familiar feeling of excitement begin to build within her.

Now, she slipped on the infra-red goggles, and instantly everything in the room took on an eerie red glow. In front of the attic door Tracy saw a beam of light that would have been invisible without the glasses.

'Slip under it,' she warned Jean Louis. 'Careful.'

They crawled under the beam and found themselves in a dark hallway leading to Count de Matigny's bedroom. Tracy flicked on the flashlight and led the way. Through the infra-red goggles, Tracy saw another light beam, this one low across the threshold of the bedroom door. Gingerly, she jumped over it. Jean Louis was right behind her.

Tracy played her flashlight around the walls, and there were the paintings, impressive, awesome.

Promise to bring me the Leonardo, Gunther had said. *And of course the jewellery.*

Tracy took down the picture, turned it over, and laid it on the floor. She carefully removed it from its frame, rolled up the vellum, and stored it in her shoulder bag. All that remained now was to get into the safe, which stood in a curtained alcove at the far end of the bedroom.

Tracy opened the curtains. Four infra-red lights transversed the alcove from the floor to the ceiling, crisscrossing one another. It was impossible to reach the safe without breaking one of the beams.

Jean Louis stared at the beams with dismay. '*Bon Dieu de merde!* We can't get through those. They're too low to crawl under and too high to jump over.'

'I want you to do just as I tell you,' Tracy said. She stepped round the back of him and put her arms tightly around his waist. 'Now, walk with me. Left foot first.'

Together, they took a step towards the beams, then another.

Jean Louis breathed, '*Alors!* We're going into them!'

'Right.'

They moved directly into the centre of the beams, where they converged, and Tracy stopped.

'Now, listen carefully,' she said. 'I want you to walk over to the safe.'

'But the beams –'

'Don't worry. It will be all right.' She fervently hoped she was right.

Hesitantly, Jean Louis stepped out of the infra-red beams. All was quiet. He looked back at Tracy with large, frightened eyes. She was standing in the middle of the beams, her body heat keeping the sensors from sounding the alarm. Jean Louis hurried over to the safe. Tracy stood stock-still, aware that the instant she moved, the alarm would sound.

Out of the corner of one eye, Tracy could see Jean Louis as he removed some tools from his pack and began to work on the dial of the safe. Tracy stood motionless, taking slow, deep breaths. Time stopped. Jean Louis seemed to be taking forever. The calf of Tracy's right leg began to ache, then went into spasm. Tracy gritted her teeth. She dared not move.

'How long?' she whispered.

'Ten, fifteen minutes.'

It seemed to Tracy she had been standing there a lifetime. The leg muscles in her left leg were beginning to cramp. She felt like screaming from the pain. She was pinned in the beams, frozen. She heard a click. The safe was open.

'*Magnifique! C'est la banque!* Do you wish everything?' Jean Louis asked.

'No papers. Only the jewels. Whatever cash is there is yours.'

'Merci.'

Tracy heard Jean Louis rifling through the safe, and a few moments later he was walking towards her.

'*Formidable*,' he said. 'But how do we get out of here without breaking the beam?'

'We don't,' Tracy informed him.

He stared at her. '*What?*'

'Stand in front of me.'

'But –'

'Do as I say.'

Panicky, Jean Louis stepped into the beam.

Tracy held her breath. Nothing happened. 'All right. Now, very slowly, we're going to back out of the room.'

'And then?' Jean Louis's eyes looked enormous behind the goggles.

'Then, my friend, we run for it.'

Inch by inch, they backed through the beams towards the curtains, where the beams began. When they reached them, Tracy took a deep breath. 'Right. When I say *now*, we go out the same way we came in.'

Jean Louis swallowed and nodded. Tracy could feel his small body tremble.

'*Now!*'

Tracy spun around and raced towards the door, Jean Louis after her. The instant they stepped out of the beams, the alarm sounded. The noise was deafening, shattering.

Tracy streaked to the attic and scurried up the hook ladder, Jean close behind. They raced across the roof and clambered down the ivy, and the two of them sped across the grounds towards the wall where the second ladder was waiting. Moments later they reached the roof of the van and scurried down. Tracy leapt into the driver's seat, Jean Louis at her side.

As the van raced down the side road, Tracy saw a dark sedan parked under a grove of trees. For an instant the headlights of the van lit the interior of the car. Behind the wheel sat Jeff Stevens. At his side was a large Doberman. Tracy laughed aloud and blew a kiss to Jeff as the van sped away.

From the distance came the wail of approaching police sirens.

TWENTY-SIX

Biarritz, on the southwestern coast of France, has lost much of its turn-of-the-century glamour. The once-famed Casino Bellevue is closed for badly needed repairs, while the Casino Municipal on Rue Mazagran is now a run-down building housing small shops and a dancing school. The old villas on the hills have taken on a look of shabby gentility.

Still, in high season, from July to September, the wealthy and titled of Europe continue to flock to Biarritz to enjoy the gambling and the sun and their memories. Those who do not have their own châteaux stay at the luxurious Hôtel du Palais, at 1 Avenue Impératrice. The former summer residence of Napoleon III, the hotel is situated on a promontory over the Atlantic Ocean, in one of nature's most spectacular settings: a lighthouse on one side, flanked by huge jagged rocks looming out of the grey ocean like prehistoric monsters, and the boardwalk on the other side.

On an afternoon in late August the French

Baroness Marguerite de Chantilly swept into the lobby of the Hôtel du Palais. The baroness was an elegant young woman with a sleek cap of ash-blonde hair. She wore a green-and-white silk Givenchy dress that set off a figure that made the women turn and watch her enviously, and the men gape.

The baroness walked up to the concierge. '*Ma clé, s'il vous plaît*,' she said. She had a charming French accent.

'Certainly, Baroness.' He handed Tracy her key and several telephone messages.

As Tracy walked towards the lift, a bespectacled rumpled-looking man turned abruptly away from the vitrine displaying Hermes scarves and crashed into her, knocking the handbag from her hand.

'Oh, dear,' he said. 'I'm terribly sorry.' He picked up her bag and handed it to her. 'Please forgive me.' He spoke with a Middle European accent.

The Baroness Marguerite de Chantilly gave him an imperious nod and moved on.

An attendant ushered her into the lift and let her off at the third floor. Tracy had chosen Suite 312, having learned that often the selection of the hotel accommodations was as important as the hotel itself. In Capri, it was Bungalow 522 in the Quisisana. In Majorca, it was the Royal Suite of Son Vida, overlooking the mountains and the distant bay. In New York, it was Tower Suite 4717 at The Helmsley Palace Hotel, and in Amsterdam, Room 325 at the Amstel, where one was lulled to sleep by the soothing lapping of the canal waters.

Suite 312 at the Hôtel du Palais had a panoramic view of both the ocean and the city. From every window Tracy could watch the waves crashing against the timeless rocks protruding from the sea like drowning figures. Directly below her window was an enormous kidney-shaped swimming pool, its bright blue water clashing with the grey of the ocean, and next to it a large terrace with umbrellas to ward off the summer sun. The walls of the suite were upholstered in blue-and-white silk damask, with marble baseboards, and the rugs and curtains were the colour of faded sweetheart roses. The wood of the doors and shutters was stained with the soft patina of time.

When Tracy had locked the door behind her, she took off the tight-fitting blonde wig and massaged her scalp. The baroness persona was one of her best. There were hundreds of titles to choose from in *Debrett's Peerage and Baronetage* and *Almanach de Gotha*. There were ladies and duchesses and princesses and baronesses and countesses by the score from two dozen countries, and the books were invaluable to Tracy, for they gave family histories dating back centuries, with the names of fathers and mothers and children, schools and houses, and addresses of family residences. It was a simple matter to select a prominent family and become a distant cousin – particularly a *wealthy* distant cousin. People were so impressed by titles and money.

Tracy thought of the stranger who had bumped into her in the hotel lobby and smiled. It had begun.

At 8:00 that evening the Baroness Marguerite de Chantilly was seated in the hotel's bar when the man who had collided with her earlier approached her table.

'Excuse me,' he said diffidently, 'but I must apologize again for my inexcusable clumsiness this afternoon.'

Tracy gave him a gracious smile. 'That's quite all right. It was an accident.'

'You are most kind.' He hesitated. 'I would feel much better if you would permit me to buy you a drink.'

'*Oui*. If you wish.'

He slid into a chair opposite her. 'Allow me to introduce myself. I am Professor Adolf Zuckerman.'

'Marguerite de Chantilly.'

Zuckerman signalled the waiter. 'What are you drinking?' Zuckerman asked Tracy.

'Champagne. But perhaps –'

He raised a reassuring hand. 'I can afford it. In fact, I am on the verge of being able to afford anything in the world.'

'Really?' Tracy gave him a small smile. 'How nice for you.'

'Yes.'

Zuckerman ordered a bottle of Bollinger, then turned to Tracy. 'The most extraordinary thing has happened to me. I really should not be discussing this with a stranger, but it is too exciting to keep to myself.' He leaned closer and lowered his voice. 'To tell you the truth, I am a simple schoolteacher – or I was, until recently. I teach history. It is most enjoyable, you understand, but not too exciting.'

She listened, a look of polite interest on her face.

'That is to say, it was not exciting until a few months ago.'

'May I ask what happened a few months ago, Professor Zuckerman?'

'I was doing research on the Spanish Armada, looking for odd bits and pieces that might make the subject more interesting for my students, and in the archives of the local museum, I came across an old document that had somehow got mixed in with other papers. It gave the details of a secret expedition that Prince Philip sent out in 1588. One of the ships, loaded with gold bullion, was supposed to have sunk in a storm and vanished without a trace.'

Tracy looked at him thoughtfully. '*Supposed* to have sunk?'

'Exactly. But according to these records, the captain and crew deliberately sank the ship in a deserted cove, planning to come back later and retrieve the treasure, but they were attacked and killed by pirates before they could return. The document survived only because none of the sailors on the pirate ship could read or write. They did not know the significance of what they had.' His voice was trembling with excitement. 'Now' – he lowered his voice and looked around to make sure it was safe to continue – '*I* have the document, with detailed instructions on how to get to the treasure.'

'What a fortunate discovery for you, Professor.' There was a note of admiration in her voice.

'That gold bullion is probably worth fifty million dollars today,' Zuckerman said. 'All I have to do is bring it up.'

'What's stopping you?'

He gave an embarrassed shrug. 'Money. I must outfit a ship to bring the treasure to the surface.'

'I see. How much would that cost?'

'A hundred thousand dollars. I must confess, I did something extremely foolish. I took twenty thousand dollars – my life's savings – and I came to Biarritz to gamble at the casino, hoping to win enough to . . .' His voice trailed off.

'And you lost it.'

He nodded. Tracy saw the glint of tears behind his spectacles.

The champagne arrived, and the waiter popped the cork and poured the golden liquid into their glasses.

'*Bonne chance*,' Tracy toasted.

'Thank you.'

They sipped their drinks in contemplative silence.

'Please forgive me for boring you with all this,' Zuckerman said. 'I should not be telling a beautiful lady my troubles.'

'But I find your story fascinating,' she assured him. 'You are sure the gold is there, *oui*?'

'Beyond a shadow of a doubt. I have the original shipping orders and a map drawn by the captain, himself. I know the exact location of the treasure.'

She was studying him with a thoughtful expression on her face. 'But you need a hundred thousand dollars?'

Zuckerman chuckled ruefully. 'Yes. For a treasure worth fifty million.' He took another sip of his drink.

'*C'est possible* . . .' She stopped.

'What?'

'Have you considered taking in a partner?'

He looked at her in surprise. 'A partner? No. I planned to do this alone. But of course now that I've lost my money . . .' His voice trailed off again.

'Professor Zuckerman, suppose I were to give you the hundred thousand dollars?'

He shook his head. 'Absolutely not, Baroness. I could not permit that. You might lose your money.'

'But if you're sure the treasure is there –?'

'Oh, of that I am positive. But a hundred things could go wrong. There are no guarantees.'

'In life, there are few guarantees. Your problem is *très intéressant*. Perhaps if I help you solve it, it could be lucrative for both of us.'

'No, I could never forgive myself if by any *remote* chance you should lose your money.'

'I can afford it,' she assured him. 'And I would

stand to make a great deal on my investment, *n'est-ce pas*?'

'Of course, there *is* that side of it,' Zuckerman admitted. He sat there weighing the matter, obviously torn with doubts. Finally, he said, 'If that is what you wish, you will be fifty-fifty partner.'

She smiled, pleased. '*D'accord*. I accept.'

The professor added quickly, 'After expenses, of course.'

'*Naturellement*. How soon can we get started?'

'Immediately.' The professor was charged with a sudden vitality. 'I have already found the boat I want to use. It has modern dredging equipment and a crew of four. Of course, we will have to give them a small percentage of whatever we bring up.'

'Bien sûr.'

'We should get started as quickly as possible, or we might lose the boat.'

'I can have the money for you in five days.'

'Wonderful!' Zuckerman exclaimed. 'That will give me time to make all the preparations. Ah, this was a fortuitous meeting for both of us, was it not?'

'Oui. Sans doute.'

'To our adventure.' The professor raised his glass.

Tracy raised hers and toasted, 'May it prove to be as profitable as I feel it will be.'

They clinked glasses. Tracy looked across the room and froze. At a table in the far corner was Jeff Stevens, watching her with an amused smile on his face. With him was an attractive woman ablaze with jewels.

Jeff nodded to Tracy, and she smiled, remembering how she had last seen him outside the de Matigny estate, with that silly dog beside him. *That was one for me*, Tracy thought happily.

'So, if you will excuse me,' Zuckerman was saying, 'I have much to do. I will be in touch with you.' Tracy graciously extended her hand, and he kissed it and departed.

'I see your friend has deserted you, and I can't imagine why. You look absolutely terrific as a blonde.'

Tracy glanced up. Jeff was standing beside her table. He sat down in the chair Adolf Zuckerman had occupied a few minutes earlier.

'Congratulations,' Jeff said. 'The de Matigny caper was ingenious. Very neat.'

'Coming from you, that's high praise, Jeff.'

'You're costing me a lot of money, Tracy.'

'You'll get used to it.'

He toyed with the glass in front of him. 'What did Professor Zuckerman want?'

'Oh, you know him?'

'You might say that.'

'He . . . er . . . just wanted to have a drink.'

'And tell you all about his sunken treasure?'

Tracy was suddenly wary. 'How do you know about that?'

Jeff looked at her in surprise. 'Don't tell me you *fell* for it? It's the oldest con game in the world.'

'Not this time.'

'You mean you *believed* him?'

Tracy said stiffly, 'I'm not at liberty to discuss it, but the professor happens to have some inside information.'

Jeff shook his head in disbelief. 'Tracy, he's trying to take you. How much did he ask you to invest in his sunken treasure?'

'Never mind,' Tracy said primly. 'It's my money and my business.'

Jeff shrugged. 'Right. Just don't say old Jeff didn't try to warn you.'

'It couldn't be that you're interested in that gold for yourself, could it?'

He threw up his hands in mock despair. 'Why are you always so suspicious of me?'

'It's simple,' Tracy replied. 'I don't trust you. Who was the woman you were with?' She instantly wished she could have withdrawn the question.

'Suzanne? A friend.'

'Rich, of course.'

Jeff gave her a lazy smile. 'As a matter of fact, I think she does have a bit of money. If you'd like to join us for luncheon tomorrow, the chef on her two-hundred-and-fifty-foot yacht in the harbour makes a –'

'Thank you. I wouldn't dream of interfering with your lunch. What are you selling her?'

'That's personal.'

'I'm sure it is.' It came out more harshly than she had intended.

Tracy studied him over the rim of her glass. He

really was too damned attractive. He had clean, regular features, beautiful grey eyes with long lashes, and the heart of a snake. A very intelligent snake.

'Have you ever thought of going into a legitimate business?' Tracy asked. 'You'd probably be very successful.'

Jeff looked shocked. 'What? And give up all this? You must be joking!'

'Have you always been a con artist?'

'Con artist? I'm an *entrepreneur*,' he said reprovingly.

'How did you become a – an – entrepreneur?'

'I ran away from home when I was fourteen and joined a carnival.'

'At fourteen?' It was the first glimpse Tracy had had into what lay beneath the sophisticated, charming veneer.

'It was good for me – I learned to cope. When that wonderful war in Vietnam came along, I joined up as a Green Beret and got an advanced education. I think the main thing I learned was that that war was the biggest con of all. Compared to that, you and I are amateurs.' He changed the subject abruptly. 'Do you like pelota?'

'If you're selling it, no thank you.'

'It's a game, a variation of jai alai. I have two tickets for tonight, and Suzanne can't make it. Would you like to go?'

Tracy found herself saying yes.

* * *

They dined at a little restaurant in the town square, where they had a local wine and *confit de canard l'aile* – roast duck simmered in its own juices with roasted potatoes and garlic. It was delicious.

'The speciality of the house,' Jeff informed Tracy.

They discussed politics and books and travel, and Tracy found Jeff surprisingly knowledgeable.

'When you're on your own at fourteen,' Jeff told her, 'you pick up things fast. First you learn what motivates you, then you learn what motivates other people. A con game is similar to ju jitsu. In ju jitsu you use your opponent's strength to win. In a con game, you use his greed. You make the first move, and he does the rest of your work for you.'

Tracy smiled, wondering if Jeff had any idea how much alike they were. She enjoyed being with him, but she was sure that given the opportunity, he would not hesitate to double-cross her. He was a man to be careful of, and that she intended to be.

The fronton where pelota was played was a large outdoor arena the size of a football field, high in the hills of Biarritz. There were huge green concrete backboards at either end of the court, and a playing area in the centre, with four tiers of stone benches on both sides of the field. At dusk, floodlights were turned on. When Tracy and Jeff arrived, the stands were almost full, crowded with fans, as the two teams went into action.

Members of each team took turns slamming the

ball into the concrete wall and catching it on the rebound in their cestas, the long, narrow baskets strapped to their arms. Pelota was a fast, dangerous game.

When one of the players missed the ball, the crowd screamed.

'They really take this very seriously,' Tracy commented.

'A lot of money is bet on these games. The Basques are a gambling race.'

As spectators kept filing in, the benches became more crowded, and Tracy found herself being pressed against Jeff. If he was aware of her body against his, he gave no sign of it.

The pace and ferocity of the game seemed to intensify as the minutes passed, and the screams of the fans kept echoing through the night.

'Is it as dangerous as it looks?' Tracy asked.

'Baroness, that ball travels through the air at almost a hundred miles an hour. If you get hit in the head, you're dead. But it's rare for a player to miss.' He patted her hand absently, his eyes glued to the action.

The players were experts, moving gracefully, in perfect control. But in the middle of the game, without warning, one of the players hurled the ball at the backboard at the wrong angle, and the lethal ball came hurtling straight towards the bench where Tracy and Jeff sat. The spectators scrambled for cover. Jeff grabbed Tracy and shoved her to the ground, his body covering hers. They heard the sound of the ball sailing directly over their heads and smashing into the side wall. Tracy lay on the ground, feeling the hardness of Jeff's body. His face was very close to hers.

He held her a moment, then lifted himself up and pulled her to her feet. There was a sudden awkwardness between them.

'I – I think I've had enough excitement for one evening,' Tracy said. 'I'd like to go back to the hotel, please.'

They said good night in the lobby.

'I enjoyed this evening,' Tracy told Jeff. She meant it.

'Tracy, you're not really going ahead with Zuckerman's crazy sunken-treasure scheme, are you?'

'Yes, I am.'

He studied her for a long moment. 'You still think I'm after that gold, don't you?'

She looked him in the eye. 'Aren't you?'

His expression hardened. 'Good luck.'

'Good night, Jeff.'

Tracy watched him turn and walk out of the hotel. She supposed he was on his way to see Suzanne. *Poor woman.*

The concierge said, 'Ah, good evening, Baroness. There is a message for you.'

It was from Professor Zuckerman.

Adolf Zuckerman had a problem. A very large problem. He was seated in the office of Armand

Grangier, and Zuckerman was so terrified of what was happening that he discovered he had wet his pants. Grangier was the owner of an illegal private casino located in an elegant private villa at 123 Rue de Frias. It made no difference to Grangier whether the Casino Municipal was closed or not, for the club at Rue de Frias was always filled with wealthy patrons. Unlike the government-supervised casinos, bets there were unlimited, and that was where the high rollers came to play roulette, chemin de fer and craps. Grangier's customers included Arab princes, English nobility, Oriental businessmen, African heads of state. Scantily clad young ladies circulated around the room taking orders for complimentary champagne and whiskey, for Armand Grangier had learned long before that, more than any other class of people, the rich appreciated getting something for nothing. Grangier could afford to give drinks away. His roulette wheels and his card games were rigged.

The club was usually filled with beautiful young women escorted by older gentlemen with money, and sooner or later the women were drawn to Grangier. He was a miniature of a man, with perfect features, liquid brown eyes, and a soft, sensual mouth. He stood five feet four inches, and the combination of his looks and his small stature drew women like a magnet. Grangier treated each one with feigned admiration.

'I find you irresistible, *chérie*, but unfortunately for both of us, I am madly in love with someone.'

And it was true. Of course, that *someone* changed from week to week, for in Biarritz there was an endless supply of beautiful young men, and Armand Grangier gave each one his brief place in the sun.

Grangier's connections with the underworld and the police were powerful enough for him to maintain his casino. He had worked his way up from being a ticket runner for the mob to running drugs, and finally, to ruling his own little fiefdom in Biarritz; those who opposed him found out too late how deadly the little man could be.

Now Adolf Zuckerman was being cross-examined by Armand Grangier.

'Tell me more about this baroness you talked into the sunken-treasure scheme.'

From the furious tone of his voice, Zuckerman knew that something was wrong, terribly wrong.

He swallowed and said, 'Well, she's a widow whose husband left her a lot of money, and she said she's going to come up with a hundred thousand dollars.' The sound of his own voice gave him confidence to go on: 'Once we get the money, of course, we'll tell her that the salvage ship had an accident and that we need another fifty thousand. Then it'll be another hundred thousand, and – you know – just like always.'

He saw the look of contempt on Armand Grangier's face. 'What's – what's the problem, chief?'

'The problem,' said Grangier in a steely tone, 'is

that I just received a call from one of my boys in Paris. He forged a passport for your baroness. Her name is Tracy Whitney, and she's an American.'

Zuckerman's mouth was suddenly dry. He licked his lips. 'She – she really seemed interested, chief.'

'*Balle! Conneau!* She's a con artist. You tried to pull a swindle on a swindler!'

'Then w-why did she say yes? Why didn't she just turn it down!'

Armand Grangier's voice was icy. 'I don't know, Professor, but I intend to find out. And when I do, I'm sending the lady for a swim in the bay. Nobody can make a fool out of Armand Grangier. Now, pick up that phone. Tell her a friend of yours has offered to put up half the money, and that I'm on my way over to see her. Do you think you can handle that?'

Zuckerman said eagerly, 'Sure, chief. Not to worry.'

'I do worry,' Armand Grangier said slowly. 'I worry a lot about you, Professor.'

Armand Grangier did not like mysteries. The sunken-treasure game had been worked for centuries, but the victims had to be gullible. There was simply no way a con artist would ever fall for it. That was the mystery that bothered Grangier, and he intended to solve it; and when he had the answer, the woman would be turned over to Bruno Vicente. Vicente enjoyed playing games with his victims before disposing of them.

Armand Grangier stepped out of the limousine as it stopped in front of the Hôtel du Palais, walked into the lobby, and approached Jules Bergerac, the white-haired Basque who had worked at the hotel from the age of thirteen.

'What's the number of the Baroness Marguerite de Chantilly's suite?'

There was a strict rule that desk clerks do not divulge the room numbers of guests, but rules did not apply to Armand Grangier.

'Suite three-twelve, Monsieur Grangier.'

'*Merci.*'

'And Room three-eleven.'

Grangier stopped. 'What?'

'The countess also has a room adjoining her suite.'

'Oh? Who occupies it?'

'No one.'

'No one? Are you sure?'

'*Oui, monsieur*. She keeps it locked. The maids have been ordered to keep out.'

A puzzled frown appeared on Grangier's face. 'You have a passkey?'

'Of course.' Without an instant's hesitation, the concierge reached under the desk for a passkey and handed it to Armand Grangier. Jules watched as Armand Grangier walked towards the lift. One never argued with a man like Grangier.

When Armand Grangier reached the door of the baroness's suite, he found it ajar. He pushed it open and entered. The living room was deserted. 'Hello. Anyone here?'

A feminine voice from another room sang out, 'I'm in the bath. I'll be with you in a minute. Please help yourself to a drink.'

Grangier wandered around the suite, familiar with its furnishings, for over the years he had arranged for many of his friends to stay in the hotel. He strolled into the bedroom. Expensive jewellery was carelessly spread out on a dressing table.

'I won't be a minute,' the voice called out from the bathroom.

'No hurry, Baroness.'

Baroness mon cul! he thought angrily. *Whatever little game you're playing, chérie, is going to backfire.* He walked over to the door that connected it to the adjoining room. It was locked. Grangier took out the passkey and opened the door. The room he stepped into had a musty, unused smell. The concierge had said that no one occupied it. Then why did she need –? Grangier's eye was caught by something oddly out of place. A heavy black electrical cord attached to a wall socket snaked along the length of the floor and disappeared into a cupboard. The door was open just enough to allow the cord to pass through. Curious, Grangier walked over to the cupboard and opened it.

A row of wet hundred-dollar bills held up by clothespegs on a wire was strung across the cupboard, hanging out to dry. On a typewriter stand was an object covered by a draped cloth. Grangier flicked up the cloth. He uncovered a small printing press with a still-wet hundred-dollar bill in it. Next to the press were sheets of blank paper the size of American currency and a paper cutter. Several one-hundred-dollar bills that had been unevenly cut were scattered on the floor.

An angry voice behind Grangier demanded, 'What are you doing in here?' Grangier spun round. Tracy Whitney, her hair damp from the bath and wrapped in a towel, had come into the room.

Armand Grangier said softly, '*Counterfeit!* You were going to pay us off with counterfeit money.' He watched the expressions that played across her face. Denial, outrage, and then defiance.

'All right,' Tracy admitted. 'But it wouldn't have mattered. No one can tell these from the real thing.'

'*Con!*' It was going to be a pleasure to destroy this one.

'These bills are as good as gold.'

'Really?' There was a contempt in Grangier's voice. He pulled one of the wet bills from the wire and glanced at it. He looked at one side, then the other, and then examined them more closely. They were excellent. 'Who cut these dies?'

'What's the difference? Look, I can have the hundred thousand dollars ready by Friday.'

Grangier stared at her, puzzled. And then he realized what she was thinking, and he laughed aloud. 'Jesus,' he said. 'You're really stupid. There's no treasure.'

Tracy was bewildered. 'What do you mean, no treasure? Professor Zuckerman told me –'

'And you believed him? Shame, *Baroness*.' He studied the bill in his hand again. 'I'll take this.'

Tracy shrugged. 'Take as many as you like. It's only paper.'

Grangier grabbed a handful of the wet hundred-dollar bills. 'How do you know one of the maids won't walk in here?' he asked.

'I pay them well to keep away. And when I'm out, I lock the cupboard.'

She's cool, Armand Grangier thought. *But it's not going to keep her alive.*

'Don't leave the hotel,' he ordered. 'I have a friend I want you to meet.'

Armand Grangier had intended to turn the woman over to Bruno Vicente immediately, but some instinct held him back. He examined one of the bills again. He had handled a lot of counterfeit money, but nothing nearly as good as this. Whoever had cut the dies was a genius. The paper felt authentic, and the lines were crisp and clean. The colours remained sharp and fixed, even with the bill wet, and the picture of Benjamin Franklin was perfect. The bitch was right. It *was* hard to tell the difference between what he held in his hand and the real thing. Grangier wondered whether it would be possible to pass it off as genuine currency. It was a tempting idea.

He decided to hold off on Bruno Vicente for a while.

Early the following morning Armand Grangier

sent for Zuckerman and handed him one of the hundred-dollar bills. 'Go down to the bank and exchange this for francs.'

'Sure, chief.'

Grangier watched him hurry out of the office. This was Zuckerman's punishment for his stupidity. If he was arrested, he would never tell where he got the counterfeit bill, not if he wanted to live. But if he managed to pass the bill sucessfully . . . *I'll see*, Grangier thought.

Fifteen minutes later Zuckerman returned to the office. He counted out a hundred dollars' worth of French francs. 'Anything else, chief?'

Grangier stared at the francs. 'Did you have any trouble?'

'Trouble? No. Why?'

'I want you to go back to the same bank,' Grangier ordered. 'This is what I want you to say . . .'

Adolf Zuckerman walked into the lobby of the Banque de France and approached the desk where the bank manager sat. This time Zuckerman was aware of the danger he was in, but he preferred facing that than Grangier's wrath.

'May I help you?' the manager asked.

'Yes.' He tried to conceal his nervousness. 'You see, I got into a poker game last night with some Americans I met at a bar.' He stopped.

The bank manager nodded wisely. 'And you lost your money and perhaps wish to make a loan?'

'No,' Zuckerman said. 'As – as a matter of fact, I won. The only thing is, the men didn't look quite honest to me.' He pulled out two $100 bills. 'They paid me with these, and I'm afraid they – they might be counterfeit.'

Zuckerman held his breath as the bank manager leaned forward and took the bills in his pudgy hands. He examined them carefully, first one side and then the other, then held them up to the light.

He looked at Zuckerman and smiled. 'You were lucky, monsieur. These bills are genuine.'

Zuckerman allowed himself to exhale. *Thank God!* Everything was going to be all right.

'No problem at all, chief. He said they were genuine.'

It was almost too good to be true. Armand Grangier sat there thinking, a plan already half-formed in his mind.

'Go to the baroness.'

Tracy was seated in Armand Grangier's office, facing him across his Empire desk.

'You and I are going to be partners,' Grangier informed her.

Tracy started to rise. 'I don't need a partner and –'

'Sit down.'

She looked into Grangier's eyes and sat down.

'Biarritz is my town. You try to pass a single one of those bills and you'll get arrested so fast you won't know what hit you. *Comprenez vous?* Bad things happen to pretty ladies in our jails. You can't make a move here without me.'

She studied him. 'So what I'm buying from you is protection?'

'Wrong. What you're buying from me is your life.'

Tracy believed him.

'Now, tell me where you got your printing press.'

Tracy hesitated, and Grangier enjoyed her squirming. He watched her surrender.

She said reluctantly, 'I bought it from an American living in Switzerland. He was an engraver with the U.S. Mint for twenty-five years, and when they retired him there was some technical problem about his pension and he never received it. He felt cheated and decided to get even, so he smuggled out some hundred-dollar plates that were supposed to have been destroyed and used his contacts to get the paper that the Treasury Department prints its money on.'

That explains it, Grangier thought triumphantly. *That is why the bills look so good*. His excitement grew. 'How much money can that press turn out in a day?'

'Only one bill an hour. Each side of the paper has to be processed and –'

He interrupted. 'Isn't there a larger press?'

'Yes, he has one that will turn out fifty bills every eight hours – five thousand dollars a day – but he wants half a million dollars for it.'

‘Buy it,’ Grangier said.

‘I don’t have five hundred thousand dollars.’

‘I do. How soon can you get hold of the press?’

She said reluctantly, ‘Now, I suppose, but I don’t –’

Grangier picked up the telephone and spoke into it. ‘Louis, I want five hundred thousand dollars’ worth of French francs. Take what we have from the safe and get the rest from the banks. Bring it to my office. *Vite!*’

Tracy stood up nervously. ‘I’d better go and –’

‘You’re not going anywhere.’

‘I really should –’

‘Just sit there and keep quiet. I’m thinking.’

He had business associates who would expect to be cut in on this deal, *but what they don’t know won’t hurt them*, Grangier decided. He would buy the large press himself and replace what he borrowed from the casino’s bank account with money he would print. After that, he would tell Bruno Vicente to handle the woman. She did not like partners.

Well, neither did Armand Grangier.

Two hours later the money arrived in a large sack. Grangier said to Tracy, ‘You’re checking out of the Palais. I have a house up in the hills that’s very private. You will stay there until we set up the operation.’ He pushed the phone towards her. ‘Now, call your friend in Switzerland and tell him you’re buying the big press.’

'I have his phone number at the hotel. I'll call from there. Give me the address of your house, and I'll tell him to ship the press there and –'

'*Non!*' Grangier snapped. 'I don't want to leave a trail. I'll have it picked up at the airport. We will talk about it at dinner tonight. I'll see you at eight o'clock.'

It was a dismissal. Tracy rose to her feet.

Grangier nodded towards the sack. 'Be careful with the money. I wouldn't want anything to happen to it – or to you.'

'Nothing will,' Tracy assured him.

He smiled lazily. 'I know. Professor Zuckerman is going to escort you back to your hotel.'

The two of them rode in the limousine in silence, the money bag between them, each busy with his own thoughts. Zuckerman was not exactly sure what was happening, but he sensed it was going to be very good for him. The woman was the key. Grangier had ordered him to keep an eye on her, and Zuckerman intended to do that.

Armand Grangier was in a euphoric mood that evening. By now, the large printing press would have been arranged for. The Whitney woman had said it would print $5,000 a day, but Grangier had a better plan. He intended to work the press on twenty-four hour shifts. That would bring it to $15,000 a day, more than $100,000 a week, $1 million every ten weeks. And that was just the beginning. Tonight he would learn who the engraver was and make a deal with him for more machines. There was no limit to the fortune it would make him.

At precisely 8:00, Grangier's limousine pulled into the sweeping curve of the driveway of the Hôtel du Palais, and Grangier stepped out of the car. As he walked into the lobby, he noticed with satisfaction that Zuckerman was seated near the entrance, keeping a watchful eye on the doors.

Grangier walked over to the desk. 'Jules, tell the Baroness de Chantilly I am here. Have her come down to the lobby.'

The concierge looked up and said, 'But the baroness has checked out, Monsieur Grangier.'

'You're mistaken. Call her.'

Jules Bergerac was distressed. It was unhealthy to contradict Armand Grangier. 'I checked her out myself.'

Impossible. 'When?'

'Shortly after she returned to the hotel. She asked me to bring her bill to her suite so she could settle it in cash –'

Armand Grangier's mind was racing. 'In cash? French francs?'

'As a matter of fact, yes, monsieur.'

Grangier asked frantically, 'Did she take anything out of her suite? Any baggage or boxes?'

'No. She said she would send for her luggage later.'

So she had taken his money and gone to Switzerland to make her own deal for the large printing press.

'Take me to her suite. Quickly!'

'*Oui, Monsieur Grangier.*'

Jules Bergerac grabbed a key from a rack and raced with Armand Grangier towards the lift.

As Grangier passed Zuckerman, he hissed, 'Why are you sitting there, you idiot? She's gone.'

Zuckerman looked up at him uncomprehendingly. 'She can't be gone. She hasn't come down to the lobby. I've been watching for her.'

'*Watching for her*,' Grangier mimicked. 'Have you been watching for a nurse – a grey-haired old lady – a maid going out the service door?'

Zuckerman was bewildered. 'Why would I do that?'

'Get back to the casino,' Grangier snapped. 'I'll deal with you later.'

The suite looked exactly the same as when Grangier had seen it last. The connecting door to the adjoining room was open. Grangier stepped in and hurried over to the cupboard and yanked open the door. The printing press was still there, thank God! The Whitney woman had left in too big a hurry to take it with her. That was her mistake. *And it is not her only mistake*, Grangier thought. She had cheated him out of $500,000, and he was going to pay her back with a vengeance. He would let the police help him find her and put her in jail, where his men could get at her. They would make her tell who the engraver was and then shut her up for good.

Armand Grangier dialled the number of police

headquarters and asked to talk to Inspector Dumont. He spoke earnestly into the phone for three minutes and then said, 'I'll wait here.'

Fifteen minutes later his friend the inspector arrived, accompanied by a man with an epicene figure and one of the most unattractive faces Grangier had ever seen. His forehead looked ready to burst out of his face, and his brown eyes, almost hidden behind thick spectacles, had the piercing look of a fanatic.

'This is Monsieur Daniel Cooper,' Inspector Dumont said. 'Monsieur Grangier. Mr Cooper is also interested in the woman you telephoned me about.'

Cooper spoke up. 'You mentioned to Inspector Dumont that she's involved in a counterfeiting operation.'

'*Vraiment*. She is on her way to Switzerland at this moment. You can pick her up at the border. I have all the evidence you need right here.'

He led them to the cupboard, and Daniel Cooper and Inspector Dumont looked inside.

'There is the press she printed her money on.'

Daniel Cooper walked over to the machine and examined it carefully. 'She printed the money on this press?'

'I just told you so,' Grangier snapped. He took a bill from his pocket. 'Look at this. It is one of the counterfeit hundred-dollar bills she gave me.'

Cooper walked over to the window and held the bill up to the light. 'This is a genuine bill.'

'It only *looks* like one. That is because she used stolen plates she brought from an engraver who once worked at the Mint in Philadelphia. She printed these bills on this press.'

Cooper said rudely, 'You're stupid. This is an ordinary printing press. The only thing you could print on this is letterheads.'

'Letterheads?' The room was beginning to spin.

'You actually *believed* in the fable of a machine that turns paper into genuine hundred-dollar bills?'

'I tell you I saw with my own eyes –' Grangier stopped. What had he seen? Some wet hundred-dollar bills strung up to dry, some blank paper and a paper cutter. The enormity of the swindle began to dawn on him. There *was* no counterfeiting operation, no engraver waiting in Switzerland. Tracy Whitney had never fallen for the sunken-treasure story. The bitch had used his own scheme as the bait to swindle him out of half a million dollars. If the word of this got out . . .

The two men were watching him.

'Do you wish to press charges of some kind, Armand?' Inspector Dumont asked.

How could he? What could he say? That he had been cheated while trying to finance a counterfeiting operation? And what were his associates going to do to him when they learned he had stolen half a million dollars of their money and given it away? He was filled with sudden dread.

'No. I – I don't wish to press charges.' There was panic in his voice.

Africa, Armand Grangier thought. *They'll never find me in Africa.*

Daniel Cooper was thinking, *Next time. I'll get her next time.*

TWENTY-SEVEN

It was Tracy who suggested to Gunther Hartog that they meet in Majorca. Tracy loved the island. It was one of the truly picturesque places in the world. 'Besides,' she told Gunther, 'it was once the refuge of pirates. We'll feel right at home there.'

'It might be best if we are not seen together,' he suggested.

'I'll arrange it.'

It had started with Gunther's phone call from London. 'I have something for you that is quite out of the ordinary, Tracy. I think you'll find it a real challenge.'

The following morning Tracy flew to Palma, Majorca's capital. Because of Interpol's red *circulation* on Tracy, her departure from Biarritz and her arrival in Majorca were reported to the local authorities. When Tracy checked into the Royal Suite at the Son Vida Hotel, a surveillance team was set up on a twenty-four-hour basis.

Police Commandant Ernesto Marze at Palma had spoken with Inspector Trignant at Interpol.

'I am convinced,' Trignant said, 'that Tracy Whitney is a one-woman crime wave.'

'All the worse for her. If she commits a crime in Majorca, she will find that our justice is swift.'

Inspector Trignant said, 'Monsieur, there is one other thing I should mention.'

'Sì?'

'You will be having an American visitor. His name is Daniel Cooper.'

It seemed to the detectives trailing Tracy that she was interested only in sightseeing. They followed her as she toured the island, visiting the cloister of San Francisco and the colourful Bellver Castle and the beach at Illetas. She attended a bullfight in Palma and dined on *sobrasadas* and *camaiot* in the Plaza de la Reine; and she was always alone.

She took trips to Formentor and Valldemosa and La Granja, and visited the pearl factories at Manacor.

'*Nada*,' the detectives reported to Ernesto Marze. 'She is here as a tourist, Commandant.'

The commandant's secretary came into the office. 'There is an American here to see you. Señor Daniel Cooper.'

Commandant Marze had many American friends. He liked Americans, and he had the feeling that despite what Inspector Trignant had said, he was going to like this Daniel Cooper.

He was wrong.

'You're idiots. All of you,' Daniel Cooper snapped. 'Of *course* she's not here as a tourist. She's after something.'

Commandant Marze barely managed to hold his temper in check. 'Señor, you yourself have said that Miss Whitney's targets are always something spectacular, that she enjoys doing the impossible. I have checked carefully, Señor Cooper. There is nothing in Majorca that is worthy of attracting Señorita Whitney's talents.'

'Has she met anyone here . . . talked to anyone?'

The insolent tone of the *ojete*! 'No. No one.'

'Then she will,' Daniel Cooper said flatly.

I finally know, Commandant Marze told himself, *what they mean by the Ugly American.*

There are two hundred known caves in Majorca, but the most exciting is the Cuevas del Drach, the 'Caves of the Dragon', near Porto Cristo, an hour's journey from Palma. The ancient caves go deep into the ground, enormous vaulted caverns carved with stalagmites and stalactites, tomb-silent except for the occasional rush of meandering, underground streams, with the water turning green or blue or white, each colour denoting the extent of the tremendous depths.

The caves are a fairyland of pale-ivory architecture, a seemingly endless series of labyrinths, dimly lit by strategically placed torches.

No one is permitted inside the caves without a guide, but from the moment the caves are opened to the public in the morning, they are filled with tourists.

Tracy chose Saturday to visit the caves, when they were most crowded, packed with hundreds of tourists from countries all over the world. She bought her ticket at the small counter and disappeared into the crowd. Daniel Cooper and two of Commandant Marze's men were close behind her. A guide led the excursionists along narrow stone paths, made slippery by the dripping water from the stalactites above, pointing downwards like accusing skeletal fingers.

There were alcoves where the visitors could step off the paths to stop and admire the calcium formations that looked like huge birds and strange animals and trees. There were pools of darkness along the dimly lit paths, and it was into one of these that Tracy disappeared.

Daniel Cooper hurried forward, but she was nowhere in sight. The press of the crowd moving down the steps made it impossible to locate her. He had no way of knowing whether she was ahead of him or behind him. *She is planning something here*, Cooper told himself. *But how? Where? What?*

In an arena-sized grotto at the lowest point in the caves, facing the Great Lake, is a Roman theatre. Tiers of stone benches have been built to accommodate the audiences that come to watch the spectacle staged every hour, and the sightseers take their seats in darkness, waiting for the show to begin.

Tracy counted her way up to the tenth tier and moved in twenty seats. The man in the twenty-first seat turned to her. 'Any problem?'

'None, Gunther.' She leaned over and kissed him on the cheek.

He said something, and she had to lean closer to hear him above the babel of voices surrounding them.

'I thought it best that we not be seen together, in case you're being followed.'

Tracy glanced around at the huge, packed black cavern. 'We're safe here.' She looked at him, curious. 'It must be important.'

'It is.' He leaned closer to her. 'A wealthy client is eager to acquire a certain painting. It's a Goya, called *Puerto*. He'll pay whoever can obtain it for him half a million dollars in cash. That's above my commission.'

Tracy was thoughtful. 'Are there others trying?'

'Frankly, yes. In my opinion, the chances of success are limited.'

'Where is the painting?'

'In the Prado Museum in Madrid.'

'The Prado!' The word that flashed through Tracy's mind was *impossible*.

He was leaning very close, speaking into her ear, ignoring the chattering going on around them as the arena filled up. 'This will take a great deal of ingenuity. That is why I thought of you, my dear Tracy.'

'I'm flattered,' Tracy said. 'Half a million dollars?'

'Free and clear.'

The show began, and there was a sudden hush. Slowly, invisible bulbs began to glow and music filled the enormous cavern. The centre of the stage was a large lake in front of the seated audience, and on it, from behind a stalagmite, a gondola appeared, lit by hidden spotlights. An organist was in the boat, filling the air with a melodic serenade that echoed across the water. The spectators watched, rapt, as the coloured lights rainbowed the darkness, and the boat slowly crossed the lake and finally disappeared, as the music faded.

'Fantastic,' Gunther said. 'It was worth travelling here just to see this.'

'I love travelling,' Tracy said. 'And do you know what city I've always wanted to see, Gunther? Madrid.'

Standing at the exit to the caves, Daniel Cooper watched Tracy Whitney come out.

She was alone.

TWENTY-EIGHT

The Ritz Hotel, on the Plaza de la Lealtad in Madrid, is considered the best hotel in Spain, and for more than a century it has housed and fed monarchs from a dozen European countries. Presidents, dictators, and billionaires have slept there. Tracy had heard so much about the Ritz that the reality was a disappointment. The lobby was faded and seedy-looking.

The assistant manager escorted her to the suite she had requested, 411–412, in the south wing of the hotel on Calle Felipe V.

'I trust this will be satisfactory, Miss Whitney.'

Tracy walked over to the window and looked out. Directly below, across the street, was the Prado Museum. 'This will do nicely, thank you.'

The suite was filled with blaring sounds of the heavy traffic from the streets below, but it had what she wanted: a bird's-eye view of the Prado.

Tracy ordered a light dinner in her room and retired early. When she got into the bed, she decided that trying to sleep in it had to be a modern form of medieval torture.

At midnight a detective stationed in the lobby was relieved by a colleague. 'She hasn't left her room. I think she's settled in for the night.'

In Madrid, Dirección General de Seguridad, police headquarters, is located in the Puerta del Sol and takes up an entire city block. It is a grey building with red brick, boasting a large clock tower at the top. Over the main entrance the red-and-yellow Spanish flag flies, and there is always a policeman at the door, wearing a beige uniform and a dark-brown beret, and equipped with a machine gun, a billy club, a small gun and handcuffs. It is at this headquarters that liaison with Interpol is maintained.

On the previous day an X-D Urgent cable had come in for Santiago Ramiro, the police commandant in Madrid, informing him of Tracy Whitney's impending arrival. The commandant had read the final sentence of the cable twice and then telephoned Inspector Andre Trignant at Interpol headquarters in Paris.

'I do not comprehend your message,' Ramiro had said. 'You ask me to extend my department's full cooperation to an American who is not even a policeman? For what reason?'

'Commandant, I think you will find Mr Cooper most useful. He understands Miss Whitney.'

'What is there to understand?' the commandant

retorted. 'She is a criminal. Ingenious, perhaps, but Spanish prisons are full of ingenious criminals. This one will not slip through our net.'

'*Bon*. And you will consult with Mr Cooper?'

The commandant said grudgingly, 'If you say he can be useful, I have no objection.'

'*Merci, monsieur*.'

'*De nada, señor*.'

Commandant Ramiro, like his counterpart in Paris, was not fond of Americans. He found them rude, materialistic and naïve. *This one*, he thought, *may be different. I will probably like him*.

He hated Daniel Cooper on sight.

'She's outsmarted half the police forces in Europe,' Daniel Cooper asserted, as he entered the commandant's office. 'And she'll probably do the same to you.'

It was all the commandant could do to control himself. 'Señor, we do not need anyone to tell us our business. Señorita Whitney has been under surveillance from the moment she arrived at Barajas Airport this morning. I assure you that if someone drops even a pin on the street and your Miss Whitney picks it up, she will be whisked to jail. She has not dealt with the Spanish police before.'

'She's not here to pick up a pin in the street.'

'Why do you think she *is* here?'

'I'm not sure. I can only tell you that it will be something big.'

Commandant Ramiro said smugly. 'The bigger the better. We will watch her every move.'

When Tracy awakened in the morning, groggy from a torturous night's sleep in the bed designed by Tomás de Torquemada, she ordered a light breakfast and hot, black coffee, and walked over to the window over-looking the Prado. It was an imposing fortress, built of stone and red bricks from the native soil, and was surrounded by grass and trees. Two Doric columns stood in front, and, on either side, twin staircases led up to the front entrance. At the street level were two side entrances. Schoolchildren and tourists from a dozen countries were lined up in front of the museum, and at exactly 10:00 A.M., the two large front doors were opened by guards, and the visitors began to move through the revolving door in the centre and through the two side passages at ground level.

The telephone rang, startling Tracy. No one except Gunther Hartog knew she was in Madrid. She picked up the telephone. 'Hello?'

'*Buenos días, señorita.*' It was a familiar voice. 'I'm calling for the Madrid Chamber of Commerce, and they have instructed me to do everything I can to make sure you have an exciting time in our city.'

'How did you know I was in Madrid, Jeff?'

'Señorita, the Chamber of Commerce knows everything. Is this your first time here?'

'Yes.'

'*Bueno!* Then I can show you a few places. How long do you plan to be here, Tracy?'

It was a leading question. 'I'm not sure,' she said lightly. 'Just long enough to do a little shopping and sightseeing. What are you doing in Madrid?'

'The same.' His tone matched hers. 'Shopping and sightseeing.'

Tracy did not believe in coincidence. Jeff Stevens was there for the same reason she was: to steal the *Puerto*.

He asked, 'Are you free for dinner?'

It was a dare. 'Yes.'

'Good. I'll make a reservation at the Jockey.'

Tracy certainly had no illusions about Jeff, but when she stepped out of the lift into the lobby and saw him standing there waiting for her, she was unreasonably pleased to see him.

Jeff took her hand in his. '*Fantástico, querida!* You look lovely.'

She had dressed carefully. She wore a Valentino navy-blue suit with a Russian sable flung around her neck. Maud Frizon pumps, and she carried a navy hand-bag emblazoned with the Hermes H.

Daniel Cooper, seated at a small round table in a corner of the lobby with a glass of Perrier before him, watched Tracy as she greeted her escort, and he felt a sense of enormous power: *Justice is mine, sayeth the Lord, and I am His sword and His instrument of vengeance. My life is a penance, and you shall help me pay. I'm going to punish you.*

Cooper knew that no police force in the world

was clever enough to catch Tracy Whitney. *But I am*, Cooper thought. *She belongs to me*.

Tracy had become more than an assignment to Daniel Cooper. She had become an obsession. He carried her photographs and file with him everywhere, and at night before he went to sleep, he lovingly pored over them. He had arrived in Biarritz too late to catch her, and she had eluded him in Majorca, but now that Interpol had picked up her trail again, Cooper was determined not to lose it.

He dreamed about Tracy at night. She was in a giant cage, naked, pleading with him to set her free. *I love you*, he said, *but I'll never set you free*.

The Jockey was a small, elegant restaurant on Amador de los Ríos.

'The food here is superb,' Jeff promised.

He was looking particularly handsome, Tracy thought. There was an inner excitement about him that matched Tracy's, and she knew why: they were competing with each other, matching wits in a game for high stakes. *But I'm going to win*, Tracy thought. *I'm going to find a way to steal that painting from the Prado before he does*.

'There's a strange rumour around,' Jeff was saying.

She focused her attention on him. 'What kind of rumour?'

'Have you ever heard of Daniel Cooper? He's an insurance investigator, very bright.'

'No. What about him?'

'Be careful. He's dangerous. I wouldn't want anything to happen to you.'

'Don't worry.'

'But I have been, Tracy.'

She laughed. 'About me? Why?'

He put a hand over hers and said lightly, 'You're very special. Life is more interesting with you around, my love.'

He's so damned convincing, Tracy thought. *If I didn't know better, I'd believe him.*

'Let's order,' Tracy said. 'I'm starved.'

In the days that followed, Jeff and Tracy explored Madrid. They were never alone. Two of Commandant Ramiro's men followed them everywhere, accompanied by the strange American. Ramiro had given permission for Cooper to be a part of the surveillance team simply to keep the man out of his hair. The American was *loco*, convinced that the Whitney woman was somehow going to steal some great treasure from under the noses of the police. *Que ridículo!*

Tracy and Jeff dined at Madrid's classic restaurants – Horcher, the Príncipe de Viana and Casa Botín – but Jeff also knew the places undiscovered by tourists: Casa Paco and La Chuletta and El Lacón, where he and Tracy dined on delicious native stews like *cocido Madrileño* and *olla podrida*, and then visited a small bar where they had delicious *tapas*.

Wherever they went, Daniel Cooper and the two detectives were never far behind.

Watching them from a careful distance, Daniel Cooper was puzzled by Jeff Stevens's role in the drama that was being played out. Who was he? Tracy's next victim? Or were they plotting something together?

Cooper talked to Commandant Ramiro. 'What information do you have on Jeff Stevens?' Cooper asked.

'*Nada*. He has no criminal record and is registered as a tourist. I think he is just a companion the lady picked up.'

Cooper's instincts told him differently. But it was not Jeff Stevens he was after. *Tracy*, he thought. *I want you, Tracy*.

When Tracy and Jeff returned to the Ritz at the end of a late evening, Jeff escorted Tracy to her door. 'Why don't I come in for a nightcap?' he suggested.

Tracy was almost tempted. She leaned forward and kissed him lightly on the cheek. 'Think of me as your sister, Jeff.'

'What's your position on incest?'

But she had closed the door.

A few minutes later he telephoned her from his room. 'How would you like to spend tomorrow with me in Segovia? It's a fascinating old city just a few hours' drive outside Madrid.'

'It sounds wonderful. Thanks for a lovely evening,' Tracy said. 'Good night, Jeff.'

She lay awake a long time, her mind filled with thoughts she had no right to be thinking. It had been so long since she had been emotionally involved with a man. Charles had hurt her badly, and she had no wish to be hurt again. Jeff Stevens was an amusing companion, but she knew she must never allow him to become any more than that. It would be easy to fall in love with him. And foolish.

Ruinous.

Fun.

Tracy had difficulty falling asleep.

The trip to Segovia was perfect. Jeff had rented a small car, and they drove out of the city into the beautiful wine country of Spain. An unmarked Seat trailed behind them during the entire day, but it was not an ordinary car.

The Seat is the only car manufactured in Spain, and it is the official car of the Spanish police. The regular model has only 100 horsepower, but the ones sold to the Policía Nacional and the Guardia Civil are souped up to 150 horsepower, so there was no danger that Tracy Whitney and Jeff Stevens would elude Daniel Cooper and the two detectives.

Tracy and Jeff arrived in Segovia in time for lunch and dined at a charming restaurant in the main square under the shadow of the two-thousand-year-old aqueduct built by the Romans. After lunch they wandered around the medieval city and visited the old Cathedral of Santa María and the Renaissance town hall, and then drove up to the Alcázar, the old Roman fortress perched on a rocky spur high over the city. The view was breathtaking.

'I'll bet if we stayed here long enough, we'd see Don Quixote and Sancho Panza riding along the plains below,' Jeff said.

She studied him. 'You enjoy tilting at windmills, don't you?'

'Depends on the shape of the windmill,' he said softly. He moved closer to her.

Tracy stepped away from the edge of the cliff. 'Tell me more about Segovia.'

And the spell was broken.

Jeff was an enthusiastic guide, knowledgeable about history, archaeology and architecture, and Tracy had to keep reminding herself that he was also a con artist. It was the most pleasant day Tracy could remember.

One of the Spanish detectives, José Pereira, grumbled to Cooper, 'The only thing they're stealing is our time. They're just two people in love, can't you see that? Are you sure she's planning something?'

'I'm sure,' Cooper snarled. He was puzzled by his own reactions. All he wanted was to catch Tracy Whitney, to punish her, as she deserved. She was just another criminal, an assignment. Yet, every time Tracy's companion took her arm, Cooper found himself stung with fury.

When Tracy and Jeff arrived back in Madrid, Jeff said, 'If you're not too exhausted, I know a special place for dinner.'

'Lovely.' Tracy did not want the day to end. *I'll give myself this day, this one day to be like other women.*

Madrileños dine late, and few restaurants open for dinner before 9:00 P.M. Jeff made a reservation for 10:00 at the Zalacaín, an elegant restaurant where the food was superb and perfectly served. Tracy ordered no dessert, but the waiter brought a delicate flaky pastry that was the most delicious thing she had ever tasted. She sat back in her chair, sated and happy.

'It was a wonderful dinner. Thank you.'

'I'm so glad you enjoyed it. This is the place to bring people if you want to impress them.'

She studied him. 'Are you trying to impress me, Jeff?'

He grinned. 'You bet I am. Wait until you see what's next.'

What was next was an unprepossessing *bodega*, a smoky café filled with leather-jacketed Spanish workmen drinking at the bar and at the dozen tables in the room. At one end was a *tablado*, a slightly elevated platform, where two men strummed guitars. Tracy and Jeff were seated at a small table near the platform.

'Do you know anything about flamenco?' Jeff asked. He had to raise his voice over the noise level in the bar.

'Only that it's a Spanish dance.'

'Gypsy, originally. You can go to fancy nightclubs in Madrid and see imitations of flamenco, but tonight you'll see the real thing.'

Tracy smiled at the enthusiasm in Jeff's voice.

'You're going to see a classic *cuadro flamenco*. That's a group of singers, dancers and guitarists. First they perform together, then each one takes his turn.'

Watching Tracy and Jeff from a table in the corner near the kitchen, Daniel Cooper wondered what they were discussing so intently.

'The dance is very subtle, because everything has to work together – movements, music, costumes, the building of the rhythm . . .'

'How do you know so much about it?' Tracy asked.

'I used to know a flamenco dancer.'

Naturally, Tracy thought.

The lights in the *bodega* dimmed, and the small stage was lit by spotlights. Then the magic began. It started slowly. A group of performers casually ascended to the platform. The women wore colourful skirts and blouses, and high combs with flowers banked on their beautiful Andalusian coiffures. The male dancers were dressed in the traditional tight trousers and vests and wore gleaming cordovan-leather half boots. The guitarists strummed a wistful melody, while one of the seated women sang in Spanish.

Yo quería dejar
A mi amante,
Pero antes de que pudiera,

Hacerlo ella me abandonó
Y destrozó mi corazón.

'Do you understand what she's saying?' Tracy whispered.

'Yes. "I wanted to leave my lover, but before I could, he left me and he broke my heart."'

A dancer moved to the centre of the stage. She started with a simple *zapateado*, a beginning stamping step, gradually pushed faster and faster by the pulsating guitars. The rhythm grew, and the dancing became a form of sensual violence, variations on steps that had been born in gypsy caves a hundred years earlier. As the music mounted in intensity and excitement, moving through the classic figures of the dance, from *alegría* to *fandanguillo* to *zambra* to *seguiriya*, and as the frantic pace increased, there were shouts of encouragement from the performers at the side of the stage.

Cries of '*Olé tu madre*', and '*Olé tus santos*', and '*Anda, anda*', the traditional *jaleos* and *piropos*, or shouts of encouragement, goaded the dancers on to wilder, more frantic rhythms.

When the music and dancing ended abruptly, a silence roared through the bar, and then there was a loud burst of applause.

'She's marvellous!' Tracy exclaimed.

'Wait,' Jeff told her.

A second woman stepped to the centre of the stage. She had a dark, classical Castilian beauty and seemed deeply aloof, completely unaware of the audience. The guitars began to play a *bolero*, plaintive and low key, an Oriental-sounding *canto*. A male dancer joined her, and the castanets began to click in a steady, driving beat.

The seated performers joined in the *jaleo*, and the handclaps that accompany the flamenco dance, and the rhythmic beat of the palms embraced the music and dancing, lifting it, building it, until the room began to rock with the echo of the *zapateado*, the hypnotic beat of the half toe, the heel, and the full sole clacking out an endless variation of tone and rhythmic sensations.

Their bodies moved apart and came together in a growing frenzy of desire, until they were making mad, violent, animal love without ever touching, moving to a wild, passionate climax that had the audience screaming. As the lights blacked out and came on again, the crowd roared, and Tracy found herself screaming with the others. To her embarrassment, she was sexually aroused. She was afraid to meet Jeff's eyes. The air between them vibrated with tension. Tracy looked down at the table, at his strong, tanned hands, and she could feel them caressing her body, slowly, swiftly, urgently, and she quickly put her hands in her lap to hide their trembling.

They said very little during the ride back to the hotel. At the door to Tracy's room, she turned and said, 'It's been a –'

Jeff's lips were on hers, and her arms went around him, and she held him tightly to her.

'Tracy –?'

The word on her lips was *yes*, and it took the last ounce of her willpower to say, 'It's been a long day, Jeff. I'm a sleepy lady.'

'Oh.'

'I think I'll just stay in my room tomorrow and rest.'

His voice was level when he answered. 'Good idea. I'll probably do the same.'

Neither of them believed the other.

TWENTY-NINE

At 10:00 the following morning Tracy was standing in the long line at the entrance to the Prado Museum. As the doors opened, a uniformed guard operated a turnstile that admitted one visitor at a time.

Tracy purchased a ticket and moved with the crowd going into the large rotunda. Daniel Cooper and Detective Pereira stayed well behind her, and Cooper began to feel a growing excitement. He was certain that Tracy Whitney was not there as a visitor. Whatever her plan was, it was beginning.

Tracy moved from room to room, walking slowly through the salons filled with Rubens paintings and Titians, Tintorettos, Bosches, and paintings by Domenikos Theotokopoulos, who became famous as El Greco. The Goyas were exhibited in a special gallery below, on the ground floor.

Tracy noted that a uniformed guard was stationed at the entrance to each room, and at his elbow was a red alarm button. She knew that the moment the alarm sounded, all entrances and exits to the museum would be sealed off, and there would be no chance to escape.

She sat on the bench in the centre of the Muses room, filled with eighteenth-century Flemish masters, and let her gaze wander towards the floor. She could see a round access fixture on each side of the doorway. That would be the infra-red beams that were turned on at night. In other museums Tracy had visited, the guards had been sleepy and bored, paying little attention to the stream of chattering tourists, but here the guards were alert. Works of art were being defaced by fanatics in museums around the world, and the Prado was taking no chance that it could happen there.

In a dozen different rooms artists had set up their easels and were assiduously at work copying paintings of the masters. The museum permitted it, but Tracy noticed that the guards kept a close eye even on the copiers.

When Tracy had finished with the rooms on the main floor, she took the stairs to the ground floor, to the Francisco de Goya exhibition.

Detective Pereira said to Cooper. 'See, she's not doing anything but looking. She –'

'You're wrong.' Cooper started down the stairs in a run.

It seemed to Tracy that the Goya exhibition was more heavily guarded than the others, and it well deserved to be. Wall after wall was filled with an incredible display of timeless beauty, and Tracy moved from canvas to canvas, caught up in the genius of the man. Goya's *Self-Portrait*, making him look like a middle-aged Pan . . . the exquisitely coloured portrait of *The Family of Charles IV* . . . *The Clothed Maja* and the famed *Nude Maja*.

And there, next to *The Witches' Sabbath*, was the *Puerto*. Tracy stopped and stared at it, her heart beginning to pound. In the foreground of the painting were a dozen beautifully dressed men and women standing in front of a stone wall, while in the background, seen through a luminous mist, were fishing boats in a harbour and a distant lighthouse. In the lower left-hand corner of the picture was Goya's signature.

This was the target. *Half a million dollars*.

Tracy glanced around. A guard stood at the entrance. Beyond him, through the long corridor leading to other rooms, Tracy could see more guards. She stood there a long time, studying the *Puerto*. As she started to move away, a group of tourists was coming down the stairs. In the middle of them was Jeff Stevens. Tracy averted her head and hurried out the side entrance before he could see her.

It's going to be a race, Mr Stevens, and I'm going to win it.

'She's planning to steal a painting from the Prado.'

Commandant Ramiro looked at Daniel Cooper

incredulously. '*Cagajón!* No one can steal a painting from the Prado.'

Cooper said stubbornly, 'She was there all morning.'

'There has never been a theft at the Prado, and there never will be. And do you know why? Because it is impossible.'

'She's not going to try any of the usual ways. You must have the museum vents protected, in case of a gas attack. If the guards drink coffee on the job, find out where they get it and if it can be drugged. Check the drinking water –'

The limits of Commandant Ramiro's patience was exhausted. It was bad enough that he had had to put up with this rude, unattractive American for the past week, and that he had wasted valuable manpower having Tracy Whitney followed around the clock, when his Policía Nacional was already working under an austerity budget; but now, confronted by this *pito*, telling him how to run *his* police department, he could stand no more.

'In my opinion, the lady is in Madrid on a holiday. I am calling off the surveillance.'

Cooper was stunned. 'No! You can't do that. Tracy Whitney is –'

Commandant Ramiro rose to his full height. 'You will kindly refrain from telling me what I can do, señor. And now, if you have nothing further to say, I am a very busy man.'

Cooper stood there, filled with frustration. 'I'd like to continue alone, then.'

The commandant smiled. ‘To keep the Prado Museum safe from the terrible threat of this woman? Of course, Señor Cooper. Now I can sleep at night.’

THIRTY

The chances of success are extremely limited, Gunther Hartog had told Tracy. *It will take a great deal of ingenuity.*

That is the understatement of the century, Tracy thought.

She was staring out the window of her suite, down at the skylight roof of the Prado, mentally reviewing everything she had learned about the museum. It was open from 10:00 in the morning until 6:00 in the evening, and during that time the alarms were off, but guards were stationed at each entrance and in every room.

Even if one could manage to take a painting off the wall, Tracy thought, *there's no way to smuggle it out*. All packages had to be checked at the door.

She studied the roof of the Prado and considered a night foray. There were several drawbacks: the first one was the high visibility. Tracy had watched as the spotlights came on at night, flooding the roof, making it visible for miles around. Even if it were possible to get into the building unseen, there were still the infra-red beams inside the building and the night watchmen.

The Prado seemed to be impregnable.

What was Jeff planning? Tracy was certain he was going to make a try for the Goya. *I'd give anything to know what he has in his crafty little mind.* Of one thing Tracy was sure: she was not going to let him get there ahead of her. She had to find a way.

She returned to the Prado the next morning.

Nothing had changed except the faces of the visitors. Tracy kept a careful lookout for Jeff, but he did not appear.

Tracy thought, *He's already figured out how he's going to steal it. The bastard. All this charm he's been using was just to try to distract me, and keep me from getting the painting first.*

She suppressed her anger and replaced it with clear, cold logic.

Tracy walked over to the *Puerto* again, and her eyes wandered over the nearby canvases, the alert guards, the amateur painters sitting on stools in front of their easels, the crowds, flowing in and out of the room, and as she looked around, Tracy's heart suddenly began to beat faster.

I know how I'm going to do it!

She made a telephone call from a public booth on the Gran Vía, and Daniel Cooper, who stood in a coffee shop doorway watching, would have given a year's pay to know whom Tracy was calling. He was sure it was an overseas call and that she was phoning collect, so that there would be no record of it. He was aware of the lime-green linen dress that he had not seen before and that her legs were bare. *So that men can stare at them*, he thought. *Whore.*

He was filled with rage.

In the telephone booth, Tracy was ending her conversation. 'Just make sure he's fast, Gunther. He'll have only about two minutes. Everything will depend on speed.'

TO:
J. J. Reynolds File No. Y-72-830-412

FROM:
Daniel Cooper CONFIDENTIAL

SUBJECT: Tracy Whitney

It is my opinion that the subject is in Madrid to carry out a major criminal endeavour. The likely target is the Prado Museum. The Spanish police are being uncooperative, but I will personally keep the subject under surveillance and apprehend her at the appropriate time.

Two days later, at 9:00 A.M., Tracy was seated on a bench in the gardens of the Retiro, the beautiful park running through the centre of Madrid, feeding the pigeons. The Retiro, with its lake and graceful trees and well-kept grass, and miniature stages with shows for children, was a magnet for the Madrileños.

Cesar Porretta, an elderly, grey-haired man with a slight hunchback, walked along the park path, and when he reached the bench, he sat down beside Tracy, opened a paper sack, and began throwing out bread crumbs to the birds. '*Buenos días, señorita.*'

'*Buenos días*. Do you see any problems?'

'None, señorita. All I need is the time and the date.'

'I don't have it,' Tracy told him. 'Soon.'

He smiled, a toothless smile. 'The police will go crazy. No one has ever tried anything like this before.'

'That's why it's going to work,' Tracy said. 'You'll hear from me.' She tossed out a last crumb to the pigeons and rose. She walked away, her silk dress swaying provocatively around her knees.

While Tracy was in the park with Cesar Porretta, Daniel Cooper was searching her hotel room. He had watched from the lobby as Tracy left the hotel and headed for the park. She had not ordered anything from room service, and Cooper had decided that she was going out to breakfast. He had given himself thirty minutes. Entering her suite had been a simple matter of avoiding the floor maids and using a lock pick. He knew what he was looking for: a copy of a painting. He had no idea how Tracy planned to substitute it, but he was sure it had to be her scheme.

He searched the suite with swift, silent efficiency, missing nothing and saving the bedroom for last. He looked through her wardrobe, examining her dresses, and then the dressing table. He opened the drawers, one by one. They were filled with panties and bras and pantyhose. He picked up a pair of pink underpants and rubbed them against his cheek and imagined her sweet-smelling flesh in them. The scent of her was suddenly everywhere. He replaced the garment and quickly looked through the other drawers. No painting.

Cooper walked into the bathroom. There were drops of water in the tub. Her body had lain there, covered with water as warm as the womb, and Cooper could visualize Tracy lying in it, naked, the water caressing her breasts as her hips undulated up and down. He felt an erection begin. He picked up the damp flannel from the bath and brought it to his lips. The odor of her body swirled around him as he unzipped his trousers. He rubbed a cake of damp soap onto the flannel and began stroking himself with it, facing the mirror, looking into his blazing eyes.

A few minutes later he left, as quietly as he had arrived, and headed directly for a nearby church.

The following morning when Tracy left the Ritz Hotel, Daniel Cooper followed her. There was an intimacy between them that had not existed before. He knew her smell; he had seen her in her bath, had watched her naked body writhing in the warm water. She belonged completely to him; she was his to destroy. He watched her as she wandered along the Gran Vía, examining the merchandise in the shops, and he followed her into a large department store, careful to remain out of sight. He saw her speak to a clerk, then head for the ladies' room. Cooper stood near the door, frustrated. It was the one place he could not follow her.

If Cooper had been able to go inside, he would have seen Tracy talking to a grossly overweight, middle-aged woman.

'*Mañana*,' Tracy said, as she applied fresh lipstick before the mirror. 'Tomorrow morning, eleven o'clock.'

The woman shook her head. 'No, señorita. He will not like that. You could not choose a worse day. Tomorrow the Prince of Luxembourg arrives on a state visit, and the newspapers say he will be taken on a tour of the Prado. There will be extra security guards and police all over the museum.'

'The more the better. Tomorrow.'

Tracy walked out the door, and the woman looked after her muttering, '*La cucha es loca . . .*'

The royal party was scheduled to appear at the Prado at exactly 11:00 A.M., and the streets around the Prado had been roped off by the Guardia Civil. Because of a delay in the ceremony at the presidential palace, the entourage did not arrive until close to noon. There were the screams of sirens as police motorcycles came into view, escorting a procession of half a dozen black limousines to the front steps of the Prado.

At the entrance, the director of the museum, Christian Machada, nervously awaited the arrival of His Highness.

Machada had made a careful morning inspection to be sure everything was in order, and the guards had been forewarned to be especially alert. The director was proud of his museum, and he wanted to make a good impression on the prince.

It never hurts to have friends in high places, Machada thought. *Quién sabe? I might even be invited to dine with His Highness this evening at the presidential palace.*

Christian Machada's only regret was that there was no way to stop the hordes of tourists that wandered about. But the prince's bodyguards and the museum's security guards would ensure that the prince was protected. Everything was in readiness for him.

The royal tour began upstairs, on the main floor. The director greeted His Highness with an effusive welcome and escorted him, followed by the armed guards, through the rotunda and into the rooms where the sixteenth-century Spanish painters were on exhibit: Juan de Juanes, Pedro Machuca, Fernando Yáñez.

The prince moved slowly, enjoying the visual

feast spread before him. He was a patron of the arts and genuinely loved the painters who could make the past come alive and remain eternal. Having no talent for painting himself, the prince, as he looked around the rooms, nonetheless envied the painters who stood before their easels trying to snatch sparks of genius from the masters.

When the official party had visited the upstairs salons, Christian Machada said proudly, 'And now, if Your Highness will permit me, I will take you downstairs to our Goya exhibit.'

Tracy had spent a nerve-racking morning. When the prince had not arrived at the Prado at 11:00 as scheduled, she had begun to panic. All her arrangements had been made and timed to the second, but she needed the prince in order to make them work.

She moved from room to room, mixing with the crowds, trying to avoid attracting attention. *He's not coming*, Tracy thought finally. *I'm going to have to call it off*. And at that moment, she had heard the sound of approaching sirens from the street.

Watching Tracy from a vantage point in the next room, Daniel Cooper, too, was aware of the sirens. His reason told him it was impossible for anyone to steal a painting from the museum, but his instinct told him that Tracy was going to try it, and Cooper trusted his instinct. He moved closer to her, letting the crowds conceal him from view. He intended to keep her in sight every moment.

Tracy was in the room next to the salon where the *Puerto* was being exhibited. Through the open doorway she could see the hunchback, Cesar Porretta, seated before an easel, copying Goya's *Clothed Maja*, which hung next to the *Puerto*. A guard stood three feet away. In the room with Tracy, a woman painter stood at her easel, studiously copying *The Milkmaid of Bordeaux*, trying to capture the brilliant browns and greens of Goya's canvas.

A group of Japanese tourists fluttered into the salon, chattering like a flock of exotic birds. *Now!* Tracy told herself. This was the moment she had been waiting for, and her heart was pounding so loudly she was afraid the guard could hear it. She moved out of the path of the approaching Japanese tour group, backing towards the woman painter. As a Japanese man brushed in front of Tracy, Tracy fell backwards, as if pushed, bumping the artist and sending her, the easel, canvas and paints flying to the ground.

'Oh, I'm terribly sorry!' Tracy exclaimed. 'Let me help you.'

As she moved to assist the startled artist, Tracy's heels stamped into the scattered paints, smearing them into the floor. Daniel Cooper, who had seen everything, hurried closer, every sense alert. He was sure Tracy Whitney had made her first move.

The guard rushed over, calling out, '*¿Qué pasa? ¿Qué pasa?*'

The accident had attracted the attention of the

tourists, and they milled around the fallen woman, smearing the paints from the crushed tubes into grotesque images on the hardwood floor. It was an unholy mess, and the prince was due to appear at any moment. The guard was in a panic. He yelled out, 'Sergio! *Ven acá! Pronto!*'

Tracy watched as the guard from the next room came running in to help. Cesar Porretta was alone in the salon with the *Puerto*.

Tracy was in the middle of the uproar. The two guards were trying vainly to push the tourists away from the area of the paint-smeared floor.

'Get the director,' Sergio yelled. '*¡En seguida!*'

The other guard hurried off towards the stairs. *¡Que birria! What a mess!*

Two minutes later Christian Machada was at the scene of the disaster. The director took one horrified look and screamed, 'Get some cleaning women down here – quickly! Mops and cloths and turpentine. *¡Pronto!*'

A young aide rushed to do his bidding.

Machada turned to Sergio. 'Get back to your post,' he snapped.

'Yes, sir.'

Tracy watched the guard push his way through the crowd to the room where Cesar Porretta was working.

Cooper had not taken his eyes off Tracy for an instant. He had waited for her next move. But it had not come. She had not gone near any of the paintings, nor had she made contact with an accomplice. All she had done was knock over an easel and spill some paints on the floor, but he was certain it had been done deliberately. But to what purpose? Somehow, Cooper felt that whatever had been planned had already happened. He looked around the walls of the salon. None of the paintings were missing.

Cooper hurried into the adjoining room. There was no one there but the guard and an elderly hunchback seated at his easel, copying the *Clothed Maja*. All the paintings were in place. But something was wrong. Cooper *knew* it.

He hurried back to the harassed director, whom he had met earlier. 'I have reason to believe,' Cooper blurted out, 'that a painting has been stolen from here in the past few minutes.'

Christian Machada stared at the wild-eyed American. 'What are you talking about? If that were so, the guards would have sounded the alarm.'

'I think that somehow a fake painting was substituted for a real one.'

The director gave him a tolerant smile. 'There is one small thing wrong with your theory, señor. It is not known to the general public, but there are sensors hidden behind each painting. If anyone tried to lift a painting from the wall – which they would certainly have to do to substitute another painting – the alarm would instantly sound.'

Daniel Cooper was still not satisfied. 'Could your alarm be disconnected?'

'No. If someone cut the wire to the power, that

also would cause the alarm to go off. Señor, it is *impossible* for anyone to steal a painting from this museum. Our security is what you call proof from fools.'

Cooper stood there shaking with frustration. Everything the director said was convincing. It *did* seem impossible. But then why had Tracy Whitney deliberately spilled those paints?

Cooper would not give up. 'Humour me. Would you ask your staff to go through the museum and check to make sure nothing is missing? I'll be at my hotel.'

There was nothing more Daniel Cooper could do.

At 7:00 that evening Christian Machada telephoned Cooper. 'I have personally made an inspection, señor. Every painting is in its proper place. Nothing is missing from the museum.'

So that was that. Seemingly, it *had* been an accident. But Daniel Cooper, with the instincts of a hunter, sensed that his quarry had escaped.

Jeff had invited Tracy to dinner in the main dining room of the Ritz Hotel.

'You're looking especially radiant this evening,' Jeff complimented her.

'Thank you. I feel absolutely wonderful.'

'It's the company. Come with me to Barcelona next week, Tracy. It's a fascinating city. You'd love –'

'I'm sorry, Jeff. I can't. I'm leaving Spain.'

'Really?' His voice was filled with regret. 'When?'

'In a few days.'

'Ah. I'm disappointed.'

You're going to be more disappointed, Tracy thought, *when you learn I've stolen the Puerto*. She wondered how he had planned to steal the painting. Not that it mattered any longer. *I've outwitted clever Jeff Stevens*. Yet, for some inexplicable reason Tracy felt a faint trace of regret.

Christian Machada was seated in his office enjoying his morning cup of strong black coffee and congratulating himself on what a success the prince's visit had been. Except for the regrettable incident of the spilled paints, everything had gone off precisely as planned. He was grateful that the prince and his retinue had been diverted until the mess could be cleaned up. The director smiled when he thought about the idiot American investigator who had tried to convince him that someone had stolen a painting from the Prado. *Not yesterday, not today, not tomorrow*, he thought smugly.

His secretary walked into the office. 'Excuse me, sir. There is a gentleman to see you. He asked me to give you this.'

She handed the director a letter. It was on the letterhead of the Kunsthaus museum in Zürich.

My Esteemed Colleague:

This letter will serve to introduce Monsieur Henri Rendell, our senior art expert. Monsieur

Rendell is making a tour of world museums and is particularly eager to see your incomparable collection. I would greatly appreciate any courtesies you extend to him.

The letter was signed by the curator of the museum.

Sooner or later, the director thought happily, *everyone comes to me*.

'Send him in.'

Henri Rendell was a tall, distinguished-looking, balding man with a heavy Swiss accent. When they shook hands, Machada noticed that the index finger on the right hand of his visitor was missing.

Henri Rendell said, 'I appreciate this. It is the first opportunity I have had to visit Madrid, and I am looking forward to seeing your renowned works of art.'

Christian Machada said modestly, 'I do not think you will be disappointed, Monsieur Rendell. Please come with me. I shall personally escort you.'

They moved slowly, walking through the rotunda with its Flemish masters, and Rubens and his followers, and they visited the central gallery, filled with Spanish masters, and Henri Rendell studied each painting carefully. The two men spoke as one expert to another, evaluating the various artists' style and perspective and colour sense.

'*Now*,' the director declared, 'for the pride of Spain.' He led his visitor downstairs, into the gallery filled with Goyas.

'It is a feast for the eyes!' Rendell exclaimed,

overwhelmed. 'Please! Let me just stand and look.'

Christian Machada waited, enjoying the man's awe.

'Never have I seen anything so magnificent,' Rendell declared. He walked slowly through the salon, studying each painting in turn. '*The Witches' Sabbath*,' Rendell said. 'Brilliant!'

They moved on.

'Goya's *Self-Portrait* – fantastic!'

Christian Machada beamed.

Rendell paused in front of the *Puerto*. 'A nice fake.' He started to move on.

The director grabbed his arm. '*What?* What was it you said, señor?'

'I said it is a nice fake.'

'You are very much mistaken.' He was filled with indignation.

'I do not think so.'

'You most certainly are,' Machada said stiffly. 'I assure you, it is genuine. I have its provenance.'

Henri Rendell stepped up to the picture and examined it more closely. 'Then its provenance has also been faked. This was done by Goya's disciple, Eugenio Lucas y Padilla. You must be aware, of course, that Lucas painted hundreds of fake Goyas.'

'Certainly I am aware of that,' Machada snapped. 'But this is not one of them.'

Rendell shrugged. 'I bow to your judgment.' He started to move on.

'I personally purchased this painting. It has passed the spectrograph test, the pigment test –'

'I do not doubt it. Lucas painted in the same period as Goya, and used the same materials.' Henri Rendell bent down to examine the signature at the bottom of the painting. 'You can reassure yourself very simply, if you wish. Take the painting back to your restoration room and test the signature.' He chuckled with amusement. 'Lucas's ego made him sign his own paintings, but his wallet forced him to forge Goya's name over his own, increasing the price enormously.' Rendell glanced at his watch. 'You must forgive me. I'm afraid I am late for an engagement. Thank you so much for sharing your treasures with me.'

'Not at all,' the director said coldly. *The man is obviously a fool*, he thought.

'I am at the Villa Magna, if I can be of service. And thank you again, señor.' Henri Rendell departed.

Christian Machada watched him leave. How dare that Swiss idiot imply that the precious Goya was a fake!

He turned to look at the painting again. It was beautiful, a masterpiece. He leaned down to examine Goya's signature. Perfectly normal. But still, *was* it possible? The tiny seed of doubt would not go away. Everyone knew that Goya's contemporary, Eugenio Lucas y Padilla, had painted hundreds of fake Goyas, making a career out of forging the master. Machada had paid $3.5 million for the Goya *Puerto*. If he *had* been deceived, it would be a terrible black mark against him, something he could not bear to think about.

Henri Rendell had said one thing that made sense: there was, indeed, a simple way to ascertain its authenticity. He would test the signature and then telephone Rendell and suggest most politely that perhaps he should seek a more suitable vocation.

The director summoned his assistant and ordered the *Puerto* moved to the restoration room.

The testing of a masterpiece is a very delicate operation, for if it is done carelessly, it can destroy something both priceless and irreplaceable. The restorers at the Prado were experts. Most of them were unsuccessful painters who had taken up restoration work so they could remain close to their beloved art. They started as apprentices, studying under master restorers, and worked for years before they became assistants and were allowed to handle masterpieces, always under the supervision of senior craftsmen.

Juan Delgado, the man in charge of art restoration at the Prado, placed the *Puerto* on a special wooden rack, as Christian Machada watched.

'I want you to test the signature,' the director informed him.

Delgado kept his surprise to himself. '*Sí, Señor Director*.'

He poured isopropyl alcohol onto a small cotton ball and set it on the table next to the painting. On a second cotton ball he poured petroleum distillate, the neutralizing agent.

'I am ready, señor.'

'Go ahead then. But be careful!'

Machada found that it was suddenly difficult for him to breathe. He watched Delgado lift the first cotton ball and gently touch it to the G in Goya's signature. Instantly, Delgado picked up the second cotton ball and neutralized the area, so that the alcohol could not penetrate too deeply. The two men examined the canvas.

Delgado was frowning. 'I'm sorry, but I cannot tell yet,' he said. 'I must use a stronger solvent.'

'Do it,' the director commanded.

Delgado opened another bottle. He carefully poured dimenthyl petone onto a fresh cotton ball and with it touched the first letter of the signature again, instantly applying the second cotton ball. The room was filled with a sharp, pungent odour from the chemicals. Christian Machada stood there staring at the painting, unable to believe what he was seeing. The G in Goya's name was fading, and in its place was a clearly visible L.

Delgado turned to him, his face pale. 'Shall – shall I go on?'

'Yes,' Machada said hoarsely. 'Go on.'

Slowly, letter by letter, Goya's signature faded under the application of the solvent, and the signature of Lucas materialized. Each letter was a blow to Machada's stomach. He, the head of one of the most important museums in the world, had been deceived. The board of directors would hear of it; the King of Spain would hear of it; the world would hear of it. He was ruined.

He stumbled back to his office and telephoned Henri Rendell.

The two men were seated in Machada's office.

'You were right,' the director said heavily. 'It is a Lucas. When word of this gets out, I shall be a laughing stock.'

'Lucas has deceived many experts,' Rendell said comfortingly. 'His forgeries happen to be a hobby of mine.'

'I paid three and a half million dollars for that painting.'

Rendell shrugged. 'Can you get your money back?'

The director shook his head in despair. 'I purchased it directly from a widow who claimed it had been in her husband's family for three generations. If I sued her, the case would drag on through the courts and it would be bad publicity. Everything in this museum would become suspect.'

Henri Rendell was thinking hard. 'There is really no reason for the publicity at all. Why don't you explain to your superiors what has happened, and quietly get rid of the Lucas? You could send the painting to Sotheby's or Christie's and let them auction it off.'

Machada shook his head. 'No. Then the whole world would learn the story.'

Rendell's face brightened. 'You may be in luck. I have a client who would be willing to purchase the Lucas. He collects them. He is a man of discretion.'

'I would be glad to get rid of it. I never want to see it again. A *fake* among my beautiful treasures. I'd like to give it away,' he added bitterly.

'That will not be necessary. My client would probably be willing to pay you, say, fifty thousand dollars for it. Shall I make a telephone call?'

'That would be most kind of you, Señor Rendell.'

At a hastily held meeting the stunned board of directors decided that the exposure of one of the Prado's prize paintings as a forgery had to be avoided at any cost. It was agreed that the prudent course of action would be to get rid of the painting as quietly and as quickly as possible. The dark-suited men filed out of the room silently. No one spoke a word to Machada, who stood there, sweltering in his misery.

That afternoon a deal was struck. Henri Rendell went to the Bank of Spain and returned with a certified cheque for $50,000, and the Eugenio Lucas y Padilla was handed over to him, wrapped in an inconspicuous piece of burlap.

'The board of directors would be very upset if this incident were to become public,' Machada said delicately, 'but I assured them that your client is a man of discretion.'

'You can count on it,' Rendell promised.

When Henri Rendell left the museum, he took a taxi to a residential area in the northern end of Madrid, carried the canvas up some stairs to a third-floor apartment, and knocked on the door.

It was opened by Tracy. Behind her stood Cesar Porretta. Tracy looked at Rendell questioningly, and he grinned.

'They couldn't wait to get this off their hands!' Henri Rendell gloated.

Tracy hugged him. 'Come in.'

Porretta took the painting and placed it on a table.

'Now,' the hunchback said, 'you are going to see a miracle – a Goya brought back to life.'

He reached for a bottle of methylated spirits and opened it. The pungent odour instantly filled the room. As Tracy and Rendell looked on, Porretta poured some of the spirits onto a piece of cotton and very gently touched the cotton to Lucas's signature, one letter at a time. Gradually the signature of Lucas began to fade. Under it was the signature of Goya.

Rendell stared at it in awe. 'Brilliant!'

'It was Miss Whitney's idea,' the hunchback admitted. 'She asked whether it would be possible to cover up the original artist's signature with a fake signature and then cover that with the original name.'

'He figured out how it could be done,' Tracy smiled.

Porretta said modestly, 'It was ridiculously simple. Took fewer than two minutes. The trick was in the paints I used. First, I covered Goya's signature with a layer of super-refined white French polish, to protect it. Then, over that I painted Lucas's name with a quick-drying acrylic-based paint. On top of that I painted in Goya's name with an oil-based paint with a light picture varnish. When the top signature was removed, Lucas's name appeared. If they had gone further, they would have discovered that Goya's original signature was hidden underneath. But of course, they didn't.'

Tracy handed each man a fat envelope and said, 'I want to thank you both.'

'Anytime you need an art expert,' Henri Rendell winked.

Porretta asked, 'How do you plan to carry the painting out of the country?'

'I'm having a messenger collect it here. Wait for him.' She shook the hands of both men and walked out.

On her way back to the Ritz, Tracy was filled with a sense of exhilaration. *Everything is a matter of psychology*, she thought.

From the beginning she had seen that it would be impossible to steal the painting from the Prado, so she had had to trick them, to put them in a frame of mind where they *wanted* to get rid of it. Tracy visualized Jeff Stevens's face when he learned how he had been outwitted, and she laughed aloud.

She waited in her hotel suite for the messenger, and when he arrived, Tracy telephoned Cesar Porretta.

'The messenger is here now,' Tracy said. 'I'm

sending him over to pick up the painting. See that he –'

'*What?* What are you talking about?' Porretta screamed. 'Your messenger picked up the painting half an hour ago.'

THIRTY-ONE

Paris
Wednesday, 9 July – Noon

In a private office off the Rue Matignon, Gunther Hartog said, 'I understand how you feel about what happened in Madrid, Tracy, but Jeff Stevens got there first.'

'No,' Tracy corrected him bitterly. '*I* got there first. He got there last.'

'But Jeff delivered it. The *Puerto* is already on its way to my client.'

After all her planning and scheming, Jeff Stevens had outwitted her. He had sat back and let her do the work and take all the risks, and at the last moment he had calmly walked off with the prize. How he must have been laughing at her all the time! *You're a very special lady, Tracy*. She could not bear the waves of humiliation that washed over her when she thought of the night of the flamenco dancing. *My God, what a fool I almost made of myself.*

'I never thought I could kill anyone,' Tracy told Gunther, 'but I could happily slaughter Jeff Stevens.'

Gunther said mildly, 'Oh, dear. Not in this room, I hope. He's on his way here.'

'He's *what*?' Tracy jumped to her feet.

'I told you I have a proposition for you. It will require a partner. In my opinion, he is the only one who –'

'I'd rather *starve* first!' Tracy snapped. 'Jeff Stevens is the most contemptible –'

'Ah, did I hear my name mentioned?' He stood in the doorway, beaming. 'Tracy, darling, you look even more stunning than usual. Gunther, my friend, how are you?'

The two men shook hands. Tracy stood there, filled with a cold fury.

Jeff looked at her and sighed. 'You're probably upset with me.'

'*Upset!* I –' She could not find the words.

'Tracy, if I may say so, I thought your plan was brilliant. I mean it. Really brilliant. You made only one little mistake. Never trust a Swiss with a missing index finger.'

She took deep breaths, trying to control herself. She turned to Gunther. 'I'll talk to you later, Gunther.'

'Tracy –'

'No. Whatever it is, I want no part of it. Not if he's involved.'

Gunther said, 'Would you at least listen to it?'

'There's no point. I –'

'In three days De Beers is shipping a four-million-dollar packet of diamonds from Paris to Amsterdam on an Air France cargo plane. I have a client who's eager to acquire those stones.'

'Why don't you hijack them on the way to the airport? Your friend here is an expert on hijacking.' She could not keep the bitterness from her voice.

By God, she's magnificent when she's angry, Jeff thought.

Gunther said, 'The diamonds are too well guarded. We're going to hijack the diamonds during the flight.'

Tracy looked at him in surprise. '*During* the flight? In a cargo plane?'

'We need someone small enough to hide inside one of the containers. When the plane is in the air, all that person has to do is step out of the crate, open the De Beers container, remove the package of diamonds, replace the package with a duplicate, which will have been prepared, and get back in the other crate.'

'And I'm small enough to fit in a crate.'

Gunther said, 'It's much more than that, Tracy. We need someone who's bright and has nerve.'

Tracy stood there, thinking. 'I like the plan, Gunther. What I don't like is the idea of working with *him*. This person is a crook.'

Jeff grinned. 'Aren't we all, dear heart? Gunther is offering us a million dollars if we can pull this off.'

Tracy stared at Gunther. 'A million dollars?'

He nodded. 'Half a million for each of you.'

'The reason it can work,' Jeff explained, 'is that I have a contact at the loading dock at the airport. He'll help us set it up. He can be trusted.'

'Unlike you,' Tracy retorted. 'Goodbye, Gunther.' She sailed out of the room.

Gunther looked after her. 'She's really upset with you about Madrid, Jeff. I'm afraid she's not going to do this.'

'You're wrong,' Jeff said cheerfully. 'I know Tracy. She won't be able to resist it.'

'The pallets are sealed before they are loaded onto the plane,' Ramon Vauban was explaining. The speaker was a young Frenchman, with an old face that had nothing to do with his years and black, dead eyes. He was a dispatcher with Air France Cargo, and the key to the success of the plan.

Vauban, Tracy, Jeff, and Gunther were seated at a rail-side table on the *Bateau Mouche*, the sightseeing boat that cruises the Seine, circling Paris.

'If the pallet is sealed,' Tracy asked, her voice crisp, 'how do I get into it?'

'For last-minute shipments,' Vauban replied, 'the company uses what we call soft pallets, large wooden crates with canvas on one side, fastened down only with rope. For security reasons, valuable cargo like diamonds always arrives at the last minute so it is the last to go on and the first to come off.'

Tracy said, 'So the diamonds would be in a soft pallet?'

'That is correct, mademoiselle. As would you. I would arrange for the container with you in it to be placed next to the pallet with the diamonds. All you have to do when the plane is in flight is cut the ropes, open the pallet with the diamonds, exchange a box identical to theirs, get back in your container, and close it up again.'

Gunther added, 'When the plane lands in Amsterdam, the guards will pick up the substitute box of diamonds and deliver it to the diamond cutters. By the time they discover the substitution, we'll have you on an airplane out of the country. Believe me, nothing can go wrong.'

A sentence that chilled Tracy's heart. 'Wouldn't I freeze to death up there?' she asked.

Vauban smiled. 'Mademoiselle, these days, cargo planes are heated. They often carry livestock and pets. No, you will be quite comfortable. A little cramped, perhaps, but otherwise fine.'

Tracy had finally agreed to *listen* to their idea. A half million dollars for a few hours' discomfort. She had examined the scheme from every angle. *It can work*, Tracy thought. *If only Jeff Stevens were not involved!*

Her feelings about him were such a roiling mixture of emotions that she was confused and angry with herself. He had done what he did in Madrid for the fun of outwitting her. He had betrayed her, cheated her, and now he was secretly laughing at her.

The three men were watching her, waiting for her answer. The boat was passing under the Pont Neuf, the oldest bridge in Paris, which the contrary French insisted on calling the New Bridge. Across the river, two lovers embraced on the edge of the embankment, and Tracy could see the blissful look on the face of the girl. *She's a fool*, Tracy thought. She made her decision. She looked straight into Jeff's eyes as she said, 'All right. I'll go along with it,' and she could feel the tension at the table dissipate.

'We don't have much time,' Vauban was saying. His dead eyes turned to Tracy. 'My brother works for a shipping agent, and he will let us load the soft container with you in it at his warehouse. I hope mademoiselle does not have claustrophobia.'

'Don't worry about me . . . How long will the trip take?'

'You will spend a few minutes in the loading area and one hour flying to Amsterdam.'

'How large is the container?'

'Large enough for you to sit down. There will be other things in it to conceal you – just in case.'

Nothing can go wrong, they had promised. *But just in case . . .*

'I have a list of the things you'll need,' Jeff told her. 'I've already arranged for them.'

The smug bastard. He had been so sure she would say yes.

'Vauban, here, will see to it that your passport has the proper exit and entrance stamps, so you can leave Holland without any problem.'

The boat began docking at its quay.

'We can go over the final plans in the morning,' Ramon Vauban said. 'Now I have to get back to work. *Au revoir*.' And he left.

Jeff asked, 'Why don't we all have dinner together to celebrate?'

'I'm sorry,' Gunther apologized, 'but I have a previous engagement.'

Jeff turned to Tracy. 'Would –'

'No, thanks. I'm tired,' she said quickly.

It was an excuse to avoid being with Jeff, but even as Tracy said it, she realized she really was exhausted. It was probably the strain of the excitement she had been going through for so long. She was feeling light-headed. *When this is over*, she promised herself, *I'm going back to London for a long rest*. Her head was beginning to throb. *I really must*.

'I brought you a little present,' Jeff told her. He handed her a gaily wrapped box. In it was an exquisite silk scarf with the initials TW switched in one corner.

'Thank you.' *He can afford it*, Tracy thought angrily. *He bought it with my half million dollars*.

'Sure you won't change your mind about dinner?'

'I'm positive.'

In Paris, Tracy stayed at the classic Plaza Athénée, in a lovely old suite that overlooked the garden restaurant. There was an elegant restaurant inside the hotel, with soft piano music, but on this evening

Tracy was too tired to change into a more formal dress. She went into the Relais, the hotel's small café, and ordered a bowl of soup. She pushed the plate away, half-finished, and left for her suite.

Daniel Cooper, seated at the other end of the room, noted the time.

Daniel Cooper had a problem. Upon his return to Paris, he had asked for a meeting with Inspector Trignant. The head of Interpol had been less than cordial. He had just spent an hour on the telephone listening to Commandant Ramiro's complaints about the American.

'He is loco!' the commandant had exploded. 'I wasted men and money and time following this Tracy Whitney, who he insisted was going to rob the Prado, and she turned out to be a harmless tourist – just as I said she was.'

The conversation had led Inspector Trignant to believe that Daniel Cooper could have been wrong about Tracy in the first place. There was not one shred of evidence against the woman. The fact that she had been in various cities at the times the crimes were committed was not evidence.

And so, when Daniel Cooper had gone to see the inspector and said, 'Tracy Whitney is in Paris. I would like her placed on twenty-four-hour surveillance,' the inspector had replied. 'Unless you can present me with some proof that this woman is planning to commit a specific crime, there is nothing I can do.'

Cooper had fixed him with his blazing brown eyes and said, 'You're a fool,' and had found himself being unceremoniously ushered out of the office.

That was when Cooper had begun his one-man surveillance. He trailed Tracy everywhere: to shops and restaurants, through the streets of Paris. He went without sleep and often without food. Daniel Cooper could not permit Tracy Whitney to defeat him. His assignment would not be finished until he had put her in prison.

Tracy lay in bed that night, reviewing the next day's plan. She wished her head felt better. She had taken aspirin, but the throbbing was worse. She was perspiring, and the room seemed unbearably hot. *Tomorrow it will be over. Switzerland. That's where I'll go. To the cool mountains of Switzerland. To the château.*

She set the alarm for 5:00 A.M., and when the bell rang she was in her prison cell and Old Iron Pants was yelling, 'Time to get dressed. Move it', and the corridor echoed with the clanging of the bell. Tracy awakened. Her chest felt tight, and the light hurt her eyes. She forced herself into the bathroom. Her face looked blotchy and flushed in the mirror. *I can't get sick now*, Tracy thought. *Not today. There's too much to do.*

She dressed slowly, trying to ignore the throbbing of her head. She put on black overalls with deep pockets, rubber-soled shoes, and a Basque beret. Her heart seemed to beat erratically, but she was not sure whether it was from excitement or the malaise that gripped her. She was dizzy and weak. Her throat felt sore and scratchy. On her table she saw the scarf Jeff had given her. She picked it up and wrapped it around her neck.

The main entrance to the Hôtel Plaza Athénée is on Avenue Montaigne, but the service entrance is on Rue du Boccador, around the corner. A discreet sign reads ENTRÉE DE SERVICE, and the passageway goes from a back hallway of the lobby through a narrow corridor lined with rubbish bins leading to the street. Daniel Cooper, who had taken up an observation post near the main entrance, did not see Tracy leave through the service door, but inexplicably, the moment she was gone, he sensed it. He hurried out to the avenue and looked up and down the street. Tracy was nowhere in sight.

The grey Renault that picked up Tracy at the side entrance to the hotel headed for the Étoile. There was little traffic at that hour, and the driver, a pimply-faced youth who apparently spoke no English, raced into one of the twelve avenues that form the spokes of the Étoile. *I wish he would slow down*, Tracy thought. The motion was making her carsick.

Thirty minutes later the car slammed to a stop in front of a warehouse. The sign over the door read BRUCERE ET CIE. Tracy remembered that this was where Ramon Vauban's brother worked.

The youth opened the car door and murmured, '*Vite!*'

A middle-aged man with a quick, furtive manner appeared as Tracy stepped out of the car. 'Follow me,' he said. 'Hurry.'

Tracy stumbled after him to the back of the warehouse, where there were half a dozen containers, most of them filled and sealed, ready to be taken to the airport. There was one soft container with a canvas side, half-filled with furniture.

'Get in. Quick! We have no time.'

Tracy felt faint. She looked at the box and thought, *I can't get in there. I'll die.*

The man was looking at her strangely. '*Avez vous mal?*'

Now was the time to back out, to put a stop to this. 'I'm all right,' Tracy mumbled. It would be over soon. In a few hours she would be on her way to Switzerland.

'*Bon*. Take this.' He handed her a double-edged knife, a long coil of heavy rope, a flashlight, and a small blue jewel box with a red ribbon around it.

'This is the duplicate of the jewel box you will exchange.'

Tracy took a deep breath, stepped into the container, and sat down. Seconds later a large piece of canvas dropped down over the opening. She could hear ropes being tied around the canvas to hold it in place.

She barely heard his voice through the canvas.

'From now on, no talking, no moving, no smoking.'

'I don't smoke,' Tracy tried to say, but she did not have the energy.

'*Bonne chance*. I've cut some holes in the side of the box so you can breathe. Don't forget to breathe.' He laughed at his joke, and she heard his footsteps fading away. She was alone in the dark.

The box was narrow and cramped, and a set of dining-room chairs took up most of the space. Tracy felt as though she were on fire. Her skin was hot to the touch, and she had difficulty breathing. *I've caught some kind of virus*, she thought, *but it's going to have to wait. I have work to do. Think about something else.*

Gunther's voice: *You've nothing to worry about, Tracy. When they unload the cargo in Amsterdam, your pallet will be taken to a private garage near the airport. Jeff will meet you there. Give him the jewels and return to the airport. There will be a plane ticket for Geneva waiting for you at the Swissair counter. Get out of Amsterdam as fast as you can. As soon as the police learn of the robbery, they'll close up the city tight. Nothing will go wrong, but just in case, here is the address and the key to a safe house in Amsterdam. It is unoccupied.*

She must have dozed, for she awakened with a start as the container was jerked into the air. Tracy felt herself swinging through space, and she clung to the sides for support. The container settled down on something hard. There was a slam of a car door, an engine roared into life, and a moment later the truck was moving.

They were on their way to the airport.

The scheme had been worked out on a split-second schedule. The container with Tracy inside was due to reach the cargo shipping area within a few minutes of the time the De Beers pallet was to arrive. The driver of the truck carrying Tracy had his instructions: *Keep it at a steady fifty miles an hour.*

Traffic on the road to the airport seemed heavier than usual that morning, but the driver was not worried. The pallet would make the plane in time, and he would be in possession of a bonus of 50,000 francs, enough to take his wife and two children on a vacation. *America*, he thought. *We'll go to Disney World.*

He looked at the dashboard clock and grinned to himself. No problem. The airport was only three miles away, and he had ten minutes to get there.

Exactly on schedule, he reached the turnoff for Air France Cargo headquarters at the Fertnord sign and drove past the low grey building at Roissy-Charles de Gaulle Airport, away from the passenger entrance, where barbed-wire fences separated the roadway from the cargo area. As he headed towards the enclosure holding the enormous warehouse, which occupied three blocks and was filled with boxes and packages and containers piled on dollies, there was a sudden explosive sound as the wheel jerked in his hand and the truck began to vibrate. *Foutre!* he thought. A *fucking blowout.*

The giant 747 Air France cargo plane was in the process of being loaded. The nose had been raised, revealing rows of tracks. The cargo containers were on a platform level with the opening, ready to slide across a bridge into the hold of the plane. There were thirty-eight pallets, twenty-eight of them on the main deck and ten of them in the belly holds. On the ceiling an exposed heating pipe ran from one end of the huge cabin to the other, and the wires and cables that controlled the transport were visible on the ceiling. There were no frills on this plane.

The loading had almost been completed. Ramon Vauban looked at his watch again and cursed. The truck was late. The De Beers consignment had already been loaded into its pallet, and the canvas sides fastened down with a crisscross of ropes. Vauban had daubed the side of it with red paint so the woman would have no trouble identifying it. He watched now as the pallet moved along the tracks into the plane and was locked into place. There was room next to it for one more pallet, before the plane took off. There were three more containers on the dock waiting to be loaded. *Where in God's name was the woman?*

The loadmaster inside the plane called, 'Let's go, Ramon. What's holding us up?'

'A minute,' Vauban answered. He hurried

towards the entrance to the loading area. No sign of the truck.

'Vauban! What's the problem?' He turned. A senior supervisor was approaching. 'Finish loading and get this cargo in the air.'

'Yes, sir. I was just waiting for –'

At that moment the truck from Brucere et Cie raced into the warehouse and came to a screaming halt in front of Vauban.

'Here's the last of the cargo,' Vauban announced.

'Well, get it aboard,' the supervisor snapped.

Vauban supervised the unloading of the container from the truck and sent it onto the bridge leading to the plane.

He waved to the loadmaster. 'It's all yours.'

Moments later the cargo was aboard, and the nose of the plane was lowered into place. Vauban watched as the jets were fired up and the giant plane started rolling towards the runway, and he thought, *Now it's up to the woman.*

There was a fierce storm. A giant wave had struck the ship and it was sinking. *I'm drowning*, Tracy thought. *I've got to get out of here.*

She flung out her arms and hit something. It was the side of a lifeboat, rocking and swaying. She tried to stand up and cracked her head on the leg of a table. In a moment of clarity she remembered where she was. Her face and hair dripped with perspiration. She felt giddy, and her body was burning up. How long had she been unconscious?

It was only an hour's flight. Was the plane about to land? *No*, she thought. *It's all right. I'm having a nightmare. I'm in my bed in London, asleep. I'll call for a doctor*. She could not breathe. She struggled upwards to reach for a telephone, then immediately sank down, her body leaden. The plane hit a pocket of turbulence, and Tracy was thrown against the side of the box. She lay there, dazed, desperately trying to concentrate. *How much time do I have?* She wavered between a hellish dream and painful reality. *The diamonds*. Somehow she had to get the diamonds. But first . . . first, she had to cut herself out of the pallet.

She touched the knife in her overalls and found that it was a terrible effort to lift it. *Not enough air*, Tracy thought. *I must have air*. She reached around the edge of the canvas, fumbled for one of the outside ropes, found it, and cut it. It seemed to take an eternity. The canvas opened wider. She cut another rope, and there was room enough to slip outside of the container into the belly of the cargo plane. The air outside the box was cold. She was freezing. Her body began to shake, and the constant jolting of the plane increased her nausea. *I've got to hold on*, Tracy thought. She forced herself to concentrate. *What am I doing here? Something important . . . Yes . . . Diamonds.*

Tracy's vision was blurred, and everything was moving in and out of focus. *I'm not going to make it.*

The plane dipped suddenly, and Tracy was

hurled to the floor, scraping her hands on the sharp metal tracks. She held on while the plane bucked, and when it had settled down, she forced herself to her feet again. The roaring of the jet engines was mixed with the roaring in her head. *The diamonds. I must find the diamonds.*

She stumbled among the containers, squinting at each one, looking for the red paint. Thank God! There it was, on the third container. She stood there, trying to remember what to do next. It was such an effort to concentrate. *If I could just lie down and sleep for a few minutes, I'd be fine. All I need is some sleep.* But there was no time. They could be landing in Amsterdam at any moment. Tracy took the knife and slashed at the ropes of the container. 'One good cut will do it,' they had told her.

She barely had the strength to hold the knife in her grasp. *I can't fail now*, Tracy thought. She began shivering again, and shook so hard that she dropped the knife. *It's not going to work. They're going to catch me and put me back in prison.*

She hesitated indecisively, clinging to the rope, wanting desperately to crawl back into her box where she could sleep, safely hidden until it was all over. It would be so easy. Then, slowly, moving carefully against the fierce pounding in her head, Tracy reached for the knife and picked it up. She began to slash at the heavy rope.

It finally gave way. Tracy pulled back the canvas and stared into the gloomy interior of the container.

She could see nothing. She pulled out the flashlight and, at that moment, she felt a sudden change of pressure in her ears.

The plane was coming down for a landing.

Tracy thought, *I've got to hurry*. But her body refused to respond. She stood there, dazed. *Move*, her mind said.

She shone the flashlight into the interior of the box. It was crammed with packages and envelopes and small cases, and on top of a crate were two little blue boxes with red ribbons around them. *Two of them! There was only supposed to be –* She blinked, and the two boxes merged into one. Everything seemed to have a bright aura around it.

She reached for the box and took the duplicate out of her pocket. Holding the two of them in her hand, an overwhelming nausea swept over her, racking her body. She squeezed her eyes together, fighting against it. She started to place the substitute box on top of the case and suddenly realized that she was no longer sure which box was which. She stared at the two identical boxes. Was it the one in her left hand or her right hand?

The plane began a steeper angle of descent. It would touch down at any moment. She had to make a decision. She set down one of the boxes, prayed that it was the right one, and moved away from the container. She fumbled an uncut coil of rope out of her overalls. *There's something I must do with the rope.* The roaring in her head made it impossible to think. She remembered: *After you cut the rope, put it in your pocket, replace it with the new rope. Don't leave anything around that will make them suspicious.*

It had sounded so easy then, sitting in the warm sun on the deck of the *Bateau Mouche.* Now it was impossible. She had no more strength left. The guards would find the cut rope and the cargo would be searched, and she would be caught. Something deep inside her screamed, *No! No! No!*

With a herculean effort, Tracy began to wind the uncut rope around the container. She felt a jolt beneath her feet as the plane touched the ground, and then another, and she was slammed backwards as the jets were thrust into reverse. Her head smashed against the floor and she blacked out.

The 747 was picking up speed now, taxiing along the runway towards the terminal. Tracy lay crumpled on the floor of the plane with her hair fanning over her white, white face. It was the silence of the engines that brought her back to consciousness. The plane had stopped. She propped herself up on an elbow and slowly forced herself to her knees. She stood up, reeling, hanging on to the container to keep from falling. The new rope was in place. She clasped the jewel box to her chest and began to weave her way back to her pallet. She pushed her body through the canvas opening and flopped down, panting, her body beaded with perspiration. *I've done it.* But there was something more she had to do. Something important. *What? Tape up the rope on your pallet.*

She reached into the pocket of her overalls for the roll of masking tape. It was gone. Her breath was coming in shallow, ragged gasps, and the sound deafened her. She thought she heard voices and forced herself to stop breathing and listen. Yes. There they were again. Someone laughed. Any second now the cargo door would open, and the men would begin unloading. They would see the cut rope, look inside the pallet, and discover her. She had to find a way to hold the rope together. She got to her knees, and as she did she felt the hard roll of masking tape, which had fallen from her pocket sometime during the turbulence of the flight. She lifted the canvas and fumbled around to find the two ends of cut rope, and held them together while she clumsily tried to wrap the tape around them.

She could not see. The perspiration pouring down her face was blinding her. She pulled the scarf from her throat and wiped her face. Better. She finished taping the rope and dropped the canvas back in place; there was nothing to do now but wait. She felt her forehead again, and it seemed hotter than before.

I must get out of the sun, Tracy thought. *Tropical suns can be dangerous.*

She was on holiday somewhere in the Caribbean. Jeff had come here to bring her some diamonds, but he had jumped into the sea and disappeared. She reached out to save him, but he slipped from her grasp. The water was over her head. She was choking, drowning.

She heard the sound of workmen entering the plane.

'Help!' she screamed. 'Please help me.'

But her scream was a whisper, and no one heard.

The giant containers began rolling out of the plane.

Tracy was unconscious when they loaded her container onto a Brucere et Cie truck. Left behind, on the floor of the cargo plane, was the scarf Jeff had given her.

Tracy was awakened by the slash of light hitting the inside of the truck as someone raised the canvas. Slowly, she opened her eyes. The truck was in the warehouse.

Jeff was standing there, grinning at her. 'You made it!' he said. 'You're a marvel. Let's have the box.'

She watched, dully, as he picked up the box from her side. 'See you in Lisbon.' He turned to leave, then stopped and looked down at her. 'You look terrible, Tracy. You all right?'

She could hardly speak. 'Jeff, I –'

But he was gone.

Tracy had only the haziest recollection of what

happened next. There was a change of clothes for her in the back of the warehouse, and some woman said, 'You look ill, mademoiselle. Do you wish me to call a doctor?'

'No doctors,' Tracy whispered.

There will be a plane ticket for Geneva waiting for you at the Swissair counter. Get out of Amsterdam as fast as you can. As soon as the police learn of the robbery, they'll close up the city tight. Nothing will go wrong, but just in case, here is the address and the key to a safe house in Amsterdam. It is unoccupied.

The airport. She had to get to the airport. 'Taxi,' she mumbled. 'Taxi.'

The woman hesitated a moment, then shrugged. 'All right. I will call one. Wait here.'

She was floating higher and higher now, ever closer to the sun.

'Your taxi is here,' a man was saying.

She wished people would stop bothering her. She wanted only to sleep.

The driver said, 'Where do you wish to go, mademoiselle?'

There will be a plane ticket for Geneva waiting for you at the Swissair counter.

She was too ill to board a plane. They would stop her, summon a doctor. She would be questioned. All she needed was to sleep for a few minutes, then she would be fine.

The voice was getting impatient. 'Where to, please?'

She had no place to go. She gave the taxi driver the address of the safe house.

The police were cross-examining her about the diamonds, and when she refused to answer them, they became very angry and put her in a room by herself and turned up the heat until the room was boiling hot. When it became unbearable, they dropped the temperature down, until icicles began to form on the walls.

Tracy pushed her way up through the cold and opened her eyes. She was on a bed, shivering uncontrollably. There was a blanket beneath her, but she did not have the strength to get under it. Her dress was soaked through, and her face and neck were wet.

I'm going to die here. Where was here?

The safe house. I'm in the safe house. And the phrase struck her as so funny that she started to laugh, and the laughter turned into a paroxysm of coughing. It had all gone wrong. She had not got away after all. By now the police would be combing Amsterdam for her: *Mademoiselle Whitney had a ticket on Swissair and did not use it? Then she still must be in Amsterdam.*

She wondered how long she had been in this bed. She lifted her wrist to look at her watch, but the numbers were blurred. She was seeing everything double. There were two beds in the small room and two dressers and four chairs. The shivering stopped, and her body was burning up. She needed to open a window, but she was too weak to move. The room was freezing again.

She was back on the airplane, locked in the crate, screaming for help.

You've made it! You're a marvel. Let's have the box.

Jeff had taken the diamonds, and he was probably on his way to Brazil with her share of the money. He would be enjoying himself with one of his women, laughing at her. He had beaten her once more. She hated him. No. She didn't. Yes, she did. She despised him.

She was in and out of delirium. The hard pelota ball was hurtling towards her, and Jeff grabbed her in his arms and pushed her to the ground, and his lips were very close to hers, and then they were having dinner at Zalacaín. *Do you know how special you are, Tracy?*

I offer you a draw, Boris Melnikov said.

Her body was trembling again, out of control, and she was on an express train whirling through a dark tunnel, and at the end of the tunnel she knew she was going to die. All the other passengers had got off except Alberto Fornati. He was angry with her, shaking her and screaming at her.

'For Christ's sake!' he yelled. 'Open your eyes! Look at me!'

With a superhuman effort, Tracy opened her eyes, and Jeff was standing over her. His face was white, and there was fury in his voice. Of course, it was all a part of her dream.

'How long have you been like this?'

'You're in Brazil,' Tracy mumbled.

After that, she remembered nothing more.

When Inspector Trignant was given the scarf with the initials TW on it, found on the floor of the Air France cargo plane, he stared at it for a long time.

Then he said, 'Get me Daniel Cooper.'

THIRTY-TWO

The picturesque village of Alkmaar, on the north-west coast of Holland facing the North Sea, is a popular tourist attraction, but there is a quarter in the eastern section that tourists seldom visit. Jeff Stevens had been on holiday there several times with a stewardess from KLM who had taught him the language. He remembered the area well, a place where residents minded their own business and were not unduly curious about visitors. It was a perfect place to hide out.

Jeff's first impulse had been to rush Tracy to a hospital, but that was too dangerous. It was also risky for her to remain in Amsterdam a minute longer. He had wrapped her in blankets and carried her out to the car, where she had remained unconscious during the drive to Alkmaar. Her pulse was erratic and her breathing shallow.

In Alkmaar, Jeff checked into a small inn. The inn-keeper watched curiously as Jeff carried Tracy upstairs to her room.

'We're honeymooners,' Jeff explained. 'My wife became ill – a slight respiratory disturbance. She needs rest.'

'Would you like a doctor?'

Jeff was not certain of the answer himself. 'I'll let you know.'

The first thing he had to do was to bring down Tracy's fever. Jeff lowered her onto the large double bed in the room and began to strip off her clothes, sodden with perspiration. He held her up in a sitting position and lifted her dress over her head. Shoes next, then pantyhose. Her body was hot to the touch. Jeff wet a towel with cool water and gently bathed her from head to foot. He covered her with a blanket and sat at the bedside listening to her uneven breathing.

If she's not better by morning, Jeff decided, *I'll have to bring in a doctor*.

In the morning the bedclothes were soaked again. Tracy was still unconscious, but it seemed to Jeff that her breathing was a little easier. He was afraid to let the maid see Tracy; it would lead to too many questions. Instead, he asked the housekeeper for a change of linens and took them inside the room. He washed Tracy's body with a moist towel, changed the sheets on the bed the way he had seen nurses do in hospitals, without disturbing the patient, and covered her up again.

Jeff put a DO NOT DISTURB sign on the door and went looking for the nearest pharmacy. He bought aspirin, a thermometer, a sponge and rubbing alcohol. When he returned to the room, Tracy was still not awake. Jeff took her temperature: 104 degrees. He sponged her body with the cool alcohol, and her fever dropped.

An hour later her temperature was up again. He was going to have to call a doctor. The problem was that the doctor would insist Tracy be taken to a hospital. Questions would be asked. Jeff had no idea whether the police were looking for them, but if they were, they would both be taken into custody. He had to do something. He mashed up four aspirins, placed the powder between Tracy's lips, and gently spooned water into her mouth until she finally swallowed. Once again he bathed her body. After he had finished drying her, it seemed to him that her skin was not as hot as it had been. He checked her pulse once more. It seemed steadier. He put his head to her chest and listened. Was her breathing less congested? He could not be certain. He was sure of only one thing, and he repeated it over and over until it became a litany: 'You're going to get well.' He kissed her gently on the forehead.

Jeff had not slept in forty-eight hours, and he was exhausted and hollow-eyed. *I'll sleep later*, he promised himself. *I'll close my eyes to rest them a moment*.

He slept.

When Tracy opened her eyes and watched the ceiling slowly come into focus, she had no idea where she was. It took long minutes for awareness to seep into her consciousness. Her body felt battered and sore, and she had the feeling that she had returned from a long, wearying journey. Drowsily, she looked around the unfamiliar room, and her heart suddenly skipped a beat. Jeff was slumped in an armchair near the window, asleep. It was impossible. The last time she had seen him, he had taken the diamonds and left. What was he doing here? And with a sudden, sinking sensation, Tracy knew the answer. She had given him the wrong box – the box with the fake diamonds – and Jeff thought she had cheated him. He must have picked her up at the safe house and taken her to wherever this place was.

As she sat up, Jeff stirred and opened his eyes. When he saw Tracy looking at him, a slow, happy grin lit his face.

'Welcome back.' There was a note of such intense relief in his voice that Tracy was confused.

'I'm sorry,' Tracy said. Her voice was a hoarse whisper. 'I gave you the wrong box.'

'What?'

'I mixed up the boxes.'

He walked over to her and said gently, 'No, Tracy. You gave me the real diamonds. They're on their way to Gunther.' She looked at him in bewilderment. 'Then – why – why are you here?'

He sat on the edge of the bed. 'When you handed me the diamonds, you looked like death. I decided I'd better wait at the airport to make sure you caught your flight. You didn't show up, and I knew you were in trouble. I went to the safe house and found you. I couldn't let you die there,' he said lightly. 'It would have been a clue for the police.'

She was watching him, puzzled. 'Tell me the real reason you came back for me.'

'Time to take your temperature,' he said briskly.

'Not bad,' he told her a few minutes later. 'Little over a hundred. You're a wonderful patient.'

'Jeff –'

'Trust me,' he said. 'Hungry?'

Tracy was suddenly ravenous. 'Starved.'

'Good. I'll bring something in.'

He returned from shopping with a bag full of orange juice, milk, and fresh fruit, and large Dutch *broodjes*, rolls filled with different kinds of cheese, meat and fish.

'This seems to be the Dutch version of chicken soup, but it should do the trick. Now, eat slowly.'

He helped her sit up, and fed her. He was careful and tender, and Tracy thought, warily, he's after something.

As they were eating, Jeff said. 'While I was out, I telephoned Gunther. He received the diamonds. He deposited your share of the money in your Swiss bank account.'

She could not keep herself from asking, 'Why didn't you keep it all?'

When Jeff answered, his tone was serious. 'Because it's time we stopped playing games with each other, Tracy. Okay?'

It was another one of his tricks, of course, but she was too tired to worry about it. 'Okay.'

'If you'll tell me your sizes,' Jeff said, 'I'll go out and buy some clothes for you. The Dutch are liberal, but I think if you walked around like that they might be shocked.'

Tracy pulled the covers up closer around her, suddenly aware of her nakedness. She had a vague impression of Jeff's undressing her and bathing her. He had risked his own safety to nurse her. Why? She had believed she understood him. *I don't understand him at all*, Tracy thought. *Not at all.*

She slept.

In the afternoon Jeff brought back two suitcases filled with robes and nightgowns, underwear, dresses, and shoes, and a makeup kit and a comb and brush and hair dryer, toothbrushes and toothpaste. He also had purchased several changes of clothes for himself and brought back the *International Herald Tribune*. On the front page was a story about the diamond hijacking; the police had figured out how it had been committed, but according to the newspaper, the thieves had left no clues.

Jeff said cheerfully, 'We're home free! Now all we have to do is get you well.'

It was Daniel Cooper who had suggested that the scarf with the initials TW be kept from the press. 'We know,' he had told Inspector Trignant, 'who it belongs to, but it's not enough evidence for an indictment. Her lawyers would produce every woman in Europe with the same initials and make fools of you.'

In Cooper's opinion, the police had already made fools of themselves. *God will give her to me.*

He sat in the darkness of the small church, on a hard wooden bench, and he prayed: *Oh, make her mine, Father. Give her to me to punish so that I may wash myself of my sins. The evil in her spirit shall be exorcized, and her naked body shall be flagellated . . .* And he thought about Tracy's naked body in his power and felt himself getting an erection. He hurried from the church in terror that God would see and inflict further punishment on him.

When Tracy awoke, it was dark. She sat up and turned on the lamp on the bedside table. She was alone. He had gone. A feeling of panic washed over her. She had allowed herself to grow dependent on Jeff, and that had been a stupid mistake. *It serves me right*, Tracy thought bitterly. 'Trust me,' Jeff had said, and she had. He had taken care of her only to protect himself, not for any other reason. She had come to believe that he felt something for her. She had *wanted* to trust him, *wanted* to feel that she meant something to him. She lay back on her pillow and closed her eyes, thinking, *I'm going to miss him. Heaven help me, I'm going to miss him.*

God had played a cosmic joke on her. Why did it have to be *him*? she wondered, but the reason did not matter. She would have to make plans to leave this place as soon as possible, find somewhere where she could get well, where she could feel safe. *Oh, you bloody fool*, she thought. *You* –

There was the sound of the door opening, and Jeff's voice called out, 'Tracy, are you awake? I brought you some books and magazines. I thought you might –' He stopped as he saw the expression on her face. 'Hey! Is something wrong?'

'Not now,' Tracy whispered. 'Not now.'

The following morning Tracy's fever was gone.

'I'd like to get out,' she said. 'Do you think we could go for a walk, Jeff?'

They were a curiosity in the lobby. The couple who owned the hotel were delighted by Tracy's recovery. 'Your husband was so wonderful. He insisted on doing everything for you himself. He was so worried. A woman is lucky to have a man who loves her so much.'

Tracy looked at Jeff, and she could have sworn he was blushing.

Outside, Tracy said, 'They're very sweet.'

'Sentimentalists,' Jeff retorted.

Jeff had arranged for a cot to sleep on, placed next to Tracy's bed. As Tracy lay in bed that night, she remembered again how Jeff had taken care of her, tended to her needs, and nursed her and bathed her naked body. She was powerfully aware of his presence. It made her feel protected.

It made her feel nervous.

Slowly, as Tracy grew stronger, she and Jeff spent more time exploring the quaint little town. They walked to the Alkmaarder Meer, along winding, cobblestoned streets that dated from the Middle Ages, and spent hours at the tulip fields on the outskirts of the city. They visited the cheese market and the old weighing house, and went through the municipal museum. To Tracy's surprise, Jeff spoke to the townspeople in Dutch.

'Where did you learn that?' Tracy asked.

'I used to know a Dutch girl.'

She was sorry she had asked.

As the days passed Tracy's healthy young body gradually healed itself. When Jeff felt that Tracy was strong enough, he rented bicycles, and they visited the windmills that dotted the countryside. Each day was a lovely holiday, and Tracy wanted it never to end.

Jeff was a constant surprise. He treated Tracy with a concern and tenderness that melted her defences against him, yet he made no sexual advances. He was an enigma to Tracy. She thought of the beautiful women with whom she had seen him, and she was sure he could have had any of them. Why was he staying by her side in this tiny backwater of the world?

Tracy found herself talking about things she had

thought she would never discuss with anyone. She told Jeff about Joe Romano and Tony Orsatti, and about Ernestine Littlechap and Big Bertha and little Amy Brannigan. Jeff was by turns outraged and distressed and sympathetic. Jeff told her about his stepmother and his Uncle Willie and about his carnival days and his marriage to Louise. Tracy had never felt so close to anyone.

Suddenly it was time to leave.

One morning Jeff said, 'The police aren't looking for us, Tracy. I think we should be moving on.'

Tracy felt a stab of disappointment. 'All right. When?'

'Tomorrow.'

She nodded. 'I'll pack in the morning.'

That night Tracy lay awake, unable to sleep. Jeff's presence seemed to fill the room as never before. This had been an unforgettable period in her life, and it was coming to an end. She looked over at the cot where Jeff lay.

'Are you asleep?' Tracy whispered.

'No . . .'

'What are you thinking about?'

'Tomorrow. Leaving this place. I'll miss it.'

'I'm going to miss you, Jeff.' The words were out before she could stop herself.

Jeff sat up slowly and looked at her. 'How much?' he asked.

'Terribly.'

A moment later he was at her bedside. 'Tracy –'

'Shhh. Don't talk. Just put your arms around me. Hold me.'

It started slowly, a velvet touching and stroking and feeling, a caressing and gentle exploring of the senses. And it began to build and swell in a frenzied, frantic rhythm, until it became a bacchanal, an orgy of pleasure, wild and savage. His hard organ stroked her and pounded her and filled her until she wanted to scream with the unbearable joy. She was at the centre of a rainbow. She felt herself being swept up on a tidal wave that lifted her higher and higher, and there was a sudden molten explosion within her, and her whole body began to shudder. Gradually, the tempest subsided. She closed her eyes. She felt Jeff's lips move down her body, down, down to the centre of her being, and she was caught up in another fierce wave of blissful sensation.

She pulled Jeff to her and held him close, feeling his heart beat against hers. She strained against him, but still she could not get close enough. She crept to the foot of the bed and touched her lips to his body with soft, tender kisses, moving upwards until she felt his hard maleness in her hand. She stroked it softly and slid it into her mouth, and listened to his moans of pleasure. Then Jeff rolled on top of her and was inside her and it began again, more exciting than before, a fountain spilling over with unbearable pleasure, and Tracy thought, *Now I know. For the first time, I know. But I must remember that this is just for tonight, a lovely farewell present.*

All through the night they made love and talked

about everything and nothing, and it was as though some long-locked floodgates had opened for both of them. At dawn, as the canals began to sparkle with the beginning day, Jeff said, 'Marry me, Tracy.'

She was sure she had misunderstood him, but the words came again, and Tracy knew that it was crazy and impossible, and it could never work, and it was deliriously wonderful, and of course it would work. And she whispered, 'Yes. Oh, yes!'

She began to cry, gripped tightly in the safety of his arms. *I'll never be lonely again*, Tracy thought. *We belong to each other. Jeff is a part of all my tomorrows*.

Tomorrow had come.

A long time later Tracy asked, 'When did you know, Jeff?'

'When I saw you in that house and I thought you were dying. I was half out of my mind.'

'I thought you had run away with the diamonds,' Tracy confessed.

He took her in his arms again. 'Tracy, what I did in Madrid wasn't for the money. It was for the game – the challenge. That's why we're both in the business we're in, isn't it? You're given a puzzle that can't possibly be solved, and then you begin to wonder if there isn't some way.'

Tracy nodded. 'I know. At first it was because I needed the money. And then it became something else; I've given away quite a bit of money. I love matching wits against people who are successful and bright and unscrupulous. I love living on the cutting edge of danger.'

After a long silence, Jeff said, 'Tracy . . . how would you feel about giving it up?'

She looked at him, puzzled. 'Giving it up? Why?'

'We were each on our own before. Now, everything has changed. I couldn't bear it if anything happened. Why take any more risks? We have all the money we'll ever need. Why don't we consider ourselves retired?'

'What would we do, Jeff?'

He grinned. 'We'll think of something.'

'Seriously, darling, how would we spend our lives?'

'Doing anything we like, my love. We'll travel, indulge ourselves in hobbies. I've always been fascinated by archaeology. I'd like to go on a dig in Tunisia. I made a promise once to an old friend. We can finance our own digs. We'll travel all over the world.'

'It sounds exciting.'

'Then what do you say?'

She looked at him for a long moment. 'If that's what you want,' Tracy said softly.

He hugged her and began laughing. 'I wonder if we should send a formal announcement to the police?'

Tracy joined in his laughter.

The churches were older than any Cooper had ever known before. Some dated back to the pagan days, and at times he was not certain whether he was praying to the devil or to God. He sat with bowed head in the ancient Beguine Court Church and in St Bavokerk and Pieterskerk and the Nieuwekerk at Delft, and each time his prayer was the same: *Let me make her suffer as I suffer.*

The telephone call from Gunther Hartog came the next day, while Jeff was out.

'How are you feeling?' Gunther asked.

'I feel wonderful,' Tracy assured him.

Gunther had telephoned every day after he had heard what had happened to her. Tracy decided not to tell him the news about Jeff and herself, not yet. She wanted to hug it to herself for a while, take it out and examine it, cherish it.

'Are you and Jeff getting along all right together?'

She smiled. 'We're getting along splendidly.'

'Would you consider working together again?'

Now she had to tell him. 'Gunther . . . we're . . . quitting.'

There was a momentary silence. 'I don't understand.'

'Jeff and I are – as they used to say in the old James Cagney movies – going straight.'

'What? But . . . why?'

'It was Jeff's idea, and I agreed to it. No more risks.'

'Supposing I told you that the job I have in mind is worth two million dollars to you and there are no risks?'

'I'd laugh a lot, Gunther.'

'I'm serious, my dear. You would travel to Amsterdam, which is only an hour from where you are now, and –'

'You'll have to find someone else.'

He sighed. 'I'm afraid there is no one else who could handle this. Will you at least discuss the possibility with Jeff?'

'All right, but it won't do any good.'

'I will call back this evening.'

When Jeff returned, Tracy reported the conversation.

'Didn't you tell him we've become law-abiding citizens?'

'Of course, darling, I told him to find someone else.'

'But he doesn't want to,' Jeff guessed.

'He insisted he needed us. He said there's no risk and that we could pick up two million dollars for a little bit of effort.'

'Which means that whatever he has in mind must be guarded like Fort Knox.'

'Or the Prado,' Tracy said mischievously.

Jeff grinned. 'That was really a neat plan, sweetheart. You know, I think *that's* when I started to fall in love with you.'

'I think when you stole my Goya is when I began to hate you.'

'Be fair,' Jeff admonished. 'You started to hate me before that.'

'True. What do we tell Gunther?'

'You've already told him. We're not in that line of work any more.'

'Shouldn't we at least find out what he's thinking?'

'Tracy, we agreed that –'

'We're going to Amsterdam anyway, aren't we?'

'Yes, but –'

'Well, while we're there darling, why don't we just listen to what he has to say?'

Jeff studied her suspiciously. 'You *want* to do it, don't you?'

'Certainly not! But it can't hurt to hear what he has to say . . .'

They drove to Amsterdam the following day and checked into the Amstel Hotel. Gunther Hartog flew in from London to meet them.

They managed to sit together, as casual tourists, on a Plas Motor launch cruising the Amstel River.

'I'm delighted that you two are getting married,' Gunther said. 'My warmest congratulations.'

'Thank you, Gunther.' Tracy knew that he was sincere.

'I respect your wishes about retiring, but I have come across a situation so unique that I felt I had to call it to your attention. It could be a very rewarding swan song.'

'We're listening,' Tracy said.

Gunther leaned forward and began talking, his voice low. When he had finished, he said, 'Two million dollars if you can pull it off.'

'It's impossible,' Jeff declared flatly. 'Tracy –'

But Tracy was not listening. She was busily figuring out how it could be done.

Amsterdam's police headquarters, at the corner of Marnix Straat and Elandsgracht, is a gracious old five-storey, brown-brick building with a long white-stucco corridor on the ground floor and a marble staircase leading to the upper floors. In a meeting room upstairs, the Gemeentepolitie were in conference. There were six Dutch detectives in the room. The lone foreigner was Daniel Cooper.

Inspector Joop van Duren was a giant of a man, larger than life, with a beefy face adorned by a flowing moustache, and a roaring basso voice. He was addressing Toon Willems, the neat, crisp, efficient chief commissioner, head of the city's police force.

'Tracy Whitney arrived in Amsterdam this morning, Chief Commissioner. Interpol is certain she was responsible for the De Beers hijacking. Mr Cooper, here, feels she has come to Holland to commit another felony.'

Chief Commissioner Willems turned to Cooper. 'Do you have any proof of this, Mr Cooper?'

Daniel Cooper did not need proof. He knew Tracy Whitney, body and soul. *Of course* she was here to carry out a crime, something beyond the scope of their tiny imaginations. He forced himself to remain calm.

'No proof. That's why she must be caught red-handed.'

'And just how do you propose that we do that?'

'By not letting the woman out of our sight.'

The use of the pronoun *our* disturbed the chief commissioner. He had spoken with Inspector Trignant in Paris about Cooper. *He's obnoxious, but he knows what he's about. If we had listened to him, we would have caught the Whitney woman red-handed.* It was the same phrase Cooper had used.

Toon Willems made his decision, and it was based partly on the well-publicized failure of the French police to apprehend the hijackers of the De Beers diamonds. Where the French police had failed, the Dutch police would succeed.

'Very well,' the chief commissioner said. 'If the lady has come to Holland to test the efficiency of our police force, we shall accommodate her.' He turned to Inspector van Duren. 'Take whatever measures you think necessary.'

The city of Amsterdam is divided into six police districts, with each district responsible for its own territory. On orders from Inspector Joop van Duren, the boundaries were ignored, and detectives from different districts were assigned to surveillance teams. 'I want her watched twenty-four hours a day. Don't let her out of your sight.'

Inspector van Duren turned to Daniel Cooper. 'Well, Mr Cooper, are you satisfied?'

'Not until we have her.'

'We will,' the inspector assured him. 'You see, Mr Cooper, we pride ourselves on having the best police force in the world.'

Amsterdam is a tourist's paradise, a city of windmills and dams and row upon row of gabled houses leaning crazily against one another along a network of tree-lined canals filled with houseboats decorated by boxes of geraniums and plants, and laundry flying in the breeze. The Dutch were the friendliest people Tracy had ever met.

'They all seem so happy,' Tracy said.

'Remember, they're the original flower people. Tulips.'

Tracy laughed and took Jeff's arm. She felt such joy in being with him. *He's so wonderful.* And Jeff was looking at her and thinking, *I'm the luckiest fellow in the world.*

Tracy and Jeff did all the usual sightseeing things tourists do. They strolled along Albert Cuyp Straat, the open-air market that stretches block after block and is filled with stands of antiques, fruits and vegetables, flowers, and clothing, and wandered through Dam Square, where young people gathered to listen to itinerant singers and punk bands. They visited Volendam, the old picturesque fishing village on the Zuider Zee, and Madurodam, Holland in miniature. As they drove past the bustling Schiphol Airport, Jeff said, 'Not long ago, all that land the airport stands on was the North

Sea. *Schiphol* means "cemetery of ships".'

Tracy nestled closer to him. 'I'm impressed. It's nice to be in love with such a smart fellow.'

'You ain't heard nothin' yet. Twenty-five percent of the Netherlands is reclaimed land. The whole country is sixteen feet below sea level.'

'Sounds scary.'

'Not to worry. We're perfectly safe as long as that little kid keeps his finger in the dyke.'

Everywhere Tracy and Jeff went, they were followed by the Gemeetepolitie, and each evening Daniel Cooper studied the written reports submitted to Inspector van Duren. There was nothing unusual in them, but Cooper's suspicions were not allayed. *She's up to something*, he told himself, *something big. I wonder if she knows she's being followed? I wonder if she knows I'm going to destroy her?*

As far as the detectives could see, Tracy Whitney and Jeff Stevens were merely tourists.

Inspector van Duren said to Cooper, 'Isn't it possible you're wrong? They could be in Holland just to have a good time.'

'No,' Cooper said stubbornly. 'I'm not wrong. Stay with her.' He had an ominous feeling that time was running out, that if Tracy Whitney did not make a move soon, the police surveillance would be called off again. That could not be allowed to happen. He joined the detectives who were keeping Tracy under observation.

* * *

Tracy and Jeff had connecting rooms at the Amstel. 'For the sake of respectability,' Jeff told Tracy, 'but I won't let you get far from me.'

'Promise?'

Each night Jeff stayed with her until early dawn, and they made love far into the night. He was a protean lover, by turns tender and considerate, wild and feral.

'It's the first time,' Tracy whispered, 'that I've really known what my body was for. Thank you, my love.'

'The pleasure's all mine.'

'Only half.'

They roamed the city in an apparently aimless manner. They had lunch at the Excelsior in the Hôtel de l'Europe and dinner at the Bowedery, and ate all twenty-two courses served at the Indonesian Bali. They had *erwtensoep*, Holland's famous pea soup; sampled *hutsput*, potatoes, carrots, and onions; and *boerenkool met worst*, made from thirteen vegetables and smoked sausage. They walked through the *walletjes*, the red-light district of Amsterdam, where fat, kimono-clad whores sat on the street windows displaying their ample wares; each evening the written report submitted to Inspector Joop van Duren ended with the same note: *Nothing suspicious*.

Patience, Daniel Cooper told himself. *Patience*.

At the urging of Cooper, Inspector van Duren went to Chief Commissioner Willems to ask permission to place electronic eavesdropping devices in the hotel rooms of the two suspects. Permission was denied.

'When you have more substantial grounds for your suspicions,' the chief commissioner said, 'come back to me. Until then, I cannot permit you to eavesdrop on people who are so far guilty only of touring Holland.'

That conversation had taken place on Friday. On Monday morning Tracy and Jeff went to Paulus Potter Straat in Coster, the diamond centre of Amsterdam, to visit the Nederlands Diamond-Cutting Factory. Daniel Cooper was a part of the surveillance team. The factory was crowded with tourists. An English-speaking guide conducted them around the factory, explaining each operation in the cutting process, and at the end of the tour led the group to a large display room, where showcases filled with a variety of diamonds for sale lined the walls. This of course was the ultimate reason visitors were given a tour of the factory. In the centre of the room stood a glass case dramatically mounted on a tall, black pedestal, and inside the case was the most exquisite diamond Tracy had ever seen.

The guide announced proudly, 'And here, ladies and gentlemen, is the famous Lucullan diamond you have all read about. It was once purchased by a stage actor for his film-star wife and is valued at ten million dollars. It is a perfect stone, one of the finest diamonds in the world.'

'That must be quite a target for thieves,' Jeff said aloud.

Daniel Cooper moved forward so he could hear better.

The guide smiled indulgently, '*Nee, mijnheer*.' He nodded towards the armed guard standing near the exhibit. 'This stone is more closely guarded than the jewels in the Tower of London. There is no danger. If anyone touches the glass case, an alarm rings – *vlug!* – and every window and door in this room is instantly sealed off. At night electronic beams are on, and if someone enters the room, an alarm sounds at police headquarters.'

Jeff looked at Tracy and said, 'I guess no one's ever going to steal that diamond.'

Cooper exchanged a look with one of the detectives. That afternoon Inspector van Duren was given a report of the conversation.

The following day Tracy and Jeff visited the Rijksmuseum. At the entrance, Jeff purchased a directory plan of the museum, and he and Tracy passed through the main hall to the Gallery of Honour, filled with Fra Angelicos, Murillos, Rubenses, Van Dycks and Tiepolos. They moved slowly, pausing in front of each painting, and then walked into the Night Watch Room, where Rembrandt's most famous painting hung. There they stayed. And the attractive Constable First-Class Fien Hauer, who was following them, thought to herself, *Oh, my God!*

The official title of the painting is *The Company*

of Captain Frans Banning Cocq and Lieutenant Willem van Ruytenburch, and it portrays, with extraordinary clarity and composition, a group of soldiers preparing to go on their watch, under the command of their colourfully uniformed captain. The area around the portrait was roped off with velvet cords, and a guard stood nearby.

'It's hard to believe,' Jeff told Tracy, 'but Rembrandt caught hell for this painting.'

'But why? It's fantastic.'

'His patron – the captain in the painting – didn't like the attention Rembrandt paid to the other figures.' Jeff turned to the guard. 'I hope this is well protected.'

'*Ja, mijnheer*. Anyone who tries to steal anything from this museum would have to get by electronic beams, security cameras, and, at night, two guards with patrol dogs.'

Jeff smiled easily. 'I guess this painting is going to stay here forever.'

Late that afternoon the exchange was reported to Van Duren. '*The Night Watch!*' he exclaimed. '*Alstublieft, impossible!*'

Daniel Cooper merely blinked at him with his wild, myopic eyes.

At the Amsterdam Convention Centre, there was a meeting of philatelists, and Tracy and Jeff were among the first to arrive. The hall was heavily guarded, for many of the stamps were priceless. Cooper and a Dutch detective watched as the two visitors wandered through the rare-stamp collection. Tracy and Jeff paused in front of the British Guiana, an unattractive magenta, six-sided stamp.

'What an ugly stamp,' Tracy observed.

'Don't knock it, darling. It's the only stamp of its kind in the world.'

'What's it worth?'

'One million dollars.'

The attendant nodded. 'That is correct, sir. Most people would have no idea, just looking at it. But I see that you, sir, love these stamps, as I do. The history of the world is in them.'

Tracy and Jeff moved on to the next case and looked at an Inverted Jenny stamp that portrayed an airplane flying upside down.

'That's an interesting one,' Tracy said.

The attendant guarding the stamp case said, 'It's worth –'

'Seventy-five thousand dollars,' Jeff remarked.

'Yes, sir. Exactly.'

They moved on to a Hawaiian Missionary two-cent blue.

'That's worth a quarter of a million dollars,' Jeff told Tracy.

Cooper was following closely behind them now, mingling with the crowd.

Jeff pointed to another stamp. 'Here's a rare one. The one-pence Mauritius Post Office. Instead of "post-paid", some daydreaming engraver printed "post *office*". It's worth a lot of pence today.'

'They all seem so small and vulnerable,' Tracy

said, 'and so easy to walk away with.'

The guard at the counter smiled. 'A thief wouldn't get very far, miss. The cases are all electronically wired, and armed guards patrol the convention centre day and night.'

'That's a great relief,' Jeff said earnestly. 'One can't be too careful these days, can one?'

That afternoon Daniel Cooper and Inspector Joop van Duren called on Chief Commissioner Willems together. Van Duren placed the surveillance reports on the commissioner's desk and waited.

'There's nothing definite here,' the chief commissioner finally said, 'but I'll admit that your suspects seem to be sniffing around some very lucrative targets. All right, Inspector. Go ahead. You have official permission to place listening devices in their hotel rooms.'

Daniel Cooper was elated. There would be no more privacy for Tracy Whitney. From this point on he would know everything she was thinking, saying, and doing. He thought about Tracy and Jeff together in bed, and remembered the feel of Tracy's underwear against his cheek. So soft, so sweet-smelling.

That afternoon he went to church.

When Tracy and Jeff left the hotel for dinner that evening, a team of police technicians went to work, planting tiny wireless transmitters in Tracy's and Jeff's suites, concealing them behind pictures, in lamps, and under bedside tables.

Inspector Joop van Duren had commandeered the suite on the floor directly above, and there a technician installed a radio receiver with an antenna and plugged in a recorder.

'It's voice activated,' the technician explained. 'No one has to be here to monitor it. When someone speaks, it will automatically begin to record.'

But Daniel Cooper *wanted* to be there. He *had* to be there. It was God's will.

THIRTY-THREE

Early the following morning Daniel Cooper, Inspector Joop van Duren, and his young assistant, Detective Constable Witkamp, were in the upstairs suite listening to the conversation below.

'More coffee?' Jeff's voice.

'No, thank you, darling.' Tracy's voice. 'Try this cheese that room service sent up. It's really wonderful.'

A short silence. 'Mmmm. Delicious. What would you like to do today, Tracy? We could take a drive to Rotterdam.'

'Why don't we just stay in and relax?'

'Sounds good.'

Daniel Cooper knew what they meant by 'relax', and his mouth tightened.

'The queen is dedicating a new home for orphans.'

'Nice. I think the Dutch are the most hospitable, generous people in the world. They're iconoclasts. They hate rules and regulations.'

A laugh. 'Of course. That's why we both like them so much.'

Ordinary morning conversation between lovers. *They're so free and easy with each other*, Cooper thought. *But how she would pay!*

'Speaking of generous' – Jeff's voice – 'guess who's staying at this hotel? The elusive Maximilian Pierpont. I missed him on the *QE Two*.'

'And I missed him on the *Orient Express*.'

'He's probably here to rape another company. Now that we've found him again, Tracy, we really should do something about him. I mean, as long as he's in the neighbourhood . . .'

Tracy's laughter. 'I couldn't agree more, darling.'

'I understand our friend is in the habit of carrying priceless artifacts with him. I have an idea that –'

Another voice, female. '*Dag, mijnheer, dag, mevrouw*. Would you care for your room to be made up now?'

Van Duren turned to Detective Constable Witkamp. 'I want a surveillance team on Maximilian Pierpont. The moment Whitney or Stevens makes any kind of contact with him, I want to know it.'

Inspector van Duren was reporting to Chief Commissioner Toon Willems.

'They could be after any number of targets, Chief Commissioner. They're showing a great deal of interest in a wealthy American here named Maximilian Pierpont, they attended the philatelist convention, they visited the Lucullan diamond at the Nederlands Diamond-Cutting Factory, and spent two hours at *The Night Watch* –'

'*Ein diefstal van de Nachtwacht? Nee!* Impossible!'

The chief commissioner sat back in his chair and wondered whether he was recklessly wasting valuable time and manpower. There was too much speculation and not enough facts. 'So at the moment you have no idea what their target is.'

'No, Chief Commissioner. I'm not certain they themselves have decided. But the moment they do, they will inform us.'

Willems frowned. 'Inform you?'

'The bugs,' Van Duren explained. 'They have no idea they are being bugged.'

The breakthrough for the police came at 9:00 A.M. the following morning. Tracy and Jeff were finishing breakfast in Tracy's suite. At the listening post upstairs were Daniel Cooper, Inspector Joop van Duren and Detective Constable Witkamp. They heard the sound of coffee being poured.

'Here's an interesting item, Tracy. Our friend was right. Listen to this: "Amro Bank is shipping five million dollars in gold bullion to the Dutch West Indies."'

In the suite on the floor above, Detective Constable Witkamp said, 'There's no way –'

'Shh!'

They listened.

'I wonder how much five million dollars in gold would weigh?' Tracy's voice.

'I can tell you exactly, my darling. One thousand six hundred and seventy-two pounds, about sixty-seven gold bars. The wonderful thing about gold is that it's so beautifully anonymous. You melt it down and it could belong to anybody. Of course, it wouldn't be easy to get those bars out of Holland.'

'Even if we could, how would we get hold of them in the first place? Just walk into the bank and pick them up?'

'Something like that.'

'You're joking.'

'I never joke about that kind of money. Why don't we just stroll by the Amro Bank, Tracy, and have a little look?'

'What do you have in mind?'

'I'll tell you all about it on the way.'

There was the sound of a door closing, and the voices ended.

Inspector van Duren was fiercely twisting his moustache. '*Nee!* There is no way they could get their hands on that gold. I, myself, approved those security arrangements.'

Daniel Cooper announced flatly, 'If there's a flaw in the bank's security system, Tracy Whitney will find it.'

It was all Inspector van Duren could do to control his hair-trigger temper. The odd-looking American had been an abomination ever since his arrival. It was his God-given sense of superiority that was so difficult to tolerate. But Inspector van Duren was a policeman first and last; and he had been ordered to cooperate with the weird little man.

The inspector turned to Witkamp. 'I want you to increase the surveillance unit. *Immediately*. I want every contact photographed and questioned. Clear?'

'Yes, Inspector.'

'And very discreetly, mind you. They must not know they are being watched.'

'Yes, Inspector.'

Van Duren looked at Cooper. 'There. Does that make you feel better?'

Cooper did not bother to reply.

During the next five days Tracy and Jeff kept Inspector van Duren's men busy, and Daniel Cooper carefully examined all the daily reports. At night, when the other detectives left the listening post, Cooper lingered. He listened for the sounds of lovemaking that he knew was going on below. He could hear nothing, but in his mind Tracy was moaning, 'Oh, yes, darling, yes, yes. Oh, God, I can't stand it . . . it's so wonderful . . . Now, oh, now . . .'

Then the long, shuddering sigh and the soft, velvety silence. And it was all for him.

Soon you'll belong to me, Cooper thought. *No one else will have you.*

During the day, Tracy and Jeff went their separate ways, and wherever they went they were followed. Jeff visited a printing shop near Leidseplein, and two detectives watched from the street as he held an earnest conversation with the printer. When Jeff left, one of the detectives followed him. The other went into the shop and showed the printer his plastic-coated police identity card with the official stamp, photograph, and the diagonal red, white and blue stripes.

'The man who just left here. What did he want?'

'He's run out of business cards. He wants me to print some more for him.'

'Let me see.'

The printer showed him a handwritten form:

Amsterdam Security Services
Cornelius Wilson, Chief Investigator

The following day Constable First-Class Fien Hauer waited outside a pet shop on Leidseplein as Tracy went in. When she emerged fifteen minutes later, Fien Hauer entered the shop and showed her identification.

'That lady who just left, what did she want?'

'She purchased a bowl of goldfish, two love-birds, a canary and a pigeon.'

A strange combination. 'A pigeon, you said? You mean an ordinary pigeon?'

'Yes, but no pet store stocks them. I told her we would have to locate one for her.'

'Where are you sending these pets?'

'To her hotel, the Amstel.'

On the other side of town, Jeff was speaking to the vice-president of the Amro Bank. They were closeted together for thirty minutes, and when Jeff left the bank, a detective went into the manager's office.

'The man who just walked out. Please tell me why he was here.'

'Mr Wilson? He's chief investigator for the security company our bank uses. They're revising the security system.'

'Did he ask you to discuss the present security arrangements with him?'

'Why, yes, as a matter of fact, he did.'

'And you told him?'

'Of course. But naturally I first took the precaution of telephoning to make sure his credentials were in order.'

'Whom did you telephone?'

'The security service – the number was printed on his identification card.'

At 3:00 that afternoon an armoured truck pulled up outside the Amro Bank. From across the street, Jeff snapped a picture of the truck, while in a doorway a few yards away a detective photographed Jeff.

At police headquarters at Elandsgracht Inspector van Duren was spreading out the rapidly accumulating evidence on the desk of Chief Commissioner Toon Willems.

'What does all this signify?' the chief commissioner asked in his dry, thin voice.

Daniel Cooper spoke. 'I'll tell you what she's planning.' His voice was heavy with conviction. 'She's planning to hijack the gold shipment.'

They were all staring at him.

Commissioner Willems said, 'And I suppose you know how she intends to accomplish this miracle?'

'Yes.' He knew something they did not know. He knew Tracy Whitney's heart and soul and mind. He had put himself inside her, so that he could think like her, plan like her . . . and anticipate her every move.

'By using a fake security truck and getting to the bank before the real truck, and driving off with the bullion.'

'That sounds rather farfetched, Mr Cooper.'

Inspector van Duren broke in. 'I don't know what their scheme is, but they are planning *something*, Chief Commissioner. We have their voices on tape.'

Daniel Cooper remembered the other sounds he had imagined: the night whispers, the cries and moans. She was behaving like a bitch in heat. Well, where he would put her, no man would ever touch her again.

The inspector was saying, 'They learned the security routine of the bank. They know what time the armoured truck makes its pickup and –'

The chief commissioner was studying the report in front of him. 'Lovebirds, a pigeon, goldfish, a canary – do you think any of this nonsense has anything to do with the robbery?'

'No,' Van Duren said.

'Yes,' Cooper said.

* * *

Constable First-Class Fien Hauer, dressed in an aqua polyester trouser suit, trailed Tracy Whitney down Prinsengracht, across the Magere Bridge, and when Tracy reached the other side of the canal, Fien Hauer looked on in frustration as Tracy stepped into a public telephone booth and spoke into the phone for five minutes. The constable would have been just as unenlightened if she could have heard the conversation.

Gunther Hartog, in London, was saying, 'We can depend on Margo, but she'll need time – at least two more weeks.' He listened a moment. 'I understand. When everything is ready, I will get in touch with you. Be careful. And give my regards to Jeff.'

Tracy replaced the receiver and stepped out of the booth. She gave a friendly nod to the woman in the aqua trouser suit who stood waiting to use the telephone.

At 11:00 the following morning a detective reported to Inspector van Duren, 'I'm at the Wolters Truck Rental Company, Inspector. Jeff Stevens has just rented a truck from them.'

'What kind of truck?'

'A service truck, Inspector.'

'Get the dimensions. I'll hold on.'

A few minutes later the detective was back on the phone. 'I have them. The truck is –'

Inspector van Duren said, 'A step van, twenty feet long, seven feet wide, six feet high, dual axles.'

There was an astonished pause. 'Yes, Inspector. How did you know?'

'Never mind. What colour is it?'

'Blue.'

'Who's following Stevens?'

'Jacobs.'

'Good. Report back here.'

Joop van Duren replaced the receiver. He looked up at Daniel Cooper. 'You were right. Except that the van is blue.'

'He'll take it to a car paint shop.'

The paint shop was located in a garage on the Damrak. Two men sprayed the truck a gun-metal grey, while Jeff stood by. On the roof of the garage a detective shot photographs through the skylight.

The pictures were on Inspector van Duren's desk one hour later.

He shoved them towards Daniel Cooper. 'It's being painted the identical colour of the real security truck. We could pick them up now, you know.'

'On what charges? Having some false business cards printed and painting a truck? The only way to make the charge stick is to catch them when they pick up the bullion.'

The little prick acts like he's running the department. 'What do you think he'll do next?'

Cooper was carefully studying the photograph. 'This truck won't take the weight of the gold. They'll have to reinforce the floorboards.'

* * *

It was a small, out-of-the-way garage on Muider Straat.

'*Goede morgen, mijnheer*. How may I serve you?'

'I'm going to be carrying some scrap iron in this truck,' Jeff explained, 'and I'm not sure the floorboards are strong enough to take the weight. I'd like them reinforced with metal braces. Can you do that?'

The mechanic walked over to the truck and examined it. '*Ja*. No problem.'

'Good.'

'I can have it ready *vrijdag* – Friday.'

'I was hoping to have it tomorrow.'

'*Morgen? Nee. Ik –*'

'I'll pay you double.'

'*Donderdag* – Thursday.'

'Tomorrow. I'll pay you triple.'

The mechanic scratched his chin thoughtfully. 'What time tomorrow?'

'Noon.'

'*Ja*. Okay.'

'*Dank wel*.'

'*Tot uw dienst*.'

Moments after Jeff left the garage a detective was interrogating the mechanic.

On the same morning the team of surveillance experts assigned to Tracy followed her to the Oude Schans Canal, where she spent half an hour in conversation with the owner of a barge. When Tracy left, one of the detectives stepped aboard the barge.

He identified himself to the owner, who was sipping a large *bessen-jenever*, the potent redcurrant gin. 'What did the young lady want?'

'She and her husband are going to take a tour of the canals. She's rented my barge for a week.'

'Beginning when?'

'Friday. It's a beautiful vacation, *mijnheer*. If you and your wife would be interested in –'

The detective was gone.

The pigeon Tracy had ordered from the pet shop was delivered to her hotel in a birdcage. Daniel Cooper returned to the pet shop and questioned the owner.

'What kind of pigeon did you send her?'

'Oh, you know, an ordinary pigeon.'

'Are you sure it's not a homing pigeon?'

'No.' The man giggled. 'The reason I know it's not a homing pigeon is because I caught it last night in Vondelpark.'

A thousand pounds of gold and an ordinary pigeon? *Why?* Daniel Cooper wondered.

Five days before the transfer of bullion from the Amro Bank was to take place, a large pile of photographs had accumulated on Inspector Joop van Duren's desk.

Each picture is a link in the chain that is going to trap her, Daniel Cooper thought. The Amsterdam police had no imagination, but Cooper had to give them credit for being thorough. Every step leading to the forthcoming crime was photographed and documented. There was no way Tracy Whitney could escape justice.

Her punishment will be my redemption.

On the day Jeff picked up the newly painted truck he drove it to a small garage he had rented near the Oude Zijds Kolk, the oldest part of Amsterdam. Six empty wooden boxes stamped MACHINERY were also delivered to the garage. A photograph of the boxes lay on Inspector van Duren's desk as he listened to the latest tape.

Jeff's voice: 'When you drive the truck from the bank to the barge, stay within the speed limit. I want to know exactly how long the trip takes. Here's a stopwatch.'

'Aren't you coming with me, darling?'

'No. I'm going to be busy.'

'What about Monty?'

'He'll arrive Thursday night.'

'Who is this Monty?' Inspector van Duren asked.

'He's probably the man who's going to pose as the second security guard,' Cooper said. 'They're going to need uniforms.'

The costume store was on Pieter Cornelisz Hooft Straat, in a shopping centre.

'I need two uniforms for a costume party,' Jeff explained to the clerk. 'Similar to the one you have in the window.'

One hour later Inspector van Duren was looking

at a photograph of a guard's uniform.

'He ordered two of these. He told the clerk he would pick them up Thursday.'

The size of the second uniform indicated that it was for a man much larger than Jeff Stevens. The inspector said, 'Our friend Monty would be about six-feet three and weigh around fifteen stone. We'll have Interpol put that through their computers,' he assured Daniel Cooper, 'and we'll get an identification on him.'

In the private garage Jeff had rented, he was perched on top of the truck, and Tracy was in the driver's seat.

'Are you ready?' Jeff called. '*Now*.'

Tracy pressed a button on the dashboard. A large piece of canvas rolled down each side of the truck, spelling out HEINEKEN HOLLAND BEER.

'It works!' Jeff cheered.

'Heineken beer? *Alstublieft!*' Van Duren looked around at the detectives gathered in his office. A series of blown-up photographs and memos were tacked all around the walls.

Daniel Cooper sat in the back of the room, silent. As far as Cooper was concerned, this meeting was a waste of time. He had long since anticipated every move Tracy Whitney and her lover would make. They had walked into a trap, and the trap was closing in on them. While the detectives in the office were filled with a growing excitement, Cooper felt an odd sense of anticlimax.

'All the pieces have fallen into place,' Inspector van Duren was saying. 'The suspects know what time the real armoured truck is due at the bank. They plan to arrive about half an hour earlier, posing as security guards. By the time the real truck arrives, they'll be gone.' Van Duren pointed to the photograph of an armoured car. 'They will drive away from the bank looking like this, but a block away, on some side street' – he indicated the Heineken beer truck photograph – 'the truck will suddenly look like *this*.'

A detective from the back of the room spoke up. 'Do you know how they plan to get the gold out of the country, Inspector?'

Van Duren pointed to a picture of Tracy stepping onto the barge. 'First, by barge. Holland is so criss-crossed with canals and waterways that they could lose themselves indefinitely.' He indicated an aerial photograph of the truck speeding along the edge of the canal. 'They've timed the run to see how long it takes to get from the bank to their barge. Plenty of time to load the gold onto the barge and be on their way before anyone suspects anything is wrong.' Van Duren walked over to the last photograph on the wall, an enlarged picture of a freighter. 'Two days ago Jeff Stevens reserved cargo space on the *Oresta*, sailing from Rotterdam next week. The cargo was listed as machinery, destination Hong Kong.'

He turned to face the men in the room. 'Well, gentlemen, we're making a slight change in their plans. We're going to let them remove the gold bullion from the bank and load it into the truck.' He looked at Daniel Cooper and smiled. 'Red-handed. We're going to catch these clever people red-handed.'

A detective followed Tracy into the American Express office, where she picked up a medium-sized package; she returned immediately to her hotel.

'No way of knowing what was in the package,' Inspector van Duren told Cooper. 'We searched both their suites when they left, and there was nothing new in either of them.'

Interpol's computers were unable to furnish any information on the fifteen-stone Monty.

At the Amstel late Thursday evening, Daniel Cooper, Inspector van Duren, and Detective Constable Witkamp were in the room above Tracy's, listening to the voices below.

Jeff's voice: 'If we get to the bank exactly thirty minutes before the guards are due, that will give us plenty of time to load the gold and move out. By the time the real truck arrives, we'll be stowing the gold onto the barge.'

Tracy's voice: 'I've had the mechanic check the truck and fill it with petrol. It's ready.'

Detective Constable Witkamp said, 'One must almost admire them. They don't leave a thing to chance.'

'They all slip up sooner or later,' Inspector van Duren said curtly.

Daniel Cooper was silent, listening.

'Tracy, when this is over, how would you like to go on that dig we talked about?'

'Tunisia? Sounds like heaven, darling.'

'Good. I'll arrange it. From now on we'll do nothing but relax and enjoy life.'

Inspector van Duren murmured, 'I'd say their next twenty years are pretty well taken care of.' He rose and stretched. 'Well, I think we can go to bed. Everything is set for tomorrow morning, and we can all use a good night's sleep.'

Daniel Cooper was unable to sleep. He visualized Tracy being grabbed and manhandled by the police, and he could see the terror on her face. It excited him. He went into the bathroom and ran a very hot bath. He removed his glasses, took off his pyjamas, and lay back in the steaming water. It was almost over, and she would pay, as he had made other whores pay. By this time tomorrow he would be on his way home. *No, not home*, Daniel Cooper corrected himself. *To my flat. Home* was a warm safe place where his mother loved him more than she loved anyone else in the world.

'You're my little man,' she said. 'I don't know what I would do without you.'

Daniel's father disappeared when Daniel was four years old, and at first he blamed himself, but his mother explained that it was because of another woman. He hated that other woman, because she made his mother cry. He had never seen her, but he knew she was a whore because he had heard his mother call her that. Later, he was happy that the woman had taken his father away, for now he had his mother all to himself. The Minnesota winters were cold, and Daniel's mother allowed him to crawl into bed with her and snuggle under the warm blankets.

'I'm going to marry you one day,' Daniel promised, and his mother laughed and stroked his hair.

Daniel was always at the head of his class in school. He wanted his mother to be proud of him.

What a brilliant little boy you have, Mrs Cooper.

I know. No one is as clever as my little man.

When Daniel was seven years old, his mother started inviting their neighbour, a huge, hairy man, over to their house for dinner, and Daniel became ill. He was in bed for a week with a dangerously high fever, and his mother promised she would never do that again. *I don't need anyone in the world but you, Daniel.*

No one could have been as happy as Daniel. His mother was the most beautiful woman in the whole world. When she was out of the house, Daniel would go into her bedroom and open the drawers of her dresser. He would take out her lingerie and rub the soft material against his cheek. They smelled oh, so wonderful.

He lay back in the warm bath in the Amsterdam hotel, his eyes closed, remembering the terrible day of his mother's murder. It was on his twelfth birthday. He was sent home from school early because he had an earache. He pretended it was worse than it was, because he wanted to be home where his mother would soothe him and put him into her bed and fuss over him. Daniel walked into the house and went to his mother's bedroom, and she was lying naked in their bed, but she was not alone. She was doing unspeakable things to the man who lived next door. Daniel watched as she began to kiss the matted chest and the bloated stomach, and her kisses trailed downward towards the huge red weapon between the man's legs. Before she took it into her mouth, Daniel heard his mother moan, 'Oh, I love you!'

And that was the most unspeakable thing of all. Daniel ran to his bathroom and vomited all over himself. He carefully undressed and cleaned himself up because his mother had taught him to be neat. His earache was really bad now. He heard voices from the hallway and listened.

His mother was saying, 'You'd better go now, darling. I've got to bathe and get dressed. Daniel will be home from school soon. I'm giving him a birthday party. I'll see you tomorrow, sweetheart.'

There was the noise of the front door closing, and then the sound of running water from his mother's bathroom. Except that she was no longer his mother. She was a whore who did dirty things in bed with men, things she had never done with him.

He walked into her bathroom, naked, and she was in the bath, her whore's face smiling. She turned her head and saw him and said, 'Daniel, darling! What are you –?'

He carried a pair of heavy dressmaker's shears in his hand.

'Daniel –' Her mouth was opened into a pink-lined O, but there was no sound until he made the first stab into the breast of the stranger in the bath. He accompanied her screams with his own. 'Whore! Whore! Whore!'

They sang a deadly duet together, until finally there was his voice alone. 'Whore . . . whore . . .'

He was spattered all over with her blood. He stepped into her shower and scrubbed himself until his skin felt raw.

That man next door had killed his mother, and that man would have to pay.

After that, everything seemed to happen with a supernal clarity, in a curious kind of slow motion. Daniel wiped the fingerprints off the shears with a flannel and threw them into the bath. They clanked dully against the enamel. He dressed and telephoned the police. Two police cars arrived, with sirens screaming, and then another car filled with detectives, and they asked Daniel questions, and he told them how he had been sent home from school early and about seeing their next-door neighbour, Fred Zimmer, leaving through the side door. When they questioned the man, he admitted being the lover of Daniel's mother, but denied killing her. It was Daniel's testimony in court that convicted Zimmer.

'When you arrived home from school, you saw your neighbour, Fred Zimmer, running out the side door?'

'Yes, sir.'

'Could you see him clearly?'

'Yes, sir. There was blood all over his hands.'

'What did you do then, Daniel?'

'I – I was so scared. I knew something awful had happened to my mother.'

'Then did you go into the house?'

'Yes, sir.'

'And what happened?'

'I called out, "Mother!" And she didn't answer, so I went into her bathroom and –'

At this point the young boy broke into hysterical sobs and had to be led from the stand.

Fred Zimmer was executed thirteen months later.

In the meantime young Daniel had been sent to live with a distant relative in Texas, Aunt Mattie, whom he had never met. She was a stern woman, a hard-shelled Baptist filled with a vehement righteousness and the conviction that hell's fire awaited all sinners. It was a house without love or joy or pity, and Daniel grew up in that atmosphere, terrified by the secret knowledge of his guilt and the damnation that awaited him. Shortly after his mother's murder Daniel began to have trouble with his vision. The doctors called the problem psychosomatic.

'He's blocking out something he doesn't want to see,' the doctors said.

The lenses on his glasses grew thicker.

At seventeen Daniel ran away from Aunt Mattie and Texas forever. He hitchhiked to New York, where he was hired as a messenger boy by the International Insurance Protection Association. Within three years he was promoted to an investigator. He became the best they had. He never demanded a raise in salary or better working conditions. He was oblivious to those things. He was the Lord's right arm, his scourge, punishing the wicked. Daniel Cooper rose from his bath and prepared for bed. *Tomorrow*, he thought. *Tomorrow will be the whore's day of retribution.*

He wished his mother could be there to see it.

THIRTY-FOUR

Amsterdam
Friday, 22 August – 8:00 A.M.

Daniel Cooper and the two detectives assigned to the listening post heard Tracy and Jeff at breakfast.

'Sweet roll, Jeff? Coffee?'

'No, thanks.'

Daniel Cooper thought, *It's the last breakfast they'll ever have together*.

'Do you know what I'm getting excited about? Our barge trip.'

'This is the big day, and you're excited about a trip on a *barge*? Why?'

'Because it will be just the two of us. Do you think I'm crazy?'

'Absolutely. But you're *my* crazy.'

'Kiss.'

The sound of a kiss.

She should be more nervous, Cooper thought. *I want her to be nervous*.

‘In a way, I’ll be sorry to leave here, Jeff.’

‘Look at it this way, darling. We won’t be any the poorer for the experience.’

Tracy’s laughter. ‘You’re right.’

At 9:00 A.M. the conversation was still going on, and Cooper thought, *They should be getting ready. They should be making their last-minute plans. What about Monty? Where are they meeting him?*

Jeff was saying, ‘Darling, would you take care of the concierge before you check us out? I’m going to be rather busy.’

‘Of course. He’s been wonderful. Why don’t they have concierges in the States?’

‘I guess it’s just a European custom. Do you know how it started?’

‘No.’

‘In France, in 1627, King Hugh built a prison in Paris and put a nobleman in charge of it. He gave him the title of *comte des cierges*, or concierge, meaning “count of the candles”. His pay was two pounds and the ashes from the king’s fireplace. Later, anyone in charge of a prison or a castle became known as a concierge, and finally, this included those working in hotels.’

What the hell are they talking about? Cooper wondered. *It’s nine-thirty. Time for them to be leaving.*

Tracy’s voice: ‘Don’t tell me where you learned that – you used to go with a beautiful concierge.’

A strange female voice: ‘*Goede morgen, mevrouw, mijnheer*.’

Jeff's voice: 'There are no beautiful concierges.'

The female voice, puzzled: '*Ik begrijp het niet.*'

Tracy's voice: 'I'll bet if there were, you'd find them.'

'What the hell is going on down there?' Cooper demanded.

The detectives looked baffled. 'I don't know. The maid's on the phone calling the housekeeper. She came in to clean, but she says she doesn't understand – she hears voices, but she doesn't see anybody.'

'*What*?' Cooper was on his feet, racing towards the floor, flying down the stairs. Moments later he and the other detectives burst into Tracy's suite. Except for the confused maid, it was empty. On a coffee table in front of a couch a tape recorder was playing.

Jeff's voice: 'I think I'll change my mind about that coffee. Is it still hot?'

Tracy's voice: 'Uh-huh.'

Cooper and the detectives stared in disbelief.

'I – I don't understand,' one of the detectives stammered.

Cooper snapped, 'What's the police emergency number?'

'Twenty-two-twenty-two-twenty-two.'

Cooper hurried over to the phone and dialled.

Jeff's voice on the tape recorder was saying, 'You know, I really think their coffee is better than ours. I wonder how they do it.'

Cooper screamed into the phone, 'This is Daniel

Cooper. Get hold of Inspector van Duren. Tell him Whitney and Stevens have disappeared. Have him check the garage and see if their truck is gone. I'm on my way to the bank!' He slammed down the receiver.

Tracy's voice was saying, 'Have you ever had coffee brewed with eggshells in it? It's really quite –'

Cooper was out the door.

Inspector van Duren said, 'It's all right. The truck has left their garage. They're on their way here.'

Van Duren, Cooper, and two detectives were at a police command post on the roof of a building across from the Amro Bank.

The inspector said, 'They probably decided to move up their plans when they learned they were being bugged, but relax, my friend. Look.' He pushed Cooper towards the wideangle telescope on the roof. On the street below, a man dressed in janitor's clothes was meticulously polishing the brass nameplate of the bank . . . a street cleaner was sweeping the streets . . . a newspaper vendor stood on a corner . . . three repairmen were at work. All were equipped with miniature walkie-talkies.

Van Duren spoke into his walkie-talkie. 'Point A?'

The janitor said, 'I read you, Inspector.'

'Point B?'

'You're coming in, sir.' This from the street cleaner.

'Point C?'

The news vendor looked up and nodded.

'Point D?'

The repairmen stopped their work, and one of them spoke into the walkie-talkie. 'Everything's ready here, sir.'

The inspector turned to Cooper. 'Don't worry. The gold is still safely in the bank. The only way they can get their hands on it is to come for it. The moment they enter the bank, both ends of the street will be barricaded. There's no way they can escape.' He consulted his watch. 'The truck should be in sight any moment now.'

Inside the bank, the tension was growing. The employees had been briefed, and the guards ordered to help load the gold into the armoured truck when it arrived. Everyone was to cooperate fully.

The disguised detectives outside the bank kept working, surreptitiously watching the street for a sign of the truck.

On the roof, Inspector van Duren asked, for the tenth time, 'Any sign of the damned truck yet?'

'*Nee.*'

Detective Constable Witkamp looked at his watch. 'They're thirteen goddamn minutes overdue. If they –'

The walkie-talkie crackled into life. 'Inspector! The truck just came into sight! It's crossing Rozengracht, heading for the bank. You should be able to see it from the roof in a minute.'

The air was suddenly charged with electricity.

Inspector van Duren spoke rapidly into the walkie-talkie. 'Attention, all units. The fish are in the net. Let them swim in.'

A grey armoured truck moved to the entrance of the bank and stopped. As Cooper and Van Duren watched, two men wearing the uniforms of the security guards got out of the truck and walked into the bank.

'Where is she? Where's Tracy Whitney?' Daniel Cooper spoke aloud.

'It doesn't matter,' Inspector van Duren assured him. 'She won't be far from the gold.'

And even if she is, Daniel Cooper thought, *it's not important. The tapes are going to convict her.*

Nervous employees helped the two uniformed men load the gold bullion from the vault onto dollies and wheel them out to the armoured truck. Cooper and van Duren watched the distant figures from the roof across the street.

The loading took eight minutes. When the back of the truck was locked, and the two men started to climb into the front seat, Inspector van Duren yelled into his walkie-talkie, '*Vlug! Pas op!* All units close in! *Close in!*'

Pandemonium erupted. The janitor, the news vendor, the workers in overalls, and a swarm of other detectives raced to the armoured truck and surrounded it, guns drawn. The street was cordoned off from all traffic in either direction.

Inspector van Duren turned to Daniel Cooper

and grinned. 'Is this red-handed enough for you? Let's wrap it up.'

It's over at last, Cooper thought.

They hurried down to the street. The two uniformed men were facing the wall, hands raised, surrounded by a circle of armed detectives. Daniel Cooper and Inspector van Duren pushed their way through.

Van Duren said, 'You can turn around now. You're under arrest.'

The two men, ashen-faced, turned to face the group. Daniel Cooper and Inspector van Duren stared at them in shock. They were total strangers.

'Who – who are you?' Inspector van Duren demanded.

'We – we're the guards for the security company,' one of them stammered. 'Don't shoot. Please don't shoot.'

Inspector van Duren turned to Cooper. 'Their plan went wrong.' His voice held a note of hysteria. 'They called it off.'

There was a green bile in the pit of Daniel Cooper's stomach, and it slowly began to rise up into his chest and throat, so that when he could finally speak, his voice was choked. 'No. Nothing went wrong.'

'What are you talking about?'

'They were never after the gold. This whole setup was a decoy.'

'That's impossible! I mean, the truck, the barge, the uniforms – we have photographs . . .'

'Don't you understand? They *knew* it. They knew we were on to them all the time!'

Inspector van Duren's face went white. 'Oh, my God! *Waar zijnze – where are they?*'

On Paulus Potter Straat in Coster, Tracy and Jeff were approaching the Nederlands Diamond-Cutting Factory. Jeff wore a beard and moustache, and had altered the shape of his cheeks and nose with foam sponges. He was dressed in a sports outfit and carried a rucksack. Tracy wore a black wig, a maternity dress and padding, heavy makeup, and dark sunglasses. She carried a large briefcase and a round package wrapped in brown paper. The two of them entered the reception room and joined a busload of tourists listening to a guide. '. . . And now, if you will follow me, ladies and gentlemen, you will see our diamond cutters at work and have an opportunity to purchase some of our fine diamonds.'

With the guide leading the way, the crowd entered the doors that led inside the factory. Tracy moved along with them, while Jeff lingered behind. When the others had gone, Jeff turned and hurried down a flight of stairs that led to a basement. He opened his rucksack and took out a pair of oil-stained overalls and a small box of tools. He donned the overalls, walked over to the fuse box, and looked at his watch.

Upstairs, Tracy stayed with the group as it moved from room to room while the guide showed them the various processes that went into making polished gems out of raw diamonds. From time to time Tracy glanced at her watch. The tour was five minutes behind schedule. She wished the guide would move faster.

At last, as the tour ended, they reached the display room. The guide walked over to the roped-off pedestal.

'In this glass case,' he announced proudly, 'is the Lucullan diamond, one of the most valuable diamonds in the world. It was once purchased by a famous stage actor for his film-star wife. It is valued at ten million dollars and is protected by the most modern –'

The lights went out. Instantly, an alarm sounded and steel shutters slammed down in front of the windows and doors, sealing all the exits. Some of the tourists began to scream.

'Please!' the guide shouted above the noise. 'There is no need for concern. It is a simple electrical failure. In a moment the emergency generator will –' The lights came on again.

'You see?' the guide reassured them. 'There is nothing to worry about.'

A German tourist in lederhosen pointed to the steel shutters. 'What are those?'

'A safety precaution,' the guide explained. He took out an odd-shaped key, inserted it in a slot in the wall, and turned it. The steel shutters over the doors and windows retracted. The telephone on the desk rang, and the guide picked it up.

'Hendrik, here. Thank you, Captain. No, everything is fine. It was a false alarm. Probably an electrical short. I will have it checked out at once. Yes, sir.' He replaced the receiver and turned to the group. 'My apologies, ladies and gentlemen. With something as valuable as this stone, one can't be too careful. Now, for those of you who would like to purchase some of our very fine diamonds –'

The lights went out again. The alarm bell rang, and the steel shutters slammed down once more.

A woman in the crowd cried, 'Let's get out of here, Harry.'

'Will you just shut up, Diane?' her husband growled.

In the basement downstairs, Jeff stood in front of the fuse box, listening to the cries of the tourists upstairs. He waited a few moments, then reconnected the switch. The lights upstairs flickered on.

'Ladies and gentlemen,' the guide yelled over the uproar. 'It is just a technical difficulty.' He took out the key again and inserted it into the wall slot. The steel shutters rose.

The telephone rang. The guide hurried over and picked it up. 'Hendrik, here. No, Captain. Yes. We will have it fixed as quickly as possible. Thank you.'

A door to the room opened and Jeff came in carrying the tool case, his worker's cap pushed back on his head.

He singled out the guide.

'What's the problem? Someone reported trouble with the electrical circuits.'

'The lights keep flashing off and on,' the guide explained. 'See if you can fix it quickly, please.' He turned to the tourists and forced a smile on his lips. 'Why don't we step over here where you can select some fine diamonds at very reasonable prices?'

The group of tourists began to move towards the showcases. Jeff, unobserved in the press of the crowd, slipped a small cylindrical object from his overalls, pulled the pin, and tossed the device behind the pedestal that held the Lucullan diamond. The contrivance began to emit smoke and sparks.

Jeff called out to the guide, 'Hey! There's your problem. There's a short in the wire under the floor.'

A woman tourist screamed, 'Fire!'

'Please, everybody!' the guide yelled. 'No need to panic. Just keep calm.' He turned to Jeff and hissed, 'Fix it! Fix it!'

'No problem,' Jeff said easily. He moved towards the velvet ropes around the pedestal.

'*Nee!*' the guard urged. 'You can't go near that!'

Jeff shrugged. 'Fine with me. *You* fix it.' He turned to leave.

Smoke was pouring out faster now. The people were beginning to panic again.

'Wait!' the guide pleaded. 'Just a minute.' He hurried over to the telephone and dialled a number. 'Captain? Hendrik, here. I'll have to ask you to shut off all the alarms; we're having a little problem. Yes, sir.' He looked over at Jeff. 'How long will you need them off?'

'Five minutes,' Jeff said.

'Five minutes,' the guide repeated into the phone. '*Dank wel.*' He replaced the receiver. 'The alarms will be off in ten seconds. For God's sake, hurry! We *never* shut off the alarm!'

'I've only got two hands, friend.' Jeff waited ten seconds, then moved inside the ropes and walked up to the pedestal. Hendrik signalled to the armed guard, and the guard nodded and fixed his eyes on Jeff.

Jeff was working behind the pedestal. The frustrated guide turned to the group. 'Now, ladies and gentlemen, as I was saying, over here we have a selection of fine diamonds at bargain prices. We accept credit cards, traveller's cheques' – he gave a little chuckle – 'and even cash.'

Tracy was standing in front of the counter. 'Do you buy diamonds?' she asked in a loud voice.

The guide stared at her. 'What?'

'My husband is a prospector. He just returned from South Africa, and he wants me to sell these.'

As she spoke, she opened the briefcase she carried, but she was holding it upside down, and a torrent of flashing diamonds cascaded down and danced all over the floor.

'My diamonds!' Tracy cried. 'Help me!'

There was one frozen moment of silence, and then all hell broke loose. The polite crowd became a mob. They scrambled for the diamonds on their hands and knees, knocking one another out of the way.

'I've got some . . .'

'Grab a handful, John . . .'

'Let go of that, it's mine . . .'

The guide and the guard were beyond speech. They were hurled aside in a sea of scrambling, greedy human beings, filling their pockets and handbags with the diamonds.

The guard screamed, 'Stand back! Stop that!' and was knocked to the floor.

A busload of Italian tourists entered, and when they saw what was happening, they joined in the frantic scramble.

The guard tried to get to his feet to sound the alarm, but the human tide made it impossible. They were trampling over him. The world had suddenly gone mad. It was a nightmare that seemed to have no end.

When the dazed guard finally managed to stagger to his feet, he pushed his way through the bedlam, reached the pedestal, and stood there, staring in disbelief.

The Lucullan diamond had disappeared.

So had the pregnant lady and the electrician.

Tracy removed her disguise in a stall in the public washroom in Oosterpark, a long away from the factory. Carrying the package wrapped in brown paper, she headed for a park bench. Everything was moving perfectly. She thought about the mob of people scrambling for the worthless zircons and laughed aloud. She saw Jeff approaching, wearing a dark grey suit; the beard and moustache had vanished. Tracy leapt to her feet. Jeff walked up to her and grinned. 'I love you,' he said. He slipped the Lucullan diamond out of his jacket pocket and handed it to Tracy. 'Feed this to your friend, darling. See you later.'

Tracy watched him as he strolled away. Her eyes were shining. They belonged to each other. They would take separate planes and meet in Brazil, and after that, they would be together for the rest of their lives.

Tracy looked around to make sure no one was observing, then she unwrapped the package she held. Inside was a small cage holding a slate-grey pigeon. When it had arrived at the American Express office three days earlier, Tracy had taken it to her suite and released the other pigeon out the window and watched it clumsily flutter away. Now, Tracy took a small chamois sack from her handbag and placed the diamond in it. She removed the pigeon from its cage and held it while she carefully tied the sack to the bird's leg.

'Good girl, Margo. Take it home.'

A uniformed policeman appeared from nowhere. 'Hold it! What do you think you're doing?'

Tracy's heart skipped a beat. 'What's – what's the trouble, officer?'

His eyes were on the cage, and he was angry. 'You *know* what the trouble is. It's one thing to feed these pigeons, but it's against the law to trap them and put them in cages. Now, you just let it go before I place you under arrest.'

Tracy swallowed and took a deep breath. 'If you say so, officer.' She lifted her arms and tossed the pigeon into the air. A lovely smile lit her face as she watched the pigeon soar, higher and higher. It circled once, then headed in the direction of London, 230 miles to the west. A homing pigeon averaged forty miles an hour, Gunther had told her, so Margo would reach him within six hours.

'Don't ever try that again,' the officer warned Tracy.

'I won't,' Tracy promised solemnly. 'Never again.'

Late that afternoon, Tracy was at Schiphol Airport, moving towards the gate from which she would board a plane bound for Brazil. Daniel Cooper stood off in a corner, watching her, his eyes bitter. Tracy Whitney had stolen the Lucullan diamond. Cooper had known it the moment he heard the report. It was her style, daring and imaginative. Yet, there was nothing that could be done about it. Inspector van Duren had shown photographs of Tracy and Jeff to the museum guard. '*Nee*. Never seen either of them. The thief had a beard and a moustache and his cheeks and nose were much fatter, and the lady with the diamonds was dark-haired and pregnant.'

Nor was there any trace of the diamond. Jeff's and Tracy's persons and baggage had been thoroughly searched.

'The diamond is still in Amsterdam,' Inspector van Duren swore to Cooper. 'We'll find it.'

No, you won't, Cooper thought angrily. She had switched pigeons. The diamond had been carried out of the country by a homing pigeon.

Cooper watched helplessly as Tracy Whitney made her way across the concourse. She was the first person who had ever defeated him. He would go to hell because of her.

As Tracy reached the boarding gate, she hesitated a moment, then turned and looked straight into Cooper's eyes. She had been aware that he had been following her all over Europe, like some kind of nemesis. There was something bizarre about him, frightening and at the same time pathetic. Inexplicably, Tracy felt sorry for him. She gave him a small farewell wave, then turned and boarded her plane.

Daniel Cooper touched the letter of resignation in his pocket.

It was a luxurious Pan American 747, and Tracy was seated in Seat 4B on the aisle in first class. She was excited. In a few hours she would be with Jeff. They would be married in Brazil. *No more capers*, Tracy thought, *but I won't miss them. I know I won't. Life will be thrilling enough just being Mrs Jeff Stevens.*

'Excuse me.'

Tracy looked up. A puffy, dissipated-looking middle-aged man was standing over her. He indicated the window seat. 'That's my seat, honey.'

Tracy twisted aside so he could get past her. As

her skirt slid up, he eyed her legs appreciatively.

'Great day for a flight, huh?' There was a leer in his voice.

Tracy turned away. She had no interest in getting into a conversation with a fellow passenger. She had too much to think about. *A whole new life. They would settle down somewhere and be model citizens. The ultrarespectable Mr and Mrs Jeff Stevens.*

Her companion nudged her. 'Since we're gonna be seat mates on this flight, little lady, why don't you and I get acquainted? My name is Maximilian Pierpont.'

Bloodline

Sidney Sheldon

The daughter of a rich and powerful father, Elizabeth Roffe is young, beautiful – and sole heir to a billion dollar fortune.

Then tragedy strikes. Her father is killed in a freak accident and Elizabeth must take command of his mighty global empire, the pharmaceutical company Roffe and Sons. It makes Elizabeth the richest girl in the world. But someone, somewhere, is determined that she must die.

From the backstreets of Istanbul to the upmarket offices of New York, *Bloodline* is a hypnotic tale of love and ambition, danger, intrigue and death.

'Absorbing and eminently well-crafted.' *New York Times*

'Contains the three basic Sheldon ingredients – glamour, intrigue and sex.' *Daily Mail*

ISBN 0 00 617501 5

Master of the Game

Sidney Sheldon

'If you want to win, you have to learn to be a master of the game.'

Kate Blackwell is one of the richest and most powerful women in the world. She is an enigma, a woman surrounded by a thousand unanswered questions. Her father was a diamond prospector who struck it rich beyond dreams. Her mother was the daughter of a crooked Afrikaaner merchant. Her very conception was an act of hate-filled vengeance.

At the extravagant celebrations of her ninetieth birthday, there are toasts from a Supreme Court judge and a telegram from the White House. And for Kate there are ghosts. Ghosts of absent friends and absent enemies. Ghosts from a life of blackmail and deceit and murder. Ghosts from an empire spawned by naked ambition . . .

'A master storyteller at the top of the game' *USA Today*

'Compulsively readable' *New York Times Book Review*

0 00 647261 3

The Other Side of Midnight

Sidney Sheldon

A gripping, glamorous novel of scorching sensuality and heart-stopping evil.

A beautiful French actress whose craving for passion and vengeance takes her from the gutters of Paris to the bedroom of a powerful billionaire; a dynamic Greek tycoon who never forgets an insult, never forgives an injury; and a handsome war hero lured from his wife by another woman.

From Paris to Washington, Hollywood to the islands of Greece, *The Other Side of Midnight* is the story of four star-crossed lives enmeshed in a deadly ritual of passion, intrigue and corruption.

'A master storyteller' *Daily Mail*

'Sheldon is a writer working at the height of his power'
New York Times

ISBN 0 00 617931 2

Are You Afraid of the Dark?

Sidney Sheldon

In New York, Denver, Paris and Berlin, four people have died in what appear to be random accidents.

When two women – widows of the dead – find themselves under merciless attack, their fear and confusion help them to form an unlikely alliance. But why are they being targeted? Is there a connection to their husbands' mysterious deaths?

Meanwhile, the Chief Executive of an international Think Tank is on the cusp of a discovery which could change the world – and deliver unbelievable power into the company's hands. Could the mysterious deaths be connected to this volatile secret?

Taut with suspense and vivid characterization, and with an unnervingly realistic premise, *Are You Afraid of the Dark?* is a *tour de force* from a master storyteller.

ISBN 0 00 716516 1